WHAT SLEEPS WITHIN THE COVE

Also by Harper L. Woods

COVEN OF BONES
The Coven
The Cursed

OF FLESH & BONE
What Lies Beyond the Veil
What Hunts Inside the Shadows
What Lurks Between the Fates

WHAT SLEEPS WITHIN THE COVE

HARPER L. WOODS

BRAMBLE

Tor Publishing Group
New York

WHAT SLEEPS WITHIN THE COVE

Copyright © 2025 by Harper L. Woods

Interior art by Shutterstock.com
Map by Abigail M Hair

A Bramble Book
Published by Tom Doherty Associates / Tor Publishing Group
120 Broadway
New York, NY 10271

www.torpublishinggroup.com

Bramble™ is a trademark of Macmillan Publishing Group, LLC.

The Library of Congress Cataloging-in-Publication Data is available
upon request.

ISBN 978-1-250-40122-9 (hardcover)
ISBN 978-1-250-40123-6 (ebook)

Our books may be purchased in bulk for promotional, educational, or
business use. Please contact your local bookseller or the Macmillan Corporate
and Premium Sales Department at 1-800-221-7945, extension 5442,
or by email at MacmillanSpecialMarkets@macmillan.com.

First Edition: 2025

Printed in the United States of America

0 9 8 7 6 5 4 3 2 1

For the ones who overcome

NOTE

The Of Flesh & Bone series is set in a medieval-style world where human women are subservient to their male counterparts. The world is a dark, dangerous place for women, particularly those who do not conform to societal standards and the purity culture that determines how they live.

The Fae realm of Alfheimr is even darker and the violence in this world gets darker and more graphic with each book. There is murder, torture, and elements of assault.

As such, some elements may be triggering to certain readers. Please proceed with caution.

- Religious purity culture
- Verbal and physical abuse (NOT by the male lead)
- References to grooming behavior and assault of a minor by an authority figure (NOT by the male lead)
- References to past physical and sexual abuse
- Ritualistic sacrifices
- Suicide
- Suicidal thoughts and ideation
- Graphic death, violence, and torture
- Attempted sexual assault (NOT by the male lead)
- Graphic sexual content
- Flesh-eating creatures

GLOSSARY

Alfheimr: The Fae realm.

Calfalls: The Ruined City that was once a tribute to the God of the Dead before he destroyed it in the war between the Fae and humans.

High Priest/Priestess: The top Priest and Priestess who profess to commune with The Father and The Mother and pass along their messages.

Ineburn City: The capital of the human realm, a gleaming city of gold.

Mistfell: The village at the edge of the Veil, where it is closest to Alfheimr. Serves as the access point between realms when the Veil does not block passage.

Mist Guard: A separate army with the sole purpose of protecting the Veil from harm and fighting the Fae should it ever fall.

New Gods: The Father and The Mother. Worshipped by humans after they discovered the truth that the Old Gods were truly Fae. The Father and The Mother make the choice of whether a soul goes to Valhalla, Folkvangr, or Helheim after the true death at the end of the thirteen-life cycle.

Nothrek: The human realm.

Old Gods: The Old Gods are the most powerful of the Fae race known as the Sidhe. Most commonly, these are the offspring of the Primordials.

Priest/Priestess: The men and women who lead the Temple in service of the New Gods and their wishes (The Father and The Mother).

Primordials: The first beings in all of creation. They do not have a human form by nature, though they can choose to take one for various reasons and are simply the personification of what they represent.

Resistance, The: A secret society living in the tunnels of the Hollow Mountains (as well as elsewhere in Nothrek) that resist the rules of the Kingdom and live their lives as they please. They also resist the Fae and offer protection to the Fae Marked and other refugees fleeing the Royal or Mist Guard.

Royal Guard: The army that works on behalf of the King of Nothrek, ensuring that the Kingdom remains peaceful and compliant with his wishes.

Sidhe: The humanlike Fae who are *not* of the first generations and are less powerful than the Old Gods. Their magic exists, but is far more limited than their older counterparts.

Veil: The magical boundary that separates the human realm of Nothrek from the Fae realm of Alfheimr.

Viniculum: The physical symbol of the Fae Marked. Swirling ink in the color of the Fae's home court extending from the hand to the shoulder/chest.

Wild Hunt: The group of ghostlike Fae from the Shadow Court that are tasked with tracking down the Fae Marked to return them to their mates in Alfheimr, as well as hunting any who may be deemed enemies to the Fae.

Witches: Immortal beings with powers relating to the elements and celestial bodies; i.e. the Shadow Witches, Lunar Witches, Natural Witches, Water Witches, etc.

HIERARCHY OF THE GODS & FAE PRIMORDIALS

Khaos: Primordial of the Void that existed before all creation
Ilta: Primordial of the Night
Edrus: Primordial of Darkness
Zain: Primordial of the Sky
Diell: Primordial of the Day
Ubel: Primordial responsible for the prison of Tartarus
Bryn: Primordial of Nature
Oshun: Primordial of the Sea
Gerwyn: Primordial of Love
Aerwyna: Primordial of the Sea Creatures
Tempest: Primordial of Storms
Peri: Primordial of the Mountains
Sauda: Primordial of Poisons
Anke: Primordial of Compulsion
Marat: Primordial of Light
Eylam: Primordial of Time
The Fates: Primordial of Destiny
Ahimoth: Primordial of Impending Doom

OLD GODS OF NOTE

Aderyn: Goddess of the Harvest and Queen of the Autumn Court

Alastor: King of the Winter Court and husband to Twyla before his death

Caldris: God of the Dead

Jonab: God of Changing Seasons. Killed during the First Fae War.

Kahlo: God of Beasts and King of the Autumn Court

Mab: Queen of the Shadow Court. Known mainly as the Queen of Air and Darkness. Sister to Rheaghan (King of the Summer Court).

Rheaghan: God of the Sun and King of the Summer Court. Rightful King of the Seelie.

Sephtis: God of the Underworld and King of the Shadow Court

Shena: Goddess of Plant Life and Queen of the Spring Court

Tiam: God of Youth and King of the Spring Court

Twyla: Goddess of the Moon and Queen of the Winter Court. Rightful Queen of the Unseelie.

The Wild Hunt

Sidhe

WHAT SLEEPS WITHIN THE COVE

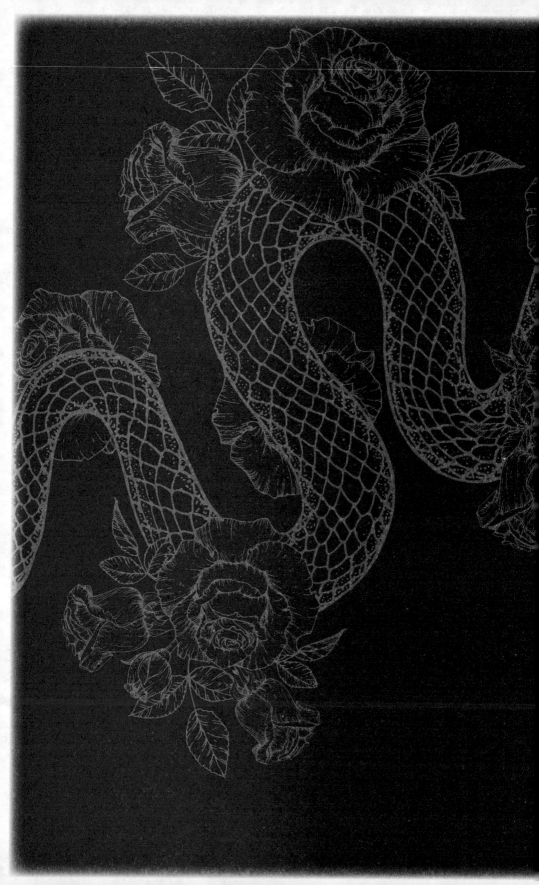

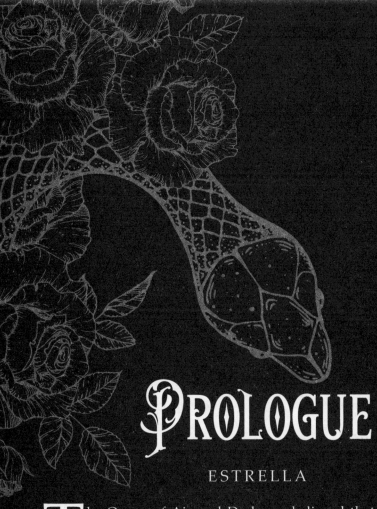

PROLOGUE

ESTRELLA

The Queen of Air and Darkness believed that to love was to weaken oneself—that the adoration I felt for my mate would be my ruination. As I floated in the water, my eyes on Caldris's as the bodies around me disappeared one by one, I couldn't even say that she was wrong.

Only that he was worth it, anyway.

My own fear was nothing compared to the terror in those helpless blue eyes that I forced myself to hold, shutting out the others watching with disdain and undisguised curiosity from the beach, even as I felt the tentacle of shadows I'd seen moving beneath the surface of the water wrap around my ankle to pull me under. I didn't let myself look away or lose sight of my mate's gaze, knowing it might very well be the last time I saw it.

I moved my hands along the surface of the water, attempting to disguise the shadowy figure below so that Caldris wouldn't see what

I saw—the jagged teeth in the open, gaping mouth waiting to swallow me whole.

I opened my mouth to tell him I loved him just one last time, but it was too little, too late. I knew it with the first feeling of that tentacle tightening around my leg, holding me firmly in a grip I had no hope of escaping.

As slowly as it had seemed to wrap around me, the tentacle jerked me beneath the surface. One moment I uttered a single word, and the next, water filled my mouth. The brine of the salt water was intense, forcing me to sputter and expend the only air in my lungs.

I stared up, watching the sun shining from above as it trickled and played with the water's surface. If it hadn't been for the pressure of the water filling my ears as the shadowed squid pulled me deeper and deeper into the cove, I knew I would have heard the roar of my mate.

I felt it in my soul, felt his anguish in every one of my limbs like the jagged edge of a blade peeling the skin from my flesh and leaving me raw. My heart lurched, desperate to offer him an apology I knew he'd demand if I survived. I'd put myself at risk to save him, but he never stopped to think about what would happen to me if he was gone.

There'd be nothing worth saving left and I too would soon follow him into the afterlife anyway.

I forced my gaze away from the surface when the ache in my lungs became too much. Even as a Fae, even with the immortality in my body and the knowledge that this would not kill me, my chest felt as if it had been stabbed with white-hot blades. The pressure in my head grew as I fought not to breathe, not to draw the water into my lungs for fear of what it might mean if I lost consciousness before emerging from the waters and into Tartarus.

The salt stung my eyes, but I forced them to remain open. I made myself watch as the limp bodies of the sacrifices to the Tithe were carried to the watery depths of the cove. In spite of the shadowed squid holding me in its grasp, the water surrounding us was filled with life.

Coral of all colors jutted out from the edges of the cove, surrounding me in a circle like a grotto as we dove straight down into the bottomless pit. The breath in my lungs faded, making my vision hazy as I fought to stay awake through the lack of air.

Others had been sent to Tartarus on Mab's behalf before. I forced myself to remember they'd returned, having survived not only the descent but the prison itself. It couldn't be all bad, not with the vibrancy that surrounded the entrance. The sheer beauty was like nothing I'd ever seen before, schools of fish swimming through the coral and brushing against the squid as if he was no threat to them. As if the great, gnawing mouth was a falsehood rather than a murderous weapon. A large turtle darted through the reefs, twirling his body around them with an elegance that seemed impossible. The turtles I'd seen that came up onto the shores of Mistfell had been awkward and slow, nothing like the smooth glide of this one through the water.

He came closer, brushing his shell against my arm as he swam past without a care in the world. I would have laughed if it hadn't been for the lack of air, for the way my head filled with the thick haze of terror and my consciousness began to slip.

The sun faded as we plunged ever deeper, darkness surrounding me as my eyes drifted closed slowly. The walls of the deepest parts of the cove seemed to shimmer, offering the only light as the sun faded out.

I forced my eyes open again, the pain in my head becoming too much to bear. Taking in the beauty of the tiny, glowing dots on the walls of the cove, I wondered if this was how it was all meant to end. My body forced me to draw in that last breath, the burn of water filling my lungs in a single, searing fire.

Surrounded by a thousand colorful lights, the pain faded as quickly as it had come.

Everything faded.

Until there was only black.

One

CALDRIS

Estrella vanished beneath the surface, leaving me staring at the water for several moments in disbelief. She was the last one taken, the last of the figures at the surface to disappear. The water rippled as she was sucked under, tiny splashes rising above the surface and crashing together in the air. The water lightened, the shadows lurking there fading as they sank into the depths.

Taking my mate with them, stripping her from my view as I knelt on the sands of the beach. I could do nothing but watch as they took her from me. Those surrounding me went quiet as they watched, as Estrella vanished so quickly there was no time to say goodbye. My heart was surrounded with darkness, the light fading out from my world in a sweep of shadows that seemed like they would never leave.

There was no sun without her—no stars to light the night sky as silence pressed in on me.

"Estrella!" I roared, the sound filling the quiet air with a shock of rage. Pushing against the hands that touched my shoulders and held me on my knees, I fought to get to my feet. Even knowing it was futile, my body could no more bear the separation from my mate than my heart could.

The daemons pinning me were unnecessary, what with the way Mab watched me intently. After the surge of power that Estrella's blood had given me, she'd have me watched constantly until she was certain the effects of it had faded from my body. She clutched her mangled hand to her chest, her repeated use of the hand only exacerbating the pain she had to feel. The flesh beneath had mostly regrown, but the shape of her severed hand was a mangled and twisted mess, as if someone had crushed her bones together.

My entire world narrowed down to the surface of the water as it went still, searching for my mate's terror down the bond. A sharp, acute emotion like that should have flooded the bond, making me suffer along with her in the interest of forcing me to save her.

The bond was a tangible thing between us, oriented toward self-preservation and the salvation of that bond above all else. Without Estrella there would be no one, there would be no life within me because I too would cave to the afterlife.

She wasn't dead; I could *feel* that she existed.

She'd closed the window.

I realized it like a bolt of lightning in my core, that even in her moments of pure, absolute terror, Estrella was protecting *me*. I'd thought, in a small comfort, that I would at least be able to feel her through our bond. That I'd know she was okay, that she wasn't in pain or suffering, but she'd taken even that from me, leaving me empty and hollow—broken.

I shouted my rage into the sky, hoping she could feel it even as she left the realm of the living. Reaching behind me with a single hand, I swiped the dagger from the thigh sheath of the male standing behind me. He gasped as I stabbed it into the side of his thigh, rotating on my knees in a move I'd seen my mate use more often than I could count. The grains of sand dug into my knees even through my trousers, the slight pain grounding me as I pulled the knife free and stabbed the male in the groin.

He screamed, his voice high-pitched and full of agony as he cupped himself with his hands, falling to his knees in front of me. I didn't waste time with delivering him to death once he was out of my way, pushing to my feet quickly and going toward the next of Mab's loyal followers who stood too close. My rage drove me into absolute determination, forcing me to take down as many of her people as possible.

She'd stripped everything from me. The right to complete my bond. The mate I loved more than anything.

"Bring her back!" I shouted, evading the blade Gunthard thrust for my gut with a sidestep. I dragged my stolen dagger across his throat, splitting the skin open and wasting only a moment of satisfaction to watch the way his blood poured over the hands he used to try to quell it. His eyes went glassy quickly as I moved on, his chest moving beneath his armor as Mab's snake chewed its way out from his flesh, fighting for freedom from its no-longer-living host.

Mab's dark eyes glimmered with morbid curiosity as she watched the display, her lack of care over those who served her dying in front of her apparent. It should have been enough to make those loyal to her hesitate, to prove to them that they would never be more than useful tools in her arsenal of weapons, ultimately disposable and re-placeable.

Another came for me, a swift sweep of my shadows lashing out like a whip to cut him in two. It cut through the air in a tangible line, the darkness held within it shimmering with the faintest golden light—like pinpricks of stars in the sky. Even now, the blood she'd given me tainted my magic with hers, offering aid in what should have been a difficult fight. His torso slid down from his legs where I'd cut him at an angle, leaving him to topple over in a disgusting pile of wasted flesh where his entrails pooled on the sand.

The whip was stronger than it had ever been—the cut far cleaner like a precisely sharpened blade. Estrella would have been horrified by the show of violence, and the knowledge that her magic had made it all the more gruesome, her human notions standing in her way sometimes when death was as necessary as the very breaths of life. It saddened me to think what Tartarus might do to the innocence of my mate, stripping it from her far more quickly than was just.

Two of Mab's personal guard stepped up, one throwing an axe at me. I sent a wave of awareness through my fingertips, imagining the way it would spread out from there until it reached the intact body of Gunthard where it lay before me. His awareness was gone, and it didn't matter that the Fae who had once called that flesh home had belonged to Mab in life. His soul had left along with her snake, escaping the prison of his body to wander without me to deliver him into the Void, and his corpse that remained as an empty shell be-came mine to control. He rose on command, taking the axe intended for me to the chest with barely a flinch, and then turning on one of my attackers.

Once hers, now he was mine.

With him to distract those who would have killed me for her benefit, I took a step closer to the true target of my wrath, staring the Queen of Air and Darkness in the face.

Mab reached out with a shadow whip of her own, catching me around the arm that held my dagger. She wrapped that tendril tight, cutting circulation and forcing the skin to part beneath the pressure she exerted. Her injured hand reached out in front of her, a warning as I turned and took a single step toward her. "Not another step, Caldris," she warned, squeezing her fingers tighter. Her voice lacked the power I was used to hearing in it, lacked the command and rage as she gave into her fear with the slightest of trembles.

My heart clenched in my chest, the snake there tightening in warning. I swallowed, taking another step through the suffocation that seemed to take the breath from my lungs with the stilling of my heart. She squeezed tighter, her eyes widening when I did not stop.

I took another step, roaring as I forced myself to move through the command she tried to instill in me. That vice around my heart came with the command, a silent word that I felt in every muscle of my body as it protested.

It wanted to give in, to do as it was told.

Fuck that.

I growled as I took another step, each one heavily weighted and leaving me vulnerable. I couldn't stomach the thought of not getting vengeance for my mate, even as my body locked up and my knee buckled and made me stumble. I kept pushing, kept going through that grip on my heart. This was the closest I'd ever come to vengeance, to overpowering the very person who had made my life a living Hel.

I was only a few steps from Mab, close enough to see the utter terror in her eyes as I forced myself closer. She could kill me; she could shred my heart. But then nothing would keep Estrella bound, the deal between them would be null and void.

With my death, she would free Estrella from the bond she'd agreed to.

It was a sacrifice we both knew I would be willing to make, were it not for the vows Estrella and I had sworn in private. I was aware of the consequence of my death and what that would mean for Estrella, but Mab was not. That lack of knowledge on her part was a strength of mine, letting her believe that my death would set my mate free.

"Caldris, stop," Mab begged, her voice quieter than normal and laced with a vulnerability I didn't recognize. She didn't want her followers to know just how desperately she'd lost control of me.

"Bring her back," I growled, forcing another step even as my knee caved in on itself, and I knelt at her feet. The dagger was still held in my hand, her whip wrapped around my forearm and pulling me away. I forced all my fight into that arm, dragging it away from her grip that was determined to keep me from killing her.

"She's beyond my reach now. Surely you know that," Mab argued softly, and for a moment I wondered if a bit of humanity peeked through those sharp, dark eyes.

"Then you shouldn't have fucking sent her," I said, yanking on my arm. Her shadows pulled tighter, fighting to hold me still as she reached down and bent my wrist back. My frustrated roar felt like it came from my very soul as she pinned me down finally, holding me still as my lungs heaved with the effort to escape her bounds. I'd been so fucking close I could smell her death in the air, the bittersweet copper of her blood coating my hands when I ripped out her fucking heart and rid all of Alfheimr of her cruelty.

Stealing the dagger from my hand, she nodded to the males behind me. Four sets of hands hauled me to my feet, fighting to control me as Mab kept that hand squeezed and her snake clenched around my heart. "Take him to the dungeon. Make sure he's locked tight," she said. I didn't miss the swallow of nerves or the glance of hesitation one of her men gave her.

She knew exactly what I knew.

I'd been so fucking close.

A laugh bubbled in my throat, chaotic and bitter, filled with the madness I felt at having freedom so close only for it to be ripped away all over again.

"I almost had you," I said, the manic sound of my own voice shocking even me. The laughter was hysterical, unhinged as the bloodlust of being separated from my mate so violently rode my body and threatened to take everything from me. "And we both know you brought enough witnesses for the Tithe, that your entire Kingdom will know it soon enough. They'll know just how close you were to death. What do you think they'll do with that knowledge?"

She shrugged, pursing her lips as she glanced toward the very witnesses she'd brought to display her strength—the same ones who had nearly watched her *fall*. "Almost does not accomplish much in the end, does it?" Mab asked, forcing her face back to the carefully controlled mask that she needed more than ever. The weakness couldn't be seen as lasting, not if she wanted to maintain control over Alfheimr in the same way she always had. "I should hope everyone watching will remember your punishment when I come to the dungeon to tear the meat from your bones and hang the ribbons of it in my throne room. I should hope they will be smart enough to avoid such a fate."

"I *almost* had you. When it was just me, with my mate as far away as she could possibly be. How long do you think you'll continue to breathe when she returns?" I asked, holding her stare with my own as her men forced me away. They shoved and kicked at my feet, making me walk toward the halls that would lead back into the palace and then to the dungeon that I'd become just as comfortable in as my own room.

My laughter echoed through the halls as we left, and I hoped the sound would haunt the Queen of Air and Darkness when she fell asleep that night.

My cell was exactly the same as I remembered it as I paced back and forth. It was still too short, leaving me with no choice but to bend over so that my head did not touch the bars at the top of the cell, but I could not simply sit and wait, not with the excess energy driven by my anger and Estrella's residual magic flooding through me. The same creaking of iron as the guards closed it. The same tang of metal and blood in the air. The same dampness to every breath with the steady stream of water that drained through the dungeon at the center of the walkway between cells. My wrists burned with the pain from the iron shackles her guards had placed on me before dragging me here, keeping me weakened enough to supervise my journey to the dungeons.

The hewn stone had worn away because of the constant flow of water in the center, only a single lantern lighting the space and the torture instruments hanging on the walls. The weapons were rusted over and covered in dried blood, any and all attempts to clean them long since forgotten. It was the slightly curved blade that drew my attention the most, the knowledge of Mab's threat to tear my flesh from my bones sitting fresh in my mind.

That knife was her favored tool when she wanted to make an example of her victim.

Lozu and Monos lingered in the cell across the hall that had once been where my mate slept, and I never thought I'd see the day when I wished for her to return to it. I would have taken her imprisonment here with me over her banishment to Tartarus any day.

I missed her already, and didn't understand how I was supposed to survive thirteen days without her at my side under good circumstances. In the worst-case scenario, it was very possible that my mate would never return. That the sight of her vanishing into the waters of the cove would be the last time I ever saw her. It was an emptiness sitting in my gut, a hollow, yawning ache that couldn't be ignored.

We'd been so close to completing our bond, so close to her being entirely mine, and nothing would stop me from completing it the moment she returned from Tartarus. The white-hot rage of her being lost to me still simmered in my blood. Seeing the moment of fear on Mab's face had reminded me of something that I'd long ago forgotten.

I was one of the strongest Gods to live. I'd brought entire cities to their knees and commanded armies at Mab's behest, but I'd forgotten what I was capable of when I acted of my own free will.

Maybe I'd never really known it in the first place—too afraid to reach my own potential because of what that would mean if it wasn't enough to overcome her. If I embraced my full power and could not win against her, what kind of weapon would I become in her hands?

But now there could be no question left. If Estrella returned, we would be enough.

And we would make Mab tremble on her knees before us.

"Where is your mate?" Monos asked, drifting from the cell she called home and coming into mine. Lozu followed behind her, somewhat reluctantly, but even the grumpy man had formed an attachment to Estrella. She collected allies with every step she took, distributing kindnesses that nobody else seemed willing to give.

"Mab sent her to Tartarus," I explained, knowing they'd been in these cells long enough to have experienced the way Mab often gave prisoners a choice: life in the cells or a quest to Tartarus.

Monos's face dropped, that ever present, hollow sort of smile fading from her expression. "All is truly lost then," she said, glancing toward Lozu and hanging her head as if she hadn't just insinuated that my mate wouldn't be coming home. At some point, they'd hung their hopes on a girl who was centuries younger than they were . . . The irony wasn't lost on me.

"Don't you fucking dare," I snapped, a growl rumbling up my throat. Monos jumped back, and the motion of the woman who had otherwise found comfort in my presence settled me some. The beast in me prowled beneath the surface, not wanting to frighten the Selkie, but he missed his mate just as much as I did. He would not tolerate anyone doubting her or the sacrifice she'd made to save me.

She'd had no choice, I knew that. So why was I so fucking furious with her for making the choice I would have made if our roles had been reversed?

"As long as she's still breathing, Estrella will do whatever it takes to come back to us. If you doubt that, then you doubt her, and you aren't worthy of the loyalty she would show you."

Monos nodded slowly, her smile returning. But there was something particularly placating in it, as if I was losing my shit, and I could no longer tell reality from fantasy.

Maybe she was right, but it would do nothing to stop me from believing I'd see her again soon.

"Okay, Caldris," Monos said, bowing her head forward in a slow display of reverence.

"So what are you going to do to help her when she does?" I asked, raising a brow to keep from punching something. The ghosts wouldn't be the appropriate target for my rage, and the only other items within my cell were made of iron and would cause far more damage than I needed to suffer through when Mab was likely to take out her anger on me all on her own.

Monos and Lozu exchanged a glance, and the gnome nodded before he spoke.

"We'll rally the Lliadhe to fight, should the Princess return," he said, nodding his head supportively in spite of the doubt in those words.

"When she returns," I corrected, lowering my bent-over body to sit in my cell.

"When she returns," Monos agreed.

"Why would the Lliadhe help? They've never concerned themselves with the politics of the Sidhe before?" In all my centuries of life, I'd never seen them even bother to follow the gossip of the Sidhe beyond passing curiosity. While we were all Fae, the lines had long since been drawn between our two classes. It was past time for the lines to be removed, for us to move together into the future in a united front.

"What difference has it made in the past? One Sidhe treats us no differently than another. We are merely servants and entertainment to most; the nobles are the worst," Lozu answered, moving to the corner of the cell to pick through any flesh that might have remained from an occupant who stayed here after my last trip to the dungeon.

"But your mate treats us as if we matter. As if we are equal. Perhaps with her in charge, the Lliadhe will finally know some peace within Alfheimr," Monos said, her gaze going distant as she glanced toward the door of the dungeon and the guard I knew waited there. "She took a lashing meant for one of our own. She danced with us when most do not acknowledge we exist. She was kind when others only brought pain. Even if there was no chance of her victory, we would stand beside her. We would do anything for your mate for she sees us as her equals."

I nodded, following her gaze to the dungeon door and wondering how many beyond it would feel the same. "So would I," I echoed.

So would all of them.

Two

ESTRELLA

Pain consumed my body, the dull thump of it striking the surface as I landed, snapping me out of unconsciousness. Coughing, I sputtered as I forced my aching form to turn over onto my stomach. The water I'd involuntarily breathed into my lungs gurgled, spewing up onto the stone beneath me.

I heaved, pushing to my hands and knees as my body revolted against me. Wiping the back of my arm against my mouth, I fought my way to my feet and froze as I glanced overhead.

The cove was above me, the waters crystal clear as the creature made of shadows writhed within it. The mouth snapped open and closed as it swam through the water. Light drifted into it from above, coming to the bottom of the cove in a filtered ray.

The shining blue of the cove was in direct contrast with the gray stone beneath my feet, with the distinct lack of all colors from the area surrounding me. The bodies of those sacrificed to the Tithe were scattered upon the stone around me, their clothing the only color to the area that felt devoid of all life.

The monochromatic stone led the way to two pillars that rested to each side of the bridge where I had landed. Daemons had been carved from stone, those horrifyingly massive figures perched precariously upon the top as they stared down at where we had landed. Their mouths were open to reveal razor-sharp teeth, their eyes glowing with red. The eeriness of those stares peering out of the darkness forced me to swallow as I looked between those pillars to the enormous gates waiting beyond them, and the three-headed dog who stood guard.

I knew him from the books I'd read, from the portraits in the forbidden texts the Resistance had managed to keep. Those drawings couldn't begin to do him justice, his very presence filling the air. Cerberus was bigger than even a cave beast, each strand of his long black fur the same length as my hair as it covered the densely packed muscle on his body. Each of his three heads was nearly identical, pointed ears jutting toward the cove above. Flames danced along his spine, sparking inside one of his mouths as he opened wide and growled at me in warning.

I took an involuntary step back, wincing as one of his paws rose and came down upon the stone steps leading up to the gate where he waited. His claws and toes spread across half a dozen steps, the sound of those claws scraping over the stone making me shiver in disgust.

His growl vibrated through the stone, the force of it making my legs tremble beneath me. Still, I was painfully aware of the faint slithering sound behind me, of the familiarity in that noise. I spun, coming face-to-face with the milky eyes of a basilisk as it crested over the ledge of the bridge.

The serpent was enormous, its neck bent to allow it to meet my gaze as it slithered forward. Its eyes were white and clouded over, shocking against the deep gray of its scales. A forked tongue slid out from its mouth, navigating the narrow gap between jagged, needle-like teeth that spread across the sides of its jaw.

The tip of its tongue touched my cheek, brushing over the skin there gently as it tasted me. I gagged, swallowing my nausea at the scent of rotten meat and decay that came from the creature's mouth.

I turned my head away from the scent, the smallest of motions so I didn't aggravate the fanged creature staring back at me. Another slithered across the stone, its enormous body curving over the edge of the bridge. I didn't want to think about what lay below for such creatures to slither from the depths, and a shudder wracked my body.

I watched in horror as the basilisk wrapped its tail around the body of one of the sacrificed humans, dragging him over the edge of the bridge. They disappeared into the nothingness below at the same moment that a third and fourth basilisk crested the ledge. I turned from the one staring me down, sprinting toward Rheaghan's unconscious body. The basilisk making its way toward him moved more slowly than I did, allowing me to reach him first and put myself between him and the coming danger.

Rheaghan's only crime had been attempting to right the wrongs he committed in the interest of saving his only sister, and the urge to protect him even in death was overwhelming. The basilisk slithered to a halt in front of me, staring down at me through milky eyes just like the other one. Its neck twisted to the side, leaving me with the distinct impression of a human cocking their head to the side in confusion.

"I won't let you take him," I said, raising my chin. The creature's eyes widened for a moment before they narrowed, its head lowering toward me in challenge.

It struck, its tail twisting around my body to reach for Rheaghan's legs. I turned, reaching for the too-large sword that was strapped to my waist. The steel handle was cool in my hand as I pulled it free, diving forward to drive it into the beast's tail.

My momentum stopped short as something slithered around my waist, pulling me back away from the attacking basilisk and Rheaghan's body as it wrapped him into its grasp. I screamed, my voice echoing off the muffling waters above and forcing the stone to vibrate with the force of my fury.

I shoved at the basilisk's tail wrapped around me, slicing through its flesh the best I could with the long blade at such a close proximity. Its body slithered around mine, wrapping me in a tighter grip as the tip of its tail grasped my forearm and squeezed.

"*He doesss not belong to youuu, Little Sssserpent,*" the snake's voice said, the words forming in my mind as the sword fell from my hand. It clattered to the stone as I wrestled with the idea of the creature who had spoken to me, communicating as if there was a bond between us.

He spun me in his grip, turning me to face him once again. I felt certain that the voice in my mind had been male, that I'd heard it as clearly as if he'd spoken the words aloud. But I also knew he hadn't, that the distinct way the words felt had been imprinted on my mind and not heard.

I struggled against his grip as the other basilisk slithered toward the edge, Rheaghan's body wrapped in its grip.

"No!" I screamed, shoving and punching at the way the basilisk held me, tightening to the point that I felt like I could barely breathe.

I screamed through it, tears stinging my eyes as the gates of Tartarus slowly parted. The portrait beyond the gates was one of hellfire and brimstone, of curved archways and abandoned ruins with no sign of life among them. A single blight flew through the gap in the doors, a whistle sounding through the air as it traveled fast. It lowered as it approached; the doors slamming shut behind it. It plummeted toward the stone, amber eyes glowing as it approached. It flung its wings wide, onyx feathers shimmering in the light of the cove above, and just before it landed, three women burst free from the blight itself. What had once been feathers in the wind transformed into three figures. Their eyes each glowed a different color, set into brown skin. The one at the center had sleek hair that reminded me of the blight's feathers, her eyes glowing the same amber as the bird's had.

"I am afraid these snakes are beyond even your control, Estrella Barlowe," she said, and the other women remained still at her side. None of them moved to help as the basilisk plunged over the edge with Rheaghan, disappearing into the smoke and steam rising from below.

The one to the right spoke next, her red eyes glowing like something from a nightmare. "Welcome to Tartarus, Child of Fate. We've been waiting for you."

THREE

ESTRELLA

I swallowed back my surging nausea, tearing my eyes off the three women standing before me. There was no sign of movement from the exact spot where Rheaghan had disappeared, and all I could do was watch as the basilisks took the rest of the sacrifices below.

"The God is none of your concern," the one with white eyes spoke, her hair a matching silver that made me miss Imelda.

"I alone determine what does or does not concern me. He is my friend," I said, stressing the words as I narrowed my glare on the one who'd spoken. That was a warning I would not heed, a reality I could not give into.

"You have far more pressing matters to concern yourself with," the one with golden eyes said, a smile making her lip twitch up at the corner. The basilisk unwound his body from around me, his scales sliding over the fabric of my clothing until he left me where I stood, making his way to the edge and retreating without taking me. His body was a deep, deep gray, so dark it was nearly black as he slithered along the stone and disappeared over the edge.

"We are the Morrigan," the one with golden eyes said. "My sisters and I have been sent to serve as your guide through Tartarus and accompany you on what will be the greatest test of your life."

"We are the harbinger of death," the white-eyed woman said, earning an eye roll from me.

"What a promising choice to serve as my guide," I said, moving to pick up the sword I'd dropped in my scuffle with the basilisk.

"Understand this, Child of Fate," the red-eyed woman said, her gaze flashing with warning as I sheathed my sword and bit my tongue to prevent a smart retort. "Estrella Barlowe will die here. The moment you pass through these gates, you can do so knowing beyond a shadow of a doubt that your life has come to an end. There is not a single path in which the Fates let you leave here without knowing the touch of death."

"Then why would I enter? Knowing I won't survive?" I asked, crossing my arms over my chest as the golden-eyed one glanced to her white-eyed sister.

"Better to die free than live on your knees," she said, holding out a hand. There was knowledge in that eerie stare, her fingers untainted by age and time, the skin smooth. Her stare left me with the distinct feeling that my choice had already been made—long before I'd come to stand in this place. The gate loomed ahead, the doors creaking open ever so slowly behind Cerberus where he stood guard. They parted as the two others turned to look back at the entrance. The red hue of the land within shimmered against the stone of the intricately carved doors, the reliefs of all the Primordials and the worst creatures they'd created carved into them. The spinning razor teeth of the creatures I'd seen in the Void surrounded them, a dark, looming threat that seemed to fill every gap.

The single eye of a cyclops seemed to stare back at me as red light illuminated it, the head of a Gorgon lurking in the shadows beside it. The sea monster Charybdis threatened to swallow them all whole, her gaping mouth opened in a perfect circle to reveal sharp, swordlike teeth. The Primordials were spread through the stone, positioned according to their rank and proximity to the male figure at the top of the archway.

Khaos, the father of everything, stared down at me where I stood. His face was familiar even though the carving lacked the details to make it recognizable, but the eerie gold of those eyes reminded me of the magic I should not have possessed.

Magic I'd seen in the man from my visions.

It was not lost on me that I had to enter a prison to free myself from Mab. That everything I needed to fight my way to freedom existed within the prison. If Medusa truly was the Queen of Serpents, then she was just as likely to be able to remove the snake from my heart and from Caldris's as she was to kill me.

Even if the odds were stacked against me, it was a chance. And that was more than I could say for most days of my life.

I took the woman's hand with my left, letting her wrap her smooth skin around my calluses. She smiled, her sharp teeth forcing me to flinch in her touch as she turned and guided me toward the entrance to the prison. "I am Macha," the red-eyed woman said, nodding her head to the golden-eyed sister who stepped in front of us and turned to face the three-headed dog. "That is Badb."

"And I am Nemain," the white-eyed woman stated, taking my right hand in hers. They led me toward the monster guarding the gates, pulling me along even though my legs had frozen in practical terror. Fenrir was huge, three times the size of a normal dog, but he was nothing compared to Cerberus.

We stepped beneath his head, narrowly avoiding the drool that fell to the stone in a puddle large enough to swim in.

Gross.

"Be a good boy, Cerberus," Macha said, reaching out to pat one of his legs. He lowered his heads in response, placing the center one just to the side of my head. His inhale drew me forward, until I felt the brush of his teeth against my cheek and neck. He wedged himself into the nook between my shoulder and head, inhaling deeply enough that my skin felt the draw of breath.

One of his other heads lowered to my other side, nudging my hip firmly so that I stumbled away from him. I forced myself to hold still, to keep my hands away from my sword and placate the creature who sniffed me, inhaling my scent into his lungs.

The third head curved around to my back, nuzzling into my hair and following it down the curve of my spine.

"That's a little rude," I whispered, turning to glare at it over my shoulder. The creature growled, the rumble coming from his chest in front of me as his long neck tensed and he bared his teeth at me.

"Cerberus needs your scent. If you try to leave Tartarus without permission, he'll be able to hunt you down and drag your soul back for eternity," Badb inserted, explaining the trauma of having three enormous dog heads sniffing at me.

I hesitated, pushing back as Macha guided my hand up to linger in front of the center head, squeezing my eyes shut as I tried to fathom the stupidity of attempting to pet such a creature. His growl worsened, the flames in his eyes glowing more brightly the closer my hand came to his snout. Flinching back, I held his stare until he turned to look down the bridge.

Three white blurs raced down the stone path, closing the distance with a speed that seemed impossible as they zipped and zagged around one another to get to us. My heart leapt into my throat at the sight of those red-tipped ears and red eyes, at the white fur I recognized.

The Cwn Annwn didn't so much as pause as they surrounded Cerberus, growling a warning. Fenrir slid his body between the enormous black dog and me, nuzzling his head into my outstretched hand even though his face didn't soften in the least.

He and Cerberus stared one another down, the other hounds of the Cwn Annwn waiting for the outcome as I pressed myself into Fenrir's side. Claiming him as he claimed me. He bared his teeth, his much smaller frame seeming so tiny compared to the might of Cerberus. But the guardian of Tartarus shocked me, his face softening in understanding before he lowered his head. I touched a hand to his snout finally, running my fingers through the length of his black fur before he pulled away with a grimace and his other heads followed.

Fenrir turned to me, nuzzling into my neck as I wrapped my arms around his. Lupa brushed up against my back, pushing against my legs and sandwiching me between the two of them. Ylfa pawed at my foot, demanding attention as I dropped a hand to the top of her head and worked my fingers through her glimmering white fur, finding the red skin beneath and scratching the spot at the back of her neck.

Nemain scowled down at the wolves as they pushed her to the side to circle me, heaving a sigh. "We cannot keep the Cwn Annwn from entering Tartarus. As part of the Wild Hunt, they are welcome to pass through the gates as they please. But they will not be permitted to interfere with the trials that await you," she said, tugging on my hand. I heaved a sigh of relief, the knowledge that I wouldn't be alone in this journey settling some of my nerves—I'd have them to look out for me at least. Nemain guided me through Cerberus's legs, stepping beneath his towering body to emerge from between his front and back legs.

The gates waited at the top of the stairs, standing wide open as the Cwn Annwn raced forward and sprinted through the doors into the fiery abyss. The Morrigan guided me forward, their touch firm as they took my hands in theirs once more and we began to ascend the steps.

I counted them as I walked, taking each step slowly as I tried to prolong the inevitable torment that surely waited for me within the prison. The gateway was veiled, that same shimmering white fabric floating through the air. I knew enough from my time in Mistfell to understand that it was the magic of a boundary, that it was not actually a transparent linen, but the mist that wafted off of it did nothing to calm me as I considered what may wait for me on the other side.

Four dozen steps separated me from the place where I would die, but I couldn't stop my feet from moving. I couldn't stop the way my heart throbbed in my chest, the snake wrapped around there squeezing as if it felt the world shift beneath my feet. I thought of Caldris on the beach, of what I'd undoubtedly left him to deal with in the aftermath of our rebellion.

I couldn't decide if I was truly the one to be punished, or if he would take the worst of it in my absence.

I didn't look back as I crossed the threshold, the shimmering haze surrounding me as the Morrigan guided me into the gateway. Magic pressed against my skin, swirling against me as if it wanted to draw my own to the surface. I stepped into the unknown, the hazy bubble popping as it allowed me to slip through. The gates closed slowly behind me, sealing me into the prison that I knew I would never leave.

FOUR

CALDRIS

The cell door creaked open in the early hours of morning the next day, bringing with it the sound of screaming from the throne room. I raised my head from where I'd laid it upon the stone, peeking at the door. Shock thrummed through me in a gentle, pulsing wave the moment my stare met Opal's, one of Mab's most loyal members of her court. She stepped back, lowering her gaze to the floor as she returned the keys to the hook on the wall. I pushed to sit slowly, not daring to move too quickly.

For the violence I'd shown in my attempt to kill Mab, I should have been locked in my cell for the duration of Estrella's trip to Tartarus.

"What are you doing?" I asked, pressing my hand to the stone beneath me. It was cold to the touch, the temperatures this far below the surface plummeting to near icy depths. Even though I was distantly aware of the cold because of the iron surrounding me and suppressing the part of me that craved the winter, it failed to affect me the way it might have some of the others when confronted with it.

Getting to my feet slowly, I made my way to the cell door and wrapped my hand around the bar, pushing it open. My skin boiled beneath the iron, splitting and bubbling as the door opened farther and the female Fae took a step back, nearly stumbling over her own legs in her haste to put distance between us. She was loyal to Mab, though one of her less enthusiastic supporters when it came to some of the more distasteful commands she gave.

She did her duty to her Queen, but she didn't enjoy it the way Octavian had.

"I need your help," she said, glancing toward the dungeon door. She'd closed it behind her, sealing us into the room, but the door did not lock from the inside.

"Why would I do anything to help you?" I asked, crossing my arms over my chest. Her pale silver eyes shone with tears as she dropped her gaze to my arms, to the harshness in them as I prepared to snap her neck. Ridding the world of all of Mab's children would never be the wrong thing, even if I suffered the consequences of it. For now, Mab needed me alive, and that provided me with some assurance to my survival.

I took a single step forward. Opal dropped back, placing her spine against the stone wall beside the dungeon door. The emerald ends of her hair swayed with the movement, the silver roots shining in the dim firelight overhead.

"You don't understand. She's out of control," she said, her words hurried. She had the rare sprinkle of freckles across her cheeks, inherited from her half-nymph mother once upon a time.

"She's always been out of control," I snapped, thrusting my arms out in frustration.

"She's killing *us*," she said, her voice a quiet whisper as she stressed the words. "I've only ever seen this kind of rage when a Fae loses their mate forever after centuries together. She's unhinged."

"So I'm supposed to care that she's suddenly killing the people who deserve it?" I asked, scoffing as I glanced toward the dungeon door and the potential escape. After centuries of killing innocents—at least her rage was finally pointed in the right direction. If there was any chance I could make it out undetected, find my way to the cove, then maybe I could enter Tartarus only a day behind Estrella.

I could find her. I could help her.

Opal swallowed, squeezing her eyes closed as she let out a heavy breath. "No, but you're supposed to care about all the others she's killing along with us. If she doesn't stop, there will be *no one left!* No Sidhe. No Lliadhe."

The reminder of the Fae that Estrella had protected at the expense of her own pain sent a pang of guilt through me. She would hate me if I left them to suffer to make my way to her, and she would have done everything she could to help them.

My nostrils flared in irritation as I grasped the handle on the dungeon door and pulled it open. "What is it you think I can do to help them? Mab killed *me* yesterday," I said, my huff of laughter echoing off the stone walls. It was only my mate's blood that had brought me back from the brink of death, making sure I lived to watch her enslaved to the woman I hated with everything I was.

"She's different with you," Opal said, taking a step toward me. Her hand came down on my forearm, a familiar touch she hadn't earned the right to. I snarled and flinched away, refusing the contact with any but my mate. It was only the softened look in her silver gaze that kept me from cutting that hand from her body for daring to touch me when I did not permit it. "You don't see it, but we do. She's . . . softer somehow. Still Mab, but not quite the same as she is with us. You're her favorite. You remind her of her husband."

"The husband that she slaughtered in cold blood in front of me?" I asked, stepping through the dungeon door. The sound of screams vibrated off the stone walls even this far into the depths of the hillside, sending a chill up my spine. "I could practically taste her affection even then."

Even still, my feet hurried up the stone steps toward the throne room. Screaming like that, in a Kingdom that was dominated by pain and suffering, I didn't want to think of the horrors being committed.

"No!" a shrill female voice screamed, the sound sinking deep into my bones. It was too reminiscent of the howl I'd felt leave my body in the moments before Estrella's death at the Veil.

Understanding struck me like a lightning bolt to the chest, driving me forward quicker than ever. "I told you she's out of control!" Opal snapped, following at my heels like the good little follower she was.

"You didn't tell me she was killing the humans!" I said, refusing to look back at her. Leave it to her to only care about what affected her and those she cared about.

I paused at the top, looking down the hall to where the entrance to the cove lay hidden. Considering my choices and my obligations, my heart and my duty pulled me in two different directions. I had sworn to burn the world to the ground if it was what was needed to save my mate, but Estrella would never forgive me for leaving the humans to such a fate.

She'd never forgive me for condemning so many others to the loss that I so desperately refused to accept.

Fuck.

Decision made, I rounded the top of the stairway, jogging forward and navigating the crowd of fleeing Fae. They raced out of the throne room, their cowardice forcing them to push through me as I made my way to the massacre I could hear more clearly now.

It wasn't one woman screaming, but a cacophony of shrill screams and howls. The torment of pain and agony resounded through the hall as I rounded the door to the throne room, glancing over my shoulder once to find Opal hadn't dared to follow me to what would be a sure death sentence.

Fucking coward.

The bodies of half a dozen humans lay at the base of the dais, Mab's hands enrobed in shadows as she twisted them through the room. A handful of Fae cried openly, curling their mate's limp bodies into their arms and rocking them as the remaining two humans watched in horror.

"I've done you a favor. You'll see soon enough," Mab said, taking a step toward one of the grieving Fae. She stroked the top of the woman's head, running her mangled hand through her hair affectionately and leaving a trail of blood in her wake. "I have rid you of the weakness that is love. Now he can never have power over you without ever doing anything to earn it."

I strode through the crowd waiting at the sidelines, nursing injuries or placing their palm over their heart as if the pain of her control was too much to bear. Mab had always had her darkness. She'd always possessed an evil so deep that none would dare to question her ability for cruelty.

Killing mates was a new descent into madness, a completely irrational outburst that hurt us all. Only through the mate bond could the next generation of Fae come to exist, and with our population already dwindling because of the witches' curse, every life mattered.

She hadn't just killed humans. She'd destroyed the potential offspring that would *never* live now.

Mab took a step back as I approached, moving closer to her throne before she seemed to regain her sense of self-preservation.

Mab did not back away for anyone, and the moment of fear was enough to show just how much my display at the cove had rattled her. The movement dragged my attention up to the bones that had crafted her seat of power, to the skull on the right side of the throne.

If I hadn't known any better, I'd have thought the jawbone moved, shifting to grind together with Mab's words. My brow knit together, but I quickly averted my gaze to not draw her attention to it. Whatever was wrong with the throne, whatever had shifted in that skull, Mab didn't need to know just yet.

One of Mab's most loyal lay at her feet, his body broken nearly beyond recognition. Only the shimmer of his Fae Mark on his neck was visible, leading up to his striking black eyes. The rest of his flesh was a swollen mass of muscle and blood, the skin missing from most of him as if Mab had been determined to remove any signs of his disloyalty from his body.

Mab stepped over his body callously, her fear of me forgotten, making her way toward a centaur woman who hurried to tuck her child behind her. The lower half of her body was a dappled gray, her hooves stomping in warning as she backed the younger Lliadhe toward the throne room door. But the crowd at her back made escape an impossibility, leaving her to stare down the Queen of Air and Darkness with her jaw set in stone and chin raised high. Her hair glimmered like the flecks of a flame in the night sky. I closed the distance between us as quickly as I could navigate those frantically trying to leave, ignoring the Sidhe who watched in silence from the sidelines as if they would be safe from Mab's wrath.

But what was once cold, cunning cruelty staring back at me in her dark, glimmering onyx eyes had shifted, changing to something feral and wild in one of her bouts of madness that struck like lightning periodically. Always a consequence of being threatened, of feeling like she was losing control over what she'd fought so hard to gain, she became a different creature entirely.

Something backed into a corner and fighting for *survival*.

Mab's mangled hand twitched at her side, dripping blood onto the stone floor. At some point since I'd last seen her, the skin had parted, rotting away from her wrist where Estrella had severed it. As if the threads still lingered there, fighting to tear their way through her flesh and bone all over again.

I stepped in front of the centaur just as the Queen reached out with her shadows, taking the onslaught meant for the centaur. Even if Mab had wanted to, there wasn't time for her to pull them back and attempt a different attack designed especially for me. They wrapped around my throat and squeezed tightly, cutting off the flow of air to my body. My hands flew to grasp them, to tug at them for a reprieve that I knew would not come. I struggled for breath, dropping to my knees before Mab as she commanded my obedience.

"Children are sacred," I rasped, feeling the centaur guide her child away from the danger. I could practically feel the centaur's hesitance, feel the similarity of what made Estrella *human* dancing over my skin.

She didn't want to leave me to suffer, not when I had taken a fate that should have been hers.

Not when I'd protected her child when no one else would.

It was in that moment that I recognized the beauty of the way Estrella saw the world, of the way she interacted with it and appreciated all life. She would not have hesitated to interfere and save the centaur and her daughter.

Because she *loved*.

"Only Sidhe children are sacred. There are plenty of Lliadhe to go around," Mab said cruelly, her words a reminder of the fact that the Lliadhe did not bear the same curse as the Sidhe. The witches hadn't felt the need to control their population as a measure to save the world, not the same way they had my kind. They'd seen something in the Lliadhe I'd never stopped to consider. Something that we lacked.

Something *good* where we had only darkness.

"My Queen, if you kill him, your bargain with the Barlowe girl will be null and void. She will be beyond your control," Eowyn said, stepping up as close to Mab as she dared. The younger girl had willingly served at Mab's command for over a century, delighting in the suffering of those around her. She'd loved the torment and the screams, but Mab glared at her all the same.

Mab turned that callous stare away from her devoted follower, stepping closer to me until her fingertips brushed my cheek.

"I would gladly die if it meant she was free of you," I rasped, using the rest of my energy to force the words free, counting on the knowledge I had that she did not. Her shadows loosened ever so slightly giving me the ability to breathe as that too-sharp mask she wore cracked. "We both know she will kill you if she returns to find me gone."

Her lips twisted as she drew her shadows back, relinquishing me under the threat of Estrella's retribution. I wasn't positive about it before, hadn't known if Mab was as aware of my mate's potential as I was.

But the fear that shone in her eyes as she reached up a hand to touch her onyx crown spoke volumes—the tremble in her hand confirming it. She'd needed Estrella to go into Tartarus and bring back the snake from Medusa's crown, but she was afraid what the consequence might be all the same—was terrified of what else my mate might find in that place of horrors.

"You're my son. Where did we go so wrong that you would hope for my death?" she asked, her voice cracking as her eyes sparkled with the threat of tears. The vulnerability in that stare shook me to my core, a peek at the girl Rheaghan remembered staring back at me.

"You killed me," I said, my voice as disbelieving as my thoughts. She'd killed my father, forced me to spend my life in abuse and violation for her own entertainment. "You killed Sephtis. All you've ever brought me is pain. Why would I not want to see your head on a spike for all of Alfheimr to celebrate?"

"If you and your miserable father had only loved me, none of this would have been necessary. Why was it so much to ask for my family to love me as I am?" she asked, her anger rising. Her fingers twitched at her sides, barely controlled as a shadow moved within the stone of her crown.

"Rheaghan loved you," I said, pushing to my feet before her. So much that he'd helped her hide the truth of her curse until after they'd effectively manipulated their way into the Court of Shadows and stolen my father's throne.

Certain that she wouldn't risk losing my mate, not even for my death, I raised my chin straight. My throat ached with the press of temporary bruises blooming beneath my skin, ones that would heal as soon as they formed. "Where did that get him?"

She flinched, swallowing as she turned her gaze away. The closest thing I'd ever seen to shame crossed her features, hardening the set of her expression when she looked around the room to those that feared her.

"Rheaghan didn't love me. He loved the girl he wanted me to be," she said, her gaze snapping back to mine with disdain. "He loved your mate. For all the ways she reminded him of me."

My jaw slackened, hanging open as I stared after her. That wasn't true in the slightest.

Estrella was *nothing* like Mab.

Before I could respond, Mab turned on her heel and made her

way to the dais. "Clean up this fucking mess before dinner. I don't want to see it again," she called, waving her hand over her shoulder to accentuate the command. "And find me whoever released the God of the Dead from his cell. I'd like to have a Gods-damned word."

She opened the shadows, stepping into the shadow realm and disappearing from sight.

Leaving the rest of us to clean up her messes like always.

FIVE

ESTRELLA

I followed behind the Morrigan, the three figures walking on sure feet that I didn't possess. The ground beneath us was the color of rust, that deep, earthy tone that gleamed like fire in the light. The vague impression of mountains lingered in the distance, stretching toward the cave ceiling above. There was no sun in Tartarus, no moon or stars in the sky above my head. As if it was trapped in a massive cave, stone covered the very existence of the prison in a way that felt impossible, as if it existed at the center of the world itself, dancing beneath the surface of the Fae and humans above.

Fires moved, shifting along the red dirt like miniature funnels of flames. They didn't stay in one place, traveling in the unnatural breeze that blew through the space.

"Where are we going?" I asked, skipping to the side as one of the fires came too close for comfort. The warmth of fire kissed my arm, the singe of heat burning the hair from my skin.

The Morrigan walked through six of the burning spirals, making their way to a stone ruin that jutted out from the reddened earth. The steps ascended toward the ceiling, an archway curving overhead that was big enough to fit two cave beasts standing on top of one another. I swallowed back my nerves and followed after them, trying not to think of what creature may be big enough to need such a large entryway.

"I am taking you to the place you need to be," Nemain said ominously, her words nearly drowning in the wind as she ascended the first steps. The wind blew through the entrance of those ruins, casting the Morrigan's hair back in a synchronized flutter.

The Cwn Annwn raced past the three women, sprinting up the steps with speed that I envied. The adrenaline of the day threatened to catch up with me, and it didn't bode well for me that I had thirteen days to be successful. Thirteen days of minimal sleep to achieve the only thing that would save Caldris's life.

"You're taking me to Medusa?" I asked, even knowing it was an impossibility. Nothing in my life was ever so simple to think that they would skip pretense.

"In time. Medusa lives with the Primordials in the Cradle of Creation. Only those who prove themselves worthy may pass through the Temple of the Fates and enter the place where it all began," Badb answered, cresting the final step as I followed behind them. Her sisters joined her at the crest, turning back to watch me ascend the steps slowly.

My skin hummed as I approached the entryway at the top of the steps, my feet moving more slowly than before—as if that part of my body knew something to dread.

The Morrigan crossed the threshold, stepping into the land beyond the ruined gate. A haze crossed over them, a sort of bubble that muffled their words as Nemain's lips parted. I reached out a hand to touch the stone, wincing back from the jolt of power that made my entire arm quake.

"If you consent to the trials of Tartarus, you must pass through the warding, Child of Fate," Nemain said, reaching out with a hand.

"What will it do to me?" I asked, taking a step back. I could feel my magic hum; drawing and calling to that well of power that existed within me made panic freeze my body.

"Tartarus is not interested in your magic or your mate's," Badb said, watching the way I faltered with keen eyes.

"Then what is it supposed to test?" I asked, wincing as Macha stepped through the haze to appear in front of me once more. She

31

smiled, her beautiful mouth shifting just a little too wide at the edges, her hair billowing around her like liquid fire.

She reached out, stretching a single pointer finger toward my chest. She touched the very center of it, digging her nail into the fabric and my skin beneath. "You, girl. Your soul. Your very being and your inner strength. Anyone can have magic, but not everyone is worthy of keeping it."

My thoughts immediately flashed to Mab, to how unworthy she'd proven to be of the magic she'd been given. The magic that was stolen by the dwarves centuries before I was born.

"How am I to survive the trials without my magic?" I asked, watching as she drew her finger away from my chest and held out her hand for me to take.

"The same way you always have. As a human," she answered, her fingers wiggling as she pushed me to accept the only choice I had.

"It hardly seems fair to have to prove myself worthy of entering a prison," I snapped, gritting my teeth. "Torture is hardly a gift."

"No place is truly good or evil, Tempest. Places as much as people exist on a continuum. For the right person, Tartarus can provide just as much as it can take."

"If I can prove myself worthy. If I'm not, it takes the ultimate price," I said, grabbing her hand despite the harsh reality of my words.

"Perhaps that, too, is a gift. If you are unsuccessful, your mate will die. This way, you may join him in the Void and find peace with The Mother in Folkvangr. The peace of oblivion is not a gift to take lightly when so many would do nearly anything for it. You would never have to know why the threads have led you here, why they've woven you through countless lives to bring you to this very place and this very decision," she said, guiding me right up to the hazy gateway. She stepped to the other side, crossing through the mist that flowed like water and reappearing on the other side to look back at me with features that felt far too familiar. "Sometimes death is a mercy, but if you live, not even you can outrun the Fates forever."

I touched shaking fingers to the mist in the entryway, wincing back from the deep cold that suffused my hand at the touch. Fenrir appeared beyond the Morrigan, his stoic face still and his eyes holding mine. His head seemed to nod, as if he understood my hesitation and wanted to tell me it would be alright.

But it wouldn't. I knew beyond a shadow of doubt that nothing would ever be alright again.

"What will the trials require of me?" I asked, hesitating at that gateway. I couldn't seem to bring myself to pass into the inner sanctum of Tartarus, not without first asking the questions that once, not so long ago, I'd have been too afraid to voice.

"That will depend on how the magic of Tartarus judges you. The trials are created around what it wishes to see of you, what it needs to test," Badb said, the cryptic answer the only one I knew I would receive.

Nemain raised a hand, lining her fingers up with mine on the opposite side of the mist. I swallowed as I pressed my hand farther, pushing it through the misty waters that spread around it, thick and viscous and so cold it burned. I gasped as my hand emerged on the other side, my arm and then my body following. Nemain moved with me, guiding me through the cold until it surrounded my face, filling my ears and my nose and my eyes with the burn of it. I couldn't escape it, couldn't breathe as it made my lungs still in my chest. I barely managed to push my legs forward before they felt like they froze solid, emerging on the other side as Nemain took a step back, her hand still raised to mirror mine.

The liquid leaked out of my nose, dripping down the sides of my neck and running over my skin in droplets. It gathered on the back of my left hand, pooling in the center of the black circle as I fought for the ability to move. It sank into my pores, eating away at my Fae Mark there.

I wheezed, dropping to my knees as it robbed me of air. As it painfully stripped my power away from me, gathering it all within itself and holding it there. The center of the circle turned the color of flesh once more, the reddish brown of my skin showing where there had been only darkness before.

My knees throbbed with the pain of hitting the stone, forcing me to acknowledge what had been lost. It wasn't just my magic, but the ability to heal from the injuries I sustained. The ability to not be fazed by such mundane trivialities.

Where I'd been semi-numbed to the pain of having the skin peeled from my bones, now I felt every stone in my knees.

I pushed myself to my feet, trying not to allow my knees to buckle. I wondered if Caldris felt the shift in our bond, felt the fact that I couldn't access any of the power that arched between us. Maybe it would mean he would have greater access to it.

Maybe it would mean he could fight.

I didn't pretend to understand the equilibrium of a bond and the magic that pulsed between two halves of a soul. Because the one thing I knew was that I didn't stand a chance when I felt like my body was too heavy to carry.

"It feels worse than you ever remember before, doesn't it?" Badb asked, nodding her head for me to walk forward. She was right, but even worse than the physical heaviness was the emptiness within me. Where my bond had once pulsed brightly in my mind, a distant light, I could no longer feel the warmth of Caldris's mind pressing against my own.

I suddenly remembered what it was to be completely and entirely alone in my head. To have him silenced.

"Let's get this over with," I said with a scowl, making my way down the steps on the other side. My knees threatened to cave with every step.

But I took them anyway. Just as I always had.

SIX

CALDRIS

I carried yet another of the fallen forms down the stairs toward the dungeons where I'd only just gotten free from hours prior. The pile of remains in front of the river exit grew with each trip as the Lliadhe and I worked tirelessly to get them out of the throne room. The remaining Fae carried their own mates, lingering beside the grouping of bodies far longer than they should have.

The sight would only torment them, would only remind them of all the moments they'd been deprived of. There would be no escaping the grief that was coming for them, or the madness that would eventually set in without the other half of them present to ground them against it, but that didn't mean they needed to stare at their mate's pain and suffering.

Mab had not been kind in her destruction.

I lowered the newest body beside the rest, a Lliadhe woman whose only crime had been to be in the wrong place when Mab snapped. She'd been the first to die, the messenger sent to deliver the humans to Mab's throne room. She'd allegedly taken too long to make the journey earning Mab's impatience as her punishment.

I stared at them, my gaze flashing between the boat waiting for me to make the journey with their souls while the Lliadhe handled their physical forms once I'd offered their spirits the true separation of the Void. I knew my place, understood my duty like a calling in my blood. It drew me toward that boat, my steps hesitant as the other part of me called from the other direction.

Only Estrella could make me abandon my duty, prolong the spirits' suffering, and increase the chances that they may condemn themselves to an eternity wandering Alfheimr. I wanted to help them more than almost anything, but my gaze wandered to the steps that would take me back toward the throne room where more bodies waited.

If I simply turned right at the top, I would go in the direction of the cove where Mab had taken my own mate from me. The need to do right by her was stronger than my need to do right by the mate of another, and I took a step back in the few moments where I did not have an audience to judge me for the selfish act.

I turned toward the door and the stairs that waited for me, coming face-to-face with Nila as she carried some of the more . . . obliterated remains down. Her dress was stained with blood and gore, chunks of flesh clinging to the fabric as she simply stared at me.

Most would think I was simply returning to gather the next body, but there was something keen in her gaze that felt weighted.

She knew exactly where I was going, and I waited to see if she would judge me for abandoning her people in their time of need. Because there could be no doubt, the people of Tartarus were Nila's. She may not have been their ruler or anything close to it, but she had ingrained herself into the community of Sidhe and Lliadhe alike so deeply that I didn't think she knew how to separate her individual emotions from theirs any longer.

"Go," she said, surprising me with the soft command. She stepped to the side, giving me the empty doorway so that I could pass her. "Go to her while you can."

I glanced back over my shoulder, hesitating as I stared at the souls lingering close to their bodies, unable to reach out and touch the mates they had probably even feared in life. But with death came clarity, came a firmer understanding that they hadn't possessed while their human upbringings and prejudices kept them from embracing the bond they felt.

"What about them?" I asked.

"I'll stay with them until it's time, do what I can to entice them to stay here and wait for you," she said, lowering the bloody body to the ground beside the others. "But they're already dead. Your mate is not."

The callous words were so unlike the optimistic female I'd come to know through her time with Estrella, but they were the ones I needed to hear at that moment. If I hadn't known better, I'd have suspected Nila possessed some magic of her own, always knowing the words a person needed to hear at any given moment.

I strode through the doorway, making my way up the steps as quickly as I could manage. I took them two at a time, pausing only for a brief moment at the top to study the halls and whatever action might exist there. They were empty, save for the Lliadhe hustling through them to bring fresh rags and cleaning supplies to rid the floor of bloodstains until Mab's next massacre. Turning away from the commotion, I made my way down the silent hall with quick steps that aimed not to attract attention to myself.

The entrance to the narrow passage that led beneath Tar Mesa was closed, the broad figure of a daemon standing guard. My heart sank with the realization that Mab had retained enough of her logic to remember to do this, to guard the place that I would be sure to go now that I was free from the dungeon.

The daemon and I made eye contact, holding one another's stares. I considered my options as I strode past him, trying not to attract further suspicion or attention.

If I was going to fight my way through a daemon, I needed to come up with a fucking plan for it. Otherwise it wouldn't end any better than it had that night in the cove when the daemon had found Estrella, damn near killing both of us.

I continued to the stairs at the other side of the palace, planning to circle around rather than passing by that passage all over again so soon. There was one phrase in my head, a mantra that I couldn't ignore as I considered my options, beating them around in my head and hoping one of them could stand the abuse.

I was no use to her dead or imprisoned.

I was no use to her dead or imprisoned.

I needed a fucking plan, and I needed it fast.

Seven

ESTRELLA

As darkness fell over the prison, the firelights gleaming at the top of the cave ceiling dimmed slowly, recreating the setting of the sun aboveground. I couldn't be sure if we were on the same cycle as Caldris would be, if he was in a place where he could appreciate such privileges.

I doubted Mab would have taken kindly to his rebellion, even if she had tried to kill him. The glimpses I'd had into the bizarre vulnerabilities she possessed were somehow even more horrifying than the brutality she exhibited.

She truly believed herself to be the victim of her story, as if her violence was warranted because her husband had been mated to another and had an affair because of it.

She saw the affair as a betrayal. If we'd been human, I might have even agreed with her. But now that I had a more full understanding of the mate bond and how all-consuming it could be, I fully appreciated the way the Fae cast all relationships aside the moment a bond snapped into place.

Nothing could compare to the love of fated mates.

Nemain stopped, snapping her gaze toward the cave ceiling and glancing at the fading cyclones of fire. They dimmed alongside the ones overhead, casting shadows that grew as we watched.

"Come with us. Quickly," Badb said, reaching out to take my hand suddenly. She guided me to the wall in the ruins, the boundary that seemed to surround this part of the prison. I wondered about the double gates, if there were other ways to get past the boundary surrounding what I had to believe was the heart of Tartarus, or if all who entered here were forced to endure the gate itself.

"What are we doing?" I asked, following as she brought me to an alcove in the stone. It was a small hollow, not big enough to allow us all to fit within it but too small for large predators to make their way in.

We stopped at the entrance, watching in awe as the prison darkened. Until all traces of light vanished, and we were plunged into the kind of darkness that could only be replicated by a moonless and starless night.

The thought immediately made me think of all those nights I'd gone wandering in the woods in the dark, of the danger I'd risked just to feel a few moments of freedom.

"We must stop here for the night. The creatures that roam the darkness of Tartarus are not for the likes of you," Macha warned, the three of them pressing me into the wall. They didn't force me into the alcove that was only big enough for me just yet. "We will begin with the first of your trials tomorrow. You must make it to the first river alive, without your magic to assist you. This place has a way of pushing you into danger, using your weaknesses against you. You should make sure you rest well tonight, Child of Fate. You'll need to keep your wits about you to survive."

"I'm not really positive I have my wits about me on a good day, let alone after sleeping in a cave with the threat of death looming over me," I muttered, looking out past where the Morrigan watched me.

The Cwn Annwn were only visible because of the white of their fur, frolicking through the darkness in a way I hadn't seen before. They were only ever so light with Caldris, when they tackled him after missing him for weeks.

Watching them play was somehow wholesome, even knowing

they were creatures of death and darkness, destined to hunt the Fae and humans who escaped punishment and deliver them to Tartarus after their trial.

Realization dawned on me so sharply it stole the breath from my lungs. "If Mab has the Wild Hunt hunting down human mates, who is delivering criminals to their punishment?" I asked, quirking a brow as Badb met my curious gaze.

"No one. We've not had a new prisoner sent to Tartarus in centuries, outside of those summoned here by the Primordials themselves," she said, gazing out into the darkness. The last of the flames flickered nearby, the cyclones barely a hint of light.

"What happens to the souls who deserve to be brought to Tartarus and die before they can be delivered?" I asked, thinking of all those who had escaped punishment during Mab's reign.

"They linger in the Void, becoming something twisted and monstrous. They cannot move on to the afterlife, not when they are not worthy of The Father or The Mother's embrace. The ferryman keeps them trapped within the river, so that they cannot harm the souls who deserve peace."

"The thing with spinning teeth," I said, more to myself than to her, thinking of the creature that had tried to eat me during my dream—when the ferryman revealed himself to be the father I remembered.

But also not.

Nemain nodded as she stepped closer, trailing a hand over the light clothes covering me. It was the same gauzy, half-transparent dress Mab had chosen for me to wear. The golden paint lines on my body were partially smeared now from my altercation, the water of the cove having made them run and bleed.

She waved a hand over it, her hand blurring with the shadow of a raven wing, the black feathers brushed over my chest, the magic within them sliding over my skin. "This will do nothing to protect you in this place."

The fabric molded, shifting higher up until it wrapped around the base of my throat. The black shimmering fabric hardened, forming individual scales like that of a snake. They shimmered with the faintest green glimmer, a raised golden snake on the breastplate that stood out from the scaled armor covering my chest and torso. It slithered down my arms, stopping only when it covered the backs of my hands with the shape of a V where it came to a point in the center of my hand.

The skirts disappeared, tightening around my legs into scaled, almost leatherlike pants. They were harder than that, firmer on the outside even though they stretched and moved with me. My dress slippers shifted to boots, curving up my calves and shins and covering me further. The soles hardened, giving me a firmer footing as Macha stepped up in front of me. Her sister, Nemain, backed away, the gift of my armor completed as Macha held out her palms.

Molding the darkness and nothingness itself, I watched in rapt fixation as two gleaming swords formed. They were shorter than the ones I'd been forced to train with out of necessity and lack of options in Mistfell, a sword designed for a man with a bigger body and different center of balance.

The form of a snake curved around the hilt, carved into the metal itself. Each sword had been marked with it, the blade itself shimmering like golden starlight. It wasn't the same silver-toned metal I'd grown up seeing, but a speckled deep midnight blue blade.

I reached out with trembling hands, taking a hilt in each hand. They were lighter than I'd thought possible, fitting in my smaller grip as if they'd been molded to my hands.

"I thought you couldn't offer me any aid in the trials," I said, raising my eyes to Macha as I took the blades from her. I wouldn't give them back, wouldn't part with the things that I felt as keenly as I felt my magic, lingering in that lightened circle of my hand.

All a part of me. With my magic just out of reach, I'd take what I could get.

"You cannot enter the trials with anything that does not already belong to you," Badb answered, gesturing toward the gifts they'd given me as the last of the fires winked out. "These were made for you long ago. We are merely delivering you your birthright," she said.

Macha's hand came down on my shoulder, pressing me into the tiny stone alcove. "In you go. Get some sleep. You'll need it in the morning," she said.

Her words were accentuated by the howl of the Cwn Annwn in the distance as the sound of them shifted from joy to hunger.

These were the hours of beasts and prey, and in this place?

I was the latter.

Sleep, a deep growl seemed to say in my head as I moved into the cave and lay down upon the stone. I tried to get settled and comfortable, the words in my head an odd comfort, surrounding me like thick fur on a cool night.

So I did.

EIGHT

CALDRIS

I worked tirelessly, contemplating ways I might lure the daemon away from the tunnel leading beneath Tar Mesa. If I could only get to the cove itself, I wouldn't hesitate to throw myself into the waters and follow after Estrella. I couldn't help the surging thoughts, the constant questioning if she was okay, even as I kept my body busy.

The Lliadhe helped me lay coins upon the eyes of the dead, letting their bodies rest upon the stone beneath the Court of Shadows. None of these creatures deserved to have their physical forms wait out eternity in the dungeons intended for human prisoners, but it was the only way for us to preserve their bodies long enough for me to take them to the entrance of the Void.

"Will they make it safely?" Nila asked, laying a hand upon my arm. She handed me a coin purse filled with gold with her other hand, having collected it from the families of Mab's latest victims. Her eyes were filled with tears, from a combination of my unsuccessful attempt to get to the cove and the loss before her. Now that it was time to say goodbye in truth, Nila was overcome with the grief for the people she'd come to know. She'd had far more experience with the human mates than I had, often tending to them when Estrella didn't need her.

She knew it was what Estrella would have wanted, but it was also just in her nature to care for those who were often ignored.

"Anyone who wishes to," I said, removing her hand, taking a step away, and approaching the boat that waited for me. I needed to be on my way, but I also felt it was necessary to reaffirm the boundary of touch even with her. Though there was nothing romantic in her touch, it still felt like something I would have despised if it had been a hand on Estrella.

I grasped the oar in both hands, holding her stare as I pushed off the stone and guided the boat into the river. "But I cannot force a soul to follow me into the afterlife. If they wish to remain and tend to any unsettled business they may have, that is their choice. But they should bear in mind that moving on becomes more difficult the more time that passes, and the things that made them who they were will slowly fade until they're mindless wanderers."

I didn't look back to see which souls chose to follow me, plunging themselves into the river and trusting me to serve as their guide. There was no reason not to, because in spite of all that Mab had forced me to become, this was my true purpose.

This was what the Fates had decided for me upon my birth, gifting me with a responsibility that most would never understand. Many would consider it a curse—the life of a nomad, traveling wherever death called me.

I could think of no better way to spend my life than seeing the world with my mate at my side, watching the awe of everything she saw settled over her adorably shocked expression.

I rowed myself downriver, watching as the jarring hills of Tar Mesa faded into the background over my shoulder. Shadows moved within the water, the banks filled with those who could sense my journey and the pilgrimage those who followed me made. They dove into the river itself slowly, one by one, filling the water with the souls of those who had been abandoned and damned because of my inability to do my job. The effects of Mab's cruel tyranny extended far beyond those within her court.

It upset the very balance of nature itself. There were those of us who had duties to the world, who were needed elsewhere but kept at her side in a desperate play for power. When those duties were ignored, the consequences could be catastrophic.

A world was overrun with lost spirits, possessing the bodies of the living who were not strong of mind enough to fight them off.

I sighed in relief with each and every soul that jumped into the river, joining me on our path to the Void. It was one less soul left to wander and become nothing but instinct. To become vengeful and driven by hatred.

The gates of the Void came into view slowly, the gleaming white marble symbols of the ferryman arching toward the sky. The eyes beneath the hood seemed to glow with gold, shimmering in the sunlight. Two black doors were carved into the hill between the figures, clamped tight with the magic of the keeper of the Void that even I could not defy.

At the base of those gates, the ferryman waited in their boat. The river narrowed just before them, making it impossible for any souls to sneak past their guard.

This place, where the underworld met the world of the living, never failed to remind me of my father. Of what the Court of Shadows had once represented before Mab twisted it into what it had now become.

Evil with thorned edges, willing to wrong anyone and anything without remorse. According to our history, there had been a time when we were simply indifferent to the politics of the Fae.

When the Court of Shadows existed as a thing all its own, part of the Winter Court but still separate and entirely ignored by the others. Our work was done in the shadows that most preferred to pretend didn't exist. That hadn't suited the Queen of Air and Darkness, who lived for attention as much as she did pain.

I rowed my boat up to the ferryman, wincing back from the golden eyes they did not hesitate to settle upon me. We had always respected one another, always understood that our purposes were one and the same, and that we merely operated on opposite sides of the boundary between life and death. Something had shifted with the knowledge that the man who had once been Estrella's father figure existed within the collection of souls that comprised the ferryman. That they still felt a semblance of attachment to my mate.

"How is she?" I asked, my desperation for news of her safety forcing me to ignore the customs that usually existed between us. They held out their palm, allowing the souls who had been fortunate enough to be given payment on the eyes of their corpse to rise from the river. The first corporeal soul raised herself up, the shadow of a golden coin gleaming in her hand. Water dripped off her, swirling around with the pure energy that a soul was made of to create a thing of beauty. The shimmering essence of her caught the light, allowing it to reflect off the water that clung to her as she dropped the coin into the ferryman's hand. They nodded to her, waving the staff they held with a skull at the top.

I'd never dared to ask what unfortunate soul had been cursed to accompany them for all eternity.

"Have you seen her?" I asked when they ignored me again to tend to the next soul, allowing the first to pass through the small gap between his boat and the river's edge.

They still didn't answer, their expression softening for the soul who cried as she handed over her coin. I didn't recognize her from Mab's court, and I realized she must have been one of the human mates who had unjustly been harmed. It went against everything the Fae believed in, especially after centuries of separation from those who should have been with us all along.

"Kharon!" I snapped, forcing them to finally shift their attention back to me.

"We have not seen your mate, God of the Dead," they said, their voice completely lacking all intonation. There wasn't a hint of the man who cared for the child he'd raised, as if he'd vanished entirely. He'd been lost to the cumulative creature of the Fates' making, the collection of souls trapped within a body for the purpose of remaining neutral to all destinies and plights.

I gritted my teeth through my frustration, knowing that if I'd had any way to get into Tartarus, I'd have moved heaven and earth to make sure I was able to see to her. Getting in through the cove would be a miracle with the daemon there to protect the passageway. Standing by while they tended to the souls, as was their duty, took every bit of patience I had and some I didn't. When the last of the souls with payment had crossed over, I reached into my pocket and pulled out the coin purse filled with gold that Nila had given me. Depositing it into the ferryman's hand, they waved their free hand and allowed the remaining souls to pass once they had their payment.

"Can you find her? See if she's alright?" I asked, already knowing the answer. The Void might not have been Tartarus, but all dimensions of the Underworld were connected. I just didn't know how.

"We alone cannot. Our purpose is to transport, not to spy . . ." they said, their voice trailing off. "But there is another way into Tartarus if you are brave enough, God of the Dead."

"Bravery has nothing to do with it," I said, because I would do anything to try to help Estrella in the prison. To shield her from all that would harm her in a place that was far worse than any nightmares I could conjure up.

"The only place where a physical form can enter Tartarus directly is the cove within the Shadow Court. But there is a back door, so to speak, within the Void itself," Kharon said, glancing over their shoulder to the doors to the Void.

"Then take me to it," I said, gripping my oar tighter. I would pass through if that was what was needed.

"Once you pay your way into the Void, you will not be able to leave the Underworld. You would die if you entered here," Kharon answered, blocking my path meaningfully. "And you will be useless to your mate if you are dead."

"I am tired of this dance, ferryman. What must I do to help Estrella?" I growled, the warning climbing up my throat. Even a God would be useless against something crafted from the Fates and used as their instrument, but that wouldn't stop me from taking a piece of them with me.

"There is a place in the human realm. A hollow in the earth that connects to all the areas of the Underworld. It will enable a traveler to enter the Void via the river of life, but you will not be able to control where you land. Left to your own devices, you may be swept into Folkvangr or Valhalla as easily as Tartarus," Kharon explained, gripping their staff tighter.

"There must be a way to make sure I go where I need? Something I can do, otherwise this is a risk I'm not sure I can take. If I go to Valhalla without Estrella, this is all for nothing," I said, digging my oar into the silt at the bottom of the river. It held my boat steady, waiting for the answer I needed even if the magic in that boat knew my natural time to return to Tar Mesa had come.

"Come to the entrance in three nights' time. I will be waiting for you on the river of life, and I will pull you out of the waters before you can go too far and take you to Tartarus," Kharon conceded, gritting their way through each word. As the souls inside of them fought against one another, trying to remain impartial while a father tried to love his daughter.

"Where do I need to go?" I asked, watching their face shift. The gold in their eyes glowed a little brighter, their words coming out pained and through clenched teeth.

"Go to the place where you first wronged your mate for selfish gains," the ferryman said, making my brow furrow in response. "I cannot tell you any more than that."

"My life depends on this riddle, you realize? Estrella's life could depend on a fucking play of words," I snapped, even knowing I would not receive any more information than that from them. The way their features shifted constantly, twitching as if they couldn't control the uprising happening within themself, led me to believe that this issue needed to play itself out inside of them.

I would be on my own to figure out where I'd first wronged Estrella.

"Caldris," they called as I turned my boat to return to Tar Mesa. "There is one important thing before you go. Only your soul may enter the river of life. Your body will be consumed if it touches the waters."

Fucking wonderful.

NINE

ESTRELLA

Hours passed in pure darkness, the sounds driving me back into the alcove slowly. I didn't want to consider the violence that existed in a place so defined by pain and suffering. Feeling so painfully alone with all this suffering to surround me, I wanted nothing more than to curl into my mate's arms and allow him to drown out the sound. As the fires lit, slowly rising off the rust-colored earth beneath my feet, a horrifying screech pierced the air. A bird made of fire streaked through the darkened sky, his feathers burning like flames. A trail of ash followed him, drifting down to land upon everything below as he followed his path.

I stepped out onto the plains, grateful for the coverage of my new armor as one of the cyclones of flame came too close. Fenrir emerged from beside the entrance to the alcove I'd called home for the night. His white fur was matted around his face and on his chest, stained with the red of blood. I tried not to think about what kind of creature he might have gotten ahold of in the night, resting my hand upon the clean fur at the back of his neck. Lupa and Ylfa approached slowly, walking through the middle of the flames to come to stand beside me. A single raven flew over their heads, its black feathers such a stark contrast to the bloodied gore of the wolves' gleaming fur.

The raven transformed into the three Goddesses of the Morrigan, and they landed smoothly in a way that I didn't think I'd ever manage. Two small birdlike wings separated into six humanoid ones, all hurrying across the sand to come to a smooth stop just in front of me.

"Is night always like that?" I asked, rolling my neck to the side. I'd only managed to get a few hours of tremulous sleep, the noises of slaughter interrupting it periodically. It was only the familiarity of Fenrir's growl that allowed me to take any comfort, knowing my wolf companion wouldn't allow me to come to any harm so long as he was near.

The Morrigan turned on their heels before answering, starting to walk farther into the prison of Tartarus. I swallowed before I followed, reaching over my shoulder to take comfort in the blades strapped across my back. It was so reminiscent of the way Caldris chose to carry his swords that it brought me extra comfort, making it feel as if he was closer than he was for just a moment. Imelda's satchel was a reassurance in my pocket, the presence and weight of it there a reminder of the friends who waited for me in Tar Mesa as well.

"Many predators hunt in the night," Nemain said, glancing over her shoulder at me and nodding her head to motivate me to follow. I did as instructed, shoving down my fear of what might be waiting for me farther inside.

My fear was irrelevant when moving forward was the only way to rescue Caldris.

"That is the way of things where you come from as well, is it not?" she asked, allowing her sisters to surround me. Nemain walked on my left, Badb at my right, with Macha taking up the rear. The Cwn Annwn guided the way, moving with an assuredness that spoke of the time they'd spent in this place.

"It is. It seems to happen more quietly somehow," I said, then laughed at the ridiculousness of such a statement. The predators in the human realm were fine, because generally speaking you didn't hear them fighting?

Okay.

The phoenix crossed his way over the sky again, cutting a different path than he had before. This time the ash rained down on us, coating my skin in warmth that didn't burn. The bird was enormous, a sprawling beast of flames. It glowed with deep red light at the core of its being, its wings and tail fading out into bright yellow at their tips. A man screamed in the distance to my right, the sound coinciding with the path of the flaming bird.

I took a step toward him, ready to intervene in whatever pain could cause a scream that shrill. "Any who suffer here are beyond your aid," Badb said, blocking my path. "To interfere in their punishment would be to incite the wrath of the Primordial responsible for putting them here. Unless you would like to risk taking their place, I suggest you leave well enough alone."

Lupa circled back, taking up position between Macha and I. She pushed her head into my back, motioning me to continue on even as I still hesitated. It wasn't in me to leave people to suffer, to let anyone feel pain.

"What did he do to deserve his punishment?" I asked, refusing to take my eyes off the distance to my right where his screams continued to echo through the void of the underground cavern.

"Never mind that," Macha said, walking forward until I had little choice but to move lest she run me over. "All you need to know is that every soul suffering here deserves it for the wrong they committed. These people are not kind. They are not misunderstood. These are the murderers who enjoyed the kill. The rapists who violated more women than you can count. They are the very kind of people you yourself would condemn if you knew them, Tempest," she added.

I found myself nodding along to her words, knowing that my constant seeking for justice would likely bring me to do just that. If I knew Mab could never escape, would I send her to Tartarus rather than give her a swift, merciful death?

The answer to that question didn't come as quickly as I wished, and I didn't want to stop to consider what that said about me. "Why do you call me that?" I asked, studying her intently.

The Morrigan shrugged with the slightest of smirks playing on her face. "A tempest is a violent storm, is it not? Would you not consider yourself to have wreaked havoc on the world that existed until he refused to let you die?"

I furrowed my brow, hating that I was to blame for the actions Caldris had taken that day at the Veil. "I've done nothing."

"And yet your very existence has changed *everything*," Nemain said, continuing on the path forward.

The ground beneath my feet seemed to glow with an increasing red pulse, and it wasn't until the scent of burning leather reached my nose that I really looked at the boots on my feet. At the soles that protected me from the hot dirt that couldn't even be called soil. The silt and sand hissed lightly where my boots touched it as I walked, tiny coils of smoke rising up from the contact.

I glanced toward Fenrir as he led the way, watching his paws touch the ground without consequence. He was unbothered by the scalding heat of the earth, his paws sinking into the dry grains with each and every step.

"The Cwn Annwn are part of this place. They are born with hel-fyre in their veins," Nemain answered, making it known just how closely they monitored my every move.

Fenrir's red-tipped ears matched the color of Tartarus, and I'd always connected it with the bright red of freshly drawn blood, but watching him stand amidst the flames, I realized I'd been wrong all along.

It was the color of pure, uncontrolled fire.

"There isn't a cruel bone in his body. How can he come from this place?" I asked, glancing toward the sharp peak to our right. It jut-ted out of the ground like sharpened stone, a pool of bright red fire churning at the base.

We avoided it, circling around it on our journey to the River Styx.

"His victims would likely tell a different story," Badb said with a disbelieving chuckle.

She wasn't wrong, and yet . . .

"Those people deserved it. I've only ever seen the Cwn Annwn kill to protect," I said, thinking only of the fact that self-defense was hardly a crime.

The defense of a loved one should be treated in the same manner.

"As do those sent here for punishment," Badb argued, a knowing gleam in her eye. She'd walked me right into the sharp edge of my own expectations and hypocrisy.

I couldn't help the huff of laughter that escaped as I leveled her with a glare.

Her lip tipped up at the corner, amusement on her face that I couldn't help but mirror. It was only the somber environment and circumstances that led to me being here in the first place that kept me from truly giving the moment the breadth it deserved.

My feet throbbed with twinges of pain, reminding me clearly of the days that I'd spent traveling with Caelum after the Veil first fell. It was strange to think of them now, with all that had changed and all that I knew. It had been so nice to avoid such human concepts of pain and inconvenience since coming to Alfheimr, and the exhaustion that riddled my bones seemed impossible to overcome. My joints ached, my back throbbed from sleeping on the stone cave floor.

Strange to think that my own ignorance had enabled me to not feel the bond pulling taut between us, when all I wanted was to feel it strengthen now.

I wanted what had been stolen from us.

The ground shifted as we walked, the soil becoming less burnt and more living, even as flames danced amongst the blades of grass that filled it. The Morrigan and I didn't speak anymore, my own dread over what would wait for me at the River Styx keeping me from asking any questions for the moment.

We walked amongst the flames, letting them tickle the fabric of my leatherlike pants. They never touched my skin, never burned me through the fabric that I'd been gifted as it formed a protective barrier.

I found myself immensely grateful for the gift, thinking about the Morrigan's words that they were always meant to be mine. But who had made them?

I thought of the snakes curving the hilt of the blades that fit perfectly into my palms. "Why would I have clothes made to withstand helfyre?" I asked, laying a hand over the flames. The warmth tickled my bare skin, forcing me to keep my distance or risk burning. Nemain met my gaze when I looked over at her, having seen her head turn from the corner of my eye. She swept a hand over a particularly large flame blocking the path, laying black feathers atop the flames. They doused beneath her magic, lowering to a height that enabled me to walk through without risking injury.

A building to our right erupted into flames as we passed, the columns burning and surrounded by fire even though the structures themselves never seemed to catch. There was no destruction in spite of the immense heat pulsing off of it in waves.

"For the same reason Fenrir was probably drawn to you from the moment he saw you," she said, taking my hand in hers. She pulled it to her side, holding it over the flame as the heat kissed my skin. She held my gaze, something silent passing between us in warning before she used both her hands to shove mine into the fire at our sides.

"No!" I screamed, attempting to yank my hand back. She held me firm, my fight barely registering against the Goddess's, faced with the truth of my power locked away by the gate. My skin erupted in agony, the burn sinking inside me and feeling as if the flesh would melt from my bones.

"Look," she said, her voice quiet but stern. I pried my eyes open, realizing that all I saw was darkness because I'd blocked out everything and closed my eyes.

She turned my arm in the flames like a spit roast. I stared at the unblemished skin of my palm and forearm, whimpering through the pain that still consumed everything.

"It hurts," I argued, yanking my hand back again. She released me finally, allowing me to cradle my uninjured arm to my chest protectively.

"Interesting," Macha hummed at my back.

"I have to assume it's a consequence of her unorthodox upbringing. Her body isn't really hers, is it?" Badb asked, the three of them shifting to stand before me and staring at me like I was a curiosity.

As if they hadn't just plunged my hand into a fire. "You didn't know it wouldn't burn me, did you?" I asked, my horror rising as Nemain turned on her heel and continued on.

"No one can know anything for certain when it comes to you. No one like you has ever existed before," she said, glancing over her shoulder at me finally. "So I made an educated guess."

"An educated guess," I repeated, blinking at the back of her head as she turned once again. "And if I'd burned?"

She shrugged, her shoulders moving with the motion of it to reveal the slender play of feather tattoos peeking out from beneath her armor. "Then I suppose you would have burned, and we likely would have known the trials to be a futile effort for us all."

"Your nonchalance is touching," I snapped, my anger rising at the casual ease of her dismissal. As if I was something to toy with, to pick apart and understand. Her lack of care regarding my life or limb . . . I was truly alone.

Fenrir growled as if he'd heard the thought.

I couldn't focus on that, not when there were far more serious insinuations to unearth.

"Why didn't I burn?" I asked.

"Because you, dear Tempest, were first born in the Cradle of Creation," she said, stealing the wind from my lungs.

TEN

ESTRELLA

My shock rippled through me at the revelation that I couldn't quite wrap my head around. Even as the implications of it sank deep into me, it didn't quite strike in the way I'd expected it to now that I knew.

My parents were from Tartarus.

That was the extent of what I could pry from the Morrigan. Nemain had immediately clamped her lips shut like she was physically unable to say more, leaving me to stare at her sisters in the hopes that they would pick up where she'd left off. Neither muttered a single word, not even when I'd probed for answers.

The beast inside of me had vanished the moment the gate stripped away my magic, but it would make sense that she was the consequence of that birthright. If my body wasn't really my body, was she what I was truly meant to be?

I swallowed, thinking of the horrific beasts I'd heard in the night. How many more nights would I need to spend in Tartarus in the endeavor to complete these trials and confront Medusa before I could return home and save Caldris?

The thought that I might have been one of them, something of this world and not my own . . .

Gods.

A very different kind of sound traveled through the ruins of what seemed to have been a village, emerging out the other side as we approached. The flames consuming the buildings disguised it, making it blend in with the surroundings until we were nearly upon it. The Morrigan and Cwn Annwn guided me through the center of the street, leading the way toward the sound.

It wasn't the strangled moan I associated with pain, but the kind that came from pure, undiluted pleasure. I swallowed back my nerves, holding my chin high and shoving down those delicate human sensibilities that had once seemed so crippling compared to Caelum's assertion and willingness to partake in more creative endeavors.

"What is that?" I asked, glancing toward Nemain. The woman smiled, her white teeth gleaming with a red tint thanks to the flames that surrounded us. Her red eyes seemed to match the fire.

"I should think you know exactly what that is," she said with a chuckle.

I paused, my feet stopping in the middle of what remained of the road. The dirt beneath my feet was all that remained, but I couldn't help but envision cobblestones having been there before.

The portrait it painted of a picturesque town vanished from my mind as soon as it had come, leaving me to scramble after the Morrigan. I couldn't afford to get left behind in a place that was just as likely to eat me as it was to make me one with it.

The flames receded as we approached a newer part of the village, the darkness settling along with a white, filmy mist that descended over the red earth. There were trees here, plants and fresh signs of life that weren't consumed by fire.

There was also a writhing mass of flesh, bodies upon bodies gathered in the center of the village. From what I could tell, the homes themselves were empty of life, as if every single soul was in the village center. Daybeds surrounded the single bonfire at the center, where my own village would have congregated around a well for drinking water.

Immediately surrounding that fire, there were strange, almost tentlike structures. But the canvas was transparent, allowing each and every person to see the activities that occurred within and offering no privacy whatsoever. But there were cushions and pillows, blankets and furs for comfort within them.

The people who hadn't found their way to the comfort of one of the tents lingered outside, already lost to the throes of passion with a partner or two or three.

Clothing was minimal if present at all, tiny scraps that covered private parts and nothing else. They were tossed out of the way to give their partners access, a forgotten and irrelevant inconvenience.

Only one man seemed separate from the passion of the orgy, a lone figure sitting on the pedestal placed atop the bonfire. He glared down at the figures below him, his hands chained behind his back. The metal clinked when he shifted, but he made no move to escape.

The wounds around his wrists where the iron touched his skin were deeper than I'd ever seen, surrounded by scar tissue as if they'd been there for countless centuries of suffering. "What is this?" I asked, sticking close to the Morrigan as we approached the village center.

The distinct pulse of music rang in my ears, though I couldn't find a single instrument that might have been responsible for it. Drums beat in a steady pulse, the rhythm of the strikes sinking into my bones. The hair rose on my arms, the distinct shiver of magic crawling up my spine and forcing me to roll my neck from one side to the other in an effort to ignore the tingle that sank into my pores.

"Phlegyas," Badb said, her voice coming from too close beside me. I'd been so fixated on ignoring the warmth coiling in my belly that I hadn't noticed her sidling up next to me. Her breath fanned my cheek, the warmth of it too hot for my skin. It made me feel like one touch and I might burn, like I might be consumed by the magic of sex that coated the air. "His daughter pledged herself and her body to one of Rheaghan's temples before the Veil. He was one of the first humans to resist the Old Gods, swearing his fealty to The Father and The Mother with the King and High Priest. I'm sure you can imagine what he thought of his daughter's participation in the Summer Court traditions."

"I know nothing of Summer Court traditions," I admitted, swallowing as a woman approached me. She separated from her male partner, striding up without a care for the Morrigan at my side or the Cwn Annwn who growled at her approach.

"They're very much like this at times," Badb said, smiling as the strange woman ran the backs of her fingers across my cheekbone.

"Aren't you hot in all those clothes?" the woman asked, her warm brown eyes running down the length of my leather and armor. "Take them off and join us," she said, trailing a hand up her belly and between the valley of her very bare breasts.

My breath hitched, and the woman's gaze was knowing as her eyes fell to my parted lips.

I swallowed, ignoring the pulsing heat in my veins. "I have a mate," I said, smiling as she reached out to take my hand in hers. She placed it on the side of her neck, slowly slipping it lower so that I could feel the distinctly feminine curve of her collarbone.

"I'm sure he wouldn't mind," she said, the words washing over me. It was like a splash of cold water to my system, forcing me to draw my hand back in the stark realization and firm knowledge that he would care.

He would care very much.

"Then you've clearly never met my Caldris," I said with a laugh, squeezing the woman's hand before I released her. She raised her chin, her head tilting to the side. I felt it in my soul that she recognized that name, that his reputation for violence had traveled even into the depths of Tartarus.

Her head tilted to the side, sadness filling her warm brown eyes as she studied me. Her deep red hair fell about her shoulders in waves, her pale skin gleaming in the shadow of all that fire.

She was beautiful.

"You're so young. Did you ever even have time to explore this side of yourself before the mate bond snapped into place?" she asked.

I swallowed, considering the answer. Thinking about the days when I'd been far more concerned with the ladies of the night than Lord Byron when they partook in their intimate activities. I'd assumed that to be because of my disdain for the Lord, because such things were so forbidden in the human realm that I dared not even think of them.

"It's just the magic," I said, with a shake of my head, denying the significance of the attraction. Always hiding it—sometimes even from myself. It had been the kind of attraction that could lead to my death in the puritan society where the High Priest controlled the very nature of sex and relationships according to expectations for breeding.

She smiled secretively, turning away from me and walking toward the man she'd left behind before. He welcomed her back with open arms, admiring the same sway of her hips from the front that I enjoyed from the back.

She murmured a few words to him, glancing over her shoulder to look at me as she sank her teeth into her bottom lip. He followed her gaze, reaching down to grip her ass in his hands while he held my stare. Putting on a show that I forced my eyes away from, giving them the privacy they hadn't asked for.

The sound of their footfalls came in our direction until the woman's long legs and thick thighs filled my vision. The hand that reached out to touch me was male, a single finger crooking under my chin to raise my stare. I couldn't help the way my eyes bounced back and forth between the man and the woman, waiting for whatever they might say and steeling myself against the rising heat of the torment around me.

"Are you certain we cannot tempt you to stay?" the man asked, reaching his hand around the front of the woman's throat. He gripped her there, and I could have sworn that I felt the whisper of the touch against my own throat.

"It can be our little secret," the woman whispered, her voice hoarse with the pressure of his hand at her throat. She reached behind her, stroking him through the thin cloth that covered his groin from view. He groaned in her ear, but his eyes were on me even as she touched him.

"My mate and I do not have secrets," I said, swallowing and shifting back. "Take your pleasure in those who are willing. I am not one of them." I continued to shift backward, putting distance between them as they obeyed the final words and engaged with one another more fully with little regard for me. The last dismissal seemed to appease something in the magic, the heated bubble around me bursting so that it felt like I could breathe through it once more. The lust was still there, ever present, but it was no longer suffocating me.

"You should always bear in mind that magic cannot create something from nothing. It is by definition the emphasis of nature, of what is already there," Macha said, and I turned to find her gaze riveted on the same woman in the way my own had been. Nemain and Badb seemed far more interested in watching a group of men with one another, their mouths moving over one another's in a slow, tantalizing dance. "If you were not attracted to her, she would not have tempted you. The magic of this place will only send someone who would be temptation for you."

"They're trapped here, aren't they?" I asked, looking at the dozens of souls lost to the throes of passion. How long had they been stuck in the same loop of intimacy?

"Any who pass through this place are tempted by the magic here as part of their trials. Should they give in to temptation, they are trapped here for all eternity and join the celebration," she said, feeding her arm through mine and guiding me through the fray. Arms reached out to touch me as I passed, gliding across my leather and armor in a way that was seductive but gentle. Pleading but not pushy. I ignored them in the interest of getting through the thickening magic that felt so dense it filled my lungs.

Only the memory of my mate and that shining golden bond pulsing between us kept me walking, pushing me forward out of loyalty.

"It is a shame you never had the opportunity to acknowledge that you are attracted to women as well as men," Macha said, running her fingers over the swell of a woman's ass as we passed where she was locked in an embrace with a man and another woman knelt before her. One of her legs was hoisted over the other woman's shoulder, her face buried between her thighs.

I swallowed back that pulse of heat, turning my stare away and wondering if Caldris could feel my need even outside of Tartarus. I'd felt nothing of him through the bond since entering Tartarus, but I couldn't be certain if that muting extended both ways.

I didn't want to join, especially not without him and in a situation where I would become trapped forever. But this only made me miss him more. It made me wish he was with me to be at my side as I had no choice but to acknowledge something that existed within me. "Is it?" I asked her, forcing myself to focus.

I could see the end of the passion ahead of me, and knowing that the end was within sight gave me some clarity of mind.

"Who I'm attracted to hardly matters now. I love my mate and would never even consider being unfaithful to him. Having an attraction to women doesn't change that any more than an attraction to men would," I said, passing by the outliers. The last groupings faded into the background as we stepped to the other side of the village, the magic of that temptation vanishing with a quick crack that made my ears pop.

Eleven

ESTRELLA

The warmth that had pulsed within me previously shifted into something darker, that monster within me simultaneously feeling like she had escaped her cage and was no longer a part of me. There were moments I didn't feel her presence at all, and then I simply wondered if she'd consumed me. If my loss of her was more because my magic being muted for the time being meant there was nothing to keep her at bay.

She was me, but she also wasn't.

She was the vindictiveness that loved seeing a man suffer for killing his child because she dared to live a life that was different than his.

Maybe that meant she wasn't really a monster at all.

I stared down at Fenrir where he'd clung to my side since leaving the village and the lust that consumed it, running my hand through the thick fur on his back. His red-tipped ears gleamed, the blood on his white fur still matted at his chest from the night before. His eyes were the same deep, haunting red of the flames around us, and watching him came with the realization that so many would consider him a beast.

An abomination or a terrifying creature, when all he did was protect the ones he loved. He might have looked monstrous in some ways, but he was just a puppy in need of love and affection at the end of the day. He nuzzled my side with his head when his sister tried to come between us, forcing me to twist so I could pet the top of Lupa's head as well.

"They're very protective of you," Nemain observed, earning a growl from Fenrir as he read the words as a threat. "Is it because they see you as an extension of your mate, I wonder?" she asked, but there was something in that tone that said she wasn't truly asking. Whatever the answer might have been, they already knew it. This like so many other questions, so many other trials, were all a game in this place. As much as I might be able to convince myself the Morrigan were looking out for me, I couldn't help my complete aggravation and frustration in this situation.

I wanted the truth. I wanted the answers, and instead of just providing them we were forced to dance around them like a childhood game.

"What else could it be?" I said, even if I doubted the words as much as she seemed to. It could have been because he was so much larger than I, but as far as I knew, Fenrir had never allowed Caldris to ride him.

The thought settled inside of me, realization dawning as I looked back down at Fenrir. His red eyes met mine, the disbelief in them so obvious it was almost as if he'd spoken the words themselves.

Duh, he seemed to say.

He stopped walking beside me, lowering his upper body so I could swing my leg over his back. I settled into position, using my thighs and calves to grip his body as he stood more fully. My hands buried in the length of white fur at his nape, using it to grip and hold on as he strode forward a few steps.

Lupa and Ylfa circled around him, pacing with an energy that was tangible.

They wanted to run, but they'd been stuck staying close to me.

"He lets you ride him?" Nemain asked. I grinned, barely refraining from pointing out the obvious. She scoffed, looking toward her sisters as they all stared at me.

"The Cwn Annwn once belonged to Sephtis, God of the

Underworld. When he died, they chose his son as their new owner," Macha explained, referring to Caldris's father.

I hadn't known the wolves had been his.

"But he wasn't their original owner. The Cwn Annwn have existed since the dawn of creation, clinging to those who are connected to death in some way because it most closely resembles the place of their birth and their original owner," Nemain added.

"What does that have to do with me?" I asked, trying not to get too impatient. I was truly growing tired of the tidbits of information they fed me in bits and pieces.

"Because the last being Fenrir allowed to ride him was his original owner," Badb answered, holding my gaze as Fenrir paused his steps. I found my fingers running through his fur, seeking comfort from the friend that went deeper than words. "The last being Fenrir allowed to ride him was the very thing that existed before death. He was the embodiment of nothingness. A distinct lack of life. He is where death comes from. He is the Void."

"*He is you,*" a deeper voice growled, the sound seeming to vibrate in my mind. I jolted, turning to look for the source and finding none but the Morrigan to accompany me.

Fenrir turned his neck slowly, peeking over his shoulders to hold my stare as that voice sounded in my mind once again. "*You and your father are one and the same.*"

I balked, staring down at those gleaming red eyes. The words didn't have time to sink in, couldn't penetrate past the haze of confusion.

Was he . . .

"He's your familiar," Macha said, forcing my gaze to snap to her suddenly. She was studying me intently, watching the exchange occur between Fenrir and I. I didn't think she could hear his voice the way I could, but she was aware that something had changed.

I looked back down at the wolf below me, blinking rapidly as the shadowed whisper of that deep, gruff voice rang in my mind like an echo. "Ilta has her owls. Bryn has her bees. Oshun has his squid . . ." She trailed off, letting the insinuation of her words hang in the air.

I had nothing in common with those names. There was no cause to lump me together with them when they were all the same.

They were all Primordials.

I swallowed, taking the moment to stop and think about the words Fenrir had growled into my mind, trying to connect the pieces. But they were all impossible, a complete betrayal of everything I'd even considered to be true about myself. I didn't even *want* to allow Macha's insinuations to pull at the fragments of my knowledge surrounding the Primordials.

"Khaos."

The golden-eyed man who claimed to be my father in the Void when I drew too much power from him was Khaos.

The father of everything and nothing.

Shit.

TWELVE

ESTRELLA

How is that possible?" I asked, staring down the Morrigan where they studied me. None of them said a word, seeming frozen. They didn't know what I knew, didn't know what Fenrir might have revealed and wouldn't risk giving me information I did not already possess. They couldn't hear the whisper of Fenrir's voice in their minds the way I could, I realized, leaving me to wonder exactly how he could speak to me now but hadn't chosen to do so before.

"You keep your mind closed to all but your mate, but your walls are weakened without your magic and I am stronger in the place I call home."

I jolted all over again, certain I would never get over the press of his mind upon mine. The way the words were growled felt like a comforting caress. It felt like . . .

"Being petted."

This was fucking ridiculous. "Stop that!" I snapped, raising my hands from the fur on the back of his neck. It made it so that I didn't have hold, but even in my panic I trusted Fenrir enough to know he wouldn't risk me falling.

He huffed, expelling the breath from his lungs in something that felt distinctly like a sigh. I snapped my mouth closed, squeezing my eyes shut as I drew in a few deep, steadying breaths. If my mental walls were weakened without my magic, then that meant that the silence I felt from Caldris was truly a result of Tartarus itself. A blockage meant to keep me isolated, no doubt, and one that I wanted to break through as soon as I could find a way.

"You cannot hear him because Tartarus's wards silence all magic other than its own, even the mate bond. You and I are both part of this place." Fenrir confirmed the path of my thoughts, offering a little reassurance as I tried to understand what the Hel was happening in my own head.

"How is it possible that Khaos would be my father?" I asked the Morrigan, feeling the press of each of their stares on mine. Nemain was the one who parted her lips first, her glare settling on the wolf who'd spilled the secret they weren't meant to share.

"Oops." Fenrir tilted his head to the side, fidgeting on his front legs in a move that made his chest rise in something like a shrug.

"He bound us to secrecy, but not you?" she asked, her glare deepening as Fenrir raised his head high in pride. I had the distinct feeling that no one and nothing could bind him, the stubborn ass.

He growled, his body rumbling beneath me. *"Heard that."*

"How?" I repeated, ignoring the fact that now that he was in my mind, I couldn't seem to shove him out. I wasn't strong enough to shield my mind from his intrusion any longer, leaving him to run rampant through my private thoughts.

My hands trembled as they touched his fur, realization settling over me. The wards had stripped away my magic, rendering me effectively human against an immortal creature and harbinger of death. He could slide into my mind and communicate with me because I was suddenly completely defenseless for the first time since the Veil fell. I was used to my body being vulnerable, but my mind had always been my safe space.

I'd known what it was to be human once, when the only beings around me were human or at the very least lacked all magic. Now I was surrounded by it, and the disadvantage it put me at felt all too familiar.

I turned to Fenrir, asking the question while I waited for the Morrigan to give me their vague attempt at an answer that would only leave me with more questions. Maybe now I would at least have

Fenrir to fill in the gaps of information I did not possess. *"Why didn't you speak to me earlier then? Why wait until now?"* I asked, letting my thoughts run rampant.

"You've been a bit busy . . ." Fenrir trailed off, his deep growl laced with humor and sarcasm and things that a wolf shouldn't be able to convey. It was so Godsdamn disorienting. *"I didn't intend to tell you at all until after you've won, but watching the three dance around answers irritates me greatly. I'd eat them if it wasn't frowned upon."*

"Your father," Nemain said vaguely, as if she couldn't quite force herself to say his name. Even with me acknowledging the truth, the binding he'd placed to protect his secret held steadfast. "He has several children. It is not uncommon for a Primordial to procreate. They are not bound by the same curse the witches placed upon their off-spring, because they are nature itself and cannot be contained."

His other children.

Rheaghan. My now dead *brother.*

Mab. My cunt of a sister.

I was going to be sick.

I pressed the back of my hand to my mouth, trying to quell the surging nausea that came with the realization that I was related to my greatest enemy. The woman who had violated my mate through the actions of others was my flesh and blood.

The woman who I would need to kill to find happiness was the only biological family I had left. Whoever had pissed them off, the Fates were cruel, unrelenting tormentors. They didn't care for kindness.

"Mab . . ." I trailed off.

"Is the daughter of Hemera. You are not," Badb said, avoiding directly calling Mab my half-sister. "Your mother is not a Primordial at all."

The distance of my maternal blood did little to ease the pain of longing for what might have been had Rheaghan not died before we ever knew the truth. He might have chosen to stand by me as the sister he'd never known he had. If he only fought for me half as hard as he fought for Mab even after she'd proven to be long past redemption, I'd have had a protective half-brother to deal with.

"Then I'm a Goddess? Like Mab and Rheaghan, or something in between God and Fae?" I asked, truly not understanding my place. There were gifts I possessed that Mab claimed were only available to the Primordials, things that I couldn't deny seemed to set me apart from the Gods I'd watched fighting on the sands outside Tar Mesa.

The threads.

"You are more than a Goddess . . ." Macha said as evasively as she could. Her voice trailed off lightly at the end, and I could tell it pained her to not be able to speak the words that lingered on her tongue. "Your father gave something to you to set you apart from his other offspring."

"What does that even mean?" I asked, feeling the press of Lupa against my thigh as she rubbed her body along the length of my leg to comfort me.

"It means he is you, and you are him."

I didn't want to be that close to anyone, let alone my biological father that I did not know. It made me uncomfortable, at best.

"The magic you possess is his gift to you. A piece of himself that he has not given to any other," Nemain said quickly, spitting out the words before the binding could stop her. She gasped, raising her hand to clutch her throat as the magic sealed itself around it. It appeared in golden threads, tightening like a noose as she fought for breath.

They wrapped around her throat twice as I flung myself from Fenrir's back, striding to her on steady feet as she dropped to her knees. Badb and Macha stared on helplessly, and I realized that they knew what was happening, even if they likely couldn't *see* it. Badb's hand twitched at her side, as if involuntarily because she wanted to interfere, but could do nothing to stop what was happening to her sister.

"Don't," Macha warned when I reached out to grasp the threads. "You gave your magic to Tartarus. It isn't there, and you cannot help her until you have it back."

The threads sank into Nemain's skin as Macha grabbed my hand, pulling me back and keeping me from attempting to interfere. The skin beneath Nemain's eyes became dotted with red as her blood vessels burst, her mouth opening wide even though she could not inhale any air. Blood welled from the wounds the threads made on her throat, trailing down her neck as the shimmering faded into her.

She drew in a deep, sudden breath finally as they vanished completely. Her stare remained fixed on the ground as she closed her mouth, a tiny whimper escaping as she pushed to her feet. To see one of the three parts of the Morrigan so vulnerable made something inside me clench with fury.

Such a foolish game the Primordials played for something as mundane as secrets. What kind of person was my father if *this* was the kind of punishment he gave out over such a minor infraction?

"Nemain?" I asked, wincing when she turned her stare to me. Her eyes seemed to bleed, the whites tinted with pink from her struggle. She nodded silently, touching the front of her throat as she opened her mouth. Her lips moved as if she was speaking, but there was no sound as she grasped the wounds that had taken something from her.

Taken her voice, I realized.

"Why are you giving me answers? Why are you risking punishment like this to help me?" I asked, turning to Badb with the question Nemain couldn't answer for herself.

She paused, hesitating for a moment before sighing. "Knowledge is power and not all here would see you stumble in the dark," she said, turning to Macha.

The two exchanged a careful look, before Macha decided to elaborate. "Everyone has their own motives, and you would be a fool to forget that. Everyone will use you to their own advantage, especially here. You are the tides, constantly shifting. We would *all* guide you in a direction that serves us. We were merely the ones fortunate enough to be tasked with it."

Badb continued, her face twisting into a smirk. "In helping you, we help ourselves and our own destinies, Child of Fate," she said. The harsh reminder settled into my gut, stern and stark. There were no friends here, only allies who would turn the moment it benefited them.

"We need to keep moving," I said, striding forward to continue on the path we'd set to find our way to the first river. I would not lose more time to wallowing in the suffering of another, not when I was merely a tool for them. The Morrigan followed at my heels as Fenrir nudged my back, lowering himself so that I could climb on. With everything I'd thought I'd known torn to shreds, I swung my leg over his back and allowed him to carry me—for just a little while.

If that was what happened for daring to speak, I shuddered to think of what Khaos would require of me to prove myself. Without magic, was I even worth anything at all?

Fenrir remained silent as we walked, leaving me to my thoughts. I could feel the distinct presence in my mind, as if he was too uncertain about my mental state to truly leave me be. I couldn't shake the memory of Nemain's throat closing, often finding myself touching my own as if he would punish me for the same if I spoke ill of him.

I hadn't gotten the impression of cruelty on the few occasions I'd met with him in the Void, and I couldn't seem to reconcile the heartless male who was capable of such things with the one who had come to my rescue when I'd taken too much magic.

From him.

I didn't dare to ask about my mother out of fear that a similar fate awaited Badb and Macha if they so much as uttered a word. As difficult as they might have been at times, and as distant and other-worldly as they seemed, I couldn't help but enjoy their company in spite of their assertions that I was a tool.

In truth, their and the Cwn Annwn's presence was the only thing keeping me sane. When my entire world was crumbling at my feet and I couldn't turn to my mate, they kept me feeling grounded in what I needed to do.

They made me believe that maybe, just maybe, I could accomplish what I'd set out to do. Even if they'd warned me I didn't stand a chance of surviving all that they'd said would come to pass, I could leave the world a better place without me in it. I could give Imelda and Fallon a chance at finding peace.

Fenrir was silent in my mind, not relaying the information to the question I knew he could hear about my mother. I didn't know if it was the fact that he didn't want to answer or something else, but I didn't dare to pry.

"It is an answer you already know deep down. It will come to you when you're ready for it," he said, earning a growl from me that felt particularly canine.

Lupa and Ylfa raced ahead, zooming through the flames without a care in the world. Fenrir moved slightly slower, but he still ran fast enough that I needed to hold on for all that I was worth as the Morrigan flew through the skies overhead. They'd disappear and then reappear when I least expected it, darting low to zoom past us in a flash of raven wings. Their feathers gleamed in the firelight, a distinctive golden sparkle showing in their amber eyes.

We made good time traveling this way, and I hated that I hadn't thought to try it earlier. It gave my feet a reprieve, even if my ass and thighs tired from the effort of holding myself on my seat as Fenrir moved.

I would need to rest soon, and I didn't think it would be an issue as some of the flames began to flicker the way they had the night before. It signaled the coming of the night, and I imagined we would need to find a place for me to hide so that the Cwn Annwn could hunt.

I hadn't eaten, and yet my stomach didn't harass me with the familiar grumbling of hunger yet. Before coming to Alfheimr, I might have gone longer than this without food and never thought anything of it. But I'd been spoiled with feasts even while being tormented at Mab's hand, and my body was no longer used to going so long.

"Time moves differently here. To your body, it has only been mere hours. A night, really."

I will need to eat soon, I thought, thinking of the way I would send emotions down the bond to reach Caldris. This felt similar, a different part of me that was connected to Fenrir. It was more complete, as if there was no part of me that was separate from him.

"Your mate bond will be similar once you complete it."

But Fenrir and I hadn't needed to complete anything.

"There is nothing to complete. I come from Khaos, and you are the Princess of it. Our bond just is."

Just was. I supposed I should have been grateful that the completion of the mate bond required my consent, because even though I didn't fault Fenrir, this somehow felt like a violation.

Which was stupid, when I wouldn't have turned him away. I just wanted to have the *choice*, in the way it felt like Caldris had done what he could, in his own twisted way, to give me as much choice as possible in something that was inevitable. It had been those I was not bound to in any way who had stripped my choice from me.

He growled, but the sound was low and calm. It didn't feel like a threat or voicing displeasure at all. It was the closest thing I thought a wolf could come to the way a cat purred, intended to soothe rather than scare. I pressed my body tighter to his back, leaning forward to lay myself along his spine as my arms wrapped around his neck more firmly. He picked up speed the moment I got a good grip, joining his sisters in the fray as they sped through ruins and rock and fire.

We sped through the fading light of the fires, Fenrir promising to find me something to eat that night. There would be an abundance of fire in the morning to cook a quick breakfast, appeasing the needs of my stomach before they could grow too distracting. I'd need my strength for the trials coming soon enough. The Morrigan swooped through the air to signal the time for safety.

"Wait!" I called to Fenrir, pushing up from his upper body frantically as the last light cast a shadow upon a perfectly rounded stone. A male form fought to push it up the only hill in the area, and he was so close to the top I bet more than anything he could practically taste the victory of it. He slipped in the dirt just before cresting the top, the stone rolling back over him and dragging him by the chains wrapped around the stone, pulling him behind it with his arms wrenched at a horrible-looking angle.

He and the stone fell into the valley beneath the hill as we watched, Fenrir slowing to a stop. His paws dug into the dirt, refusing to move any closer but respecting my wish to not move past without offering aid.

I climbed off Fenrir's back, dropping to the ground less than gracefully and starting my path toward the man as he slowly pushed to his feet. I moved closer even though I knew I needed to find shelter—an irrational tug pulling me forward. I needed to know, needed to see the person before me.

His arms snapped, the bones cracking as they righted themselves under invisible, magical hands. He approached the stone, positioned himself below it, and began to push it up the hill all over again before he dropped to his knees with exhaustion.

He slumped forward, pressing his forehead to the stone as I approached. I knew that bone-tired exhaustion, had felt it every day after harvesting in the gardens and knowing I had a night at the manor still awaiting me. The man turned his head toward me as my boot crunched in the dried, burnt grass surrounding his valley. Everything in this area was dead, unlike the lushness of the area surrounding Phlegyas and his feast. Blond hair barely showed in the darkness, light golden skin on a form taller than any human I'd known before. His warm brown eyes widened with shock as he stared at me, our gazes connecting for a single, brief moment before everything plunged into total darkness.

"Brann?"

THIRTEEN

ESTRELLA

"Estrella!" his voice called back frantically. Something furry pressed into my spine, drawing a panicked squeak from me as I spun to face it.

"*Calm*," Fenrir ordered, nudging me in the darkness to guide me onto his back. I couldn't see anything as the noises of beasts rang through the night, forcing me to follow his direction and climb onto his back. I pressed fully into his fur, making myself flat to get as much protection from any predators that might have been in the area.

"Estrella!" Brann called again, his voice ringing through the darkness. A flutter of wings brushed against my back, fluttering over me as I felt the magic in the air. The Morrigan shifted at my side, wings disappearing in a wave of air and then a very humanlike hand touched the center of my back.

"You must be quiet," Badb warned, and I felt the moment her sisters surrounded Fenrir. "There is no shelter here."

I clamped my mouth shut, the distant sound of growling predators emerging from their lairs forcing me into silence. It took everything in me not to call out to my brother, to the man I thought was
dead. As much as my feelings about him had become a jumble of
love and hatred and confusion, I couldn't just leave him to be eaten.
"That's my brother."

"*Guardian*," Fenrir corrected.

"I can't just leave him," I said, aware of the way Fenrir's feet
moved. He wasn't going anywhere fast, but he kept moving. The
Morrigan, Lupa, and Ylfa surrounded us, moving in a synchronized
pattern meant to keep me hidden. In this place, in this moment, I was
the weak link.

Daughter of a Primordial or not. Princess of Khaos or not. The
wards had taken all of that and Caldris's magic from me as well,
leaving me as defenseless as a newborn fawn in this place filled with
monsters.

"He'll be fine come morning," Macha said, but the words didn't
reassure me.

"What does that even mean?" I whispered, my voice coming out
too much like a scathing hiss. I couldn't stand the thought of Brann
hurting, of him suffering, but I'd never felt more helpless than I did
in this place in spite of the swords strapped across my back.

"It means something will probably eat him tonight, but the phoenix will revive him come morning as she does all those who are punished here. It is an eternity of death and suffering," Badb answered.

"No," I said, swallowing back my fear. I wouldn't be able to live
with myself if I heard him scream and did nothing to help him. Survival or not, that would leave a stain on my soul that could never be
washed clean.

"No?" Macha asked as Fenrir's body sagged with a sigh. He
knew damn well I wouldn't leave it alone, and I felt him shift his
body to head back in the direction of Brann's continued cry for me.
"You won't survive. The phoenix will not revive you in the morning
if you die. You have a physical form here as a visitor for the trials.
You are not a prisoner of Tartarus."

"Then I guess I'd better not fucking die, yeah?" I asked, grimacing as I thought of it. "I walked away before, but I cannot this time. A
stranger you implied is a terrible person is one thing, but this is my
fucking brother!"

"You cannot even see in the darkness," Badb argued. I had to
concede that she had a point there, but fortunately the wolves could

see. The Morrigan could see, and while they weren't allowed to intervene in the trials, nothing said they couldn't protect themselves from the consequences of my stubbornness.

"*Yet you called me stubborn,*" Fenrir growled.

"No!" Brann cried as we came closer, and I suspected it was because he couldn't see in the dark either.

"It's alright," I murmured as Fenrir stopped and stood in front of Brann. I jumped off Fenrir's back, sliding my body next to my brother's and searching for his hand. The ground shook beneath us, a warning of the monstrosities that were about to emerge in the night.

"Find shelter. Quickly," he snapped, yanking his hand back in rejection. I tumbled sideways, falling over as the ground cracked beneath the stone. It split beneath my hand, darting over the surface and opening a chasm in the ground. Fire erupted from it as Fenrir grabbed me by the back of my armor, carefully snatching the fabric between his teeth and tossing me to the side.

He leapt after me, his massive body coming to stand over me as fire emerged from the gasping wound in the earth. The flames crept higher, resulting in a sudden wave of light that was so bright it blinded me. Shoving a hand to cover my eyes against the worst of it, I protected myself the best I could as I looked for the other wolves, the Morrigan, *Brann.*

They'd escaped the chasm, for the most part landing on the opposite side of where Fenrir had tossed me. Only Brann had come to this side, leaving most of our protection separated from us by the massive cavern that opened in the ground.

"The fire, Estrella!" Badb yelled, the words not making any sense. I might have been immune to the flames, but that didn't mean I could use them as a weapon either. "Your blades!"

I crawled out from beneath Fenrir as he growled at the chasm, rolling to my feet and pulling my swords from their sheath in a quick, fluid motion that had nothing to do with magic and everything to do with training so deep it became muscle memory. I leaned over the chasm, plunging my hands and blades into the flames that erupted.

Something began to climb out of the fire, an enormous mass of flesh and muscle that forced me to swallow. The chasm began to close the moment it ascended the gap, stepping onto the ground closer to Fenrir. He vanished into the darkness as I tried to allow my blades to burn in the flames for as long as possible, my pulse rising with every moment where it was out of sight.

The chasm closed in a ripple behind him, making me pull my blades back sharply to avoid being crushed in the process. The blades continued to burn, the flames licking along the metallic surface as if it were a tree limb for kindling, even as my hands and armor refused to catch fire, offering me the slightest bit of light as I pushed to my feet and used the light from the blades to find my way to Brann.

He crouched on the ground beside the stone, his chains clanking as he tried to make himself small. I shoved him to the side, raising one of my swords above my head and bringing it down upon the chain in a quick, swift slice. Metal clanked against metal, the chains giving beneath the sharp edge of my blade as I did it again and again, letting the fire burn through the iron in a way I never would have been able to do.

I was so close to cutting through the last of the chain when Fenrir growled and Brann cried out in pain. I jumped to my feet, positioning my blades at the ready. One remained by my waist, one rising to the level of my eye to help me see in the darkness.

Fenrir had clamped his mouth down on the creature that was even larger than him, his teeth digging into the leather-looking flesh of an arm. He tore his head from side to side, working to shred the skin and muscle of whatever he'd latched onto. Lupa and Ylfa used the closed chasm to cross the distance, launching themselves at the creature's back. They slammed into him with all their force, knocking him forward.

I shifted my blade, allowing myself to see the creature who had crawled out of the abyss with greater clarity while the wolves occupied him.

Two angled eyes of flame existed below a strong, protruding brow. The creature had no nose or lips, only a gaping maw of razor-sharp teeth that snapped at me as I raised my blade in response. I blocked his bite at the last moment, cringing back as his teeth clamped down on it and he cut his gums as he tried to bite his way through it.

I jabbed my second sword forward while he was distracted, sinking the flaming blade into his gut. The resounding howl he gave echoed through Tartarus, a high-pitched scream that sounded wrong considering his height. I pulled back, yanking my blade free. It wasn't fast enough as his free arm thrust forward, his fist connecting with the side of my face. Thrown to the side, I scrambled to hold onto my blades and keep them from stabbing myself as I landed on the dirt, skidding across it and feeling all the little pebbles and rocks scrape the skin of my cheek. Heat bloomed beneath where he'd struck me, the distinct memory of bruising forcing me to shift my jaw from side to side as I got to my feet.

My face throbbed as it swelled, my lip already feeling too large for my face.

I raced forward as Fenrir fought to climb the creature with teeth and claws. I lunged forward, racing toward them as Ylfa and Lupa jumped back.

I threw myself to the ground as he reached for me, his arms grasping thin air as I turned to my back and skidded across the dirt, keeping my blades tucked in close as I slid between his feet. I spread my blades as I passed through, cutting the sinew at the backs of his knees and watching as he stumbled forward.

His knees struck dirt, making him short enough for Fenrir to get closer to his throat, but not close enough. He sprawled on the dirt, rolling onto his back as Fenrir lunged.

The creature caught Fenrir by the jaw, grasping his top and bottom teeth in enormous hands. Fenrir yelped as he fought to free himself, forcing me to my feet as I raced toward the creature holding him captive.

Not *my* fucking murder puppy.

I ran over his body, tucking one of my blades back in its sheath. Standing on top of his chest for a brief moment, I watched the creature's flaming eyes go wide as he tossed Fenrir to the side to focus on the new, impending threat. I dropped, placing both hands on the hilt of my remaining sword as I drove it down toward the ground, catching the creature directly in the center of his throat.

The blade pierced his flesh quickly, sinking into the dirt beneath him. The flames in his eyes flickered as his hand grasped me by the waist, tearing me free from my sword as he threw me sideways.

I brushed against Fenrir's back as I flew through the air, his resounding whimper letting me know he was still breathing as I tumbled over him. I crashed into something cool and hard, my head pounding for a brief moment.

Reprieve from the pain came with the return of darkness.

Fourteen

ESTRELLA

A wet, rough tongue dragged over my face. I raised a hand, swatting it away and peeling my eyes open slowly. The motion was too much, forcing me to acknowledge the pain on the right side of my face. I raised a hand to touch it, wincing when my fingers connected with the swollen flesh.

"You shouldn't be here," Brann said, shoving his back against the stone as he fought to push it up the hill all over again.

The fires had returned for the day, illuminating the valley and the way the Morrigan and the Cwn Annwn watched me warily, waiting to see if I'd be able to function. I pushed to sit up, shoving Fenrir and his wet tongue away as I gently wiped the slobber from my swollen face.

"Dogs lick their wounds. He thinks he's taking care of you," Macha said, pressing her lips together to contain her amused chuckle.

"How sweet," I said, smiling saccharinely at Fenrir when he dropped to lay at my side. He draped his enormous head over my lap, the weight of it pinning me to the ground as I sat and stared down at him. There was little sign of any injury on him, just a few scratches and some claw marks where the creature had gripped his jaws and fought to crush them. I ran a hand over his snout gently, soothing him as much as he soothed me with his presence.

"Why are you in Tartarus?" I asked, leveling Brann with a glare. He paused, planting his feet so that the stone couldn't roll back over him.

"I came here intentionally to find someone and convince him to help you," he paused, seeming to contemplate how much I might already know about the truth of his involvement in my life.

"You mean the same person who appointed you as my guardian within the Lunar Coven? My father?" I asked, wishing Fenrir would move so I could get to my feet.

Now that Brann wasn't in danger, I needed to smack the shit out of him for his secrets and deception.

Brann blinked, swallowing as it became obvious I wasn't as ignorant as I'd once been. "My mate and I have had a number of revelations since you *died*," I snapped.

"You do not need to accept the mate bond as fact. You can choose to reject it," he said, clearly hating what had come of Caldris and I in the time since he'd vanished from my life. "And I'm not dead," he said, sighing. His chest sagged with it, leaving me to fully realize the level of his exhaustion. "I was pulled out to sea. I'm not human, so the fall wasn't enough to kill me. There's a secret entrance to Tartarus, and I was able to perform a ritual to separate my soul from my body so that I could enter. It was the only thing I could think to do to help you. *Really* help you."

"Separate your soul from your body," I said, considering those words. "I walked into Tartarus body and all. Why wouldn't you have just done the same?"

"Only the main gates will allow a living person to enter in their physical form," Macha answered, and I glanced over to find Nemain nodding silently. She smiled slightly, seeming to reassure me about the fact that she couldn't speak.

Reassuring *me*. When it was my fault she'd lost the ability.

"So you just let me believe you were dead," I said. Fenrir raised his head as he sensed my growing frustration, dropping it onto the ground beside me. He clearly wasn't happy about it, the dirt much harder and less comfortable than my thighs.

"I could do nothing to protect you against the Wild Hunt. This was the only way. I never expected to get trapped here in eternal punishment. I didn't think Khaos would hate me quite that much," Brann said, the chains that kept him strapped to his stone clanking together. "The only way I can escape it is if I manage to get this stone to the top of the hill by the time the fires fade at night. I've tried, every single day."

"You kept his daughter from him for years longer than agreed upon. Of course he's furious with you," Badb snapped, striding up to Brann and only stopping when I got to my feet. "You were supposed to return her when she was reborn into her final life cycle. There's no telling what kind of damage you have caused by not allowing her to grow in the Cradle of Creation."

"If Mab ever discovered she existed, she would have killed her. I made sure to get her away from the rest of the coven before the Veil fell. I protected her. I made it so she would never have to know the truth of her purpose and the suffering it would bring," Brann explained as I strode up to his side.

"At the cost of everyone else!" Macha yelled, her rage palpable in the air. It was something I'd never thought to experience from the Morrigan, who seemed so detached from all things resembling human emotion most of the time. "She would have been safe in the Cradle."

"If that was the case, they'd have allowed her to stay there in the first place. They *chose* to send her away. I raised her. Not *him*," Brann snapped, the words filled with a rage I hadn't ever seen from him. He took a moment to compose himself, pinching the bridge of his nose between two fingers. "I can get her out now," he said, his voice going desolate at the thought of me being in this place after all he'd given to try to keep me away. "Out the same way I came in. You don't have to be here."

"How is it that you think I came to be here?" I asked, tilting my head to the side as I studied the man I'd believed to be my brother. "I just happened to wander into the cove?"

He swallowed as I approached, his eyes shuddering against the judgment I cast upon him. Imelda had spoken of Brander with respect whenever she was willing to speak of him at all, unable to believe the crime he'd committed against his own people and the vows they'd made to return Fallon and me when the time came. "You escaped Mab. The Fates guided you here to serve their agenda."

"Mab sent me here herself. She doesn't have the slightest clue who I am aside from the fact that I somehow have the power of the

Primordials at my disposal. I'm to collect a snake from the crown of Medusa and return it to her, or she will kill my mate as punishment," I answered, watching as he winced.

"Then let him die," Brann said, the hollowness of the words shocking me. He didn't care for the pain that would cause me, completely ignoring the fact that I would likely be unable to continue on without him.

"Let him die?" I asked. For someone who'd lived alongside the Fae for centuries, he was a fool to the truth of the bond.

"If Mab has him, it would be a mercy," he said, his gaze sliding to the side. He couldn't be bothered to look at me, to witness the devastation his words caused with his lack of care.

I knelt in front of him, drawing my blade from the sheath. "I would burn this world and the next to the ground before I ever lived a day without my mate in it," I snapped, glaring and grimacing in warning. Fenrir growled behind me, echoing the sentiment with his own rage. He might have belonged to me, been my familiar, but he'd been at Caldris's side for centuries before that.

Over my fucking dead body.

"Estrella," Brann warned, his gaze dropping to the short sword I held in front of me. He looked at me as if I was something to fear, as if he saw me for the first time, and it shocked me how much I reveled in that moment. All my life, he'd treated me as something to be protected.

Something to contain.

He was *my* prison.

Never again would I allow someone to make me small.

I shifted my sword to the side, raising it above the last bit connecting his chains to the stone. "If you free him, the Primordial responsible may require you to take his place," Badb warned, echoing the warning she'd given me earlier.

Brann deserved to be punished for going back on his word, especially when we would never know what his choices might have caused. But he would suffer while he watched the world suffer at Mab's hands, knowing he'd chosen to protect me against the best interest of *everyone else.*

I cracked the sharp edge of the blade down upon the chain, severing it entirely. "Let Khaos come and imprison me, then. I'd like to have a word with him," I said, standing and making my way back to Fenrir. He stood but lowered himself to the ground so that I could ride him, leaving me to collect the sword from the dead creature's throat. I yanked it free, staring into the hole it had created as Brann grimaced back from the squelching sound of it pulling out of flesh.

I shoved the bloodied blade back into my sheath, swinging a leg over Fenrir's back and settling in comfortably. Brann would slow us down. I knew that, and yet I couldn't exactly leave him behind.

Badb stepped up before me, her gaze weighted and heavy. "He wronged you," she said, her eyes darting over my face. I knew she could see every emotion playing out within me, the hurt, the betrayal, the confusion, the rage.

"He was my brother," I said with a shrug, downplaying all the ways I fought to understand if I could trust him going forward. I couldn't decide if he was being honest or continuing to lie, if this was just another twist of reality and a way to attempt to manipulate me back into the cage he wanted for me.

If he'd put me there out of love or some selfish motivation.

"And still, he wronged you. Yet you forgive him enough to free him from his punishment for doing so, anyway, at risk to yourself," she responded, tilting her head to the side in thought. "You have passed your second trial."

"No more fucking secrets, Brander," I said, using his true name to display just how much knowledge I had of him. Of the way he'd used magic to grow at my side, making it seem like he'd been a child growing up with me when he'd really just been using the moon and lunar magic to glamour himself.

"You know who your father is? And still you're here?" he asked, pushing to his feet.

"I would do anything for my mate," I said as Fenrir started walking in the direction of the river. "After a lifetime of being lied to, I'd also do just about anything for the truth, and I have a feeling Khaos is the only one who can give it to me," I said, ignoring the way Brann stepped back from the accusation in those words.

I didn't allow the guilt of them to sink inside me, telling myself he'd deserved my anger for all the things he'd kept from me over the years.

I was done believing in the value of secrets.

FIFTEEN

CALDRIS

I stared at the wall in front of me, ignoring the carnage happening. Mab had once again killed one of her loyal followers, showing no discrepancy in who became a victim of her violence. All I wanted was for it to stop, but after a certain point, the constant screams would desensitize anyone to it.

I'd reached that point centuries prior, and the carnage of her court was nothing like this. Not normally.

Something was wrong—even more wrong than usual.

It was the third death since I'd returned from the entrance to the Void. The third death in a matter of hours. It would give me a reason to return and tell the ferryman that I would be able to meet him at the secret entrance to the Void.

If only I knew where that place was.

I couldn't be bothered to care about the fact that she was reducing the numbers of her own followers, but those who got caught up in her violence and weren't loyal were unfortunate. Another Lliadhe had suffered at her hands, and as much as I hated to think of it in such a callous manner, all I could think about was the fact that she was fanning the flames of the rebellion.

It was churning away, burning brighter than ever as innocent Sidhe and Lliadhe were murdered next to one another.

Their differences didn't matter all that much once they were dead. They all looked the same when she reduced them to a pile of meat and bone.

"She's unhinged," Nila said, stepping up beside me.

A Lliadhe woman, a satyr, approached her other side, leaning forward on her goat legs and hooves to hold my gaze as she spoke. "Pay close attention to the stone within her crown," she said, her brow furrowed in confusion.

I looked to Mab, risking her wrath by looking at her when all else tried to fade into the background. A shadow of a figure moved within the gem, mouth parted to reveal sharp teeth and a serpent-like forked tongue. In all my years at Mab's side, I'd never seen the woman in the stone.

Some claimed to have seen it when she was most angry, when she seemed to become less strategic with her killing. While I'd witnessed those occasions from time to time, I'd never found myself in the position to look at her straight on. Mab's attention shifted to me, her gaze narrowing as she witnessed the company I kept for a brief moment.

"What is it?" Nila asked, standing in the center of the satyr and I, doing her best to look as if we weren't actively engaged in conversation. She too was all too aware of Mab's attention, having spent the better part of centuries trying to keep to the shadows and avoid her attention.

"I'm uncertain," the satyr woman said. "My brother, Sisko, said there were stories in our village when we were children. A passing traveler spoke of the Gorgon who haunted the stone after it was stolen by the dwarves. He was not summoned to Tar Mesa when I was as a child, so he has not seen it in person. I can't be certain of the origin."

"A Gorgon? Are you certain, Maeryn?" Nila asked, gripping the satyr's human arm with perfectly polished nails.

"Yes. That is what he said," Maeryn answered, nodding her head as she looked back to Mab. The Lliadhe had not been present on the beach when Mab had sent Estrella into the cove. She hadn't been there to know that the sole purpose of Estrella's journey was to gather a snake from Medusa's crown. Most in Tar Mesa did not know the reasons for Mab's constant need to send her prisoners into Tartarus to earn their freedom, but it seemed a far stretch to imagine this to be a coincidence.

I'd thought a snake from Medusa's crown would be a trophy or make her control over snakes stronger somehow. I hadn't begun to anticipate that there might be something more to it. Did the journey she sent Estrella on have more to do with her sanity and the woman in the stone that haunted her than we could have ever anticipated?

I chanced another look to Mab, her attention diverted as I stared into the stone itself. The figure was gone, vanished without a trace as if I had all but imagined it, but I couldn't shake the knowledge that there was something more to the combination of circumstances than I'd expected. Nila's knowing gaze confirmed my own suspicions, letting me know that I wasn't alone in my desire to connect the pieces of the puzzle I hadn't known I held.

"Mab sent Estrella to retrieve a snake from the crown of Medusa," I said, echoing Nila's train of thought. Was Medusa responsible for the cursed gem itself? Had she been its owner before the dwarves had stolen it?

Was she angry that Mab had sent someone to steal from her yet again and getting revenge upon her through her own rage?

"My brother will be most interested in that turn of events," Maeryn said, retreating. Her hooves clomped against the floor as she made her way out the door of the throne room, retreating to safety as quickly as she could.

Her brother.

The thought tickled the back of my brain, the fact that she'd been so quick to want to go share the news with him, striking a thought into my head. There'd been a time when Estrella's brother had been her confidante, when he would have been the first person she turned to when she learned something new about herself and her life.

Her fucking brother.

I'd watched him jump over that cliff, and while I hadn't been in position to intervene during that first leap when he'd aimed to take Estrella with him, I could have intervened in their struggle after. I'd let the bastard die when I *could* have saved him. It would have ruined everything, all my plans for glamouring myself wasted. I wouldn't have been able to stop Holt and the Wild Hunt without revealing my identity to them and to Estrella and her brother in the process. I'd let him die, knowing damn well he would have only gotten in my way if he'd survived. His disdain for me and the Fae had been obvious, even before I learned that he'd been an elder of the Lunar Coven. There would have been no chance of convincing Estrella to fall in love with me if she knew the truth of my identity then and there, but especially not with that bastard whispering in her ear.

In doing so, I'd betrayed my mate the very first night I'd met her.

I retreated out of the throne room without another word, ignoring the duty I had to collect the bodies upon the floor. Mab would only make more in the time it took for me to return anyway.

I had a riddle to answer.

Sixteen

ESTRELLA

B rann followed behind us, forcing us to move slower than I
cared for. I urged him to move faster, pushing him to walk as
if his life depended on it.

"Would you hurry the fuck up?" I snapped, all patience gone. If
it came down to a choice between him and Caldris, I would choose
my mate. Especially when I'd already lost time to save Brann, and his
slow speed seemed deliberate and intentional as a method to delay
the inevitable. I'd condemned my mate for saying he would sacrifice
the world to save me if it came to it, but I was no better.

I was willing to sacrifice my own brother to make it to him in
time, and that wasn't a choice that I would have made lightly not so
long ago.

Now it wasn't a choice at all.

"I'm going as fast as I can, Estrella," he snapped in return, that
old sibling rivalry pulsing between us. Even if I knew better now
and understood that Brann hadn't truly grown up alongside me in

anything more than an illusion, he still *felt* like my sibling in my heart.

"I hope that's true, otherwise I'm going to leave you behind. Either keep up or don't, but I don't have time for this," I said, sending a pulse of love down the mate bond that arched between Caldris and I, hoping he could feel it even if I couldn't see the threads or feel my magic in the same way. The lack of my magic had mostly stripped those from me, leaving me with only the shadow of them when the strongest magic was at play.

I'd seen them when Nemain lost her voice, felt the connection to the magic that was the same as mine. The magic that flowed through me was the same as what he'd used to torment and punish, and I couldn't shake the distinct feeling that it would change me into something I never wanted to be.

The sound of raging water was such a stark contrast to the silence of the burning plains. It lingered in the distance long before I could see the river itself. My heart felt like it dropped into my stomach, leaving me with a distinct mix of dread and anticipation. We were finally approaching the site of the first river. While I dreaded what I might endure, it was one step closer to being reunited with Caldris.

To seeing him safe.

"What should I expect at this trial?" I asked, running my fingers through Fenrir's fur. Speaking to him didn't come naturally, my own discomfort with having another being present in my mind forcing me to give the words voice. The Morrigan flew overhead, leaving me with just my Cwn Annwn to protect Brann and I. I had little doubt they would return to their human forms if needed, but answering these types of questions obviously wasn't necessary for them.

"Trial?" Brann asked, glancing between me and Fenrir. He swallowed, turning his gaze forward with a grimace. "Please tell me he is not forcing you to undergo the Trials of the Five Rivers."

I said nothing, waiting for Fenrir to murmur his answer within my mind. He was silent, leaving me to deal with the furious brother at my side who sucked his teeth and hung his head in his hands. "All who enter Tartarus in their physical forms are required to endure the trials," I said, forcing my voice not to tremble with my own frustration. I didn't care to admit that it seemed even more pointless now that I knew who my father was. If any one being was responsible for the laws that governed this place, it was him.

He was the only person who could condemn me to such a fate, and simultaneously the only one who could save me.

He hadn't bothered. The man who'd come to me when my magic became too much for me and took the excess away so that I could survive felt like a distant memory, like it was disconnected from what I knew now. This version of Khaos did not seem to care if I suffered during the trials, and it left me with a bitter taste on my tongue.

He'd been kinder to me when I thought him a stranger, but now that I knew he was my father, I was disappointed.

"The Trials of the Five Rivers were designed to determine a person's worthiness of the magical gifts that would be bestowed upon them if they were to reach the Cradle of Creation," Brann explained, his gaze going distant. Something in that expression was so *old*, so tired that I wondered how I'd never seen the weariness he must have felt when we'd been living in Mistfell.

How many times had he watched me struggle through a human existence? How many times had he watched me make the same mistakes over and over and never been able to stop me from repeating a vicious cycle?

"I'm aware. That doesn't tell me what *this* trial will entail," I said, looking down at the side of his face. His features had thinned during his time in Tartarus, as if even his soul was damaged from his prolonged starvation and separation from his body. I didn't know if his magic could sustain his physical form even when his soul was separated, or if he'd effectively already died during his time here.

"Each of the rivers represents a strong human emotion. Something that could turn even the most innocent of humans into a tyrant if left unchecked. The trials are a safeguard of sorts to keep humans or Fae who lack the ability to overcome those emotions from reaching the Cradle," he explained, turning his brown-eyed stare toward me finally.

"The dwarves stole Mab's crown from the Cradle," I said, the sudden realization striking me in the chest. If that was the place where all the strongest of magical gifts originated, nothing else made sense.

"Yes," Brann answered, nodding along to the words. Lupa nuzzled up to him, pressing her body against the length of his and looking for attention. He rested his hand atop her back uncertainly, looking entirely too awkward as if he'd never considered an animal might want affection. "The trials weren't always necessary. They didn't exist in the same way and the Primordials were more trusting of those who came to them looking to bargain. The dwarves stole the Cursed Gem from the Cradle in the dead of night, and the Primordials created the Trials of the Five Rivers to make sure they would never again contribute to the rise of a tyrant like Mab."

I nodded, wondering what sort of gift might await me when I made it to the Cradle. If the Cursed Gem had been stolen, what would be given willingly?

"What have the previous victors been gifted after they completed the trials?" I asked, watching as Brann's face fell into sad resignation.

He drew his bottom lip between his teeth, looking away from me in silence. I waited, expecting an answer that he seemed unwilling to give.

"*None have survived the trials,*" Fenrir said, that deep voice confirming everything Brann wasn't bold enough to say.

Well then.

"I guess there's a first time for everything," I said, swallowing back the rising trepidation of what was to come.

The Morrigan dove toward us, shifting as they landed. The flutter of feathers bursting through the air never stopped amazing me, leaving behind three shining Goddesses when they settled to the dusty earth.

"While none have survived the trials as a whole, some have survived one or two. But the trials are about more than *just* surviving," Macha explained, flipping her hair over her shoulder. "Many survive a trial only to return home because they weren't able to procure a gift for the Primordials. You must perform in a way that is befitting of someone *worthy* of power in order to be granted the gift. You have to prove that you are stronger than the emotion that makes you human."

"But the Fae aren't human," I argued, thinking that if that was all there was to it, one of them would have won the trials already.

"They're not, but that doesn't mean the humans are the only ones with emotions. The Fae feel things like rage and sadness, love and loss. To say that they don't is to grossly underestimate their capacity to feel. Only the Primordials are immune to such emotions," Badb said, striding forward as the chasm that held the river opened up.

The waters below me rushed downhill, the current fast enough to pull even the strongest of creatures beneath the surface.

My father couldn't feel emotion. That didn't feel entirely true from my interaction with him before coming to Tartarus, and I couldn't help but feel frustrated by the inconsistent information. It was in direct opposition to what I felt like I knew already.

If the Morrigan was right, I was worth nothing to him if I didn't win. There would be no love lost beyond whatever purpose he had for me.

Whatever the Fates had in store.

I hated the notion of being nothing to one of the only people in this world who were supposed to love me unconditionally, and while I didn't expect to have a normal relationship with Khaos by any means, one that was absent of all affection was too dark a reality to face.

I climbed down from Fenrir's back, striding up to the very edge of the river and staring down into it. The waters churned angrily, waves crashing against one another in a chaotic rhythm that made no sense. There was no rhyme or reason to the current, just pure, unrelenting rage.

"What is the trial?" I asked, turning to look back at the Morrigan. The riverbank was void of any life aside from ours, leaving me to wonder exactly how I was to prove myself. There was nothing for me to defeat, no monster for me to fight.

That's only for you to know.

"The trial changes for every being who enters the river. No two trials are alike, because it is tailored to you. It is meant to test *you*, no one else," Badb answered, laying a hand upon my shoulder. "And you must face it alone, Tempest."

I nodded, glancing over my shoulder at the raging river. Of all the things I'd thought I might need to do in the trial, jumping into white waters and expecting to come out alive hadn't been one of them.

I didn't even know how to swim, thanks to spending my entire life in Mistfell where the waters were entirely forbidden.

I swallowed, my gut churning like the waters below. Badb's hand pushed at my shoulder, toppling me off balance as my foot slid down the edge of the muddy bank.

She smiled sadly as she pressed more firmly, sending me careening backward. I toppled head over foot, spinning as I fell backward into the waters below.

My world stopped the moment I crashed into the surface, the impact stealing the breath from my lungs. The current caught me immediately, thrashing me about in the waters as it filled my lungs. I hadn't had time to get a breath, couldn't breathe beneath the white currents and couldn't find any bearings as my chest burned.

The burn spread, filling every corner of me with a fire that I couldn't remember feeling, that I only remembered seeing staring back at me through the eyes of my enemies who thought me an abomination.

Hatred.

Pure, fiery hatred filled my lungs and my veins, making my blood boil beneath the surface of my skin.

My world went red as the river sucked me under the current completely.

SEVENTEEN

ESTRELLA

I fell through the bottom of the river, the water vanishing as I landed on the dirt. My cheek smacked against the surface as a strangled growl rumbled in my chest. Pushing to my feet, I found my blades in hand before I even had time to stand, spinning them dramatically as I looked about the arena I'd found myself in. The sand I stood upon was shaped in a circle, burning hot. A glance overhead showed the river flowing above me, held back by some kind of magical barrier. The water looked cool, refreshing somehow, even when logic told me it was the reason for the hatred churning in my gut.

Still, I couldn't deny that hatred. Couldn't see past the blinding rage as I looked into the arena. Countless spectators cheered from their seats, sitting upon the stone-crafted benches of a stadium.

They'd come to watch me die. To watch me fight and struggle against something that would be futile in the end. There would be no stopping me from demanding blood, no stopping me from slaughtering them all.

I did not exist for their entertainment. I did not exist to be used and looked upon like a curiosity—whether it was trapped within a gilded cage or sacrificed to a battle I hadn't chosen.

I felt nothing but rage as I studied the faces staring back at me, spinning in a circle, my twin blades held tightly within my hands. Nothing compared to the complete, mind-numbing anger I felt as I paused, my gaze landing on the golden-eyed man standing beneath a canopy. He was sheltered from the sun, his shaded oasis filled with living plants and greenery. A jug of water rested beside him, and it was only then that I acknowledged the truth of my own thirst.

He raised the jug, pouring the water into a sheepskin canteen slowly. Screwing the lid on tight, he tossed it down the sands of the arena below him, quirking an eyebrow as if he expected me to thank him for the gift.

I remained standing still, even though every bone in my body wished to move for the water. The river that had filled my lungs had done nothing to quench my thirst, only making me crave true refreshment more. Khaos pursed his lips, running his tongue over his teeth. "You disappoint me, daughter," he said, seeming so confident that I didn't know the truth of his identity. He'd silenced Nemain before she could reveal it, after all. He'd expected the word to rattle me, to get a reaction from me when I already knew the truth of who he was.

And I suspected he couldn't hear the words Fenrir whispered in my mind. Whatever bond he had with the wolves, it was unique to mine. Separate enough in the end.

"I live to please," I said, keeping the truth I knew to myself. There was no telling when such information might come in handy, and if *this* was what he had in store for me as his child?

I wanted no part in any of his grand plans.

"I had thought your survival instincts were greater than your foolish pride," he said, dropping into his seat gracefully. The golden cloth that was draped over one of his shoulders shifted as he did so, moving to keep him covered equally no matter the position he assumed.

"Then you clearly do not know me at all," I said, smiling sweetly as I contemplated how long it would take me to climb the mantle and reach his seating area. I doubted I'd make it before he struck me down with the golden power that shimmered behind his eyes.

I took a step forward, preparing to risk his wrath in my anger over the position he'd put me in. If he possessed any kind of love or loyalty for his child, he'd have allowed me to skip the trials alto-gether and given me just what I needed to defeat his other daughter.

A monster of his own making. Created through his own igno-rance and foolishness.

I knew my anger was unreasonable—that my hatred for him not telling me the truth wasn't like me and yet . . .

The heavy footsteps of something massive made the entire arena shake. My knees wobbled beneath me with each step as a creature stepped out from the shadows beneath the pedestal where Khaos sat. The creature's head appeared first, emerging just above my eye level. A familiar ring hung from his snout, the gold of it shining in a way that matched the shimmering golden marks painted onto the black hair covering his body. He walked on four legs unlike the Minotaur had, his hooves enormous with a cleft separating the toe. His neck was thick and corded with muscle, covered in scales of golden armor that followed a path down his spine. His breastplate was made from the same golden armor, covering his more sensitive areas from my swords.

His body tapered toward the back, thinning out in comparison to the muscle and fat of his front torso. He was bigger than one of the draft horses we used to till the soil in Mistfell. He stopped several paces away, his deep brown eyes glaring at mine with a rage that matched my own.

"The bull has taken a vow of revenge and agreed to act as cham-pion for someone you may recognize," Khaos said, drawing my gaze back up to the real source of my ire. The puppet master who pulled all of our strings and expected us to dance to his song. A man stepped up beside him, his coiffed silver hair as pristinely kept as I remembered from my worst nightmares.

The Lord who had ordered me to be beaten into submission and groomed me stared down from the platform, his place alongside my supposed father making my skin crawl. Everything in me tightened, a harsh familiarity growing into a yawning, massive pit in my stom-ach. Complete and utter rage filled the hole, swirling within me until my hands clenched into fists at my sides and my vision was tinted with the distinct haze of red. Khaos shifted on his feet, putting more distance between himself and the man who had somehow found himself summoned to the prison of Tartarus.

"How very unpleasant to have to suffer your insolence even in death, Miss Barlowe," Byron said, his smile twisting into a sneer of hatred.

"How fitting that you would be around to fucking haunt me," I muttered, my toes curling in my boots. They gripped the soles, as if it would help me grip the sand beneath my feet. It was the only thing preventing me from launching myself toward him and scaling the platform.

Khaos sighed, rolling his eyes as if exasperated by the hatred that I was right to feel in this situation. Any who would side with someone who abused a child to make her into a good wife was not someone I wanted to call my blood. "Only one of you will leave this arena alive as his revenge for a wrong you committed against them both," Khaos said, his stare on me feeling pointed as he ignored Byron and didn't engage with him further.

"I've never seen him before in my life," I snapped, shrugging my shoulders as I nodded my head toward the bull pointedly. I reached behind me to grasp the hilt of my swords, twirling them in my hand as I dragged them over my head and brought them down into a fighting position.

Not knowing him wouldn't stop me from killing him, not with the craving I felt for his blood and the blood of all who had gathered to watch me *die*. Not with my hatred for Byron like a breathing, tangible thing in my veins.

"You killed my son," the bull said, his words shocking me. His mouth moved with them, leaving me feeling certain that they were not spoken into my mind the way Fenrir's would have been.

I tilted my head to the side as I studied him, the golden ring in his nose bringing a smile to my face as realization set in.

Whoopsies.

"He had your hooves," I said, the quiet murmur snapping through the arena as a bark of laughter rang through the crowd. "Considering he was trying to eat me, I hope you're not expecting an apology."

"There is no apology large enough to make up for the pain and loss of a child," he snorted. He stomped his front hooves against the ground, dragging dirt backward and kicking it beneath him. Waiting to be unleashed upon me I realized.

"I think my daddy dearest must have missed that memo," I said, leaning in to whisper the words as if they were some great secret. The bull drew his head back sharply, his eyes widening in a moment of shock. It passed as soon as it had come, leaving him to blink through his rage once again. Even though I spoke the words with a sardonic edge, I couldn't help but feel the truth in the conversation. Here was a father, however misguided, who was willing to risk his life for the very *memory* of his son, while mine sat there beside a man who had tormented me for years.

"Enough, Estrella," he said, the words a quiet admonishment. It was the first moment I saw the potential for a father in the disinterested male who stared down at me. A moment that reminded me of my father when he discreetly attempted to get me to behave in a way that was for my best interest. "Begin," he said, waving his hand passively. All thoughts of paternal bonds faded away in a flash. There was no longer time to think of my own revenge against Byron, only time to think of survival.

The bull's hooves beat against the sand as he charged, leaving me to throw myself to the side to avoid his strike. I rolled to my feet, spinning back to face the creature who ran in a circle around the arena. He couldn't turn quickly, needing a great deal of space to get his enormous body to change path.

I filed the information away in the place where I knew it would come in handy, readying my blades as he came at me a second time. I sidestepped his charge, swinging one of my knives down onto his back as he passed by. The clang of metal rang through the arena, confirming my sinking suspicion that the armor had been crafted by something magical. The same as my swords, as my own armor.

Where I suspected my swords would have cut through most armor that came from the land of the living, it was evenly matched.

I kept my eyes on him as he charged me, moving out of the way and finding that I couldn't get close enough to his vulnerable, unprotected parts to connect with flesh. The only time I did, a swipe of my blade across the fatty part at the top of his rear leg, was barely more than a flesh wound.

I *felt* the humor of the crowd as I struggled. Felt the way they were entertained by the difficulty with which I fought. The horns atop the bull's head posed a great threat if he managed to connect with me, his hooves and body weight big enough to crush me if he managed to get me on the ground.

My anger rose, that fury becoming blinding. The red that filled my vision in the river returned, forcing me to blink past the stain of blood in my eyes. I held my stance as the bull charged me again, his own bloodred stare meeting mine as he came closer.

Closer.

I struck, shoving my knife into the front of his leg. It collapsed beneath him, but his momentum didn't end there as he toppled forward.

Blinding heat filled my stomach, the pain agonizing as a scream tore free from my throat and threatened to shred the flesh there. Gasping for breath, I tore myself back just before the bull flipped over himself, landing on his back on the dirt before me.

He fought to get to his hooves, leaving me to press a hand to the gaping wound in my stomach. Blood coated my skin, dripping down to coat my leather as I wheezed.

The bull got to his feet, stumbling over himself as his leg gave out beneath him again.

The tip of one of his horns gleamed with my blood, gold shimmering within the red even without any of the power flowing through me.

Fuck.

EIGHTEEN

CALDRIS

Pain seared my insides as I returned from the entrance to the Void, stepping into the front doors of the palace at Tar Mesa. All thoughts of the timing of my meeting with the ferryman forgotten, I staggered sideways and clutched my abdomen with one hand as the other thrust out to catch myself against the wall.

Pulling my hand back to glance down at it, I found it clean of blood. There was no injury on me, no indication that I should be feeling the burning hot pain of being stabbed through the middle.

Estrella.

"No," I mumbled, striding forward. I pushed through that pain, knowing that it wasn't responsible for anything wrong within me. The injury was hers without the emotion to accompany it.

I'd felt nothing from Estrella since she'd disappeared into the cove, completely unaware of how much of that silence might have been a result of her slamming the window shut on our bond or how much was a consequence of her location. The very notion that what-

ever she was suffering through was severe enough to shatter that silence was horrifying. This was more than the emotional connection
of our bond—our lives were connected—her body and mine.

Her *life* and mine.

I sent back calming thoughts, drawing in deep lungfuls of air as
I tried to soothe her through whatever had happened.

The pain of the unknown was so much worse than witnessing it
for myself. It was the greatest pain I could imagine, not knowing if
the injury preceded the end of everything that mattered to me, or
if she would be able to rally despite it.

I hurried toward the hall that would lead me to the cove, sinking down into the darkness that came with going farther below the
surface. I didn't dare to breathe, hoping that I would find the entrance unguarded by some miracle. The need to reach her was all-
consuming, forcing me to ignore the secret entrance to the Void and
Tartarus by extension. This was closer.

This would take me directly to my mate if I could get through.

One of Mab's daemon's waited in the entrance to the narrow passage that led beneath the palace. I reached for my sword, wincing
when I found the sheath strapped across my back empty. I wouldn't
be given my weapons back until I was allowed to leave Tar Mesa on
a longer basis.

The daemon turned toward me, taking slow, solid steps toward
me as I bolted forward and tried to use my speed to get past it. I slid
along the ground as I darted through the gap between his thigh and
the stone wall, skinning my knees and wearing down the fabric of
my pants as I spun to my feet when I was past him.

Estrella wasn't healing. Her pain continued to ebb and flow, that
agony in her stomach driving my concern higher. Why wasn't her
magic healing her?

I sprinted down the passage, not daring to touch anything as the
daemon chased after me. His heavy footfalls came down against the
stone beneath our feet, the vibrations echoing through the hall as I
raced toward the cove.

I turned the corner, sprinting when I hit the straightaway and I
could see the twinkling light of the cove at the other end of the passage. *So close.*

The light faded from view as something stepped into the opening,
blocking my sight entirely and leaving me to attempt to stop quickly.
The daemon reached out with two hands, blocking the opening on
either side of his wide frame.

My boots slid across the stone. I spun as I approached, unable to stop my momentum and using it to my advantage instead. My boot struck his knee, forcing him to fall down onto one leg. I jumped into the wall, pushing myself off of it and trying to vault myself over him as he fell.

The daemon I'd snuck past grasped the back of my armor, his slimy, thick fingers touching my skin as they sank beneath the leathers. He yanked me back, sending me sprawling across the stone as I gasped for breath and pushed to my feet.

Ice and shadows gathered at my fingertips, preparing to help me with the fight I knew I couldn't win. Any magic I used, any power I sent toward the daemon, would only end up absorbed. It would only fuel him and weaken me.

One spun to face me as the other got back to his feet, and they moved toward me in a single unit. One mind, one soul. All their thoughts and very being were tied to the woman who had summoned them here from the depths of Tartarus. All they cared for was the orders she'd given them, and a third stepped into the passageway from the cove, resuming the guard that the one I'd kicked vacated as they moved toward me.

One wrapped his heavy hand under my jaw, lifting me by the neck as I glared down at him. If this was how it ended, at least it would be in a moment I'd spent trying to reach Estrella.

At least I would go to the Void knowing I'd tried to get to her, hoping that she lived long enough to make me wait for her to join me.

He slammed the side of my face against the stone wall, the sound of my skull cracking ringing in my ears. Dropping me to the ground when he finished, I watched in horror as the other reached for me, slinging me over his shoulder as it all faded to darkness.

My eyes flitted open, the feeling of my skull healing itself pulling me from a sleep that was tormented by the memory of Estrella's pain. It had lingered in my dreams, conjuring up all my worst imaginings of what she might have endured. I searched down the bond for the place where her life throbbed, shimmering brightly.

It was there, dimmed, but alive.

I pushed to sit, staring at the cell that surrounded me once again. It seemed I was doomed to spend the last days of my life in this realm trapped in a cell surrounded by iron, forcing me to be unable to help Estrella when she needed me most.

What was the fucking point in being a God if I couldn't help the one person who mattered the most?

"I thought you were smarter than this. I showed you kindness by letting you roam Tar Mesa after that bitch Opal released you," Mab said, stepping out from the shadows. She so rarely deigned to bother herself with the prisoners she locked away here, and seeing her standing amidst all the iron only reminded me that she *could* be weakened.

She could be killed.

We just needed someone stronger than her to run her fucking through with it.

I didn't answer as I got to my feet, bending forward because of the shortness of the cage that surrounded me. I was too tall for such a prison, but I couldn't warn Mab of what was coming while I sat on my ass.

"You have no understanding of what you've fucking done," I accused, feeling in my soul that the loss of Estrella wouldn't just be something I felt. It wouldn't just be something the rebellion suffered. I knew beyond the shadow of a doubt that the loss of her would mean something even more catastrophic for us all.

"Is she dead?" she asked, her voice rising with her laughter. I'd thought she sent Estrella into Tartarus believing her to be the only one who could succeed in the task she required. But that laughter . . .

That was the laughter of a woman who'd won.

"No," I said, my jaw clenching with the words. Anger like I'd never known rose in my veins, funneling down the bond between Estrella and I. She gave me her rage, gave me whatever she needed me to take for her to find her focus, and I drank it down greedily.

I let it energize me.

"Too bad," Mab said with a pout, the malicious part of her insanity playing at the front of her disposition. She sank her teeth into her lip hard enough to draw blood, leaning toward my cell with wide eyes. The figure of the Gorgon woman danced in the gem atop of her head, the snakes writhing as Mab's dark eyes flashed. "I was looking forward to watching you fall into insanity with me because of that stupid little bitch."

I grabbed the iron bars of my cell, feeling them burn the skin from my flesh. Mab took a step back, staring down at the bars in horror as I held steady, forcing all my magic and all my strength into the metal. The shadows in the room gathered around the iron, surrounding me as I shoved at the gate.

My skin remained attached to it when I pulled my hands back finally, shoving the ice of winter that so often didn't come to me naturally at those iron bars. They froze over, the magic making my hands burn with the cold. The temperature was so at odds with the burns from the iron, making me gasp as I pulled back and shoved my shoulder into the frozen bars.

Mab flinched back, staring in shock as I did it again, and again.

Until the bars gave beneath me, the top of the cage crashing down as I fell through the opening I'd created. I pushed to my feet slowly, the carnage behind me forming twisted metal as I wrapped a single blood-soaked and bony hand around Mab's throat. My power was tangible in my veins, stronger than I could ever remember it being. The taste on my tongue was sweet and metallic all at once, Estrella's familiar scent accompanying it and leaving me to wonder *why*.

She gasped, raising her own hand to touch my chest. The snake around my heart clenched, forcing me to my knees. I took Mab down with me, drawing her to the floor as I refused to let her go. The rage inside me knew nothing but red, saw nothing but the nearness of her death. If I'd had a weapon, I'd have driven it through her heart and been done with it.

Even knowing I probably wouldn't survive. That the very last thing she did would be taking me down with her.

I gasped through the pressure in my chest, my hand loosening as I fought for breath. "If anything happens to her . . ." I trailed off, shoving my anger down long enough to pull my hand away from her throat. Her grip on my heart lessened, allowing deep breaths to fill my lungs once again.

That rage that had come from Estrella was so unlike my mate and her more peaceful nature.

"What?" Mab asked, the threat hanging between us as she pushed to her feet. She ran a hand over the red marks on her throat from my grip, trying to gather her composure. But her voice was rough, distorted, and pained.

"I'll have nothing left to live for," I warned, glaring up at her. I didn't bother to get to my feet, having made my point already as I cradled my injured hand to my chest. "So you better fucking believe I will take you down with me. She is the only bargaining chip you have to control me now, so you had better hope she doesn't die."

NINETEEN

ESTRELLA

The bull paused to stare at me, his snout twisted into glee. I stood on shaking feet, my lungs heaving with the effort to breathe through the pain. My hand was drenched in blood, the hilt of my blade slipping along the wet skin as I shoved it into the sheath at my back.

"How can you just sit there and watch?" I asked, the quiet of my voice traveling up to where Khaos sat on his platform.

The pain cut through the haze of rage as Khaos blinked down at me, my mate's calm assurance reaching me in the moments where I wondered if my death had finally found me.

No.

I shoved my second blade back into the sheath, focusing on that glimmering, bright bond that existed where I couldn't see it. I sent my rage to my mate, allowing him to take what I couldn't keep. I couldn't be so blinded by the rage coursing through me if I wanted to win.

I needed to overcome it.

I realized with stark clarity that it hadn't been *his* rage I needed to overcome. My enemies would always be wrathful and violent, drawing me into battles I wanted no part in. I couldn't control the actions of those around me.

But I could control mine.

I shoved it down, ignoring the bitter tang of that anger on my tongue. It was tangible in the air now that I acknowledged it, filling the stadium with the raucous cheers of those who wanted blood.

They too were affected by the magic of the Styx, their hatred for me induced by the spell coating the air.

The bull charged, racing toward me on thundering steps. His body leapt across the distance, his gait larger than I could ever dream to achieve. I thrust my hands forward, grabbing him by each of his horns. My feet slid back along the dirt as he pushed me, but I managed to keep him from goring me again. "Stop," I said, my voice quiet and meant only for him.

He kept pushing, forcing me back toward the wall where I knew he would overpower me. If he pinned me, I was as good as dead.

"Stop!" I screamed, wincing when he ignored me and the red in his eyes flashed even brighter. In the background, I watched as Khaos got to his feet slowly, staring down at me as he realized I'd overcome my own hatred. My eyes no longer burned with the flow of blood, feeling more human than I had in a long time.

I glanced over my shoulder, repositioning my hands on his horns carefully and using that grip to pull myself up. I flipped my body over, coming down to sit on the bull's back as he slammed into the wall horn-first, impaling the stone itself.

I held on as he bucked, attempting to dislodge me as I thought of a way to end this without bloodshed. With my anger gone, I had no desire to kill a creature that was being ridden by the same magic that had nearly turned me into a monster.

I gripped his horns as he yanked them free from the wall, using them to hold myself in my seat as I flattened toward his back, gripping as tightly as I could. The words came easy as I leaned toward his ears, a soft murmur that rang through the arena in spite of the quiet nature. "I am sorry for your son," I said, the words ringing true in spite of the circumstances of his death. I wasn't sorry he was dead when it meant I was alive, but I *was* sorry that we'd been in that position in the first place. I was sorry it was him or me, and I was sorry that I'd had no choice because of the bitch who'd put me there.

He flipped me off his back, my hands clinging to his horns as he raced forward and dragged me beneath his body. I managed to avoid the heavy footfalls of his hooves by hooking my boots around his armor, releasing one hand to work the straps connecting it around his body loose. The armor flapped open, giving me a vulnerability finally.

A fail-safe.

He shook his head sharply, finally forcing me to release his horns as I fell to the ground. He stood over me, pressing a single hoof onto the top of my arm while I fought to get my small dagger free from the holster at my waist.

"You cannot defeat hatred with kindness. Nothing can overcome pure, absolute hatred, you fool," he said, his deep voice too loud as he leaned in close, preparing to take a bite out of my face. I held his gaze, knowing that it might not be enough to overcome *his* hatred.

But it was enough for mine.

"You're wrong," I said, thinking of all the moments I'd allowed my own hatred to take over. Every time I'd stabbed Aramis when he'd only done what was necessary to save my life from the brother determined to kill me. When I'd made stupid choices because of that rage within me, picked fights I could never fucking win. I forgave them all, but more than that.

I forgave myself.

"I forgive you. You are more than what they've made you become," I said, feeling the burn of tears in my eyes. This trial, this battle, was about more than a bull who wanted revenge for his son. But it didn't stop him from becoming one more thing I needed forgiveness for.

He pulled back, preparing himself and then lunged forward. His horn was only a breath from my eye when I slipped my dagger between his ribs in his side, sliding it under the armor that I'd parted to give me access to his heart.

The bull froze, staring down at me and blinking past the red haze in his eyes. It faded from view as I shoved his leg off my arm, scrambling back to get free before he fell to the sand. With my dagger clutched in my hand, I watched him collapse, the brown eyes of an animal staring up at me as he bled.

"I'm sorry," I said, holding that gaze and watching as it glazed over with death. "May you find peace in the meadows of Folkvangr with your son."

He blinked, long and slow, his snout parting to reveal an already graying tongue. "You are forgiven, Child of Fate."

I dropped to my knees, allowing the burning in my eyes to consume me. My tears fell to the sand, offering them a moment of hydration as I stood and stumbled toward the canteen Khaos had dropped.

I flung it open, pouring it into my mouth and allowing the sweet crispness of water to cool my insides. I turned my stare up to the Primordial who hadn't stepped in, who had been more than willing to let me die for his trial. "What does my father wish for me to bring him as a gift to prove my worth?" I asked, attempting to keep the anger out of my voice.

In this place, this river filled with so much hatred, my own had no place.

I'd hold onto mine, filing it away for only the moments when it was needed.

"The horn that bled you," he said, his jaw clenching. He shoved the emotion away quickly, and I was immediately reminded of the way Macha had said he couldn't feel any emotions. Primordials didn't feel. They just were.

So why did my father watch me saw the horn from the bull's body as if he wished I could desecrate his corpse more?

When I finished and held the horn in my hands, I turned to look at my father and the man who still stood beside him, his face twisted into a scowl I recognized all too well. "How can you not take vengeance against the man who hurt me?" I asked, all trace of energy fading from my body. I didn't know if it was the absence of the Styx toying with my hatred or the injury that continued to bleed, but I couldn't find it in me to close the gap and take my revenge all over again.

"Oh, foolish daughter," Khaos said, shaking his head sadly. "I already have."

Byron faded from view, his body disappearing into a gust of wind as if he'd been a specter all along and not really there.

A figment of my imagination, brought by the trials to use my past against me.

I blinked, and the Lord of Mistfell was gone.

TWENTY

ESTRELLA

I gripped the horn in my hand, making my way to the center of the arena where a circle of golden flames had begun to form. Khaos raised a hand, waiting for me to step into the circle before the flames completed it. They surrounded me, sinking deeper into the sand and carving through the ground beneath me.

"Until next time, my daughter," he said, the words feeling far too emotional. He opened his mouth as if he might speak again, then thought better of it and clamped it shut. Again, that feeling of emotions danced over my skin.

He shut them down as quickly as they'd come, his face retreated back to that blank mask. I felt the gap in them, the unfortunate snapping of a bond that would never truly flourish. It was like a vice around my throat, like those threads he'd wrapped around Nemain's so callously pressed in on mine.

I didn't want to dare to hope that he cared, didn't dare to let myself believe that the Morrigan's statements about him not feeling anything were wrong.

But I couldn't deny that he didn't seem to *want* to feel something as powerful as love or affection, clamping down on that and shutting it out quickly.

Again, the bittersweet torment of having a father dangled in front of me only for him to be this twisted, detached version of what I'd once known. His failure only made me miss the man who'd raised me more.

"I had a father," I said, turning my gaze away from him as I fought to swallow the emotion clogging my throat. "And he was ten times the man you will ever be."

Khaos clenched his teeth, pursing his lips as he raised his hand. "Because I am not a man at all," he said finally, clearly needing the last word. A stream of water shot straight toward me from the river, swallowing me up and pulling me out of the arena.

The water surrounded me once again, thrashing me about as I fought to hold onto the horn that would be a gift for a male who didn't deserve it. Until *he* proved himself to me, he was worthy of none of my sacrifice.

Only Caldris could make me keep going, could make me keep fighting.

I emerged from the water, breaking through the surface with a sudden gasp for breath. Fenrir howled on the bank, racing forward. His feet slipped along the muddy bank as I jabbed the horn into the ground, using it to steel myself against the racing current of the river as it tried to pull me downriver.

Fenrir grabbed me by the back of my leather armor, sinking his teeth into the collar and using it to pull me out. I helped when I could, pushing a hand beneath me and using my feet to push myself off the muddy bank out of fear I would simply slip back in and drown.

Of all the ways to die, drowning in a river of my own hatred sounded terrible.

I collapsed on top of the mud where the bank crested. Half of my body was draped over the mud, the other half lying on the dry, burnt sand of the Fields of Hatred. Brann approached, touching a hand to the wound in my abdomen that I couldn't heal on my own. He grimaced as he stared at the blood seeping from it, tearing a strip of cloth from the bottom of his shirt. He pressed it to my waist, lifting my limp body as he tied it around and tried to stem the flow of blood.

It wouldn't matter. I couldn't continue to the next trial in this state.

I wouldn't survive the night when the flames went out if I couldn't find the energy to move.

"You just have to survive the night," Brann said, seeming to read my thoughts. My resignation that this would be the end. "The phoenix returns everything to its natural state in the morning."

"Not her," Macha said, contradicting what Brann believed to be true. His stare was wide as he turned it to me, understanding knitting his brow.

There was no firebird coming to save me.

I sighed, nodding my head and fighting back the urge to cry. Brann stood, giving me space like I'd always wanted when I was upset. Even after the time we spent apart, he knew what I needed. Fenrir nuzzled into me, laying himself along my side and offering me warmth as I shivered with shock.

I was cold. Too fucking cold to be sitting on a plain of burnt earth with fires spiraling all around me.

The Morrigan stood over me, three shimmering faces staring down at me. "Is this how it will be? You watching me nearly die? Over and over and over again?" I asked, the words sticking in my throat as that burn of tears returned. I'd taken another life. Killed another being when it was entirely avoidable outside of the meddling Primordials who had no business deciding who lived or died. Who fought who.

"The journey is about discovering the path to the truth," Macha said, her voice solemn as Badb knelt at my side. She smiled sadly, reaching out to wipe a tear from my cheekbone. Everything I'd known about myself felt like it was breaking.

Everything I'd known about the world was a lie.

"What truth can be in this?" I asked. I didn't want any part in whatever truth existed in lies and secrets, death and destruction.

Badb leaned down to touch her mouth to my forehead, shocking me into silence as she pulled back. She held my gaze, looking more maternal than she had any right to be, as her thumb swept another tear away. "Yours."

With everything I'd already learned, what more truth could there be?

Twenty-One

ESTRELLA

Night fell.

The sound of creatures howling in the distance forced me to curl myself tighter into Fenrir's side. Brann sat across from me and stared at me in the dark; even if I couldn't see his gaze, I felt the weight of it.

Felt his focus on my torso, on the stab wound that leaked blood faster than I could prevent. The scent of it permeated my senses, lingering in the air around us. I knew that the creatures of Tartarus could smell me. They smelled the blood of a living being, the real kind of blood they couldn't gain from those who were already dead.

I was prime prey.

Something growled, far closer than they had been before. Fenrir stood, nudging me with his snout. The female wolves lingered not far, their growls meeting those that came in the distance. I forced my eyes to close, sinking into that hollow within me where there was no pain. Allowing Fenrir to help me to my feet, I absorbed the complete and utter darkness surrounding me.

Night in Tartarus wasn't just dark. It was the complete and total absence of all light. Without a fire to guide my way, I stumbled into Fenrir's side and winced as a fresh flow of blood trickled down over my hand.

The creatures of the night were drawn to my blood, the scent reaching them across the distance. I would only bring harm to the others, but particularly to Brann who was next to defenseless here. I needed to leave him, but couldn't bear to say goodbye again.

"Estrella," Brann said, his voice coming from the void around me. He stumbled around in the darkness, searching for me and tripping over the stones lining our way.

I didn't dare to move, holding perfectly still until his fingers brushed against mine. He threaded those fingers through my own, lacing our hands together so that I could feel his lack of a pulse against my hand. My own beat so quickly I could barely hear past it, the steady thrum of blood roaring through my veins.

"Don't you dare say it," I snapped, shaking my head side to side even though I knew he could not see it.

He squeezed my hand, lending me the strength I didn't have. "You have to go. Fenrir can outrun them," he said, and the biggest wolf curled his head around my shoulder, nuzzling into me to offer a silent confirmation.

"You can ride Lupa," I said, gesturing to the other wolf. Brann was larger than me, but she was still big enough to carry his weight.

Lupa growled in response, telling me exactly what she thought of that suggestion.

"A wolf only has one rider," Brann said sadly, and I felt his fingers brush against my cheek. They were wet with the blood he'd gotten from touching my hand, my scent all over him. "And I am not hers."

"You could be," I argued, even knowing it was useless. "She hasn't chosen one yet."

Even if I had no clue if the words were true, they *felt* it. Fenrir did not object.

"She cannot choose someone who is just a soul, Estrella," Brann said, his bloodstained hand cupping my cheek.

I paused, the distinct burn of tears in my throat making it hard to find the words. Life was forcing me to choose, to separate from my brother knowing it was the best choice for my mate, or to stick together and risk it all trying to protect Brann.

Him or Caldris.

Because if I died here, my mate would follow soon after.

It wasn't a choice at all.

"I don't want to lose you again," I said, but the weakness in my voice was the first sign of my lack of options. I would give anything, sacrifice anyone, to save Caldris.

Even Brann.

"We must hurry," Fenrir said into my head, his body snapping taut. He went alert, preparing for the attack we both knew approached.

"I have protected you in all your lives," Brann said, his voice soft enough to make me wish I could see it. See him one last time. "Allow me to do it one last time."

A strangled sob erupted from my throat as he released my hand, the slow glide of his fingers pulling through mine making my heart ache. It left a stain, an imprint on my soul that I would never release— the day I chose my love and my purpose over protecting my brother.

It wasn't only Caldris who waited for me in Tar Mesa. It wasn't only him who needed me to return and help them fight a war.

"Go back to your body. Go find a happy corner and live out your life in peace like you wanted," I said, the words soft as he took a few steps backward.

"No," Brann contradicted me, shaking his head. "I'll meet you in the Cradle. If you are determined to do this, then you won't do it alone."

"He will not die here," Fenrir said, the reminder sharp and meant to soothe me. Brann stepped away, the sound of his footsteps fading as he moved in the other direction. The steps came slowly at first, as if he hesitated to leave me, but eventually they increased in pace.

He ran, leaving me in the darkness behind him. He was a part of Tartarus, and he would rise once again when the phoenix flew overhead when she returned the flames to the land.

Lupa stepped up behind me, placing her nose beneath me and using it to lift me onto Fenrir's back as he lowered. I did my best to pull myself into position, laying my weight atop his and sinking a hand into the fur at the side of his neck. I gripped it tightly as he stood, rising to his full height.

The sound of wings fluttering nearby was my only confirmation of the Morrigan taking their raven form, soaring overhead to avoid the creatures coming for me.

Fenrir walked forward, offering me a silent warning that I should hold tight. His gait increased to a trot, and then an outright sprint. The sounds of Lupa and Ylfa running beside us brought me comfort as I stared into the darkness, doing everything in my power to keep my eyes open.

I wanted nothing more than to fall asleep and give into the weakness plaguing my limbs, but I couldn't.

"If the phoenix will bring Brann back in the morning, wouldn't she bring me back, too?" I asked, the sleepy sound of my voice jarring even me.

"*You are not a part of this place,*" Fenrir said, the words growled in my mind. Despite how quickly he ran, he did not sound even remotely out of breath.

I hugged Fenrir tighter, snuggling the side of my face into his fur as Brann's screams of pain ripped through the night. I'd never be the same after hearing them, not knowing if I could have saved him. Turning my back on him was something I never could have imagined, never picturing a life without him in it.

The uncle to my children one day. The protector I'd never asked for that I couldn't get rid of.

I didn't know if I'd ever get to see him and my mate argue over my well-being, and while that might have seemed like an inconvenience to deal with a few hours before, now I wanted it more than anything.

I drowned out the sound of his screams as the wolves ran with a quiet hum in my head, even knowing that Fenrir could hear the pathetic noise. His body rumbled with a deep purr-like growl, as if he was answering a song that no one else could hear.

Brann's screams stopped finally, and the silence was deafening for more than one reason.

There was only one place the monsters would go next, one more meal to hunt with the scent of my blood more clearly imprinted on their senses than ever.

They were coming for me, and I would be able to do nothing to help the Cwn Annwn fight them off.

Fenrir leapt over a boulder, jarring me on his back as I clung on for dear life. The creatures at his back blended into the darkness, but I could feel them closing in on us. I could practically feel their breath beating down my neck as Fenrir fought to move faster.

The Morrigan flew overhead, their caws sounding out warnings. Fenrir moved in tune with those noises, as if he understood the instructions in them. Ylfa and Lupa ran at our sides, fighting for just a little more time. They defended us against any of the creatures who braved Fenrir's wrath to come at his flank, taking them down one by one.

They'd fought for hours, their exhaustion finally catching up with them. We'd lose precious time to sleeping during the day if we survived the night, all of us needing to take whatever opportunity we could to rest.

"Look out!" I called, the dimmest lights of the fires swirling behind us as dawn broke out.

Fenrir jumped to the left, loosening my grip as he bucked me to the side to avoid the gnarled hand that reached for me. The creature missed only barely, his claws raking down Fenrir's spine as the wolf howled in pain. That same hand struck me in the side, knocking me farther sideways until my only remaining grip slipped through Fenrir's fur.

"*Neamhai!*" his panicked voice called as I tumbled off his side, rolling onto the red earth where it had only just begun to illuminate. The creature behind me snarled, skidding to a stop as Fenrir collapsed beneath his own weight.

I rolled over in the dirt, wincing in pain as I shoved my hands into the earth and forced myself to my knees. The creature spun for me, but it was the mass of red streaming down Fenrir's back that I couldn't take my eyes off of.

I stood slowly, staggering to the side as I reached over my head and pulled my swords from their sheath. The creature stood on its back legs, rolling its neck as it ran straight toward me. It was an almost-human motion, a reliever of tension right before devouring its meal.

I forced my legs shoulder width apart, leading with my blades as I waited for the impact I knew was coming.

Ylfa charged the creature, slamming into its side and knocking it off course as Lupa jumped on its back. She wrapped her teeth around the creature's neck, sinking her teeth deep as blood poured down its chest. I kept my distance as long as I could, watching them grapple with the creature as two more closed in.

The phoenix was nowhere to be found, the sky clear of all things that flew except for the Morrigan where they circled overhead, swooping down to claw at the creature and offer brief moments of distraction.

I turned my attention to the coming wave of creatures, swallowing as I readied myself for what was sure to be my death. I glanced toward where Fenrir bled on the ground, attempting to get to his feet and falling beneath his weight each time.

Putting one foot in front of the other, I positioned myself between him and the coming creatures. He whimpered as he looked back at me, the pleading in his eyes nearly melting my resolve. *"Run, you foolish girl."*

But there was no force to the command, because he knew as well as I did that I wouldn't make it ten steps before they descended upon me.

The creatures came, running forward in a wave of terrifying skin and teeth, of fur and claws that would tear me in two. I met the beady red eyes of the one closest to me, determined to take him down with me as I raised my swords to position.

I drew in a deep breath, letting the air fill my lungs as the phoenix cried in the distance.

Too far.

She would never reach me before they devoured me.

Even if she had, *this* was not something I could overcome. It was not something the Cwn Annwn and I could fight at once.

This was the end.

The creatures came forward until I could make out every line of fur on their skin, only slowing when a group of basilisks slithered over the ground. They moved as one unit, all six of them coming to rest in front of me. The creatures charging me tried to stop, their feet and paws skidding over the ground.

The basilisks rose up onto their tails, their bodies leaving the ground as they shifted into something *else*. What had once been a single tail split into two legs, the scales fading off in favor of scaled armor and boots. The figures of six women came into being, from their feet up to their heads. The hair on their heads writhed, moving as if it was alive as it came into view and the scales of the basilisks fell to the earth.

"Do not look, Neamhai," Fenrir said, using that name once again. *"Just to be safe."*

Celestial one.

One by one, the creatures froze in place, expressions of terror trapped on their faces. Starting from the area surrounding their eyes, skin cracked and fur hardened.

The creatures turned to stone, blending in with the red earth below their feet. Plants lingered in the distance, offering a bright pop of green to an otherwise monochromatic landscape.

The creatures became statues, unmoving and part of the earth. The sheer number of them when they were stone took my breath away, but I couldn't stop to think about what the implication of that meant as the phoenix finally flew overhead.

His call echoed through me, making me gasp as the wound in my stomach gushed with blood anew. The skin warmed but didn't heal, but Fenrir pushed to his feet with a whimper. His gaze was cast toward the ground, his stare not meeting the basilisks as his back healed.

I kept my gaze firmly rooted to the ground, wincing when one of the women stepped around me. Her boots filled my vision, the scales on her pants intricate and fascinating. She touched a finger beneath my chin, grasping me there and applying pressure to raise my head.

I closed my eyes as she moved my head to face her, squeezing them closed in desperation. What had been the point in saving me if she wanted to turn me to stone?

"Open your eyes, Little Serpent," she said, the voice low and melodic. Something in that voice called to me, making me want to obey her. I wrinkled my nose, keeping my eyes closed out of spite. "You have nothing to fear from usss."

I believed her. Believed the honesty in her voice.

"Estrella . . ." Fenrir warned, the irritated sound of him in my head doing nothing to dissuade me.

The woman pressed two firm hands into my wound, her touch cold compared to the flaming heat of the wound. I screamed out as I tried to shove her back, but she held firm. My eyes flew open and found the eyes of a snake within the face of a beautiful woman. A Gorgon, I realized, my gaze darting over the snakes slithering around her head. They reached toward me, lingering close to my face as if scenting me. She accepted a scrap of cloth from one of the others, wrapping it tightly around my waist into a bandage to help contain my bleeding.

"Welcome home, Estrella Barlowe," the woman said, and I felt Fenrir's sigh of relief at my back. Lupa and Ylfa nuzzled my side, keeping their gaze averted as I stared into the eyes of the Gorgon woman.

But I didn't turn to stone.

I turned to Fenrir, my mind dancing with questions. He'd suspected I would turn to stone like the others, so why hadn't I?

"You can never be too cautious, Neamhai."

TWENTY-TWO

CALDRIS

I stepped into the abandoned hallway outside Estrella's rooms. Nila lingered in the room, tending to the space as if Estrella would return at any moment and require her services.

The table was covered in wildflowers, a slow procession of Lli-adhe making their way in and out of the room in silence in direct opposition to Mab. I imagined she hadn't wandered into this part of the palace, hadn't had any reason to with Estrella gone from it, but if she ever did, she'd be furious to find the quiet rebellion in support of my mate.

"What's going on?" I asked, clearing my throat. Nila and the wide-eyed *acalica* Estrella had drawn into her dance in the throne room looked up from where they worked to carefully arrange the display. The *acalica*'s fingers were long and spindly, her teeth razor-sharp as she turned her stare to me.

"Does she have a favorite flower?" Nila asked, glancing around at what remained on the table. Her energy was nervous, her movement frenzied as she tried to straighten them as if it wasn't likely to take Estrella days to return yet.

I ran through the possibilities in my mind, examining the memory of the flowers we'd passed in our journeys. There were few options with the approach of winter upon us, most of the true flowers had died already. But there was one memory, a drawing in a book during our stay with the Resistance that she'd run her fingers over, pausing to study it.

I imagined she'd never seen it before, the trees responsible not likely to be favored in a village designed for growing crops to feed Nothrek.

"Night Blossoms," I said, referring to the flowers that budded on the Loreth trees in the peak of summer. They existed only at the fringes of the Summer Court where it touched Spring and Autumn, favoring sticky, balmy nights. The flowers emerged from their buds beneath the light of the full moon, their petals the deepest purple of the midnight sky.

Nila turned to the *acalica*, nodding her head in encouragement. "Tell the others. They can relay the message to those who are free to find the flowers."

The Lliadhe faerie fled the bedroom, leaving Nila and I alone. Her eyes were sad, her features expressing every bit of worry she felt for my mate. "She'll come back," I said, attempting to keep my voice strong. My mate collected people, collected the souls of those who earned kindness and had been denied it by those who would force them into submission.

The Lliadhe saw something of themselves in Estrella. They saw a woman the world had been determined to make small, standing up to her oppressors even if it meant carrying the weight of her punishments.

"How do you know she'll be back? How do you know she'll survive this?" Nila asked, her voice barely a whisper. She looked to the door, and it struck me that Nila had taken the duty of keeping their hope alive. She'd been forced to remain strong for the others, but in this moment, she knew she could be vulnerable.

She knew I missed more than what the Llaidhe saw as their savior. I missed the woman I loved.

"Because she would never allow anything to force her to leave us to suffer. She would never leave this world knowing there are people who need her help," I said, taking a step toward Nila. I didn't touch her, and she didn't dare to cross the gap between us either.

"She would never leave *you* here without her," Nila said, a small smile appearing on her face.

"She would never leave me. She'll do whatever it takes to survive," I agreed, allowing the confidence of those words to sink deep inside me. Estrella was distant, the bond pulled taut between us and leaving me at the fringes of her emotions. I couldn't make them out, but I still felt closer to her than I had in those moments after she discovered my true identity.

Then I'd had to wonder if my mate would ever forgive me, accept me, *choose* me. Now I was settled in the knowledge that she would choose me every day for the rest of her life, doing whatever it took to return to my side.

That was love. It was the undeniable bond between us that even she couldn't deny any longer.

It was what had driven her to forgive my deception in the first place.

"They need her to come back. She gave them hope," Nila said, looking toward the empty doorway as if she expected another Lliadhe to appear at any moment. She rubbed her hands over her face, wiping away any traces of emotion and donning the mask she must have worn to keep them all going.

"These are offerings," I said, my voice quiet as I studied the flowers on the table.

"They don't have much," Nila said, explaining the lack of gold that the humans had once left in the temples of the Gods they worshipped.

Estrella wouldn't have wanted gold or coin anyway. Those things meant nothing to her but suffering.

"But they give what they can," I said, smiling as I thought of a young Estrella who might have done the same in a different life.

"The humans have their Gods," Nila said, even now with the knowledge that they'd chosen The Father and The Mother over the Fae Gods of Old, they still made offerings to the beings they believed would bring them eternal peace. "Now the Lliadhe have theirs."

"They'll die before she returns," I said, glancing down to the flowers.

"And every day, they will bring more. Maybe she can feel it, feel our belief. The Fae Gods were said to be stronger when the humans *believed*. Maybe she will be, too," Nila said, studying my face for any sign that it might have been true.

It was so long ago, I didn't know when I'd settled into my life of servitude to a Queen I hated. Once, I'd been strong enough to oppose her in my own way, but it wasn't until Estrella that I felt like I could rid us of her in truth.

"Maybe she will," I said, agreeing with Nila's belief. Even if it didn't help Estrella, it helped those she'd been forced to leave behind.

It would help the army she had at her disposal when she returned.

"What if Mab sees them? Aren't you afraid of the consequences for you?" I asked. Given that Nila had been tasked with caring for Estrella and her rooms during her time at Tar Mesa, she would be the first suspect on Mab's warpath if the time came.

"Then let her see," Nila said with a shrug that felt so defeated compared to the hopeful woman I'd witnessed at Estrella's side. "But she has no reason to come to this part of the castle now."

"And what of her spies?" I asked, glancing back to the open door. The others who had come and gone from this space did so hurriedly, but Nila was willful enough to know there was no point to her hiding this with the location being what it was.

"None are willing to stand before her long enough to report what we've done anymore. They're too busy hiding from her wrath, and I must admit that has brought us some freedom to move throughout the castle. Mab's real power has always been her far reach and the eyes she has everywhere. Without that outright loyalty, she's weakened herself slightly at least," Nila said, returning to fussing over the contents of the room. She'd clearly taken to keeping the space perfect for Estrella, for when she returned, but she was riddled with anxious energy in a way that felt unnatural.

She stopped, sighing and forcing herself to be still as she finally looked at me. Her smile was hesitant. "Is there anything else we can do?" Nila asked, studying my face.

"I need to leave Tar Mesa," I said, watching her eyes widen. To not be here when Estrella returned was unthinkable to both of us, but I would need to do it to be there for her while she was gone. "I have a way to sneak into Tartarus, but it will require me to soul-walk for a time. The ritual is risky without a witch at my side, and I haven't seen Imelda since that day at the cove." Worry laced my words as I spoke them, and Nila's pinched brow was all I needed to know that she had not either.

"The Wild Hunt is here," Nila said, reaching out to grasp my arm in shock. She jolted back immediately, turning for the door. "They've brought more of the human mates to the dungeons below. If you hurry, you may catch them before they leave."

Holt would need to disobey his Queen to play the song that could pull my soul from my body in the night, but he could do it.

I turned, leaving Estrella's bedroom behind me without a second thought. I kept my pace controlled but quick as I navigated the halls of Tar Mesa. Carefully avoiding making eye contact with any of Mab's followers, none of them interfered as I moved through the shadows and stepped into the shadow realm.

My magic took me where I needed to go, the inky darkness surrounding me as soon as I'd put enough distance between Estrella's room and the wards placed there and myself. It was like coming home, like a cool winter's night by the hearth enveloping me in its warmth. The shadows drifted over my skin, tickling against the edges of my armor affectionately.

I emerged within the human dungeons, staring at Holt as he and the Wild Hunt ushered the newest batch of mates into a cell. His eyes widened as I stepped out of the shadow realm, placing one foot in front of the other and coming to a stop in front of him. "Caldris," he said, his voice dropping low.

He looked over my shoulder, studying the space behind me for my mate or the witch he so desperately wished to see. He wouldn't admit it out loud, not when she clearly detested him for what had transpired between them centuries before.

"I need your help," I said, glancing over his shoulder to find Aramis standing behind Holt. Behind them, the other members of the Wild Hunt grimaced as they closed the doors to the cells that now occupied dozens of human mates. I couldn't stop to think of what fate might wait for them here when Mab realized I was missing. Not when Estrella's life, and all our lives, depended on me finding her in Tartarus.

"Anything," Holt said, stepping forward. He raised his hand, allowing me to place mine in his and gripping it tight in the male version of affection.

"What do you need?" Aramis asked, stepping forward with the rest of the Wild Hunt at his back.

"Estrella is in Tartarus," I explained, watching as Holt flinched. We both knew the horrors that waited for her there, the torment she would need to endure in her efforts to find Medusa.

"Caldris," he said, shaking his head as he pulled his hand back from mine. I gripped him tighter, pulling him close enough that the breastplate of my armor touched his tattooed skin.

"She was injured, Holt," I said, staring him in the face and daring him to deny me this. Centuries of friendship did not equate to turning his back on me when I needed him the most. "I don't need to explain to you what happens to me if she dies."

"You're a fucking idiot," Holt grumbled, but he nodded his head anyway. "There's a doorway."

"I know," I said, already certain of the placement where I would need to meet the ferryman. "But I cannot enter into it with my physical form."

Holt scoffed. "You want me to call you to join the Hunt for the night," he said, a disbelieving laugh bubbling up in his throat. While some of the souls Holt called to join the Wild Hunt came from those who were already dead or dying, others were people who simply slept too soundly, feeling compelled to the call and joined instead of resting peacefully.

"It's the only way," I said, not bothering to deny my plan.

"It's dangerous. You'll be little more than a shade, and that will make you susceptible to the claims of Tartarus. If you stay too long, you'll never escape," Holt said, the warning on his tongue sounding like something I should heed. Hopefully I would have enough time to aid Estrella in her quest and see her home safely, because I didn't think I would be able to leave her.

"We'll need somewhere to hide my body. Otherwise Mab's minions will run me through while I sleep to be rid of me once and for all," I said, looking around the dungeon. It was too risky to leave the dungeon again, the chances of Mab realizing I was up to something slim, but possible.

If she interrogated me, I'd have to tell her the truth. I couldn't lie.

"Through here," Tara said, breaking off from the rest of the Wild Hunt who watched and rushing to the side of the dungeon. She rounded the corner, going out of sight of the humans as Holt and I followed behind her. She held a finger to her lips, warning us to be silent as she groped along the stone. She touched the stones on the wall, feeling across them as she searched for something that only she could feel. Finally pressing her fingers more firmly into one of the rocks, she stepped back as the panel slid to the side as if by magic.

The small room within was littered with bones. The dead who had once been placed in solitary in this place long since forgotten.

"What is this place?" I asked as I stepped into the little room.

"It was your father's favored cell for his prisoners that he didn't want Mab to know about," she said, gesturing to the skeletons that littered the room. "He tended to them personally. No one but us knows of this room's existence."

I ran my hand over the stones within, to the dangling instruments of torture on the walls. "How do you know of it then?" I asked, watching as she wrung her hands in front of her.

"There was a time when he used this room to have secret rendezvous with your mother," she said, watching as my eyes lit with understanding. My parents had shared more than the one forbidden night that led to my birth.

My mother had been in Tar Mesa to see him.

But they'd never allowed me to join, because my curse to serve Mab had made it impossible for me to guard their secret.

Everything in me went cold, and my hand dropped off the stone as hurt flashed through me. It radiated with heat, a burning, writhing thing with a mind of its own.

"I brought her here through the river entrance. There was no reason for Mab to believe I had any ties to either of them," she said, finishing the thought as I sank to the floor and found a spot that was cleared of bones.

I lay back on the stone, staring up at the ceiling and refusing to think of what had transpired in this cell.

Our fate would not be the same as that of my parents.

"She was never the same after she lost him," Tara said, continuing on. "I served her in the Winter Court before my death, and she was always so full of life. So vibrant, but now even she dances on the edge of madness. If you were to take your rightful place on the throne, I believe she would pass into the Void willingly to join him."

Abandoning me yet again, but I couldn't even muster up the energy to be angry with her for that.

A life without Estrella wasn't worth living at all.

I placed my hands behind my head, attempting to get comfortable as I let my eyes drift closed. Holt seemed to realize that my need for understanding had passed, the history between my parents and I no longer relevant.

They'd chosen one another over time with me, and I couldn't fault them for it.

Not when I would have sacrificed them both to save her. Holt spoke, silencing Tara with his voice.

"Sleep, God of the Dead. For when you wake, we ride."

Twenty-Three

ESTRELLA

The Gorgon woman stared back at me, her lungs heaving as she studied my face. My hands tightened around the hilt of my sword, my fingers running over the scales of the snakes engraved into the metal.

The woman standing before me was a breathtaking beauty. Her eyes were the bright, vivid green of the serpents dancing within her hair, specks of brown forming the pattern of scales within her irises. Her hair was wavy and a deep brown so dark it almost possessed a blueish undertone. She had brown skin, her lips a deep rose color. Her facial structure was sharp, with high cheekbones and a defined brow.

She was a great and terrible beauty in a timeless way, the kind of breathtaking that men waged wars for.

She wore armor of the deepest green, her shoulders bare where it curved to wrap around her throat at the center before plunging into a sweetheart neckline. Each of her arms was wrapped in a snake, their teeth embedded into her flesh. The skin around the snakes' fangs was gray, as if their bites threatened to turn her to stone at any given moment.

An intricate band of metal curved over her forehead, the gold sparkling in the firelight. It continued around her head like a band, complementing the gold tones in the scales of the snakes that stared back at me. Their eyes glimmered with the same golden color, heads tipping to the side as they studied me in curiosity.

They'd saved our lives. There was no denying that.

I swallowed, forcing down my trepidation at what they might expect in return. In this place, no one did anything out of the kindness of their hearts.

"Thank you," I said, the sound coming out far too quiet. The Gorgon woman tipped her head to the side in a manner that was so reminiscent of the snakes in her hair that I almost chuckled, standing on my own as the others couldn't risk meeting her stare.

There were no Gorgons left in Nothrek, but that didn't mean I hadn't seen the remains of the statues they'd left behind during our war with the Fae all those centuries ago. People turned to stone where they stood, with no ability to defend themselves.

I looked to the Morrigan where they had turned their backs on the Gorgon women, my own relief peaking. It wasn't without a hint of surprise, but given my father's bloodline, maybe such magics weren't a threat to me.

Was that why I hadn't turned to stone?

"You've no need to thank me, Little Sserpent," she said, taking a single step toward me. I braced myself, placing my feet shoulder width apart on instinct. My swords rose at my sides automatically, my elbows bending to prepare for an attack. "Your father might have sworn not to interfere in the trials, but I made no such promise."

"What do you want in return for your aid?" I asked, pursing my lips as I studied her. Whoever she was, whatever she thought to gain from sparing our lives, Fenrir seemed to know she wouldn't harm me.

Even if he thought he would turn to stone, the beast would interfere to save me if he saw a threat.

"*Beast*," Fenrir scoffed in my head. "*Do not insult me, Neamhai. I am no more beast than you.*"

"Fenrir," the Gorgon woman said, but the affection in her voice caught me off guard. My wolf kept his eyes to the ground, rising now that his injuries had healed thanks to the phoenix. He approached the Gorgon women, standing at their feet and allowing them to run their hands over his fur.

"You know my familiar," I said, my swords lowering at my sides.

"*Family,*" Fenrir said, his words full of warmth as he rubbed his head against the scaled pants of the woman who wouldn't turn her gaze away from me. She petted him absentmindedly, allowing him to lick her hand sweetly as Ylfa and Lupa approached the other Gorgons behind her and rolled to their backs, letting the snakes tickle their bellies.

Family, I thought, echoing his word. I knew he heard the disbelief in the thought, knew he understood it for what it was.

I didn't have much in the way of family. A mother who was hidden away in the Winter Court and my not-brother I'd left to suffer in Tartarus under the thin promise to meet him at the Cradle of Creation. Could he be trusted to uphold his word? After all his lies?

"Fenrir and I have been family for a very long time," the woman said, quirking her brow at the swords still held tightly within my grasp.

"I fail to see the resemblance," I said, the snark in my tone taking even me by surprise. It was stupid, foolish to think that someone else could lay claim to the wolf that felt so like a part of me already.

What would it be like when we'd had decades, *centuries*, to exist within one another's head?

The Gorgon woman smiled, revealing straight, perfectly white teeth. Only the fangs peeking out from the corners of her mouth were enough to remind me that she was far from human. Her smile reached her eyes, genuine glee consuming her features in a way that made any retort I might have continued with vanish. She took a step toward me, her hand outstretched cautiously as if it might placate me.

"Fenrir was bonded to my hussband, once upon a time," she said, making everything in me go still. Fenrir was silent. The sound of the rushing fire and the slithering of the serpents in her hair was all that reached me through the haze in my mind.

It meant nothing. Caldris's father was married to a woman that was not his mother.

The woman smiled softly, showing the gleam of those fangs as her eyes softened.

"Who are you?" I asked, feeling incredibly alone. The Morrigan made no move to interfere as she took another step toward me, and the Cwn Annwn remained with the other Gorgons as they were reunited.

"You already know the answer to that question, Little Ssserpent," she said, her voice soft as she stopped so close to me that I could reach out to touch her. I raised my sword, holding the point to her throat in warning. She grinned, the low hiss of her snakes echoing as they shifted to stare down at me. "Just as you know why you have not turned to stone."

"Fenrir believed I might," I said, glancing down at the wolf at my side. I didn't want to consider the implications in her words, didn't want to face the reality staring me in the face.

Her connection to Fenrir. Her affinity for snakes.

No.

"You can never be certain with mixed bloodlinesss such as yours, but you are jusst as much mine as you are hisss. Perhaps more, looking at you now," she said.

The Gorgon wrapped her hand around the blade, the clink of stone touching the sword. She shoved it away, her skin unblemished as I thrust my other toward her in defiance. It touched the skin of her arm, bouncing off as pain radiated through my hand and up my wrist as if I'd struck it against a boulder.

"Ssay it," she said, blocking each of my blows as I attempted to strike her and put distance between us. "Sssay my name, Essstrella."

I winced, tossing my sword into the dirt at her feet. She didn't so much as flinch away from it as I reached up with my other hand, attempting to grab a snake from her hair. It bit me, sinking its teeth into the fleshy part between my thumb and forefinger.

Jerking back, I stared down at the two puncture holes and the blood that welled from them.

Turning my gaze up to the woman staring down at me, her face a mask of patience, I realized how impossible my task would be.

I realized why so many others had failed.

"*Medusa,*" I said, the word coming out half a hiss. I'd never felt more serpentine than in the moments after the venom of her snake slithered through my veins. It burned a path through me, turning everything within me cold and hard.

Turning my insides to what felt like stone.

"If you want ssomething from me, all you need to do is *assk,*" she said, reaching out to cup my cheek in her hand. Her touch was somehow soft in spite of the way my blades had bounced off her body, her thumb brushing over my cheekbone as I fought through the burn within me. "Claim your birthright, Esstrella."

I shoved aside the pain, blinking through it as I tried to focus on her speckled green eyes. "I need a snake from your crown. Will you give me that willingly?" I asked, understanding what Mab hadn't.

No one would ever be able to take from this woman by force. Never again would she allow something to be stolen from her, not after how she'd been wronged when she was cursed to this form in the first place.

The legend of Medusa had been passed through countless books, countless stories that the village of Mistfell had thought to burn. I'd seen mention of them, only learning the full truth of the horror she'd endured during my time in the caves with the Resistance.

Medusa reached up with her free hand, allowing one of the snakes from her hair to coil itself around her hand and wrist. She lowered it to mine, threading her fingers through my own as the snake passed from her forearm to mine.

She wound her way up over my wrist, slithering over the armor covering my forearm and sliding into the tiny slit in the scales at my elbow. She squirmed her way underneath it, slithering along bare skin and tickling the inside of my elbow as Medusa held me still with her iron grip. The snake was small, thinner than my wrist and the deepest purple as she turned her body and situated herself. Her tail wrapped around my shoulder, settling against my breast as it curled around my arm twice. The head rested just below my elbow, those eerie golden eyes staring up at me through the slit in my armor. She unhinged her jaw, spreading her mouth around my forearm and burying her fangs into my skin once again.

Fire burned through me, but she made no move to separate. Settling in for the long haul, she stared up at me as she pumped her venom into my flesh.

The skin around her teeth cracked, graying as it turned to stone just like the Gorgon woman in front of me.

It didn't spread, leaving me to wonder what the fire in my veins would do.

Medusa ran her finger over the snake's head, watching as the creature's eyes closed happily. She turned her stare back to mine, those freckled green eyes boring into mine as she spoke. "I would give you anything, my daughter."

TWENTY-FOUR

CALDRIS

The music of the Hunt rocked through me, calling me from the depths of sleep. I woke, opening my eyes and moving to sit. My body was lighter than normal, my form moving with ease as I met Holt's stare. He stopped playing the song, not wanting to risk summoning any of the others within Tar Mesa to join us on this night, particularly not when it would risk exposing my location.

I stood, staring down at my body where it slumbered peacefully. It was only my soul that moved freely in the room, the weight of my physical form discarded like a cloak.

We wasted no time making our way out of the secret chamber, and I followed Holt and the other members of the Wild Hunt through the halls of Mab's palace. Most of the palace slept or had retired to their beds for the night at least, only the posted guards lingering as we ascended the steps from the dungeon and emerged into the main hall. My feet never touched the ground beneath me, gliding over the surface as the members of the Wild Hunt surrounded me and hid me from view for any who might have looked a little too closely and caught sight of my shade.

It wasn't every Fae who could see the spirits who left their body or the spectral form of the dead who lingered, only those with an affinity for the magics of death, but the Shadow Court possessed more of those Fae than any other place.

Their magic was just minimal if they were not Gods. Diluted as their blood became more distant from the Primordials who had birthed the first of us.

Holt did not stop once on his way out of the hallowed halls of Tar Mesa, ignoring the screams that came from the throne room. The Huntswoman at my side winced at the sharp, shrill sound of suffering, her face conveying exactly what she thought of what had become of us.

Enslaved to a tyrant Queen, we would all die out soon enough. She had no respect for life or harmony, not even caring if she ruled over nothing but ashes when this was all done.

The skeletal horses of the Wild Hunt waited for us at the castle gates, and I immediately missed Azra. Riding him would be impossible, even if Mab was clueless to my departure for the time being. The snake around my heart could not alert her to something changing within me, not when my physical form merely slept. No one but me ever rode my horse, and it would only alert the guards watching as I stepped up beside Holt's horse and put the creature between me and the watchful eyes. Holt mounted his horse, not speaking a word as one without a rider took up place beside him.

Reserved for the next member of the Wild Hunt who could join at any moment, choosing a life of hunting over the peace of the Meadows of Folkvangr.

We walked away from Tar Mesa, going slowly enough that I could keep up with the horse's gait until we crossed over one of the sandy hills. When the guards could no longer see us, I lifted myself into the saddle.

And the Wild Hunt rode.

We rode at a pace that no human could sustain, stepping into the Shadow Walk as a unit. It carried us to Nothrek, taking a mere hour to travel a distance that might have otherwise taken us days. The Wild Hunt would need to travel back the slow way for fear of losing humans to the shadow realm, but there was nothing to stop us on our journey.

We all knew the consequences that waited if we wandered off the path. The creatures who waited to collect us and feast on us for an eternity. The power of a soul was valuable to the shadows.

Even a human's.

We emerged on the cliffside I recognized from my memory of the first night I'd laid eyes on my mate. I dismounted the horse, patting the side of his neck as I made my way to the narrow path that led down to the water.

Holt followed behind me, leaving the others to wait on top of the cliff.

We walked in silence until I stopped on the shore, watching the water lap against the sand and mud. Estrella had once thrown herself into these waters, not knowing the dangers and the passage that lingered in the distance of the chasm. Holt stopped at my side, pointing into the distance.

A ways out, just before the horizon faded into the mists that surrounded the human realm, a tree grew out of the water. It was massive, its trunk twisted and gnarled. The roots stuck out from the water, the very tiny hint of land beneath it that formed a bridge over the water.

"There," he said simply, allowing me to step into the freezing waters. They lapped at my ankles, chilling even me as I made my way out to waist-deep. My magic seeped out of my soul without a body to contain it, freezing the water behind me as I made my way.

My hands trailed over the surface, turning to face Holt in what we both knew could very well be a final goodbye.

"Staying in Tartarus for too long will have disastrous consequences. You are a shade, the undead, and therefore you are susceptible to the pull of the Five Rivers. Make sure you return before Tartarus traps you forever," he said.

I nodded as I felt him release the call of the Wild Hunt, letting me wander freely. I was too far from my body to return in spite of the lack of call, pushing my way through the water until it lapped against my throat.

"I'll return," I said, reassuring him with words that neither of us knew if we could believe.

"I'm coming with you," Holt said.

"No," I argued, shaking my head. As much as I appreciated the thought, it did not make sense for him to risk everything to make this journey with me. Not when there were others here who needed his help far more than me. "Someone has to transport the souls to the Void in my absence. Don't let them suffer because I've gone."

Holt nodded, his jaw clenching as he acknowledged the truth in those words. Estrella would have me to help her, and I would have her to watch out for me. The souls that needed help passing had no one with me gone. "Be safe," he said instead of arguing, and neither of us spoke of the other reason he could not come. The Wild Hunt may not have been dead, but they were not truly alive either. Who knew how they would be susceptible to the prison of Tartarus in this form?

I lay my body out, swimming as quickly as I could toward the bridge formed by the tree.

As I came closer, the pit of darkness between the tree came into view. The water rushed toward it, forming almost a river within the sea as the current picked up, catching me within it.

Even if I'd wanted to, I wouldn't have had time to catch myself on the tree roots before the current sucked me beneath the surface.

Darkness surrounded me, a familiar cold comfort sinking into my bones that felt chilled enough to shatter.

The water turned to ice as it surrounded me, chunks floating through the current beneath me.

Above me, the sky vanished as I passed beneath the bridge underneath the tree. Tossing and turning through the water, all light disappeared.

And I plunged into the Void.

Twenty-Five

ESTRELLA

Daughter," I whispered, stumbling back from her. It wasn't a question, not in truth, because I'd already not dared to admit that the possibility was there. She looked so much like me, with the same eyes and similar mannerisms that seemed impossible given I hadn't spent time with her to commit them to learned behavior.

She let me go, leaving me to pry at the snake that had embedded its teeth within my skin. It didn't release, as if it was a part of me now. I fell back, landing on my ass and wincing as the burn of venom flooding my veins centered in my palms.

The dirt beneath me hardened, the grains turning to pebbles as I forced myself to my feet and stared down at it in shock. I stumbled to the side, confusion lacing my vision as I looked back and forth between my palms and Medusa, desperately trying to make sense of what had happened. Had she been the one to turn the sand to stone, or had I?

I tripped, catching myself at the last minute. The weight of something moved within the tiny pocket in my scaled trousers, forcing me to reach down and touch it on instinct. The armor didn't react to my touch, giving me a brief moment of reprieve in the feelings of horror washing over me.

I reached into my pocket, my fingertips brushing against the velvet satchel I'd nearly forgotten Imelda had given me. The soft fabric shifted at my touch, changing to hardened stone before I could pull it free. The stone was beautiful, rather than the pebbles I'd left at my feet, a translucent amber with the herbs she must have given me for my journey trapped within its shell.

My hands trembled at my sides, the implications of what my touch had done forcing me not to even look at Fenrir.

Gods.

"Estrella, look at me," Medusa said, stepping up in front of me. She took my hands in hers, the gentle touch doing nothing to soothe me.

What if I couldn't touch anything without turning it to stone?

What if I could never look Caldris in the eye?

"What have you done?" I asked, shaking my head from side to side. She'd done to me what had been done to her, the reality of that fate making me murderous.

"You can control it," she said, releasing my hands to grasp my face. She forced me to meet her gaze, holding my stare as she leaned forward and touched her forehead to mine. The snakes around her head slithered over mine, brushing against my face and inhaling the scent of my hair.

Badb stepped forward, keeping her eyes averted as she held out her hand for me to take. I shook my head, unwilling to risk adding to the garden of stones that lingered behind the Gorgons. "You are more than the power that you possess," Badb said, crossing the distance between us.

She wrapped her fingers around my wrist, stilling as her fingers turned to stone where they touched me. I drew in a deep breath, willing the stone to retreat back into my body.

I wouldn't let her become a statue of the past, not because of me.

It burned as it seared my skin, turning my forearm gray with the flash of rock that passed over me. It faded into my flesh, making me feel heavy for a moment before it disappeared. Badb raised her gaze to meet mine, her chest failing to rise and fall with breath as she waited for the sure fate that my eye contact would leave her with.

"Why would you do that to me?" I asked, backing away from Medusa.

She tipped her head to the side, a look of confusion crossing over her face. "I only gave you what you asked for."

"I didn't know it would make me—"

"A Gorgon?" she asked, taking a step back as Fenrir moved toward me. He nuzzled against my arm, using his massive head to nudge my hand until I had no choice but to pet him. "You are not a Gorgon, Esstrella. You merely possessss the blood of one. The other half of your heritage is far more potent."

"So if I give Mab this snake, it won't give her the ability to turn her victims to stone?" I asked, waiting for her response.

"No. She does not possessss the blood of the Gorgon. The ssnake will do nothing for her but drive her further on her path to madness. No matter what she believesss it will do," Medusa answered. Fenrir and the wolves moved on, walking in the direction of the next river as the Morrigan followed behind them. It left me with no choice but to take up pace beside Medusa, beside my mother, as she walked behind them. The other Gorgons strolled behind us, their bodies and faces alert as they scoured the land for threats.

Somehow, I didn't think I'd be at risk of dying between trials any longer.

"The cursed stone," I said, realizing that the face of the woman I'd seen in it was so similar to the breathtaking face of my *mother*. I had a mother waiting for me, one who was probably confused and terrified in the Winter Court, while I stood face-to-face with a woman who also held the same title. It was disorienting, at best, nauseating at worst. "It was yours," I added, forcing myself to focus in on the conversation and the answers I could gain from it.

"I created it yesss; your father imbued it with his power. He'd intended for it to be yourss one day, but we struggled to conceive. He'd ssired his children with Hemera a few years before we met, but we struggled greatly. The Primordials bear offspring easily, but it is not sso easy for Gorgonss. It took us centuries, much like it would for a Fae couple after the curse," she explained, her voice like the softest melody. I wondered if she'd have read me bedtime stories in that same voice in a different life, instantly feeling guilty because I had a mother who *had* done that. "We didn't anticipate the sstruggle. We expected it to occur much more quickly because of who your father was. We should have waited to put his magic into the sstone. If we had, the dwarves never would have been able to steal it."

"The stone was made for me?" I asked, choosing to focus on that one detail.

"Yes. Your father wanted you to have some of his magic at your disposal so that he could teach you the ways of the Primordials as you grew. It was his greatest wish to be able to share that with one of his children and raise you to be his protégé."

"Then why didn't he just take Mab?" I asked, watching as Medusa winced.

"He was determined that it should be our child who followed in his footsteps. He loved me enough that he didn't want me to have to raise the child he'd sired with another woman, and Rheaghan and Mab had their mother and stepfather who loved them more than anything," she said, sighing sadly. "To take Mab as his protégé once she ended up with the stone, he would have needed to destroy two families. He wasn't willing to do that."

"Instead he condemned the world to her cruelty," I said, snapping as I thought of all that Mab had done since the stone had corrupted her.

"We failed to anticipate what my influence on the stone would do to someone who did not share my blood," she said. "By the time she'd come to power, the Primordials had all taken a blood vow that they were done interfering in the ways of the Fae. They had long since retreated to the Cradle of Creation, leaving the living to decide their own fate."

Macha scoffed. "Leaving the Fates to decide their fates, you mean."

Badb glared at her sister. "We've wasted enough time. The Acheron waits up ahead," she said, forcing the red-eyed third of the Morrigan to silence her opinions.

I stopped, brushing my fingers over the snake wrapped around my arm. She squirmed into my touch, the impression distinctly affectionate. "I already have what I came for," I said, staring at the Morrigan as they turned to look at me.

Badb and Nemain exchanged a knowing look, but they never turned it on Medusa herself for fear that they would turn to stone. I wondered if the Gorgons had the same ability to only turn things to stone when they desired it, or if it was an involuntary act on their part.

"You entered into the Trial of Five Rivers," Badb said sadly. "If you choose to leave now, you will do so without the magic you gave to Tartarus upon entry as a consequence for abandoning your quest."

"What?" I asked, glancing back and forth between Medusa and the Morrigan. "No wonder you were willing to give me the snake. I can't even fucking use it without leaving all my strength here, and that's not an option if I want to defeat Mab."

"You can. You can go back and save your mate. You will just do so as his human mate, because Tartarus and your father will accept your withdrawal as proof that you are not worthy of the gifts the Cradle has in store for you," Medusa said. She pressed her mouth tight, her lips sealing together as if she hated the situation as much as I did. "Should you choose to return as you are now, there is a possibility that Caldris can win this fight once you complete your bond, but the only way to do so will mean murdering Mab."

"Why would I care if she dies?" I asked, my brow furrowing as I studied Medusa. Even if the sinking pit in my stomach did feel sorry for the little girl she'd been before the stone corrupted her, that girl had been gone for centuries.

"Because that is the kind of person you are, Estrella. She is your sister, and there is a weapon that awaits you in the Cradle that will have the power to lift the curse from Mab. She would be free to be herself for the first time since childhood, and I would think that you of all people would want to free her from the prison that her own body has become," Medusa said, the words feeling like a stern reprimand.

"I shouldn't have to prove my worth to any of you," I griped, stalking forward. I *hated* that this woman I'd never met seemed to know so much about me and my motivations, let alone that she felt like she had the ability to discipline me like a parent.

"Estrella, we both love you," Medusa said, quickening her pace to keep up at my side. In spite of the harsh words, we continued on toward the next river, because I knew I needed that magic to help Caldris. Returning to save his life now was only a bandage on the festering wound that was Mab, when I had the ability to do something that could heal it altogether.

"What do the two of you know of love?" I scoffed, thinking of the arrogant male who had stared down at me in that arena and done nothing to help me when I'd been gored by a bull.

"We know enough of it that we sent you away to keep you safe. We sacrificed our relationship with you for your well-being," Medusa said, her voice stern and low. The red sands beneath our feet deepened as we walked, and ahead of us I took in the fertile black sand that reminded me of the rumors of the volcano on the other coast of Nothrek.

"I might have believed that of you, if not for the fact that you're married to Khaos. He's the original Primordial. What could he possibly have to fear?" I asked, the words giving me pause.

Either both my parents were truly incapable of love as the Morrigan believed, or they'd found a way to love one another despite the rules of nature. The Primordials didn't feel; they didn't care about anything but themselves.

"Somebody allowed those dwarves entry to the Cradle," she said, her voice melancholy as she considered the betrayal. "Someone we trusted allowed the dwarves to raid our home and take anything of value. We never discovered who was responsible, and the fear that they would return and take you was crippling."

"Why would anyone care about me? I'm just another child of the Primordials. They have more than they know what to do with," I said, thinking back to the number of Gods that had once plagued Nothrek. Gods were the children of two Primordials. The children the Primordials sired with something else took different forms, shaping the various creatures and Lliadhe who existed in both our realms.

"You're not just another child of a Primordial, Estrella," Medusa said, reaching down to scoop a handful of black sand into her hand. We came upon the Acheron river more quickly than I'd expected, the sight of the glowing green water in the distance making me shift my weight nervously.

Where the Styx had been a raging river, the Acheron was still. There was no movement on the surface of the water as it set in the wide canal it called home, no current to speak of.

"Then what am I?" I snapped, tired of the evasive answers. I doubted Khaos had bound her to secrecy in the way he had the Morrigan, but even still she didn't outright say what I was to them.

Why he'd placed his magic in the stone.

"You are our *daughter*," she said, turning to face me. Those snakes on her head stretched toward me, and I couldn't resist the urge to reach up with a single hand so that they could wrap around my finger and hug it.

"And Mab is also his daughter, is she not?" I asked.

"It's not the same," she said, shaking her head. "Everyone knows he has no love for his other children. They were created purely out of a need to populate the realm at a time when there weren't many living souls, when he was still bleeding from the betrayal of his first wife. But you were conceived in love, Estrella. Our intention was always to raise you ourselves, but after I got pregnant, he became more paranoid than ever. Mab was seeking out her other siblings and killing them, collecting the heads of the Gods as trophies. He fell asleep seeing that fate for you every night, and we knew it was only a matter of time before the rumor of your birth reached her and she sent an assassin to kill you in your crib."

"So you sent me away," I said, resisting the burn of tears in my throat.

Whoever Khaos might have been to me, whatever kind of father he'd intended to be, there was little evidence that the man Medusa spoke of still existed. If that had been true to begin with, was it still true now? Or had the years I'd lived and grown without them to raise me hardened him?

"He loved you enough to give you up," Medusa said, her voice sad. "As did I."

"He might have loved me then, but no father would put the daughter he loved through these trials. He wouldn't force me to be human while I endure—"

"There are rules that even he cannot break, Estrella. If he intervenes in your trials, he forfeits them for you. Why do you think I'm here?" Medusa asked, cocking her head to the side. "It is not a coincidence that we knew you would be in danger and came to you. It is a long journey from the Cradle. We traveled all night to get to you in time because he warned me you were in trouble."

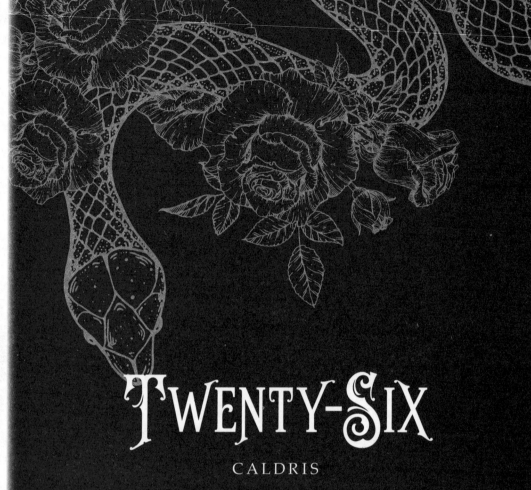

TWENTY-SIX

CALDRIS

The current swept me up, cradling me as it thrashed me back and forth in the darkness. I became weightless entirely, feeling as if pieces of my soul might be lost to the river.

Just when I thought I couldn't take it anymore, the river finally spit me out.

I sucked back a deep breath, letting it fill my lungs as water splashed around me. I fell through the air, lost in a waterfall as it poured me into a pool below. The crash of my spirit against the surface filled my ears, and then fluid quickly filled them soon after as I plunged beneath the surface.

Struggling to swim in the strength of the current, I fought to raise my head above the surface and took what breaths I could manage in the moments I won.

The area surrounding me was black, completely devoid of all things living and dead. Nothing existed but for that darkness, not even the twinkle of starlight to ease my passage as I plummeted below the surface of the pool. It sucked me down into its depths, pulling me deep enough that I could no longer see the surface. In a moment, the current slowed, and I found myself trapped in darkness, not knowing which way was up any longer.

This current was slow, an easy movement that felt deceptively calm compared to the raging river that had carried me here. The River of Life held me in a cool embrace, and I might have given into the temptation to stay if it hadn't been for the figure that drifted over the top of me.

His body was stretched out longer than was normal, as if someone had drawn and quartered him in life and his soul wore the signs of it. He opened his eyes, blinking down at me with a haunting red stare before he reached for me.

His nails were overgrown, sharp and curved as they grasped the wisps of my clothing, tugging at my tunic to pull me closer as I drifted through the water. I touched two hands to his chest, shoving myself back just as he opened his mouth to reveal three rows of jagged teeth. They spun in a circle within him, threatening to pull me in from the current it created.

He released me as I gave him a full shove, swimming for the surface of the water frantically as a golden light shone through. I passed by countless others of those creatures, wincing as they reached for me and turned their long, stretched bodies to follow after me.

I swam with all the strength in my soul, hating the fact that I did not possess the same magic as a soul as I had as a Fae. In death, we were all the same.

In this space between life and death, I might as well have been human.

Fuck.

I struck the top of the water, flinching back when it refused to release me. As if a glass barrier existed between me and the dark void above, I banged my fists against it.

Hoping the ferryman would hear me, hoping they would follow through on his promise to pull me from the river.

Clawed hands wrapped around my ankle, threatening to pull me farther beneath the surface as I struggled. I swam, attempting to resist that pull but losing momentum with every second that passed.

A skull popped through the surface, pushing through the barrier that reminded me of the softness of spring moss. I wrapped a hand around the staff attached to that skull, tugging on it to let the wielder know that I'd grabbed ahold.

The ferryman pulled me out, draping me across the corner of their boat. The wood dug into my ribs as I fell in, releasing their staff when they tugged it away from me.

They used it to beat at the head of the creature who held tight to my ankle, using me to pull himself from the river. They didn't stop until the being's head was a mass of blood and gore, his brain exposed on the side.

He slunk back into the water as the springy barrier reappeared, leaving the ferryman to turn their attention to me.

"You're early," they grunted, using their skull-topped oar to resume rowing. They continued down the river, leaving me to stare over the edge of the boat at the sheer number of souls trapped within.

The Void left no ability to discern how long we traveled before we reached the entrance to Tartarus, leaving me to sit in silence. "Thank you . . . for coming for me," I said, swallowing my pride to thank the being who had given me my only chance at reaching Estrella.

"We didn't do it for you, God of the Dead," the ferryman said, golden eyes flashing in defiance.

I wondered how much longer the ferryman would be able to show preference for Estrella before the Fates intervened, suspecting it wouldn't be much longer at all from the tension on their face.

I turned my attention back to the river and the odd boundary that kept the creatures contained within the water. They'd become something monstrous, so distorted by their time there that I couldn't help but swallow and wonder if that had been what might have become of me had the ferryman not pulled me free.

However much longer we had where they were still an ally to Estrella, I would never not be grateful for the love a father felt for his daughter in spite of all the odds stacked against him and the interference of the Fates.

Something rested upon the top of the pool as we continued, a stone figure of a woman that seemed to float at the water's edge. I studied it intensely, the figure far too familiar for my comfort. Had she not been crafted from a pearlescent quartz, I might have questioned whether or not my mate had somehow found her way into the Void to meet me.

The cloak framed her face, the intricate way the stone was carved mimicking even the wrinkles in the fabric. I knew in my heart that it was meant to depict my mate, felt that tug on my soul as the ferryman rowed us past her, but where Estrella's face should have been was only a mask of darkness. Like staring into the night sky, she was entirely featureless with only the gold and purple sparks of starlight to shine through the void of light. Her hands were the same where they rose at her sides, reminding me so much of the way her fingers looked as if they'd been dipped into the night sky itself.

The Void beside her shifted, a spark of purple and blue light spreading from an epicenter. It morphed and molded, spreading into a gateway of sorts as a male figure emerged through the gap it created. He was nothing but a twist of shadows and starlight, golden eyes gleaming through the galaxy he created.

I knew who he was immediately, had seen this likeness depicted so many times in the books I'd read as a boy, hiding away in the library archives with my father when Mab was on a rampage.

Khaos.

"Kharon," I said, drawing their attention to the Primordial in our midst. They didn't seem fazed by the being's presence, grunting under their breath before he continued rowing. Khaos glided his way across the surface of the water, abandoning his place beside the statue of my mate in favor of keeping up with the boat. He did not hurry or rush to get there, but as the view of light on the other side of a small cavern appeared, illuminating the void with a reddish hue, Khaos moved his form into our path and blocked the way.

Kharon sank their staff into the waters, making the boat come to a swaying halt. My balance shifted as I fought to find my footing, my body slamming against the edge of the boat inevitably. Khaos's eyes were a burning gold as he studied me, the light of a thousand stars glowing from the form on his body.

He was darkness made flesh, the night sky made real.

The power of the galaxy held within a single breath.

The ferryman bowed their head low as they kept to the back of the boat, leaving me to kneel before Khaos like a sacrifice. "What business do you have in my Void, God of the Dead?" the Primordial asked finally. I wished more than anything for facial features I could read, for even a hint of emotion, but there was nothing of the sort to be found.

The Primordials were not human, though they could take humanoid forms when they chose. They were the personification of their magic, a home for the various aspects of nature to be contained.

"I only seek passage into Tartarus," I said, keeping my voice calm and quiet. Using this entrance to Tartarus felt like trespassing, like a defiance of the Gods and the natural order of things. I would do it anyway for the sake of my mate, but Khaos had to allow it.

He did not answer immediately, the weight of that burning golden gaze on me heavy, studying me and finding me completely lacking. I hated the familiarity of that feeling, the knowledge that I'd felt it before and couldn't place where I might have encountered such judgment.

"She does not belong to you any longer," he said finally, making my head snap up to fully meet that gaze.

"She is my mate," I argued, swallowing back my unease. What business did Khaos have with Estrella, so much so that he would meet me here to warn me off? "We belong to each other."

"Our Child of Fate has finally returned home. You will not interfere in her purpose in this place, Caldris. Swearing to that will be the only way I permit you to pass into Tartarus so that you may offer her comfort in her trials here," the Primordial said, and I shoved down my resentment over the warning.

I never wanted to get in the way of Estrella's destiny or her purpose.

"I will not interfere in anything she herself desires to do during her time here. I will swear to that," I said, considering how she might feel if she knew that her destiny was so tightly wound with the Primordials.

"Very well," he said finally, nodding his head forward with a final foreboding look. "If you hurt her, you will answer to us." The darkness spread open once more, leaving him to disappear into it and leave the path clear for us to make our way out the cavern and into Tartarus.

The ferryman did not hesitate to row forward, bringing us into the gap and allowing us to flow down the river. The cavern was bright, with crystals shimmering on the cave walls as the light from the prison reflected off of them. It added an eerie hue to the space, making the walls seem as if they too burned like the pits of Hel.

The current swept us along, dragging us down a decline that was so sharp I felt unbalanced. Sitting on the floor of the boat, I held onto the edges as we careened down into the light.

Just like that, we'd left the Void behind us and entered into the prison of Tartarus.

Twenty-Seven

ESTRELLA

The glowing green waters of the Acheron were so different from the Styx that it took my breath away. It looked the way I imagined poison would, shimmering in a vial and just waiting for someone to ingest it. I swallowed as I approached the shore, turning my attention to the Morrigan who were to serve as my guide.

In spite of Medusa's presence, I wouldn't shun the Goddess who had shown me loyalty and honesty. I didn't know that I could trust a word out of Medusa's mouth, her own self-interest a mystery to me.

Perhaps she really did care for me when I'd been a baby, maybe she'd wanted me when I'd been born.

I had no doubt she would quickly come to realize that whatever she'd imagined for my life and my upbringing hadn't been the case, and the woman I'd become had been a product of those acts.

They could argue that my life had made me stronger, but that was bullshit.

I'd made me stronger. I'd survived what was done to me and come out the other side in spite of the hardships of my life, *not* because of them. Suffering to gain strength was a ridiculous excuse crafted by abusers and the privileged.

"What's the Acheron?" I asked the three-fold Goddess.

Badb stared down at the green waters sadly, wringing her hands in front of her. She picked at her black nails that were sharpened into talons, sighing before she met my eye.

"The River of Pain," she said finally, earning a scoff from me.

"Of course it is," I said, rolling my eyes as I took another step closer to the water. I'd endured enough pain in my life, and I was so fucking tired of it being the test for everything.

Medusa stepped up beside me, taking my hand in hers as I snapped to look at her. Her bespeckled green eyes met mine, a silent plea in them. "The river will use your worst fears against you," she said, the warning resonating between us. "Fear is your worst enemy. Fear makes pain and suffering so much worse. If you can numb your mind to the agony of those fears, you will be able to numb your body *some* as well so that you can overcome whatever the river deems your challenge to be. I have seen people persevere through burning, drowning, being skinned alive—"

I drew my hand back from hers, my gaze sharpening. "You know nothing about me if you think being skinned alive or burned could be my greatest fear. You cannot fear what you've already overcome," I said, earning a twisted brow in response. I smiled, the bitter expression feeling callous even to me. "You may have given birth to me thirteen lives ago, but that doesn't mean you know a single thing about me now. I don't fear anything they could do to *me*," I said, staring down at the green water.

Only those who hadn't suffered could underestimate what the greatest pains were.

I dove into the water, swimming through the green, cloudy fluid as every corner of my body throbbed. It felt like being struck with lightning, like tiny fires exploding on my skin and shriveling me into pieces.

I swam for the bottom anyway, continuing on even when my body wanted to stop and my muscles locked in agony.

Sinking deeper, I let the river take me down.

TWENTY-EIGHT

CALDRIS

The ferryman rowed the boat through Tartarus, the landscape changing as the current swept us down the Acheron river. The darkness of the Void left us in a sudden, blinding burst of pulsing red light, fires gleaming on the land beside the green tinted shore. The dirt here was as black as Mab's soul, continuing on in what seemed like endless monotony.

We continued to row, the ferryman pausing as something came into view in the distance. We could only see the heads over the rolling black hill that stood between the river and the figures, but the gray of stone was unmistakable.

"What is that?" I asked, standing in the boat to try to get a better view. The creatures that the statues had been modeled after were enormous, monstrous things crafted from my worst nightmares. Some were larger than cave beasts, the teeth curving out of their open mouths far longer and bigger than the creature I'd once fought to defend Estrella. The thought that she might have been forced to face them down on her own sent a pang of unease through me.

She was alive. I knew it without a doubt.

But that didn't mean she was safe.

"The Gorgons were here," the ferryman said, his mouth pursed into a tight line. The sheer volume of creatures—both humanoid and not—that they'd turned to stone was horrifying, knowing that they'd never stood a chance against the simple stare of the very creature Estrella had come here to seek out.

Fuck.

The ferryman continued rowing, the tension in his face the only sign that any part of him cared for the woman we rowed in search of. "What if she's one of those statues?" I asked, turning back to him with wide eyes.

He paused in his rowing, his arms stilling as he stared at the water of the river for a moment. When he finally turned to face me, his golden eyes glowed from beneath the fabric of his hood. "She isn't," he said simply, tipping his head to the side as he studied me.

I couldn't see beyond the glow of his stare to anything that might have resembled a man beneath the hood, as if the ferryman was nothing more than the energy of the Fates beneath his cloak. I wondered what I might find if I pulled it back, if it would be an all-consuming darkness or the shadow of a man. If his face would pull tight with his annoyance or his brow would rise in his confusion.

"You can't know that," I said, attempting to ignore the way I felt that gaze slither against my skin.

Kharon guided the boat around the corner, using the shoreline to maneuver us so that we entered the transparent, toxic waters of the Acheron.

"Your mate will not be harmed by the Gorgons," the ferryman answered, guiding us to the shoreline ahead. A small group had gathered there, women with snakes for hair standing on the sand. I recognized Fenrir even from a distance, his sisters standing in his shadow as he nuzzled his face against something that remained hidden on his other side.

Three women with different-colored hair took a step toward the water, speaking to the woman that emerged from behind Fenrir and approached the dizzying green water that made me sick to even look at. Estrella's hair was bound into a tight braid, black, tailored armor covering her body from her neck to her wrists and feet.

She shook her head, and I could imagine the disdain-filled scoff she emitted as she stepped into the edge of the water.

"Estrella!" I shouted, but we were too far for her to hear me over the rushing of the Styx at my back.

My mate dove face-first into the Acheron, disappearing beneath the surface as I scrambled to the front of the boat and frantically searched the waters for her. Kharon rowed us forward, swiftly approaching the place where Estrella had gone under. They stopped only when we were alongside the group she'd traveled with, allowing me to step over the edge and place my feet on the shore.

I searched the water from my new vantage point, stepping into the river and shrinking back from the sudden, burning agony that shot up my legs. I fell to my ass in the sand, my legs trembling as the muscles felt like they shriveled and died.

"Estrella!" I shouted, searching the water for her once again. There was no sign of her within the waters, as if the silt at the bottom had swallowed her whole and claimed her as part of it.

Forcing myself to my feet, I dove headfirst into the water after her. Pain tore through me, making my muscles lock up as the agonizing cramps and burning filled me. I couldn't move, couldn't function as it stole through me and trapped me in the river itself.

I screamed, water filling my mouth and pouring down my throat. It lit me on fire from the inside, sinking me deeper as my body could not fight to swim. Something gripped the back of my tunic, a monstrous force pulling me from the river. As we slid along the sandy bank, the pain lessened with each moment of fresh air on my skin.

Fenrir stood over me, shaking his massive white head at me in what I had to guess was disappointment. I sighed, reaching up and petting him in thanks even as I stared at the river where Estrella had disappeared. Had she not felt the pain? Was it a consequence of not truly having a body to protect me from the magic of the river?

"Where is she?" I asked Fenrir as I sat up, ignoring the small, pained whimpers of Lupa and Ylfa at my back. They pressed their noses into my spine, offering gentle assurances that I did not ask for. I scrambled to my feet.

"Where is my mate, Fenrir?!" I asked, throwing a hand out to the river.

The three non-Gorgon women stepped forward, coming to rest beside the wolf that should have protected Estrella at all costs. "This is not your test, God of the Dead," the woman with the black hair said, her amber eyes shining in the dim, green lighting of the river-bank. "You should not have come."

"She shouldn't be alone," I said, raising my chin as I stared down at her. Whoever the women were, there was something eternal in their stares as they watched me.

"Estrella Barlowe will never be alone in Tartarus. This is her home," the black-haired woman retorted, her features twisted in anger. Lurking beneath that eternal stare was affection, as if my mate had wormed her way beneath the skin of her companions here as well as she did in the land of the living.

"The Child of Fate is among family. You may return to your realm, Caldris," a Gorgon said, stepping up beside me. I noted the stance of her feet, the relaxation of her posture even as I refused to meet her gaze. I knew what would happen to me should I discover the color of her eyes.

A snake stretched toward me, appearing in my line of sight and placing itself beneath my chin. It applied pressure there, the strength in the curve of its body taking my breath away as it forced my gaze to meet the Gorgon's.

Her eyes were the same mossy, *serpentine* green of Estrella's, like looking into a mirror of what I'd seen in my mate's eyes every day since meeting her. "You have nothing to fear from me, mate of my blood," she said, and though I felt the cold, stonelike magic of hers pressing over my skin, it did nothing to turn me solid.

"I don't understand," I said, my brow furrowing as the snake left my chin. I looked around the group in confusion.

"Just as your magic lives within Estrella, so does hers live within you," the Gorgon said, turning her gaze down to the river where Estrella had vanished. "You have simply never considered what the reality of your bond with her means, probably because you do not understand who or what she is. You've spent centuries believing you would be given a weaker human mate and your mind has not caught up with your reality."

"What are you talking about?"

"You may be a God, Caldris," she said, scoffing as if the magic I possessed came down to mere parlor tricks. I'd made cities tremble, destroyed mountains in my rage. "But you are nothing next to *my daughter*. None of us are."

"Medusa," the black-haired woman warned, forcing the Gorgon to take a step back. The name washed over me, the reality that Estrella had already found the very being she was intended to search for.

And the very same creature was her mother.

TWENTY-NINE

ESTRELLA

I sank through the water, until the ground beneath me gave way. Dirt fell through the opening, the chasm spreading until I fit through the riverbed. Looking toward the surface, I would have sworn I'd seen the familiar ashen white hair of my mate through the shimmering water.

Just before the river swallowed me whole.

I fell through air, the wind of my fall whipping against my skin as I dropped. The surface I landed on was soft, leaving me to bounce off a cushion filled with the plushest of material. My cheek came to rest upon the velvety smooth surface, my fingers running over the buttons sewn into the cushion as I forced my body to sit.

The area around me was a tropical oasis, the clearing surrounded by trees and lush greenery. The vines that hung between the trees were longer than the roads in Mistfell, the trees taller than the ruins I'd seen in Calfalls.

Across the way, a single obelisk stood with a handful of people waiting at the top. Khaos stood front and center, his face as expressionless as I'd ever seen it as the Primordial who oversaw the trials. I wanted nothing to do with the lack of emotion and care I found there as I got to my feet, the fresh wounds of Medusa's words bleeding like open sores.

Whatever Medusa thought to be true of the man that was supposed to be my father, there was no trace of that affection as he stared down at me.

Gold jutted out from the earth below me, a single spike striving for the sky and the river that flowed overhead. A scale hung from a support beam overhead on either side, and it was on one of them that I stood.

I looked toward the other, finding the figure of a woman who glowed with golden light. It was far more faint than Khaos's own light, as if she was a step removed from the power he possessed. Her skin was milky white, her hair split down the middle. One side of her head was straight hair the color of night, and the other was the complete absence of color. The pure white of it shown against the night sky of her other side, and the colors of her dress mimicked the pattern of her hair.

She nodded at me slowly, glancing down to the ground below us. An enormous lion prowled through the grass of the clearing, pacing around the scales that held us aloft. Its fur was the softest muted gold, each of his paws the size of my head and tipped with claws that would easily tear the eyes from my skull. Its face was surrounded by a mane of darker brown that framed its broad-chested, long body.

"Melinoe is the Goddess of Nightmares and Madness," Khaos said, his voice carrying over the distance between us. "She will guide you through a series of nightmares, giving you pain and fear in unison. It will be your job to overcome each and every one, for every nightmare that you fail to pull yourself out of, for every dream that you succumb to and fail to overcome your greatest fear, your side of the scale will drop."

"What if I do not succumb?" I asked, glancing toward the Goddess who took her seat on the scale. She laid back, staring up at the river overhead as I lowered myself to sit once more.

"Then she will lower. By the end of the trial, only one of you will survive the beast's hunger. The Fates have chosen this as your trial for the River of Pain," Khaos said, forcing me to look toward the other woman. With her own life on the line, she would do whatever it took to make me suffer. To make me *forget* who I was and where I was.

She'd bring me back to the weakest moments of my life, and I couldn't even blame her for it.

I laid my head down, staring at the waters above for a moment before my eyes drifted closed unwillingly. It should have been impossible to fall asleep under the circumstances, knowing that a test and trials of my worst imaginings would wait for me as soon as I did.

The warm shimmer of magic coated my skin, forcing my eyes open to find specks of golden light falling from the river above. Melinoe stood on her own platform, holding my gaze as the magic in that golden light turned my insides warm and brought me comfort, easing my path to sleep.

My eyes drifted closed once more, the sounds of the onlookers fading as my ears rang.

And the nightmares began.

The cool wind of autumn blew across my face, teasing my skin with the familiar smell of home. The salty brine of the sea lingered just beyond the scent of freshly harvested earth, the tingle of Twilight Berry sweetness tickling my senses as I slowly pried my eyes open.

All sense of comfort faded as I watched the High Priest take his place at the edge of the Veil, the upturned earth between him and I telling me more than I cared to know about the time of year. His face was less weathered by the elements, less wrinkled with the stain of time to hint at a much younger age. I vaguely remembered a time when he'd looked this way.

He ran his thumb over the edge of the ceremonial dagger, testing its sharpness on his own skin as my throat caught in horror of the day that had changed everything for me. For my mother and my brother, for the path my life had taken for the next fourteen years. That first drop of blood sliding down the edge of the blade had been forever committed to my memory, a slow and tormenting glide that I saw when I closed my eyes.

To relive this moment all over again, as an observer watching one of my worst memories unfold . . .

This was true agony.

"Macario Barlowe," the High Priest announced, raising his chin as sighs of relief echoed through the group of villagers gathered at the edge of the Veil.

My mother's familiar sob caught my ears, forcing me to look back to where my family stood.

My father's mouth dropped open in shock, letting me observe the subtleties I hadn't seen when I was a girl and so lost in the grief that consumed me. Brann's eyes closed, his arms wrapping around himself as if he could shut out the desire to interfere. At the time I'd thought him just as lost as I'd felt, but I saw it now for what it was.

Restraint.

My father pulled my mother into his arms, ignoring the soft encouragement from the High Priest at the front of the gardens. His words were lost to time, the ringing in my ears drowning out all traces of sounds around me. Lips moved, but I couldn't see past the pain in my head that came with that ringing.

I watched their gazes hold steady, stepping closer in an attempt to hear those words he'd given to her that had escaped me. The childlike version of me stood at his side, clinging to his legs desperately as he held my mother's gaze and murmured to her with their foreheads pressed together. I snagged Brann's gaze finally, something in that familiar warmth chasing away the ringing in my ears.

Sound rushed in all over again, so quickly that my head throbbed and I couldn't help the whimper of pain. No one noticed me, no one but Brann anyway, an unseen intruder watching an event of the past.

"No one can know, Elora. Promise me," he said, waiting until my mother nodded through her tears and glanced down at me. My father pulled away from her, reaching down and grasping the younger me at the waist to lift her into his arms. He propped her up on his hip, wiping the tears away from her cheeks with the warmest expression I could ever remember until seeing the way that Caldris looked at me.

"Don't cry, Little Bird," he said, touching his forehead to hers. I hurried closer, stopping behind him so that when he turned I'd be able to see the warmth of his face for myself. "I gladly make this sacrifice. Do you know why?"

She shook her head, her lips pursed tightly as she tried to keep her sobs quiet. The suffering of a child made the grateful people around us shift uncomfortably with guilt. It was a strange mix of feelings, to be both thrilled that one's own loved ones were safe all the while feeling horribly for our neighbors. It kept families ostracized from one another, and I supposed that was the point.

Loyalty to the faith above all else became far, far easier to achieve if they could limit the people we cared about and turn us against one another. It was easier to keep us subservient if we were stranded islands living in proximity to one another, rather than a community that looked after our own.

"Why, Daddy?" the younger me asked, sniffling through her sobs. Watching the exchange, I shoved back the surge of emotion that made the inside of my nose sting and closed my throat. I knew the words that came next. They'd haunted me all my life, following me with the inevitable feeling that he'd be disappointed in me.

I hadn't managed to do the one thing he asked of me.

"Because it means you'll be safe here for another year," he said, and the words took on new meaning with all I now knew. With all he'd known in that moment about what I was—who I was. "But promise me, when the time is right, you'll leave this place. Fly free, Little Bird," he said, and my heart clenched as he lowered me to the ground and stood. He smiled at her one last time, his cheeks tipping up even from behind as he turned toward me slowly.

He paused, as if he could see me lingering in the nightmare of this memory. I held his stare, the mossy green of his eyes searching mine as I waited for him to continue on. To turn away from the adult version of me, just as he'd had to turn away from the child. I didn't know that he could see me, not until he gave me the smallest of smiles. It was a bittersweet thing, as if grateful for the opportunity to see me grown, as if he knew I was there watching.

Reliving.

He cleared his throat, a single tear trailing down his cheek that I hadn't seen when I'd been a child and his back was to me. It was the final straw in my restraint, pulling a strangled sob from my throat. I pressed the back of my hand to my mouth to try to suppress it as my childlike voice rang out when he took the first step forward.

"Daddy, no!"

He stepped through me, the mists of my dreamlike body parting to allow him to pass as I turned to watch him go. He put one foot in front of the other, and I had a newfound appreciation for the strength required in something that seemed so simple under other circumstances.

Knowing he was walking to his death took a different kind of strength, a peace with one's life that I didn't know I had any longer. There was so much left for me to do, so many wrongs left to right.

It had been easy enough to walk to my death when there was no one counting on me. It had been easy to justify it to myself. The world would go on, my loved ones would heal in time, the wounds of my loss scabbing over enough to get through the day.

I may not have been a parent, and I didn't know if that was ever in the Fates for me given what I knew of the evils of this world, but I knew what it was to feel responsible for the lives of others now. I knew what it was to feel the pain of letting them down.

"Hush now, Child," a deep male voice said behind me. I spun to glare

at the man who had taken up his place behind my six-year-old self, placing stern, rough hands against my shoulders. I stilled, everything in me going taut as I realized this had been the place where it all began. That the tears streaking my cheeks had been what made Byron spend the next fourteen years tormenting me, preparing me for a life as his wife even then. "What's her name?" he asked my mother, lifting a lock of wavy, dark hair from my shoulder. He twirled it around his fingers, forcing me to glance back at him.

"Estrella, my Lord," my mother said, her brow furrowing in confusion even as she forced her body into a curtsy. Her face twisted with the pain of it, and my anger over Byron's need for ceremony even in such dire situations only rose.

At the front of the fields, my father was readying himself to die. These were the last moments my mother could look upon the man she loved more than anything, and instead of having the privilege of embracing those moments, she was stuck entertaining a pompous and arrogant lord who cared nothing for her grief.

My hand tingled with warmth, magic coating the surface of my skin as I glanced down at my fingertips. They throbbed with pain as I gritted my teeth, feeling as if my fingers had pulled the agony from my heart and trapped it there. My breathing was uneven, ragged and rough, and I could do nothing to stop the strangled scream that wanted to escape. Pain and fear and hatred mixed together, marking me in a way I would never escape. Stained in the paint of the night sky, those fingers were so different from the unblemished skin of my child self. Of the innocence I'd lost to monsters like Byron—a reminder of what they'd turned me into.

My nails elongated where my hand rested at my side, forming the familiar black talons I'd seen on Caldris when he was lost to his feral side and his anger won out over his senses—when he called to the storms and made the earth shake with his rage.

Byron lowered himself to kneel at the younger me's side. He was the same height as me when he placed a single one of his knees on the earth, putting his blue eyes level with hers. His silver, coiffed hair was far more polished than anything about her dirt-streaked face.

I'd spent my morning playing with Loris in the woods, racing through the trees without a single thought for what the day might bring. The adults all knew better, but I'd been foolish—blinded by the innocence of a child who didn't understand the ways of the world around me yet.

Byron raised a hand, a handkerchief clutched in his grasp. He used it to wipe at her cheeks, using the moisture of her tears to wipe the dirt from her face. I glanced forward toward where my father approached the Veil, turning back to look at us while the High Priest watched the exchange in irritation.

Younger me's voice shook as she forced out the words, her breath catching as she tried to avoid panic. "Please don't take my daddy." She didn't yet understand that men like Byron didn't do anything that was of no benefit to them. She couldn't comprehend that the man who seemed so interested in becoming her friend wanted her weak and afraid. He wanted her fatherless and available for the taking.

Byron could have intervened. I knew that now, given his offer to save me from the very same sacrifice, but he'd never wanted to.

I closed my eyes, watching the hope die on the girl's face as Lord Byron tilted his head to the side. "Please don't take my daddy, my Lord," he said, correcting her etiquette as she forced her head to nod enthusiastically. "You think your grief is more important than the safety of Nothrek?"

I swallowed, pinching my eyes closed as my mother's eyes flew wide and she turned to Byron to make excuses for her daughter. To explain that I was just a child, that I didn't know what I was saying. He held up a hand to silence her without so much as glancing away from me.

"No, my Lord," she said, stumbling over the words she knew she was supposed to say. What did a child care for the safety of the Kingdom when her father was about to die before her?

"I'll ask you this, Estrella. Would you give yourself in his place? Who would you offer to save him?" he asked, and I ground my teeth together at the guiding words. At the deception in them, the hope he gave only to rip it away.

I saw it now for the test it had been, an evaluation of how much I would come to love and inspire love in my children one day. All because of the impression my father had left on me, on the ability to love fully and completely.

He'd been grooming me, even then and there. Even on that day.

"I'd give myself," she sobbed, ignoring my mother's shocked protest behind me. It felt like the brave thing to say, and I remembered being so proud of the words as I jutted my chin out and pursed my lips.

I'd been so proud in that moment, and looking back, I couldn't help but wonder if this was the moment I was meant to tear down the Veil. If Byron had deviated from what the Fates predetermined. How would I have returned to Alfheimr and the Cradle as I was meant to, or would I have just . . . died?

Byron smiled, his face lighting with something disturbing as he stroked a hand over her hair. "Unfortunately, The Father has already made his choice, Child," he said, grasping a handful of her hair and turning her to face the Veil where the High Priest nodded finally and my father dropped to his knees before him. He scolded the child, shaking her head from side to side when she pinched her eyes closed to avoid seeing. "He makes this sacrifice for all of us. The least you can do is bear witness to it, Estrella."

"We thank you for your sacrifice, Macario Barlowe of Mistfell. May you find peace in your next existence, warmly embraced by The Father," the High Priest said, his voice spreading through the gardens as he touched his dagger to my father's throat.

Behind me, the child version of myself whimpered as Byron pulled harder at her hair anytime she tried to close her eyes, forcing her with the pain I could still feel yanking at my scalp after all these years. He leaned over her, his voice seething as his nostrils flared. "Do not disappoint me, Child."

My father's throat split as I watched, the stream of blood falling to the ground before him. His head rolled back, his eyes connecting with mine briefly.

It was enough. That agony of loss flooded me, becoming something so all-consuming that I didn't know where I ended and where I began. My body was weightless, everything around me going dark as I was lost to that pure hatred that came from my pain.

When light returned to my vision, I found myself staring up at Byron. His hand was buried in my hair and my mother stood before me sobbing as my father died. Tears stained my cheeks with wet, and Byron's blue gaze tracked each and every one with interest.

I was the child once again, trapped and helpless in Byron's hold. I knew the years of suffering that would come from this moment, I knew the way those hands would cause me so much pain only to try to bandage it and wipe it away—to soothe the hurt he caused.

I'd placed my hands before me, wringing them together as I fought not to scream out my grief. I watched as my fingers shifted, as the darkness inside of me climbed to the surface and consumed my innocence right then and there. It clawed its way up my throat with a rumbling growl that felt more beast than human, far more animal than a child could be.

I rolled my head to the side, fighting against his grip in my hair as I touched my hands to his chest. Darkness bloomed over the fingertips of a child, talons spreading from my nail beds into something from my worst imaginations— becoming a reflection of the monster I'd become.

I sank my nails into his skin and watched his shirt bloom with red beneath my touch. Tears streaked down my cheeks, drenching my dress where it met my throat, as the innocence of a child warred with the monster I'd become. I felt her within me, the little girl who was so completely horrified by what I was doing.

Not even death and loss could excuse murder, not to a child who saw the good in people.

I shoved my hand into Byron's flesh, enjoying the way his bones cracked beneath my touch and scraped at the surface of my hand so similarly to the thorns of the Twilight Berry bushes he'd made me harvest all those years in the gardens so that he could tend to my injuries later after the sun went down.

These were the scars I would gladly wear for the rest of my life, the ones written in vengeance and justice.

My mouth parted into a scream, the shrill sound of a child's horror filling the air as Byron's eyes faded to white. I pulled my hand free from his chest, my fingers completely wrapped around the delicate flesh of his heart. I stared into the hollow void I'd created within him, feeling nothing but relief that he couldn't hurt her.

He couldn't spend the next decade erasing everything of the child who'd been kind and sweet and forgiving and molding her into a monster who could kill without mercy.

I split from my childhood form the moment he collapsed to the ground, shoved free from her and becoming weightless once more. Her eyes were wide as she stared at me, seeing me before her for the first time.

Her horrified eyes were the purest of night skies, the glimmer of starlight shining up at me as she tipped her head to the side. Tears covered her cheeks, her face a mangled red mess of terror as she studied me.

I stumbled back in shock, dropping Byron's heart as I tripped over a swell in the earth and fell through space and time.

I'd thought I was protecting her from the monster who meant to harm her.

But I'd only shown her the even worse monster she would become.

THIRTY

ESTRELLA

The platform dropped, lowering me closer to the sands beneath me. I sat suddenly, my stomach becoming weightless for a moment that lasted far too long before the platform stopped suddenly, the chains holding the scale swaying above my head as they worked to halt my descent. My gaze snapped to Melinoe on the other platform, her face carefully blank but for the victorious gleam in her eye. Her platform had risen, taking her farther from the wild-cat prowling the sands beneath me and waiting for its next meal.

I glanced across the distance to the obelisk where Khaos had risen to his feet. His hands grasped the edge of the platform he'd made into his home, his fingers digging in so that the wood of the structure cracked beneath his grip.

There was a moment of panic in that gaze, of horror that I'd failed in my task as Melinoe's golden sleep powder drifted over my head once more to drag me into another dreamscape. I held that starry gaze, seeing the same stare in his eyes that I'd seen in my childlike face as a memory even as the first hints of sleep made my upper body sway.

"Overcome your *fear*, Estrella," he said, his voice dropping low. It carried across the distance to me, his eerie calm filling me as I let my upper body lie back on the platform once more. The river churned overhead as my eyes slowly drifted closed, the poisoned green of the water hiding the flames of Tartarus above.

My eyes closed finally, and my body tensed as sleep took it— preparing for the horror that would wait for me in my mind.

I woke, the grit of sand on my hands as I shifted. The leather armor I wore was wet, creaking with every movement as I got to my hands and knees and pulled myself out of the azure waters of the cove that served as the entrance to Tartarus. I scrambled along the sand, racing for the corridor that I knew would take me to Mab's court.

To Caldris.

To my mate.

I didn't know how I'd gotten here, how I'd managed to return without completing the trials. The snake from Medusa remained wrapped around my bicep as I moved, hurrying for the body laying upon the sand and scanning the beach for signs of any others who might have remained in this place.

Caldris's familiar black armor was covered in sand, the grit sticking to him as the tide lapped at his legs. He didn't move as I placed my hand on his ankle, using his boot to pull myself toward him as everything went hazy in my head.

The world around us faded from view, leaving only the sight of my mate laying still upon the sand.

Too still.

The wheeze of his breath reached me as I curled myself over him, staring down at the way his golden skin had paled. His lips were nearly blue, his hands grasping a gaping wound in his chest. He clung to the final threads of life as I shook my head, my eyes burning with shocked tears that didn't dare to fall.

I touched a hand to his chest, covering the hole that led to the mangled mess of his heart. The snake that had once been wrapped around it slithered free, wrapping itself around my wrist with a gleam of iron teeth.

I shook it off, sending it skittering into the sands as Caldris's blood coated my hand—staining it red like the thickest paint.

"Min asteren," he murmured, his voice too weak. I pursed my lips together, trying to think of the words to say. Trying to figure out what I could do.

There had to be a way to save him, a way to keep him here with me even without a functioning heart.

"I don't know what to do," I said, the gasping sound of my voice relaying the horror I didn't think I could feel. Shock coursed through my veins, agony like I'd never felt lingering just behind the strange numbness that tried to protect me in my final moments with the man I loved.

Because I knew in my heart that's what this was. That Caldris would die.

That I'd failed him.

I shifted, ignoring the pained look on his face as I pulled his head into my lap and ran my fingers through his ashen silver hair. It threaded through easily, allowing me to offer just a few moments of comfort. "Just stay with me," Caldris said, his voice weakening. His eyes began to close, but he forced them open one last time, the blue of them staring so deeply into me that I choked down a sob. "I want your face to be the last thing I see."

"I'm sorry. I'm so sorry I couldn't save you. You deserved a better mate, someone stronger than me," I said, my voice breaking.

Caldris raised a single hand, his blood-covered finger touching my lips to stop me from the path my thoughts had wandered. "Don't you dare. I'm sorry for many things, my star, but being your mate is not one of them. I'm only sorry we didn't have more time. That I never gave you peace," he said.

I leaned forward, touching my mouth to his gently and swallowing the sigh that he let loose. Trapping it within me, holding it for the remaining time I would have before I followed after him. "You are my peace," I said, touching my forehead to his.

He did not sigh again, as his eyes drifted closed. His chest refused to rise again, even though I waited and watched, begging the universe to give him back to me. "Please," I whispered, the words barely audible.

I felt the moment his soul left to make its way to the Void to wait for me. The deep, splintering crack that struck down my center seemed to cleave me in two. I jolted with the force of it, a mangled scream tearing free from my throat.

My hands shook as I wrapped Caldris in my embrace, cradling his body to my chest and rocking back and forth. My tears wet his hair, and I could not say how long I spent there waiting for death to claim me.

With our blood pact, I would follow. I felt immense gratitude for it, *knowing I would only need to exist without him for a while. I couldn't say how long, minutes, hours, or days, but my suffering had an end.*

I got to my feet, staring down at my mate's lifeless body. Reaching down, I closed his eyelids the rest of the way before I pulled one of my swords free from the strap across my back. Turning to the entrance to the cove, I met the gaze of the daemon who thought to block me from getting to its master.

From getting to the bitch Queen that I would kill with my own hands before I left this world.

His twisted, razor-sharp teeth snapped together tauntingly. The four tusks spreading off his face gleamed in the moonlight as he leaned forward, preparing to fight me.

In our last fight, I hadn't been skilled enough in combat to not rely on my magic, but I'd spent the entirety of my time in Tartarus fighting without it. But the Estrella who had walked out of Tartarus was stronger. I was far more capable of fighting him, of killing him with my bare hands and then seeking the revenge I deserved. My eyes warmed with the swell of that beast within me, her growl rumbling in my chest as I took another step forward in spite of my fear of what she would do to me.

I'd survived the bull. I'd survived the . . .

I shook my head, my arms dropping at my sides with my swords still held tight as I glanced over my shoulder at Caldris's prone form. My throat closed all over again, but I forced myself to stop.

To fucking think.

What was the second trial?

I couldn't remember, couldn't grasp the memory of the trial. I stared down at Caldris, forcing myself to feel past the surface of that absolute blinding agony and search for our bond. I couldn't see the thread, but I could feel it.

It swayed in the wind as I reached out a single finger to stroke it, feeling it tickle my skin exactly where I'd thought it might be. The shimmering of its light came slowly, filling my vision until it glowed brightly.

Glowing with life.

I held out a single hand, uttering very simple words that I felt the truth of in my soul. It chased away the pain, forcing the grief away. "It isn't real."

My body was weightless for a moment, my feet flying off the sand as I became airborne.

And I landed on the platform once again, staring across the gap to find Melinoe's shocked gaze upon mine.

Our platforms were even once again. Hers having dropped so that mine could rise with my victory.

Caldris was alive. And I?

I was fucking murderous.

Thirty-One

ESTRELLA

I turned my attention to the obelisk that held Khaos, watching him loose a subtle sigh. His lips tipped up too much to be a smirk, but he suppressed it before it could become a full-blown smile, glancing over his shoulder at the Primordials watching him carefully.

I hated that smile and everything it embodied. I hated the notion that it was a moment of pride for him. Yes, I'd won.

But at what cost? What weight would that vision have on my future, haunting me through my years with my mate?

From where I sat on my podium, I shifted my stare back to Melinoe's seething face. She bared her teeth, malice churning behind her gaze. I couldn't even fault her, not when the catlike beast paced below us and waited for a meal.

She tipped her mouth up into a devious grin as I laid back down. She might think that she could break me, but she wouldn't. I'd been created of flesh and bone, forged in the fires of abuse and tyrants.

Gold glittered above my head, falling down to land on my face and drag me into the deep sleep where Melinoe ruled. She controlled my dreams and nightmares, holding the power in her hands to give me the greatest dreams or the worst memories.

I dragged back a deep breath, my body feeling ragged and torn in the wake of my traumatic experience. Losing Caldris had nearly broken me, and only the knowledge that he still lived in Mab's clutches kept me going as sleep dragged me under.

I held Khaos in my mind, the gleaming gold of his stare following me from behind closed lids.

I was the daughter of Khaos.

So chaos was what I would embrace.

The cane came down against my mother's shoulders, sending her flying forward. She fell from the chair, landing on the rough wood of the floor. The smack of her palms against the surface was audible, echoing through the Temple where I'd spent so many days learning to kneel obediently.

My mother's arms shook as she tried to push herself up to sit, her body jolting with the force of the cane when Lord Byron struck it down across her back once again. His gleaming, malicious blue eyes held mine as he beat my mother, and I strode forward to snap that cane from his hand and shove it into his belly.

I'd been deprived of his death the first time; I wouldn't lose it this time.

My mother looked up, her tear-filled brown eyes meeting mine in the mirror at the front of the room. The Priestesses used it to force us to see our own flaws, to gaze upon them as our husband would one day.

In it, I saw my mother's sheer exhaustion.

I hurried forward, smacking into an invisible barrier that kept me from reaching her. I slapped a palm against it, feeling for any breaks in the magic that had no home in this place. Mistfell condemned magic. The Priestesses and Lord Byron condemned it.

"All those you love suffer. All those you love die,*" the High Priestess said, her voice a gentle whisper in my ear. I spun to look for her, finding nothing and no one behind me. My mother and Lord Byron existed just beyond that magical boundary, leaving me to consider if this had been how Caldris felt when he knew I was going to die and the Veil stood in his way of reaching me.*

He brought the cane down on the small of her back, leaving her body to jolt as I fought for a way to reach her. My fists banged on the glass between us, pressing as if I could push through. Byron merely smirked at me in the reflection of the mirror, forcing me to meet his gaze.

"You'll never be enough," the High Priestess said, forcing my stare to turn to myself.

How many years had I spent staring into my own reflection in this mirror and finding myself lacking? How many years had I looked upon myself and believed the hatred in her words?

I'd never be enough. I'd never be good enough for this realm.

Because I hadn't belonged here.

The sunlight reflected off the mirror, making my head tip to the side as I tried to hold my own stare. Something danced beneath the surface in my eyes, a glimmer of golden light shimmering behind my irises. Glancing down to the fingers tipped in darkness and the starry sky, I raised them to look at them in front of me.

When I lifted my stare to that mirror once again, my eyes had delved into the dark, starry-eyed stare Caldris had seen that day at Blackwater. The creature that existed within me, allowed to escape and take ownership of my body.

I didn't know what she was or who she would make me become, only that I'd never felt stronger than those moments when she rode my body and we had to fight to pull me back.

She was not helpless or afraid.

She was enough.

My mother shook her head at me subtly, warning me from doing the very thing I feared. It was in that moment I realized facing my greatest fears hadn't been losing my loved ones. It hadn't even been my own death.

It was that creature stalking beneath my skin, waiting to take over and erase my will. My greatest fear was the inevitability of accepting her and what that meant for my future.

Accepting that she always had been, and always would be, the most dangerous part of me.

I sunk into the darkness of that stare, studying the constellations in my own eyes as I tipped my head to the side. My reflection shifted, turning her gaze down to look at my hands even though I hadn't moved.

My heart caught in my throat, forcing me to swallow as I followed her stare.

Faint golden threads rose up from the floor and came in through the open windows at the sides of the dream. They strained toward me, leaving me to fear what would happen if I embraced them. The last time I'd attempted it, Khaos had needed to intervene because I'd taken too much magic.

But I hadn't truly embraced the beast then, and she nodded to me in encouragement as if she held all the answers.

To who I had been, who I was now, and who I would one day become.

I stretched out my hands, accepting the first brush of the threads against my skin. It was as if air returned to my lungs, filling me with warmth as they touched the tips of my fingers. Each thread embraced me, winding around my fingers and then my hand. My Fae Marks faded, disappearing beneath the golden light of the threads as they wound their way up my arms. I forced myself to still, holding my own gaze even as panic made my heart stutter in my chest.

There was no fear greater than this—greater than being consumed by power.

The threads of fate covered my shoulders, wrapping around my torso and my legs until I was covered in the golden shimmer. I saw the panic in my own eyes as well as the reassurance of the dark stare looking back at me.

The threads tickled my throat, wrapping around it and twining until they covered my face. They consumed my mouth, the frayed edges sinking between my lips to rest against my tongue as the rest of my face fell to the tomb I'd created.

I struggled to move beneath their weight as they slid over my nose, hardening into a cage as I felt the air rush out of my chest.

There was only the gold glimmer of the threads surrounding me, my body trapped in excruciating pain as they tightened on my skin and broke through the surface. They sank into my body, into the Fae Marks that filled with warmth.

I forced myself to hold still through the agony, letting the power take root in my soul and flood my veins.

I would never again be helpless.

I would never again be afraid.

I would take back what was mine and what Tartarus had stolen from me.

I saw through the threads finally as they sank into me, becoming part of me and allowing me to see Byron posture the cane above his head and ready to drive it down onto my mother once more.

Those hardened threads held me still, giving me no choice but to force through. My fingers flexed at my sides, fighting against the restraints.

No.

I was not just a tempest. I was the storm as something new surged through me.

Byron lowered the cane, swinging it forward sharply with a shout that hinted at the force he put into this one.

I struck out, breaking through the threads and glass barrier between us in one step. I burst free from the threads, a flash of gold lighting the room as my hand connected with the cane and stopped it in midair. Byron's shocked gaze met mine, his fear coating my tongue. I drank it down, consuming it like a meal. It should have terrified me to feed on such a thing, but the creature side of me purred.

Grasping the cane from midair, I shoved him back and watched as he faded into the shadows at the corner. The sun had fled the room, leaving the brightest light in the room to be the shimmer of gold.

My Fae Marks that had once been white glowed with the color, lighting the darkness like the brightest star to match the gold stars swimming in the depths of my dark eyes.

My mother's tear-filled eyes faded from view, her form disappearing from the temple as I made my choice.

As I chose to overcome.

Clutching the cane tightly in my hand, I turned my back on my own reflection and stepped through space and time.

I left the nightmare of my own volition.

And landed within my own body, the cane still clutched in my hands as I rose to my feet, my wound in my abdomen healed.

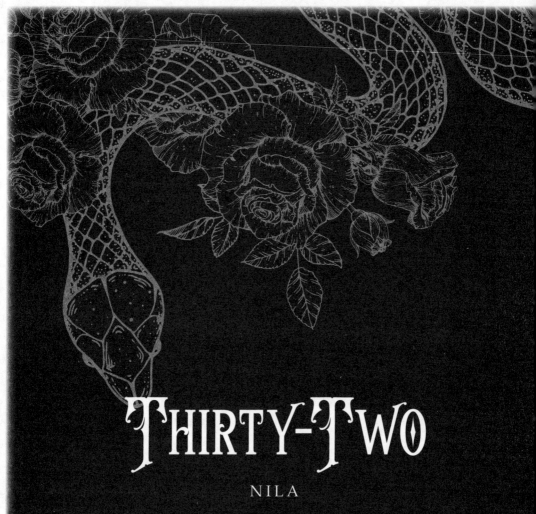

THIRTY-TWO

NILA

I walked through the halls, keeping my head down as I passed by guards who made their way through the halls of Tar Mesa. They were unusually quiet, ignoring me as much as I tried to evade their notice.

None of them wanted to do anything that would bring them into Mab's notice either, meaning that those of us who worked and lived just outside of what Mab would tolerate had an unusual sense of freedom.

The consequences for being caught might have been even more extreme than normal, but the odds of someone turning us in were greatly lessened.

I intended to take advantage of the moments I had where there were less eyes prying into my business. I intended to spend every waking moment I had working to embolden those who might have remained in the shadows.

If I died, so be it. It was only a matter of time before I succumbed to the madness after losing my mate, and I wanted to do something that *mattered* before I went.

I wanted to help. The way *he* would have.

I made my way to the back of the palace, where the mountains made of sand were larger. The Lliadhe worked to sort deliveries of food and supplies that came from the more lively courts of Alfheimr, fresh fruits and vegetables and all the things that Mab took advantage of having access to.

I ran my hand over a crate that had come from the Summer Court, the red-tinted wood calling to me. Where there might have once been the familiar call of sunlight in my veins, the magic that had belonged to my mate was no longer at my disposal.

I was not a God, and without him to share his magic with me, I was nothing but another Sidhe.

I moved on, slinking past the guards who monitored the distribution of supplies. Catching the eye of a Lliadhe I knew well, I waited for her to nod in confirmation that she'd managed to track down the very thing I'd asked for.

The Night Blossoms.

She lifted a crate into her hands, keeping her head ducked low as she walked past the most careless of the guards. He didn't stop her as she made her way to me, striding past and retreating into the palace as I followed at her heels with a nonchalance I didn't feel.

The guard gripped me by the forearm, his bright green eyes staring down at me when I finally turned to meet his stare. "Where do you think you're going so quick?" he asked, the scent of smoke on his breath. There was a deep, herby hint to it, a reminder of the white leaves some Fae burned to inhale the smoke of.

"To help distribute the produce," I said, the words rolling off my tongue. I would be helping in the kitchens, sorting through the deliveries as soon as I brought the Night Blossoms to Estrella's rooms and arranged them for her return.

"Got another job for you," he said, leering down at me in that way that so many of the guards had grown used to getting away with.

"I'm not interested in being your plaything for the ten minutes it will take you to finish," I snapped, jerking my arm back from his grip. He scowled down at me, the fury on his face twisting his mouth into a snarl as he leaned closer.

I could make out each and every imperfection on his face, every scar that had marked him as dangerous and having lived a difficult life. He wrapped his arm around my back, tugging me closer until his breath coated my face and body pressed into mine fully. "Have you forgotten your place here, girl? I wasn't asking," he said, leaning forward to run his tongue along the surface of my cheek.

"And what are you going to do about it if I have forgotten my place? Will you make a scene and risk any of your friends turning us both into Mab for the disturbance? Or maybe you'll take me to her yourself?" I asked, shoving at his chest.

He let me go, leaving me to stumble backward before I caught my own balance on a stack of crates. The darkness around us was so complete I couldn't see into the distance, only the illuminated area for the delivery. But every set of eyes had turned to us, Sidhe and Lliadhe alike witnessing our altercation and observing it.

The Sidhe who were part of Mab's army were undoubtedly hoping he would put me in my place for all to see, but I saw the doubt in his glare. He didn't want to risk Mab's wrath for ruining any of the shipments needed for her feast. While I might have to deal with his rage later on if he caught me alone, it was worth it to bear witness to the way the Lliadhe remained hopeful.

"A storm is coming for us all, and with it will come a shifting of the Fates. I wonder who will be *owned* when it is all said and done," I said, turning on my heel. I waited for him to strike out, to attempt to punish me for my insolence.

There was nothing but the faint whisper of those Mab had forced to work at her behest, and the guards barking for them to get back to work.

Never again would we allow ourselves to be owned, not after finding a taste of the freedom we could have if we managed to overcome Mab and her tyranny.

I met up with Tindra, the Lliadhe carrying the Night Blossoms, on the stairs, hurriedly making our way to the shrine we'd made from Estrella's rooms. She raised a brow at me as I finally shoved open the door to the Princess's rooms, taking the crate from her and carefully placing it on the seat of one of the chairs.

Removing the lid, I stared down into the blossoms that had not yet opened, the petals curled tightly into a ball in the hopes that the flowers would bloom when Estrella returned. She'd brought dozens of the flowers, giving me plenty to arrange over the surface of the table and the bedding, positioning them to form a star in her honor.

"You shouldn't have angered Pyralis," Tindra said, referring to the guard that I'd refused. His temper was one of the worse ones among

Mab's guards, and he fully reveled in the control he had over Mab's victims under threat of exposure. He wouldn't allow my insolence to go unpunished, but I found that mattered very little to me now.

I was numb to the reality of the consequences of my action. My death was certain, and it seemed prudent that, with that in mind, I did everything within my power to leave a better world for those who came after me.

"There are a lot of things we shouldn't do," I said, shaking my head as I worked to perfect the placement of the blossoms along the bed. They were somewhat similar to the lotus flowers that bloomed on the water in the Spring Court, and Tindra had used the little magic she possessed to spell them so that they would continue to grow with their own personal supply of water to keep them alive.

"Nila . . ." She trailed off, as if wanting to talk about the very thing that none of us spoke of. My mate was off-limits, a secret that remained unspoken for fear of Mab's discovery.

"Don't . . ." I warned, trailing off as the air around us went still. My eyes snapped to Tindra's, trying to decide if the Spring Court Fae felt it the same as me. She pressed her hand to her chest, her lungs heaving as she fought for breath. The torches on the walls went dark, the fires extinguishing as they too felt the suffocation that stole the breath from my lungs. It felt like all magic had been sucked from the atmosphere, as if something had taken everything it needed and held it hostage.

It was like the stillness around us had sucked out all the air, leaving everything eerie and frozen. My ears rang, the piercing screech of pressure in them making me cover them with both my hands as my mouth dropped open.

Just as suddenly, the air erupted. A wave of it crashed into my back as it returned, sending me sprawling forward. It felt different, balmy and humid as it filled the room with the warmth of a summer's night. Tindra hurried to the window at the edge of the room, throwing open the shutters to see if the air outside felt the same.

The stars had disappeared from the night sky, and we watched a ripple glide through the darkness. That same wave of air and sensation that had erupted in our room continued out through the sandy mountains of Tar Mesa, the stars and moon returning to the sky as it went.

I followed Tindra to the window, staring out as she turned back to look at me. "Nila," she whispered, the reverent awe in her voice forcing me to turn back as well.

The Night Blossoms had bloomed, the petals freckled with golden spots that gleamed in the darkness of the room.

Tindra and I exchanged a look between us, only one name coming to the forefront of my mind for who could have caused such a ripple in the worlds.

Khaos.

THIRTY-THREE

ESTRELLA

Impossible," Melinoe murmured as her platform dropped, bringing her closer to the lion who waited at the bottom. She looked at him fearfully, watching as I cracked the cane in half. The ends shimmered with golden threads, the magic of chaos coursing through them. I had little doubt that was what allowed me to remove the cane from the dreamscape, taking it back to the waking world with me.

"They were my memories. My dream," I said, taking a step closer to the edge of the platform. "Only I can decide what happens within it."

"You said she'd given her power to Tartarus before entering the trials!" Melinoe said, turning her glare to Khaos. "She should not have been allowed to compete."

"I did give my magic to Tartarus upon entering," I said, standing with my toes hanging over the edge. I tossed the broken cane to her feet on the other platform, reaching behind my back and pulling one of my swords free.

I stretched out a hand, calling to the thread of life waving in the breeze as it swayed off of Melinoe. Grasping it in my hand, I entwined it as I smiled at her, the same malice I'd seen on her face stamped onto mine.

I stepped off the platform, tugging at that thread as I fell and landed on my feet, rolling forward to soften the blow to my knees. I stood as the lion stalked toward me, moving slowly as its tawny eyes dropped to the sword in my hand.

Glancing up to Melinoe, I found her gasping at the edge of the platform as it dropped. Without my weight on the opposite side, she was the heavier of the two scales no matter what any victory said. Holding firmly to her thread of life, I tugged it toward me and watched as she tumbled over the edge, landing on the sand below face-first.

She sputtered, spitting the sand everywhere as I finally released her thread and stepped toward her. The lion tracked my movement, its massive paws sinking into the sand as it pivoted to follow my movements.

It seemed even larger from this vantage point as I closed the distance between Melinoe and I. She got to her hands and knees, backing away from me as I stalked toward her. The lion followed at my side, and I watched as the Goddess's eyes went back and forth between us as if she couldn't decide which threat was greater.

Which one she should fear more.

It should have horrified me to admit that the answer was me.

I stopped in front of her, watching as she panted in fear. Squatting down in front of her, I stared into her eyes. There was no anger, even though I should have hated her for the things she'd made me live through.

For the pain she'd caused. It was the kind of pain that would always linger in the back of my mind, even after waking and knowing it hadn't been real.

It was the kind of pain that would drive every one of my actions from this day forward.

"Where are your nightmares now?" I asked, watching as her eyes wet with the threat of tears.

She swallowed as I gripped her hair in my hands. "I'm looking at it," she said, her voice a quiet reminder of my own fears.

Snarling, I pulled her hair forward until I managed to get the spot where the black locks met the white, cutting a chunk of both colors and shoving them into my pocket as a keepsake to offer.

I dragged the tip of my sword across her cheek, drawing a thin line of blood to entice the beast. She touched her hand to the cut in horror, her gaze tracking over my shoulder to stare at the lion as it approached.

It walked up behind me, and I spun with my sword in hand. Tawny eyes met mine, its massive head only a breath away as I held its gaze in a silent warning. I raised my sword, pressing it to the underside of his neck. He raised it to allow me better access, allowing me to saw off a chunk of hair from his mane.

His purr echoed through the space, igniting one in my own chest as he rubbed the side of his face against mine.

Moving past him, I ignored the sounds of his feast as his teeth met flesh. I ignored Melinoe's screams, feeling nothing as I made my way to stand on the sands before the obelisk.

I stood before the Primordials waiting on the dais at the top, glaring up at them and holding my father's gaze. His mouth spread into a wide smile as amusement lit up his eyes.

"What am I to do with you, daughter?" he asked, watching as I tossed the collection of hair onto the sands before me in an offering. "Never before has someone taken their power back from Tartarus in the middle of the trials."

I shrugged my shoulders, shoving my sword back into the scabbard behind my back. "Good," I said, smiling up at the man I refused to think of as my father. He might have given me my magic, but every other trace of him within me had to be gone after centuries of rebirth. "I would so hate to be predictable."

His smile widened, a laugh bubbling up his throat as those around him stared at him in shock. I gave a mock bow, grinning slightly when he returned it with a flourish.

"Until the next river, Khaos," I said, using his name instead of the word he thought he deserved and the respect that went with it.

"You can avoid calling me father all you want, Estrella, but you are more my daughter on this day than you ever have been before," he said, and my smile faltered at the words. They were an echo of the fear I felt, a reminder that the creature I'd embraced was probably the part of me that came from him. "Until the next river."

The water came down, sucking me into the vortex of green. Pain and sorrow struck through me, forcing me into a pit of anguish even as the waters thrashed me in all directions.

THIRTY-FOUR

CALDRIS

I sat, sinking my hands in the sand at my sides. There'd been no sign of Estrella since she plunged into the river while I watched, sinking beneath the green surface of the water. I watched it relentlessly, running a hand through Fenrir's, Lupa's, and Ylfa's fur as they took turns trying to comfort me, while simultaneously restraining me from wandering into the depths of the river I would not survive. The ferryman lingered on his boat, hesitant to leave until he knew Estrella was alright. I was grateful for the diligence, knowing he would take me to the Void himself if she didn't emerge.

But I felt nothing of her, no symptom of her death.

I knew in my heart I would know the moment she was gone. I would feel her soul leave this world, knowing it had taken the better part of me with it.

I didn't want to live without her, and for that, I needed to be the one to die first. I needed to never be forced to experience a single moment without her here with me.

Fenrir nudged my arm with his snout more forcefully, making me turn my stare away from the river. I jolted to my feet, seeing the spin of gold light from within the white lines of my Fae Marks.

"Caldris," Medusa said, closing the distance as I rose. She wrapped her hands around my arm, turning it in the light to watch the delicate shine of gold. It was just the faintest hint of a sparkle, barely noticeable if Fenrir hadn't sensed it. The Goddesses who had introduced themselves as the Morrigan stepped closer to join us at the edge of the river.

Medusa and I watched in fascination as the faint golden light spread through the winding marks of my tattoo, filling every last space that had once been white and gleaming like the golden city of Ineburn. "What's happening?" I asked, remembering the way the last time my marks had turned gold, I'd consumed Estrella's blood.

But it had been days since I'd fed from her, and the sudden influx of power didn't make sense.

"She took her power back," Medusa said, her disbelieving grin spreading across her face as she tipped her head to the sky and laughed. The Morrigan sisters studied one another, their mouths open in shock as they too studied my arms.

"What do you mean she took it *back*?" I asked, staring at the three birdlike women. They shuffled their feet uncomfortably, until finally the one with the black hair opened her mouth and answered me.

"All who enter the Trials of the Five Rivers must willingly offer their magic to Tartarus for safekeeping until they've completed the tasks set before them," she said, her chin rising in defiance.

"You mean to tell me," I said, pausing as my hands clenched into fists. Medusa gentled her arm on mine, the touch turning to something reassuring instead of urgent. "That my mate has been forced to survive *Tartarus* and fuck knows what kind of *trials* as a human?"

"You would be wise to remember your mate was raised as a human. She is no stranger to functioning without magic," the red-eyed Morrigan answered. As if the fact that Estrella had been forced to suffer through a human existence for all this time somehow justified doing it to her again, but in a place that could kill her at any moment.

I didn't want to consider what manner of creatures hunted under the cover of darkness in a place like this.

"What could possibly be achieved by taking away her magic? What can she prove that way?" I asked, pulling my arm back from Medusa.

"Estrella has been chosen for a fate that you cannot even begin to imagine. There is more to her future than simply having the power to do as she pleases. She must prove herself to have inner strength as much as outer strength. She must prove that she is kind, but fair, that she cannot be controlled by the human sensibilities that are undoubtedly a part of her given her upbringing," Medusa answered, her voice quiet. "I don't like it any more than you do, but he needs Estrella to prove who she *is*. Not the strength of her magic."

I paused, studying her as my brow furrowed. "Who is *he*?" I asked, staring back over the water.

"He is the origin of everything and nothing all at the same time. He is the here and now, as well as everything that came before," she said, her words somehow making no sense even though I understood them perfectly. My throat closed, fear of the finality of the words that would relieve any doubt I'd had as to what Estrella could become. "And if he is everything that has already been, she is what has yet to come."

"She's the daughter of Khaos," I said, swallowing past the implications. That would mean she was Mab's half-sister, that she'd witnessed her half-sister murder the half-brother she'd only just begun to get to know.

"Yes and no," Medusa said.

Badb protested, her panicked expression transforming the sharp features of her face. Her mouth drew open into something resembling a beak more than I'd seen since my arrival, but there was no doubt to who the women were.

They were legend.

Medusa silenced her with a raised palm, her stare never leaving mine. She raised her chin, her chest thrusting out with her pride. "She is more than just a daughter of Khaos. She is *the* daughter of Khaos," she said, a knowing grin spreading her lips wide. "Estrella is his chosen heir. She is chaos incarnate."

Shock forced me to take a step back from the Gorgon, my eyes widening even as I ground my teeth together. "The Primordials do not *have* heirs," I said, doing everything in my power to keep my voice steady.

My eyes flashed to the ferryman where he waited atop his skiff, the golden gleam of fate shining in the eyes that stared back at me. He nodded his head once, but his mouth pressed together into a thin line.

Medusa wasn't supposed to tell me, that much was clear based on his displeasure and Badb's attempt to intervene. "They do now," the Gorgon said, her voice smooth and confident in spite of the fact that she'd flipped my world upside down. "And you will not speak a word of it to Estrella."

I rubbed my forehead, shaking my head from side to side. She was out of her mind if she thought I would keep something like this from my mate. "Why wouldn't I tell her? Why would you tell me if she cannot know?"

"Estrella will discover the truth of her fate soon enough. Her time here is all leading her to that point, but she is not yet ready to know what the future holds for her," Medusa said, stepping forward to cross the distance between us. She gave me a weak smile that hinted at sympathy or pity, something I hadn't experienced often. "But I know what it is to live in the shadow of something far greater than I can ever hope to be. You have lived for centuries believing that one day you will have a human mate, a queen to sit at your side when you rule over the Winter Court. But what are the courts of Alfheimr to a woman who can move the stars and the moons themselves? Who can plunge the world into eternal darkness with a snap of her fingers? To the woman who will control the Void and all who exist in it?"

"Estrella doesn't want all that. She just wants a simple life, something warm and comfortable, with books to keep her company," I said, as if that changed anything.

"And since when have women with that kind of power ever been allowed to have a life of comfort? I think deep down, you have always known that she was made for *more*. I think you've always known, in your heart, exactly what she is and what she was born to be. There is a darkness in her that you'll need to accept," she said, the softening of her smile feeling like a double-edged sword.

"I'm the God of the Dead," I said, returning her smile. I was no stranger to darkness and the elements of that reality that would also plague my mate.

It never failed to shock me, the influence of fate in our lives and the way every piece of who we were lined up with the path that had already been chosen for us. It was easy to forget sometimes, to pretend that we had any sway in our destiny—until reality came sweeping in and took our legs out from under us.

"*Until chaos reigns*," Medusa said, turning to look at the river as she spoke the words that struck me straight in the heart. The words I'd spoken to my mate in love, meaning it as an impossibility to indicate I would never stop loving her.

The water rippled, something moving beneath the depths. Estrella broke through the surface, flipping her head back to splash water onto the opposite shore. Her hair was still trapped in the loose braid she wore, but stray strands had broken free, cascading around her face as she scrubbed a hand over it to wipe away the drops of water where they clung to her.

Her hands trembled as she did it, the pain of the Acheron making her quake. She didn't make a sound as she took her first step toward us, her eyes remaining closed as she glided through the water that had brought me to my knees. I felt her magic crawl along my skin, our bond reunited as she used her power to sense her way toward the shore.

What had she suffered, what had she lived through, that the agony of that river was so tolerable to her?

Her Fae Marks glowed with golden light from within, reflecting off the water beneath her to make her look as if she was bathed in sunlight. Her hands dropped to her sides as she walked, sucking back a deep breath of air that filled her lungs.

The light pulsing off her glowed brighter, and I stared unabashedly at her as she emerged from the river. Step by step, until she was nearly to the edge of the water.

"*Min asteren*," I said finally, taking a step toward her.

Her eyes flew open finally, forcing me to suck back a breath as I met her dark stare. Gold stars glittered at me from within the depths of black that had stolen over the green of her irises. Gone were the green eyes I'd fallen in love with, changed into something that felt more right even if I missed the innocence of the woman I'd known. There was a thin ring of green around her pupil that was a nod to that human girl I'd found in the barn, but she'd shifted and changed even in the mere days we'd been apart. The woman in front of me was crafted from darkness and something wild, a destiny written in the stars and trapped within the galaxies of her eyes.

Until chaos reigned.

"Caldris?"

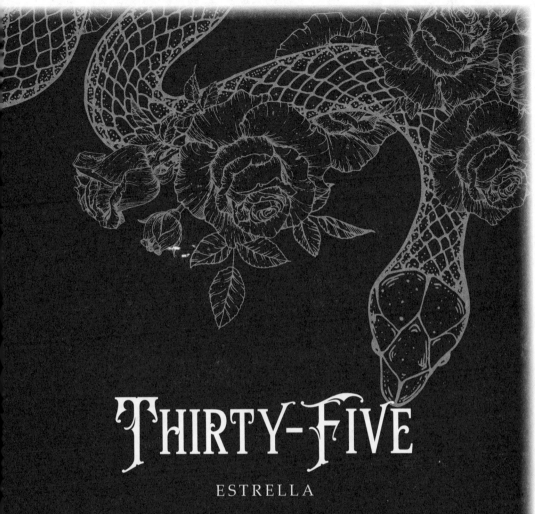

THIRTY-FIVE

ESTRELLA

He stood across from me, the exact picture of the man from my nightmare. I closed my eyes, squeezing them tight against the pain of that memory and what had followed me into my waking thoughts. Reaching over my head without opening my eyes, I took comfort in the familiar hilt of my sword in my palm.

I drew it free slowly, relishing in the sound of metal against leather. My eyes only opened when I swung it forward, catching the vision in the front of the throat as he took a step closer to me. The pale blue eyes staring down at me were a mockery of everything I loved, a twisted manipulation meant to weaken me in a place that had already caused me so much pain.

"Little One," he said, his voice dropping to a quiet whisper. He held his hands up at the side of his head, his palms facing me as he froze in place. I pushed my sword tighter to his throat, halting when it met the resistance of flesh.

Caldris sensed my hesitation, pressing forward so that my blade cut a shallow line across the front of his throat. It was such a callback to that first time we'd met, when he'd snuck up on me in the barn and terrified me.

"You're not here," I said, swallowing past the burn of the words in my throat. It wasn't possible, not given Mab's determination to keep us separated. She was so determined that we shouldn't be permitted to complete our mate bond, knowing that our power would rise if we did.

The breath caught in my lungs, my bottom lip trembling as I fought back the tears that wanted to fall. For him to be here, trapped in Tartarus . . .

"You can't be here," I insisted.

For him to be here, he'd have to be dead. He would have had to die, and I had to believe I would feel that deep into my marrow. My sword dropped to my side as I shook my head. The thought that after all of it, after everything I'd been through to get back to him, he might have died while I was gone.

He might have died alone.

Medusa lingered nearby, holding out a hand with a snake coiled within her palm. The tiny creature's tongue eased out, poking at my armor and drawing my attention to it as Fenrir nuzzled into my side. He raised his head high, snuggling his face into my neck and grounding me in reality.

"*He's alive,*" he said, holding my gaze with the stern red of his eyes.

"He's not dead?" I asked, resting my forehead against his snout.

I was vaguely aware of Caldris's attention bouncing between us, studying every moment of the interaction as if he didn't understand what was happening.

"*Yes.*"

"I'm not dead, Estrella," he said, his voice making me turn back to look at him finally. I dropped my arm, letting my sword clatter to the sand at my feet. He took it for the invitation it was, closing the distance between us immediately and wrapping his arms around me. One pressed into my spine, pulling me so close I thought he might suck me into the middle of him, and the other wrapped around the back of my head and tugged me into his chest.

I touched my hands to him slowly, feeling the familiar strength of his muscles beneath my hands. It had only been a few days, and yet it seemed as if I'd been gone for months, like my entire being had been changed by my time here.

But I still fit into his embrace like I belonged. He still held me like he loved me—even though I felt forever changed. Tipping my head to look up at him, I drank in the sight of that tense, clenched jaw and the face I'd come to so heavily depend on even though the world seemed determined to keep us apart.

He tipped his head down, studying my face before he leaned forward and touched his mouth to mine. His mouth was gentle at first, giving me time to protest the connection. He didn't forget that I'd been about to slit his throat only a moment before, that whatever I'd lived through, it had nearly forced me to do the unthinkable.

He pried my mouth open with his tongue, his urgency growing as he fought to drag me closer. Lifting my feet from the sands, he raised me high enough for me to wrap my legs around his waist, capturing his face in my hands as I returned his fervor.

I didn't care how. I didn't care why.

My mate was here, his mouth moving on mine, and all was right in my world. A life in Tartarus would be bearable if I had him at my side, and maybe we would be better off staying here.

Hiding away the same way the Primordials had.

I winced at the thought, hating the selfish nature of it. I could never really accept a life like that when I knew people were suffering at Mab's hands. That it was my own blood who caused such pain.

What of Fallon and Imelda? Nila and Soren?

"Your mother is watching you," Fenrir said, forcing me to pull my mouth off of Caldris's. He followed after me, clearly not wanting the separation any more than I did. Unwinding my legs from his waist, I let myself slide down the smooth, hard expanse of his body until I stood in front of him. "How is this possible?" I asked, looking up into the sad smile he offered in return.

He tucked a stray hair behind my ear, raising his chin to gesture behind me. Looking over my shoulder to follow his gaze, I found the boat of the ferryman floating at the edge of the riverbank. Their oar was placed on the sand, the bottom sinking in as they held themself perfectly still. The eerie gold of their eyes never left me as I turned fully, approaching them slowly as they waited for me.

"You brought him here?" I asked, watching as his hood moved with his nod.

"One last favor, Little Bird," he said, the quiet tone of his voice making something within me crack. My chest felt tight, my lungs caving in on themselves. In the wake of reliving his death, I couldn't face the possibility of losing what I had left of him all over again. The nickname in that voice that was so different from my father's in my memory made the sting of tears in my throat worsen, the tenseness of my jaw making my head ache.

"When will I see you again?" I asked, stepping off the sand to put both feet in the boat with him. He glanced down at where I touched the surface of the skiff, as if he couldn't believe I'd been willing to set foot on it.

"I suspect you'll see us often in your immortal life, but we will not be as we are now the next time you see us. There will be consequences for what we've done," he said, his grip tightening on his oar as he held the boat steady.

"He'll be gone, you mean," I said, referring to the part of Kharon that was my father. That had been my rock during my childhood until the High Priest took him from me.

"It is against the rules to interfere. We have disobeyed the Fates themselves by giving you something to hold onto while you break," he said, acting as if it was not going to break my heart that I would lose him.

Having Caldris was a gift, the greatest gift I could have asked for. But I hated that the gift had cost me dearly.

"I have so many questions," I said, wincing when the gleam of sharp teeth came through the hood. I wanted nothing more than to sit down with him, to ask him every question that I had about my childhood and what Brann might have told him, what the Fates might have said.

"And I fear there is not enough time in all of eternity to give you the answers you seek. Your very existence was woven into the tapestries long before you were born," he said, his voice sad and melancholy. As if he would miss me as much as I could miss him.

I reached out slowly with tentative fingers, catching his hood on either side. I pushed it back carefully, narrowly avoiding touching the thin skin that covered his skull. It was the faintest, most transparent skin I'd seen, firmly stretched across bones to give only the hint of a face. His golden eyes shone out from the eye sockets, and there was nothing of the father I remembered in the face that stared back at me.

Still, I swallowed back my unease and leaned forward. Touching my mouth to the skin of his cheek, I breathed softly through the only sign of affection I could offer. "Thank you for bringing him to me," I whispered, pulling back as I adjusted the hood to cover his face.

I stepped off the skiff, holding his stare as Caldris stepped up behind me. I'd recognize his touch anywhere, the comforting set of his hand around my waist and his mouth at my temple.

Kharon pushed off the sands of the shore, using his oar to guide his way to turn to paddle upriver.

I watched him go, holding back the tears that threatened to fall. I would not betray the sacrifice he'd made by grieving for him, allowing myself to feel the joy that his sacrifice had brought me.

Thanks to him, I had Caldris at my side.

With him, I could do anything.

THIRTY-SIX

ESTRELLA

T hunder clapped in the sky, the sound drawing my gaze up to the clouds that formed along the surface of the cave structure that was Tartarus.

Medusa looked to the sky, meeting the Morrigan's gaze briefly before she turned her eyes back to the group of Gorgon women waiting behind her. She reached out, taking my hand and squeezing it tightly.

"Come quickly," she said, tugging me away from the river at my back. The clouds above us turned more menacing with every moment, blackening the sky as Caldris hurried after us.

"What's happening?" I asked, following after her as the wolves snapped at Caldris's heels, forcing him to keep up. He grunted at them, his steps far larger than mine.

He wasn't at risk of falling behind or being too slow. The urgency of the Morrigan as they shifted into their bird form took me by surprise, and they fluttered into the distance until they were gone from sight.

"Rain is coming. The rain of the Acheron causes pain all the same as the river itself," she said, but instead of taking us downriver where I assumed we would attempt to reach the safety of the next river, she brought us inland.

"We'll never make it," I said, glancing up at the clouds as they swirled in the sky. The storm brewing seemed like one that would tear through all the homes in Mistfell, like it would obliterate anything in its path. The swirling motion of the clouds formed a cylinder above, the winds picking up to blow sand through the air.

Caldris was at my side in an instant, using his body to shield mine from the worst of the wind. Sand pelted into his armor as he raised an arm to shield his face, tucking me into his side as Medusa guided us forward. The rest of the Gorgons took up the rear, keeping their eyes peeled for any threats that may have tried to follow us.

The cave Medusa led us to was tiny, so small it felt like Caldris would never fit inside. There wouldn't be room for all of us, but she ducked her head low and walked inside without hesitation. Caldris and I shared a glance, but the first drops of rain fell. It sizzled on the leather of his armor, smoke rising as it burned a tiny hole into the protection.

"What about the wolves?" I asked, turning back to look at Fenrir and his sisters. He lowered his head to me, a sign of respect as his voice rang through my mind.

Do not worry for us. We will go to a cave nearby.

I returned the wolf's nod, ignoring the pointed glance Caldris gave me as he observed the communication he couldn't hear. With a swallow, he shook it off and nodded as the wolves raced in the opposite direction, pushing me forward gently. I ducked down, reaching out to grasp his hand in mine as I pulled him to follow. His fingers were like ice, even without his physical form, his magic keeping him cool in what was otherwise a balmy, too warm setting with the flames that often surrounded us.

He had to bend himself in half to fit within the cave, but he maneuvered himself through the narrow passage. It plunged into darkness, leaving me to grope the fingers of my free hand along the wall to feel for the path to take. I could no longer see Medusa as she faded from view, disappearing into the depths of the narrow cave ahead of me.

"Keep going, Estrella!" she called, her voice echoing off the walls as I fumbled and came to a stop. The walls felt like they were closing in, getting narrower. My shoulder bumped against the rock, and if it hadn't been for the leather protecting me, I might have lost a layer of skin against the porous surface.

I took another step, continuing on the path and choosing to trust the woman who had birthed me into my original life. Caldris grunted behind me as he squeezed through the narrowing passage, and I could just imagine how he struggled to fit.

I continued on, guiding him with me and refusing to risk separation. I stepped, tipping forward when the rock vanished beneath me. I yelped as I fell forward, falling through a gap in the stone. My fingers slipped through Caldris's, neither of us prepared for me to drop so suddenly.

My stomach dropped out as I fell, finally splashing into a pool of water at the bottom. I swam, kicking for the surface desperately.

I was so fucking tired of water.

I burst through the surface, gasping for air as sound returned. "Estrella!" Caldris called, leaning over the hole in the floor to stare down at me. I couldn't see anything but the shadow of his form, blinding by the dazzling lights around me.

"I'm okay!" I called up, turning in the water to meet Medusa's stare. She treaded water, floating on the surface as serpents slithered across the surface to touch her affectionately. They glowed from within, reflecting light upon the water. "You need to see this!"

"Are those snakes?" he asked, and I smiled, knowing that he could see down into the cavern. I caught a tiny ball of light in my hands where it floated through the water, raising it to my face to stare at the tiny creature held in my palms. Her body glowed with a mix of turquoise and purple, her upper body humanoid on a much, much smaller level.

Her arms were barely visible, so small and thin as she ran them through the pool of water cupped in my palms. From the waist down was the tail of a serpent, reminding me of the sirens but somehow snakelike.

I lowered her to the water, kicking my legs to keep afloat as Caldris dropped into the water. The other Gorgons followed behind him, sending ripples through the water as they splashed beneath the surface.

"What is this place?" I asked Medusa, looking around the enclosed cavern. The walls were covered with a deep purple flower, the vines nearly silver as they slithered along the stone.

"Welcome to the home of the Gorgons," she said, swimming to the shoreline at the edge of the water. She strode out slowly, tiny ripples of glowing water sliding off her body as she turned to wait for Caldris and I. She held out her hand, leaving us to swim for her as Caldris flipped his ashen silver hair out of his face. It glowed with the colors of the cavern, illuminating the metallic sheen in a way I'd never seen before.

I stepped out of the water, my drenched armor feeling so much heavier with the added weight of the water. Medusa looked over my shoulder to one of the Gorgon women swimming with the serpents contentedly. "See that we're informed the moment the storm passes," she said, turning on her heel after she received a confirming nod.

She guided us to a much more open tunnel through the caves, tiny creatures skittering and slithering through the flowers that lined the walls. "This is where you live?"

"I spend most of my days in the Cradle of Creation with your father, but this is the home I built for myself before I fell in love with him. This is the home of my family," she explained, pausing at the entrance to a larger alcove. A few Gorgons lingered in it, sliding hands and feet through the shallow pools of water scattered across the floor.

She turned to look at me, meeting my stare with a furrowed brow. "Do you love him? Truly?" she asked, glancing to Caldris. My mate jerked his head back in shock, his mouth dropping open as if he might convey his outrage. He hadn't reacted in the slightest when Medusa revealed who my father was, confirming my sinking suspicion that they'd had time to speak before I emerged from the Acheron.

"Of course I do," I said, taking his hand in mine. I squeezed it reassuringly, wondering what the point to her question could possibly be. Why now? Why hadn't she asked the moment I climbed out of the river?

"Your bond is incomplete," she said by way of explanation, glancing down at our hands. I followed it to the way the golden threads of our bond wound around our touching palms, but the threads glowed with a dim, almost brassy tone instead of the bright sheen of something that was truly flourishing.

"Mab prevented us from completing it," I explained, pursing my lips together. I wanted nothing more than to know Caldris so completely that I couldn't tell where he ended and I began any longer, existing on one equilibrium with him.

"You can complete the ceremony here, if you so choose," Medusa said, making the breath freeze in my lungs. I turned my surprised stare up to Caldris, finding the cool blue of his eyes on me. He didn't speak, allowing me to consider our options. "You would need to do it in our ways and according to our traditions, rather than those of Alfheimr," my mother said to my mate.

He didn't take his eyes off of me, reaching up with his free hand to trail delicate, gentle fingers over the swell of my cheek. "How I marry Estrella matters little to me, so long as she is my mate."

I smiled, turning to nod at Medusa. "Yes," I said, no hesitation in the word. If we were to die here, if I was to fail my task, I wanted to die having at least gotten to know what it was to be complete.

"You did not even ask what our customs dictate must occur. I could demand you both light yourselves on fire, for all you know," Medusa said, raising a brow.

"Then I guess we will burn, but at least we'll burn together," Caldris answered, his words making a shudder run down my spine. The pure and utter possession in the deep growl of his voice took my breath away, the notion that I would be his in death as I was in life bringing both of us a distinct, perverse kind of pleasure.

"So be it," Medusa said, but her mouth twitched into a subtle smile. She turned to a male Gorgon waiting nearby, signaling him over with a motion of her hand. "Deiseus, take the God of the Dead and help him prepare for the handfasting ceremony. Estrella, you will come with me."

"Why do we need to separate?" I asked, squeezing his hand tighter. I'd only just gotten him back, and already she wanted us to part.

"It won't be long, but there are things you both must do to prepare yourselves to join together as one," she said.

I hesitated for a moment, waiting to see how Caldris reacted to the man attempting to lead him away. He smiled at me gently, loosening his grip on my hand in encouragement. "Let your mother prepare you for me, Little One," he said as I released his hand and turned to face him more fully. "Enjoy your alone time while it lasts. After the ceremony, you're mine."

A shiver crept up my spine. It wasn't so long ago that such a proclamation would have terrified me, the thought of being bonded to one person for the rest of my days absolutely horrifying to me. Now the dark promise of his words made something within me tighten in anticipation, a flutter of wings within my stomach making my heart pound.

It wasn't solely the thought of being alone with him, of maybe finding the time for us to consummate the bond in truth without an audience. While I might have come to terms with Caldris's, and mine if I was honest, tendency toward exhibition, that didn't mean I wanted my mother to witness such things.

It was the intimacy that I knew would come with the completion of our bond. The same way I felt Fenrir in the back of my mind as he hunted for something to eat, zooming through the cave system the Cwn Annwn had discovered to hunt down a beast that prowled through the tunnels . . .

Soon I'd feel my mate in the same way. Soon, I'd be able to hear his voice in my head and his feelings as if they were my own. And so he would be able to feel and hear the same from me.

Leaving me never truly alone in this world.

Where that might have once brought fear, there was only comfort.

He leaned down, touching his mouth to mine without breaking the eye contact between us. I bit my lip as I backed away, holding his gaze until the male Gorgon chuckled and broke the moment. "Nothing like a newlywed," he said, looking at my mother with a gaze that lingered just a moment too long. She turned her attention away, holding out a hand for me to take as she guided me in the opposite direction. I accepted it, looking over my shoulder as Deiseus led Caldris away. He smiled at me as if there was nothing to be concerned about, and I knew in my gut that he was right.

I may not have been able to trust Medusa with my heart and my love, but she could have harmed me at any moment. She could have allowed me to die instead of saving me. She didn't mean me or my mate any harm.

It was the nightmare giving me pain in separating. The memory of his death clung to me like the ominous rain clouds outside, and I knew I would never truly be rid of it.

The snakes in her hair swayed toward me as she tucked my hand around her arm. They slithered down her arm, winding themselves around mine and settling across my chest and neck. Gentle, cautious tongues snaked out to touch my skin, scenting me as they got comfortable.

"They like you," she said, smiling approvingly.

I swallowed, holding out a hand for one of the smallest serpents to curl up in my palm. He snuggled into my touch, leaving me to smile down at him.

The feeling was mutual.

THIRTY-SEVEN

ESTRELLA

Medusa led me through one of the tunnels, the walls spreading farther apart to allow the passage to widen. The purple flowers on the stone walls swayed in a breeze I couldn't explain, as if something blew through them and them alone. It wasn't until I stepped closer, running my palm over the surface of one of the petals that I realized the dark things I'd seen between those flowers were not vines at all.

They were the slow-moving tails of snakes, slithering leisurely along the stone walls. Each one was covered with more of them than I dared to count as I swallowed and took a step back. Medusa watched my realization with amusement, her stare alight with humor. The green of them was so close to the eyes I'd had, even born from a mortal woman instead of her. I couldn't look into my mother's face and not see the similarities between us. Her skin was a few shades darker than mine, the tone a rich, sepia brown. Her nose was the same shape as mine, her lips slightly puffier.

But the eyes were the same as what I'd grown used to seeing in my own reflection.

"This is a haven for all the serpentine creatures who reside in Tartarus," she said, encouraging me to continue walking forward. The cave floor at my feet was dry, but up ahead the shimmer of luminescent water reflected on the flowers.

Shimmering white crystals lined the shallow pools of water as we approached, reflecting light from the tiny, glowing faeries in the water, and the snakes that seemed to possess the same pulsing light beneath their dark scales.

I moved through the passage, my feet sinking into the water as Medusa continued on as if it did not faze her to enter the pool. She ran her hands through the water as she walked, allowing the water to sluice over her skin.

I touched a hand to a crystal as I passed, the golden glow emanating from my touch catching me by surprise. "Why was I able to take my power back from Tartarus?" I asked, releasing the crystal to continue on.

"Many have entered into the Trials of the Five Rivers," she said, looking to the cave ceiling. I followed that gaze, studying the turquoise snakes where they seemed to hang from the ceiling and stretch toward her. "Of those who have dared, none have been born here. You are just as much a part of Tartarus as any who reside here. Perhaps more so. Perhaps this place recognizes you, or perhaps you're just stubborn enough to dare to try."

I snorted a laugh, hanging my head forward as the sound bubbled up my throat. "Caldris would say it was the latter," I answered her, stepping out of the pool as a bridge of land appeared in our way. We climbed the bank, ascending to look down into another cove.

Whereas the others had been littered with snakes, the creatures swimming happily, this felt different. Beside us, snakes slithered over the land, lowering themselves down into the water that was already filled to the brim. I could barely see the sheen of water upon their scales with how tightly they'd packed themselves in.

"Somehow I can imagine why," Medusa said, watching the rest of the snakes following us slither into the cove.

"What is this?" I asked, trying not to think of what purpose there could be for snakes to overcrowd this severely. They weren't typically shy about touching one another from what I'd seen, but this seemed extreme.

"This is your birthright," she said, taking the end of my braid in her fingers. She raised her chin in a gesture, calling my attention to the hill at the other side of the cove. "All Gorgons who wish to marry must descend into the pools and allow their chosen cardinal snake to claim them. You will strip yourself of all mortal belongings and descend into the pool, and when you emerge, if a snake finds you worthy, you will have one of your own to bring with you into your future and your handfasting ceremony. When you've been chosen, you will rise and climb to the other side of the partition. We will be waiting to prepare you in the bridal cove," she said, unwinding my hair and taking the bit of rope that had been used to secure it.

She stripped my swords from my back slowly, placing them upon the ground with a gentleness that brought me comfort. She unlaced the back of my armor, unknotting it so that I could slip the leather from my shoulders and my arms, dropping the top to the ground beside me and trying not to think about my own nudity. It shouldn't continue to bother me, not when I'd spent a great deal of time naked in front of people since meeting Caldris.

Many had seen me in far more compromising positions, but something about standing nude before the woman who had birthed me felt more vulnerable somehow.

I shifted, peeling the leathers down my legs and tugging off my boots. Medusa gathered my belongings into her arms, stepping back as I turned to look at her over my shoulder. "I'll see you on the other side, Estrella," she said, her reassuring smile making me grin as I took a single step forward.

I stepped down, my feet sliding through the clay beneath the thick ferns that covered the floor in this spot. Even if I'd wanted to descend into the snake-filled waters slowly, I wouldn't have been able to.

My feet hit first, sliding through water as the snakes parted instinctively to allow me to join them. They brushed against me as my body lowered, their scales rubbing on my skin as I fell into the depths.

My face plunged beneath the surface, leaving me sputtering beneath the water. But something touched the bottom of my foot, lifting me when I could not even try to swim for myself. There was nothing but snakes around me, no way for me to tread water. I tried not to think of what was beneath me, the large, scaled surface being thicker than my thigh as it raised me to the surface. I gasped, sucking back air as I broke through and stood still, watching the snakes slither around me. They surrounded me completely, rubbing against me as they moved.

Even being on good terms with snakes thanks to my heritage, I swallowed back my unease. They parted in front of me, leaving a gap in the water. I took a half step forward, faltering when the water before me rippled. Snakes pressed against my belly, pinning me still. I ran my hands over each one, the difference in their sizes easier to determine in this way. I could not make out where one ended and the other began, a mixture of colors swimming through the water in an array of purple, blue, green, and black.

Something shifted in the water, something *large*, and I attempted to take a step back as it broke through the surface in front of me.

Its head was white, its body a gleaming, shining silver speckled white. With eyes of green, it stared down at me as it raised its massive neck out of the water and curled forward. My eyes widened as I studied the serpent, a thinner, more agile version of the basilisks that had swallowed men whole on my command.

It felt familiar, that stare gleaming down at me. Like something strangely comforting when it had no right to be. I met its gaze as a purple snake slithered up the side of its body, winding itself around to peek over the white snake's head.

It felt like Medusa, I realized, as I stretched out a hand. The white serpent scented me, leaning forward to touch its nose to my hand as the smaller purple snake slithered over its forehead. The purple one gleamed with specks of gold, the scales shimmering as it touched my fingers and rose up my arm.

It crossed over the stone snake with teeth still sunk into my skin, draping itself over my neck. She was larger than the one who had helped me with the sword in Mistfell, larger than the one Medusa had given me. Not so large that I wouldn't be able to bear her weight, but large enough to be intimidating all the same.

I met her shining golden gaze, feeling a familiarity staring back at me. If the white snake was Medusa's counterpart, then this one was mine. She pressed the side of her face into mine, leaving me to lean my head to the side and return the moment of affection.

The white snake nodded, lowering itself down and maneuvering its body. It rose us up, bringing me to the clay on the other side of the cove so that I could step out. I was still nude, walking up onto the bank a few paces before I turned to look back. The white snake sunk into the cove once again, the smaller snakes spreading out and beginning the process of vacating the cove to go back to wherever they'd come from.

"Do you have a name?" I asked, raising a finger for the snake draped across my shoulders. I held her gaze, wondering if I would ever be able to understand her in the same way I could speak to Fenrir. "How about Amethyst?"

She huffed, air puffing out of her nostrils as she rolled her eyes to the ceiling. I chuckled, smiling down at her. "Okay, so not Amethyst. What about Vox?" She shook her head. "Gwen? Belladonna?" I asked as I crested the top of the hill and looked down into the room in front of me. It immediately reminded me of the way Byron had murdered his wife, slowly poisoning her without anyone suspecting him of it. Sneaky and insidious.

Unsuspecting.

"Belladonna suits her," Medusa said, staring up at me as I glanced around the cavern in awe.

Holy fucking Hel.

THIRTY-EIGHT

ESTRELLA

The shimmering lights of the cove waters glistened off the crystals that filled the chamber. Bioluminescence illuminated what should have been a dark, dreary place—so separated from the light of the surface. The crystals shone from within, a low, pulsating light that was in tune with the rhythm of my heart in a way that erased any doubt.

In another life, in other circumstances, this would have been my home.

The thought was sobering, taking away a little of the overwhelming joy the prospect of uniting with Caldris gave me. What would a life in a place like this have been like? The beauty here couldn't drown out the horror outside of these caverns.

But Tartarus lacked one thing in particular that I wouldn't have given up for anything.

My mate.

I made my way down the embankment to approach Medusa

where she waited with a group of three other Gorgon women. I tried not to allow myself to be bothered by my own nudity, drawing comfort from where Belladonna had perched herself across my shoulders comfortably. Her weight felt like it belonged there, like she had always been a part of my body when she was as new to me as the cove that surrounded me.

Medusa had changed out of the armor she'd worn previously, donning a simple white gown that draped over her shoulders and cut low in the front. A strap wound around her waist, the fabric woven into a braid that held the loosely flowing skirt tight at the smallest part of her body. The other Gorgons wore similar gowns, their arms covered in bioluminescent shimmers that clung to their sepia skin.

They looked so much like Medusa that I felt the stall of my heart in my chest, somehow knowing that these women were family to her . . . family to me by extension.

There'd been a life here that I'd never been a part of. A family unit that I'd been deprived of.

Time I could never get back.

The cove was stunning, with a waterfall at the back corner of the room. The water plunged into a pool below, the sound of rushing water filling the small space. Somehow, it wasn't as loud as I thought it should have been, offering a simple kind of peace to the humming of my mind and the thoughts that constantly plagued me.

"Step into the waters, Estrella," Medusa said, nodding her head over to the cove itself. I stepped past the three Gorgon women watching me, both simultaneously wishing I knew their names and needing nothing more than to continue on. Whatever this tradition was, whatever else was needed to prepare me, I wanted to be with Caldris once again.

I wanted to feel his heart beat in time with mine, and I wanted to feel complete for the first time in my life. Coming here, to this place so filled with the things I'd missed out on in my life on the other side of the Veil, reminded me of everything I'd lost.

I wanted to think of everything I could have now. The love that waited for me.

My toes touched the warm, balmy waters of the cove first. The water spread along my skin, coating me in warmth that was all-consuming. I felt it sink inside of me, warming me through the barrier of my skin. Belladonna shifted on my shoulders as I stepped deeper, drawn into the water until I lowered to my shoulders.

"You must pass beneath the falls," one of the Gorgon women said with a gentle smile. "Cleanse yourself of everything that came before this day and the handfasting that awaits you. You must go to one another as you are, not as the world would have you be."

I moved deeper into the cove as Belladonna lifted from my shoulders, twisting through the water at her leisure. My hands moved just beneath the surface as the water grew too deep for me to stand, my feet kicking as I moved slowly to the falls. I paused just before passing beneath it, drawing in deep breaths of air.

The moment I swam beneath the fall, the pressure of it beat against the top of my head. Pain blossomed there, any breath I'd attempted to store being stolen from my lungs as it pushed me beneath the surface. I hurried to kick myself forward, seeking an out in desperation. I swam until my feet could brush the silt below me, pushing myself to stand and breaking through the surface as I flung my hair back and water splashed out of my face.

It dripped down me, leaving me to stare at my bare skin that was covered in the same sparkle the Gorgon women had donned. I raised my hands above the surface, splaying my fingers and watching the turquoise and purple lights glisten as I moved. Medusa stepped into the shallow waters, uncaring for the way the water drenched her dress. She bent low, holding out a hand that Belladonna approached without hesitation. The purple snake nuzzled into Medusa's hand, the moment of affection beautiful in the uniqueness of it.

Here, the snakes and the serpents were not feared, but existed happily alongside the Gorgons. In Mistfell, they'd been killed if they were discovered in the gardens. Long before I'd understood *why*, I'd snuck them into my pocket when I discovered them, setting them free in the forest later after I'd finished harvesting.

Even then, I hadn't been able to suffer their deaths when all they wanted was food just the same as me.

"By our customs, the day of your handfasting should come with a gift from each of your families. Something you can carry with you always and one day give to a child of your own," Medusa said as Belladonna sank her teeth into her wrist. I watched the fangs penetrate Medusa's skin, sinking deep into the vein there and drinking. "I have nothing of my mother to offer you, and even if I did, I wouldn't. She condemned me when the Goddess turned me into this, and she does not get to be a part of my legacy."

"Your legacy is this place," I said, shrugging off the tightness in my chest to gesture to the home she'd carved out for herself in Tartarus. "Your sanctuary will live on forever."

"*You* will always be my true legacy, Estrella," she said as Belladonna pulled her fangs free from her wrist finally. "My daughter of chaos."

I swallowed as the bright violet snake slithered toward me, glancing back and forth between her and Medusa. "I don't need a gift. My mate is all I need, and I wouldn't have a gift from Khaos anyway."

"Your father would never allow you to be married without his knowledge or permission, Estrella. Surely you know that," she said, reaching up a hand to the snakes in her hair. They parted, allowing her to reach into the strands beneath them and pluck a single, golden thread from her head. She held it out before me, distracting me as I watched it shimmer in the lights of the cove.

My hands hung at my sides as I stared at the thread, attempting to trace where it went. What it touched and what it might change if I pulled on it.

Belladonna brushed against my hand, giving me a moment to look at her before she bared her fangs and sank them into my wrist. My knees buckled beneath me, dragging me deeper into the water as her body wound around my arm and cold filled my body. It was such a contrast to the warmth of the water surrounding me, filling me with stone and attempting to drag me beneath the surface.

I would drown. I would turn to the very rock at my feet and drown in this place, condemned by my mother's "gift."

Just when I thought I could not take any more, Belladonna released me. I got my feet beneath me, pushing to the surface once again and emerging from it as the snake swam around me. Medusa had closed the distance between us, standing just in front of me as I sputtered for breath.

She touched a finger to the space above my breast, dragging a long, black talon across my skin slowly as I gasped and stared down at the blood that welled in response to her touch. She slid a finger into the parted flesh, never taking her gaze off mine as I wheezed in pain. Belladonna pressed her body against my back as she bit into my other wrist, making everything inside of me still.

I couldn't move as Medusa's serpentine green eyes held mine rooted to the spot. She hummed, the sound a quiet song, as something emerged from the cavity in my chest, wrapping around her finger and turning to stone the moment it touched her. The snake Mab had wrapped around my heart hardened and turned to ash, falling into the water below us as Medusa raised that small, short piece of thread and pressed it into my wound.

"Let your father's gift be a reminder," she said, reaching up to cup my cheek as the wound healed over, glowing with golden light from within. "That no matter what the Fates may weave, you command the threads themselves."

Belladonna released me with an affectionate brush, following after Medusa as she turned to walk out of the cove. I followed after her, breathing through the odd freedom in my heart. There was no vice pressing down on it, only the distinct feeling that I could conquer anything.

That fate itself was in tune with my wants and needs.

I followed after her, emerging from the water and stepping onto the sands at the edge of the cove. I stumbled over jagged grains, turning my attention to where the tan sand turned to pebbles, hardening beneath me once more. "Soft, Estrella," Medusa said, the words a gentle reminder. "You are soft and gentle, and you want the things around you to remain so. You are not cursed like I am, but gifted with another means to protect yourself."

I breathed, the very threat of turning Caldris to stone enough of a reprimand. I couldn't afford to let my magic slip, to lose control of this power for even a moment. The rock at my feet lifted, raising me higher as I focused on the sound of Medusa's breathing. She breathed out, and I followed suit, feeling the rock sink back down at my feet. The grains of sand returned, correcting my slip up with ease.

"You are the master of your magic, my love. Do not ever doubt that or let it control you," Medusa explained, using her grip on my hand to guide me toward the three other women. One held up a deep blue dress that matched the colors of the home the Gorgons had created here. It was the blue of deep water, of the night sky on a cold winter's day. She slid the fabric over my head, letting it settle at my breast as one of the other women tore my braid free and splayed my damp hair over my shoulder. She ran her fingers through it as the last woman stepped up beside me, yanking at the laces across my back and pulling the dress tight. It was fitted through the breast, without straps or anything to cover my shoulders. It left the entirety of my Fae Marks visible and remained fitted through my hips before flaring out to the floor.

As soon as the dress was tightened, they worked as a team to braid my hair anew and brush the blue lights of the water onto my cheekbones. There wasn't any of the pomp and circumstance I thought I would have experienced had I ever married in the human realm. No formalities beyond the gifts given to me by those who had created me.

A simple dress. A braid for my hair. There was no kohl to line my eyes or intricate makeup to cover my face. I felt nude without it on a day like this somehow, as if Caldris would see the real me beneath the surface.

It didn't matter that he already had more times than I could count, only that this would be different.

In this, I would be his wife. He would see inside of me as well as outside, claiming the last parts of me as his.

"How do you feel?" Medusa asked, her face soft as she nodded to one of the Gorgons. The woman left my side, moving to an opening in the cave we occupied. It was narrow, as if it led to a hallway or tunnel, and she disappeared from view as Medusa settled Belladonna around my shoulders. She draped there comfortably, twining her tail around one of my arms as her head rested over my heart.

My heart that was free to love and do as I choose finally.

"Nervous," I said, sinking my teeth into my bottom lip.

"There is no need to be nervous about love, Estrella. You only need to fear all that comes after," she said, the ominous words making my brow furrow. "To that end, I have one more gift that may help."

She nodded behind me, making me turn slowly to find Caldris walking toward me. His steps faltered as his gaze swept over my body, moving from head to toe and back again in a way that made me fidget. Those stormy blue eyes glazed over with heat, burning a hole into me as he finally settled on my face once again.

I drowned in the depths of them, the breath sweeping out of my lungs as he strode closer to me. Medusa left my side, approaching him and placing a hand over his heart.

He faltered, his stare dropping from mine and leaving me bereft.

Medusa drew back, her fingernails lengthening as she tipped her head to the side.

And plunged her fist into Caldris's chest.

THIRTY-NINE

NILA

I slinked through the halls in the dark cover of night. All was silent as I made my way through the narrow corridors, a momentary reprieve offered to all who called Tar Mesa home as Mab slept. It was as if the palace itself breathed a sigh of relief, as if the very stone walls that surrounded me relaxed along with the residents who were trapped in this Godsforsaken place.

Even Mab's guards who usually patrolled the halls while she slept were conspicuously absent. They too undoubtedly took advantage of the opportunity to rest without fear that she would kill them in a mad fit while they slept.

I'd only told one person of my plans for my night, instead choosing to take this part of my journey on my own. Countless others had attempted it before me, and few had made it past the guards Mab surrounded herself with. My only hope in this was that she was less protected than ever, her own who were usually loyal to her even coming to fear her in such a way that they could no longer defend her.

Their risk of being murdered was as high as any of ours, and that tended to put things into perspective for those whose loyalty could be purchased with the promise of survival.

The knife I had tucked away into one of the drawers in Estrella's sitting room burned a hole in my pocket. I didn't dare to reach in to grasp the hilt for fear of burning myself upon the iron of the blade, particularly when I turned to the staircase that would take me to the upper floor of Tar Mesa. On this top level, only Mab resided and no others were permitted entrance apart from the guard who waited outside and her lady-in-waiting. Any others who were summoned here had come to fear this place, and I couldn't help but think of the day that Mab had brought Estrella here. I rounded the corner at the top of the staircase, keeping my head low as I carried a tray with a teapot and cup and small bites of food placed upon it.

I hoped her guard would pay little attention to the servant bringing Mab her midnight tea. Even if she had already succumbed to sleep earlier than normal this evening, Aligan, her lady-in-waiting, would always make sure that her tea was there for her should she wake and desire it. The consequences of not providing that service were too dire.

While Aligan slept off the harsh reality of the herbs I'd put into her own tea, tucking her into the kitchen closet so that no one would find her before I'd done what I'd set out to do, I would bring Mab her tea and stab her through the heart before she could ever wake.

I kept my head down as I approached the carved metal of the doors to her bedroom. Mab's pet snakes slithered through the gaps, making the door look alive in the darkness. I kept my head down with my hood raised high around the edges of my face, hoping the guard couldn't see past the faint hint of glamour I'd managed to summon. Any hint of Rheaghan's magic had left me when he died, but it mattered little now.

I wouldn't need it for much longer anyway.

"Nila," the guard said, my name on his voice making everything in me tighten. It was the worst possible outcome of this quest, the one guard on duty being the one who would recognize me. He'd been kind to me where all Mab's other loyal members had been cruel, and I knew without a doubt he was the only one who'd taken time to know my name, let alone recognize the lines of my face through my glamour.

"Dravenor," I said, meeting his stare finally. I released my hold on the glamour, letting it slip away and preserving my energy. The presence of the iron had already made it weak enough, giving me little hope of victory unless I managed to sneak into Mab's rooms undetected.

"What do you think you're doing?" he hissed, grasping me by the forearm and pulling me away from the doorway and the prying eyes of Mab's snakes who may or may not alert her to my deception now that he'd spoken my name out loud.

The alcove he took me to was secluded enough, tucking us out of view from the prying eyes as he pressed me into the wall and leaned into my space.

"I'm ending this for all of us," I said, jerking my arm out of his hold. I set the tray upon the table next to a vase in the alcove beside us, my deception no longer necessary.

"What makes you think you'll be successful when so many others have tried and failed? She'll kill you before you can even get close," he said, scoffing as he ran his hand through his hair. "Don't waste your life on this misguided attempt that will only get you killed. Do you want your painting to hang in this hallway?" he asked, gesturing an arm out to the portraits of some of those who had tried to kill Mab through deception and tricks. They decorated her halls now, their likeness a morbid reminder of what happened to those who dared.

Few bothered anymore, her reign of terror so complete that there was no form of bravery that could account for an action such as this. Only recklessness and a disregard for one's life could bring someone to this moment. "And what kind of life is it that I'll have if I don't do this? Eternal fucking servitude?" I snapped, shaking my head with a bitter laugh.

"At least you'll be alive," Dravenor hissed, his anger tangible in the air. "Rheaghan was a good male. Deserved far better than he got, and he would want better for you than to die at Mab's hands."

I wanted to kill him for daring to speak his name. For offering me the reminder of all that I'd lost, and all that we hadn't hidden as well as we'd thought.

"Don't tell me what he would want. He never got to have what he wanted while he was alive because of that fucking bitch of a Queen, and I'll be damned if she gets to continue controlling my life now that he's gone," I argued, glaring into Dravenor's face. I was determined to keep him distracted, to allow for the backup to this endeavor to slide into place while I kept him occupied. I hated that of all the guards I needed to use in this, it had been him who would bear the consequences.

If we didn't succeed, Mab would kill him, too.

But that was a sacrifice I was willing to make for the rest of Alfheimr and the lives we would save if we were successful.

"Many here find a way to go on without their mates for a time. Some find companionship that fills some of the hole left behind by the mates they never got the opportunity to meet. Your bond was never completed. You could have centuries before you're lost to the madness and you want to throw that all away?"

I raised a hand, placing it on his chest gently. I didn't miss the flare of his eyes at the intimate touch, even if his armor did separate us from having skin-to-skin contact. It was a strict reminder of what I'd already learned in my time in the Shadow Court.

Kindness never came free in this place.

It always came with the weight of expectation and a pulsating reality that lingered just behind the kind words and gentle assurances.

He was no less a monster than the others. He just hid it better and used emotional manipulation rather than violence.

The door to Mab's bedroom creaked as Imelda pulled it open, slipping inside quickly but as quietly as she could manage. Dravenor too heard the sound, his head snapping to the side to lean back and look down the hall. I hoped Imelda was already inside Mab's quarters, tucked out of sight and out of mind as I did the only thing I could think to do in order to distract Dravenor from the second intruder looking to kill his Queen.

I lunged forward, grasping him by the collar of his tunic where it peeked out from beneath his armor. Tugging him back to me, I waited until he'd turned to face me, his mouth parted to ask me a question he never got to voice.

I pulled him down until his mouth crashed against mine, his reaction immediate. The moment his lips pressed into mine, he shoved his tongue into my parted lips and deepened the kiss, his distraction fully immersed when his hands dropped from the stone of the wall to my lower back. He guided me where he wanted me, shoving the tray of tea to the floor and lifting me so that I sat on the edge of the table with the vase pressed into the small of my back.

He tasted of ale as I let him take what he wanted, shoving the fabric of my dress down from my shoulder to get bare skin. As his mouth dropped there, I reached into the pocket of my gown and wrapped my fingers around the hilt of the dagger I'd brought with me.

Any hesitation I might have had was erased as he nipped at the flesh of my collarbone with sharp teeth, marking me in a way that should have belonged to only one male.

I moved slowly, not alerting him to anything that was wrong as a fake moan slid free from my mouth. Tugging at the hem of his shirt, I motioned to raise it above his head. He let me unlatch his armor as he raised his arms for me to slide it over his head, the leatherlike fabric parting on the side. I shoved it out of the way, using my free hand to tear it over his head and toss it to the side. He hadn't even lowered his arms before I slid my knife free from my pocket, immediately thrusting it forward into the center of his chest.

He froze as I shoved it forward, the motion too slow as it penetrated his rib cage. The crack vibrated through my hand as the blade finally sank into the fleshy meat of his heart, his body freezing immediately as the iron worked its magic and pulled everything from him.

This was not an injury he would survive, and he lowered his forehead to mine to stare at me in shock. I groaned, disgust rolling through me at the contact now that I didn't have to keep up any appearances. I shoved him forward, watching as he fell to his back on the stone floor before me. The knife still protruded from his chest, his eyes going blank as I jumped down from the table, adjusted my dress, and strode past him to help Imelda in the Queen's bedroom.

I shoved the door open, ignoring the snakes that slithered along the surface. The gilded bedframe against the back wall shouldn't have come as a surprise, a symbol of complete and utter opulence. Imelda stood beside the bed, her fingers touching the crown. Her arms shook, her face twisted into a pained expression. I watched in horror as her fingers that were so like Estrella's turned to stone against the crown, but still she fought to remove the crown from Mab's head.

She shook her head, her mismatched obsidian and white eyes turning to meet my gaze. The panic on her face was all that I needed to stride forward, taking the dagger Imelda had placed upon the nightstand. I turned it in my hand, prepared to plunge it down into Mab's heart.

I made the motion, raising the dagger over my head to gain the momentum to make this wound much more quickly than I had

Dravenor's. There was no time to spare with the Queen of Air and Darkness, no guarantee that she would die as quickly as he had.

Mab's eyes flew open as she thrust out a hand, launching Imelda and I back as she sat up with a shrill scream. I crashed into the door, the snakes slithering down to touch my shoulders. I'd thought Mab would kill us both immediately for our insolence, but instead she pressed a hand tightly to her chest, her face pained as her lungs heaved with the exertion of breathing.

"*No*," she rasped, her nails clawing at her own skin. "That's not possible."

Imelda recovered first, grabbing my hand and slipping us both out the door and into the hallway. Mab hadn't seemed to see us at all, so lost in whatever had happened to make her so distracted the only thing to save us from her vengeance.

"Dravenor!" she screamed, but the guard would not answer her. She didn't seem to care, instead continuing on as if he was there to do her bidding as Imelda guided me toward the stairwell. We paused there to listen for a moment that we probably shouldn't have risked, curiosity getting the best of us. "Bring me Caldris! I want to see his fucking heart for myself when I rip it from his chest."

There was a moment of silence while Mab waited for a response, and Imelda took my hand in hers and dragged me down the first set of stairs until we disappeared from view. We heard the door creak open as she poked into the hallway, furious energy reaching us as we moved quietly. Half to listen, half to hide from her notice as we fled the site of the murder I'd committed. My hands were covered in Dravenor's blood, but I couldn't make myself regret his death.

Not when we'd come so close to killing Mab and still had our lives intact. Not when we knew something had happened to infuriate her so.

Imelda pulled me into an alcove that was tucked into the stairwell, pressing a finger to her lips as we listened in the silence of the night. Mab's voice was a hushed whisper from this far away, accompanied only by her footsteps as she paced back and forth in the hall outside her rooms.

"Impossible. Only I can remove you from still beating hearts, my loves," Mab said.

Imelda's face spread into a wide smile as she pressed a hand to her mouth to silence her laughter, pulling me down the rest of the stairs. I didn't dare to speak until we'd returned to the sanctuary of the kitchen, surrounded by Fae who wanted to know if we'd been successful.

While we hadn't, the room was quiet as Imelda relayed the story of all we'd heard.

"What does it mean?" one of them asked as Imelda and I exchanged a knowing smile.

"It means Estrella and Caldris are both free from Mab's influence," Imelda said, her teeth gleaming brightly in the dark with the joy we both felt.

I added the truth of the meaning, the underlying message that we needed to cling to. "It means we have hope."

FORTY

CALDRIS

Medusa's smile was apologetic even as the feeling of her fist burst through my chest. I felt her fingers, and the long black talons that adorned them all the way to the thick muscle of my heart. Estrella cried out, motioning toward us as if she might interfere. A single look from her mother silenced any further attempt to interfere on my behalf, and though her body remained tense, she froze in place and I nodded even though the pain was excruciating.

Medusa could have killed me already if that was her intention, with the way her hand was wrapped around my heart. She could have pulled it from my body, could have taken the very core of my soul from me before I dared to blink.

"I'm okay," I said, reassuring my mate's wide-eyed stare. Medusa's gaze turned to the hole she'd made in my chest, remaining fixated as her fingers shifted and moved within me. I grimaced, a growl rumbling in my throat that Estrella echoed.

Only the hope that she might be able to offer freedom from the imprisonment that had existed within my own body for longer than I could remember was enough to keep me still. Medusa's finger glided over a particularly sensitive spot, her mouth twitching into a smile as she pressed into whatever she'd found. Something loosened within me, like cords snapping in two, and then suddenly I was dropping. I fell to my knees, relief like a shock to my system, Medusa moving with me as she pulled her hand free. The small stone figure of a snake rested in her palm, fading into ash and blowing in the breeze as I watched.

Estrella moved for me immediately, dropping onto her knees so harshly that the ground shook beneath her. She grasped my face in her hands, staring down at my chest as the wound healed over and Medusa got to her feet beside me.

"Are you alright?" Estrella asked, her gaze bouncing over my face and looking for any sign of pain. I smiled, the lack of pressure in my chest bringing a disbelieving laugh with it.

"Am I alright?" I asked, pushing to my feet. I took Estrella with me, pulling her into my arms and relishing the warmth of her skin. Her hand touched my chest above my heart, sliding into the fabric where the deep blue shirt they'd given me was open. Where that fucking serpent might have once recoiled from her touch and been so at odds with the way the rest of me swayed toward her orbit, there was only the warmth of our bond and the desire to get closer. I spun her in a circle, centuries of subservience gone in the blink of an eye.

What no one had been able to do for centuries, Medusa managed with a press of her finger.

"Mab may command the snakes on the surface, but the power she holds over them is only because she wears the stone that I crafted for my daughter upon her head like the thief she is. That magic is stolen, and one day," she said, turning her attention to Estrella's broad grin, "you will take it back."

Estrella swallowed, the reminder of the conflict that was coming far too grounded in reality. I pulled her tighter into my chest, giving her any reassurance I had.

I was no longer Mab's captive, and I could only assume Estrella was not either given her mother's ability to free her. We were free, and soon enough, we would be *one*.

"The storm will not last forever," one of the Gorgon men announced as he stepped into the cave, crossing his arms over his chest. There was a smile on his face that belied the tension of his posture, quirking an eyebrow as he studied us. "I assume you would also like time to consummate the bond before leaving us."

Estrella blushed, the pretty pink tint to her cheeks leaving me with no choice but to reach up a hand and stroke a thumb over the swell at the high point of her cheekbone.

"He's right, as brash as he may be," Medusa said, smiling as she took Estrella's hand and guided her to the edge of the pool. My mate dragged me alongside her, refusing to allow us to separate for even one moment longer.

Estrella stepped into the water, allowing it to soak the bottom of her dress. My trousers dampened on my calves as I stepped in beside her, only the shallow depths touching us as we turned to face one another. I clutched one of her hands in each of mine, staring down into the starry sky of her eyes.

Medusa touched a hand to Estrella's heart, smiling at her daughter. "Guide me to the thread of your bond," she said, watching as Estrella reached out a hand without hesitation. She wrapped something in her finger, placing her hand in her mother's and allowing the Gorgon woman to wrap our united hands in the thread. I felt the press of it on my skin where I normally might not have sensed it, felt every bit of the length as it draped over our forearms and hung down, until we were utterly connected by that dull connection that pulsed with desire. "Will you spend every one of your days proving to the Fates that the soul they split in two was better united as one?" Medusa asked her daughter, forcing Estrella to turn her attention away from mine.

"Always," Estrella answered, her voice soft as emotion clogged her throat.

Medusa reached down to the water below, picking up the thin but long purple snake that swam at our feet. She draped it over our united hands, covering the pulsing thread of our bond where it beat in tune with our hearts. I grimaced as the snake wound herself around my bare arm, shuddering as she rubbed into me tighter like she sensed my discomfort and wanted to toy with me. "It just had to be snakes," I muttered.

But Estrella's resulting laughter was light, happier than it had felt since her world came crashing down with the revelation of who and what I was, with the danger that had plagued our relationship from the very beginning.

I wanted to stroke that lightness to the surface, to coax it from her every chance I got.

"Will you love your mate on her worst days, embracing the monster as much as the woman?" Medusa asked me, chuckling as the snake settled her face on my forearm at the perfect moment.

"I'll love her in all her forms," I said, squeezing Estrella's hand in mine. Her eyes glistened with the threat of tears, but she swallowed to keep them at bay as she leaned forward and tilted her head up, inviting me to lean down to her height.

I met her lips with mine, the gentle touch sending a surge of magic through me.

"Not yet!" one of the women who witnessed our union called, making Estrella laugh into my mouth before I pulled back from her.

"Call to your ice with your other hand, God of the Dead," Medusa commanded, watching as my fingers frosted over. That same ice coated Estrella's skin, but she did not flinch back from the cold. She'd learned to welcome that part of me long ago. "Will you take your mate for all the sharp edges formed from his centuries of life, and take it upon yourself to soften them with your love?" she asked Estrella.

Estrella scoffed, as if the very idea of softening me was ludicrous. She liked me hard.

"When it suits me," she said, echoing my thoughts and drawing a rumble of laughter from my lungs.

Medusa shook her head as if she hadn't wanted the image that planted in her mind. "Shadows, Caldris," she said, pressing her lips together.

I called to them, watching them wrap Estrella's and my hands in darkness. "Will you accept your mate's eternal darkness, and help her so that she may always find the light?" Medusa asked, and I couldn't help the smile that came over me as I stared at my mate and reiterated our vows.

Only I knew the new significance of them, knew the way that the Fates had determined those words long before we'd ever spoken them.

"Until chaos reigns," I murmured, leaning forward to touch my mouth to Estrella's. She surged forward, leaning into my embrace as my hands warmed. That pressure where the threads had been draped scalded my skin, the lights shimmering off it glowing so brightly even I could see it. Estrella gasped, her deep intake of breath drawing me into her.

My soul searched for hers, colliding so suddenly it blinded me. The shimmering edges of where we'd been torn apart healed over with a slow progression of golden light in the dark abyss that existed within her.

I looked for the light, as I'd vowed I would always do for the woman that I loved more than life itself, but I found something so much more.

I found *her*.

FORTY-ONE

ESTRELLA

The burst of gleaming, golden light was nearly blinding. It shimmered so completely, making everything within me feel whole. It was impossible to realize how empty I had been before, how I'd truly only been half of myself without him and his soul fully entwined with mine.

Now feeling complete for the first time, I wondered how I'd ever lived without the comfort of his mind with mine, his soul making itself at home within my body. Just as quickly as the light had blinded me, the darkness of the shadows surrounding our bond plunged me into night.

The breath was stolen from my lungs, catapulting me into a darkness that I wasn't certain I would ever be able to find my way out of. I followed that single thread of gold that connected Caldris and I, tugging on it with my mind in desperation.

The pressure from the other side reassured me that he was still there, that he was still with me. The fear of being completely alone was immense, the darkness vibrating over my skin like the low, tormenting touch of a lover in the night. It was far too familiar with me, as if it knew each and every point on my body to touch to draw a shiver from me. That touch lingered over my skin, touching every part of me as it pressed in and surrounded me, but there was no arousal in spite of the tickle on my body.

There was only fear. A fear that struck so deep inside of me that when my breath finally returned, it came in deep, ragged gasps.

I fell back, landing on my ass on a surface that sprang in response to my touch. My fingertips were wet as they drifted below the surface, digging into the flowing water beneath me. I stared down into the waters of the Void in horror as I drew my touch back, ensuring that none of the creatures within could grasp me. The ferryman was nowhere in sight, and after his words when he left Caldris with me, I wasn't so sure he would interfere on my behalf a second time.

The Void was empty, devoid of life in a way that felt wrong. With all the souls who lingered here too long trapped within the waters of the flowing water, I had one pressing question that I couldn't seem to answer.

Where was everyone else?

The Void should have been teeming with souls as they waited for The Father and The Mother to wrap them up in their eternal embrace, but time and time again when I made my journey into the Void, I found it empty of such creatures.

I got to my feet slowly, rocking on unsteady heels as the strange boundary between the river and I wobbled beneath me. Spinning in a circle, I looked for any sign of my mate. I felt him at the other side of the bond, his presence shimmering away with a mix of shadows and the first winter's frost. I wrapped the thread around my hand, pressing it to my heart and holding it tight as I turned in the direction it guided me.

Something was wrong.

I felt it in my flesh, felt the simmering in my blood and the hardening in my bones. Caldris and I had completed our bond, connected in a way that was permanent and could not be severed by any but through death. I'd been awake, when the only other times I'd been dragged into the Void had been when I slept or was on the brink of death. When my suffering was too much, this place protected me from the agony and sheltered me in a cocoon of numbness.

I took a single, cautious step, halting suddenly when the waters swirled at my feet. Stumbling back, I watched transfixed as they rose up out of the river and formed an archway. Barely taller than myself, the surface of the water hardened as if Caldris had kissed it with the cold of winter. A smooth sheen of ice waited in front of me, forming a perfect mirror as I stared at myself in shock.

I was as I remembered being before leaving Mistfell. My eyes were the deep green I'd come to recognize in Medusa, my hair braided neatly in spite of my tattered and torn green dress. There were no Fae Marks gracing my collarbone or slithering out from beneath my sleeve to touch the back of my hand. I raised it to my face, studying the fingertips that were covered in tiny scratches from the Twilight Berry bush. I shook my head as I stumbled back, refusing to acknowledge the hollow that formed inside me at the thought of losing everything I'd worked for. Everything I'd suffered for.

I would *not* go back.

I would never go back to that life, to that girl.

I pressed my lips together, turning my back on the mirror that showed me my past. The water swirled again as I shook my head and attempted to flee in the other direction. I didn't want to see whatever it had to share with me.

Waters rose all around me, the chill of a winter breeze blowing through the Void around me. It swirled over the surface of the water, picking up a spray that reminded me of the sea and splashing it over my face and skin as mirrors hardened all around me. I spun in a circle slowly, looking for a place to squeeze through. The mirrors were empty except that first, leaving me trapped without showing me anything.

A flicker of slow movement appeared in the mirror to my left, forcing me to raise my stare from the water at my feet to squint at what moved in the distance. The figure was a woman, clad in a white dress that draped over one of her shoulders and fell to her feet. There was a shimmer of golden jewelry across the front of her throat, the lights of the swirling golden and black lines tattooed over her hand and arm playing off the shimmering surface. Her dark hair flowed freely around her shoulders, swaying lightly as she made her way toward me.

Her eyes were the depth of the night sky, a universe trapped in her gaze. In the mirror behind her, the stars seemed to pulse in tune with her Fae Marks as they slithered over her skin, the twin moons shining behind her as I swallowed. I recognized her at the same time I didn't, her immortal skin far more smooth than mine could ever dream to be. Her ears were pointed, her mouth set into a neutral line as she looked me up and down. There wasn't a trace of emotion of any kind on that cold, impassive face of the monster that was both me and not me.

No disdain for my humanity. No sympathy for the panic that made my heart beat so quickly I thought it might fail.

She leaned into the surface of the mirror, pressing a hand to the other side of the ice. Golden light pulsed against her skin, warming the ice just enough that a trickle of sweat dripped down my side.

She tipped her head to the side, studying me as her mouth tipped up into a cruel, callous smirk and she spoke a command that made me swallow and shake my head.

"Let. Me. Out." Each word was carefully enunciated, her voice hoarse from disuse. It was both mine and not, the power within it making the ice of the mirror quake.

"I won't," I said, shaking my head at the figure in front of me. I knew without a doubt that she was that monster I felt lingering beneath my skin, the one that intervened when the horrors were too much for me to handle on my own.

The one I could turn to who would kill my enemies without batting an eye.

She was a part of me, and I had accepted that and accepted her during my trials, but that didn't mean I would ever willingly let her erase the person I had fought so hard to become. She belonged within me, within *us*.

"Let me out!" she screamed, banging her fist against the ice between us. My body jerked, as if I could feel her thrashing against my rib cage and trying to fight her way out through my flesh and bone. She grinned as she did it again, forcing my body closer to the ice until I was certain I would be able to scent her if it were not for the barrier between us. My ribs ached with the force of her blow, even as I watched her do it before me. I let out a loose rasp, gritting my teeth against the pain as my palm touched my ribs that throbbed in pain.

"He is not yours," she said, the cruel smile on her mouth revealing lightly pointed teeth at the corners of her mouth. They were so similar to the ones Caldris possessed that had terrified me that first day when he revealed himself in Calfalls, a sign of the immortality she possessed that remained just out of my reach.

"He's my mate," I said, arguing the words she spoke. There was no truth to them. I knew and felt Caldris in my soul like a tangible thing, but the sight of my Fae Marks upon her skin pushed at every insecurity I possessed.

"No. He is *our* mate," she argued, raising one of her hands to trail over the Fae Marks on her skin. Not so long ago, I would have done anything to get rid of them, overjoyed at the sight of them upon someone else and the freedom that offered me.

But now? Now I just wanted to rip them from her flesh and wear her skin if that meant Caldris belonged to me and me alone.

I bared my teeth at her, snarling as I stepped closer to the mirror. She tipped her head to the side, studying my anger as her smile broadened. "Don't worry, little human. Neither of us can exist without the other. I cannot have him without you, just like you cannot have him without me," she said, pressing both hands to the ice. Her fingers curled against the surface, sharp black talons digging into the ice. I resisted the urge to raise my hands to meet hers, keeping them firmly pressed against the sides of my thighs.

"What are you?" I asked, swallowing back that part of me, that tiny, insignificant voice that remembered what it had been like to deny myself answers. To avoid asking hard questions because sometimes ignorance was far better than truth.

But this truth had haunted me through space and time, followed me from Nothrek to Alfheimr and finally Tartarus. There was no freedom from the truth that was already before me.

I could no longer remain ignorant to my own potential.

"I am you," she said, her smile softening as those dark eyes flashed with gold. They lit something within her, power striking against the ice as I stared down at my hand. My Fae Marks returned, the glamour she'd placed on me fading in a smooth line up my arm to reveal the truth of who I'd already become. "I am your future and your past. I am what you were meant to be before your humanity tainted you."

"My humanity protected me when Mab would have killed me," I argued, dismissing the notion that to be human automatically meant weakness. It meant caring in a way that the Fae didn't seem to understand, and I would *never* believe that love was weakness.

"Maybe so," she said, nodding her head in agreement, leaning in until her breath fogged the ice. "But it is not you who needs protection any longer. It is the rest of the world who needs to live in fear now."

The words struck inside my chest, making my hands curl into fists at my side. "I don't want to be a monster," I said, swallowing back the fear that Melinoe had picked up on and attempted to use against me. I wondered if she possessed some power of foresight in addition to her control over the realm of dreams, understanding that the moment when she'd shown me myself had been so similar to this. I'd thought I'd already embraced the nightmare, but I still saw her as a separate entity to myself.

Still saw her as something within me that I could suppress until she was needed.

"Every monster is the hero of their own story, and every hero the villain of someone else's. You will always be Mab's villain, just as she is yours," the woman in the mirror answered.

"That doesn't mean I need to be like her," I snapped. "It doesn't mean I need to accept you as part of me if it means becoming cruel."

"Even with me as part of you, you are not capable of cruelty like that. The Fates made sure of it," she said, her eyes widening ever so slightly as I stepped closer.

"No," I snarled, refusing to allow any of that credit to go to the creatures who had made my life miserable. I could have just as easily descended into the cruelty of the world as a result of my suffering, but I hadn't. "The Fates didn't do that. *I did.*"

She smirked, raising her head as if to agree. "Very well. You made sure of that."

"What was our name? Our first name?" I asked, watching as her nostrils flared. It was the name of the monster, the name of the creature who could have and should have been if it hadn't been for the threat to my life.

I'd been forced to the other side of a Veil and had my immortality stripped from me, the child of the King of the Primordials carefully crafted into a mortal girl and kept oblivious.

The Fae believed there was power in names, that they could be used against you if the wrong person learned them.

I wanted to know mine.

"Aella," the woman said, the ice melting at her hands as I studied them. Her skin was pink as it poked through the ice, heat rolling off her flesh as that name thumped inside of me. I reached out my own hands, taking hers in mine and embracing her.

Embracing Aella.

FORTY-TWO

CALDRIS

She stood before me, bathed in darkness that clung to her skin as if it were a part of her. She didn't seem frightened of the dark, and though she looked the same as the woman I had bound myself to, there was something distinctly different about the mate that raised a hand, gliding it through the void that surrounded her. She had yet to become aware of my presence as she spun her fingers through the air, and I sucked back a shocked breath at the thread of gold she wound around her fingers and clasped within her hand.

The threads of fate.

They were more than merely gold, I realized as I watched. They pulsed with power and magic that the Fae could only dream of achieving with the mediocre hint of power that flooded through our veins. The Primordials had given their offspring nothing but a taste of the magic at their fingertips, and I watched as Estrella tugged on the thread. Her gaze went skyward, her eyes gleaming with golden light as a star appeared in the darkness. Estrella's face split into a blinding smile as she stared up at the star she'd brought into exis-tence, the light she'd created in the darkness that attempted to swal-low her whole. That was the moment I realized what had changed in her in the brief moments since I'd plummeted into the bond between us.

Estrella had found her peace.

I lingered in the background even when I wanted to go to her, allowing her the moment of joy and watching. A smile curved my lips, witnessing a moment of pure, uninterrupted joy in a life that had not offered many.

Estrella gathered threads, making them appear from the darkness. I could not see them until the moment she touched them, whether that was because she created them or a limitation of our bond, but the shimmer of magic was breathtaking as she gathered them between her hands. She waved her hands slowly, her movements dance-like as she swayed to music that only she could hear—the music of the Fates.

When she finished, the loosely tied knot of threads floated before her without her touch, and she tilted her head as she watched it. The mannerism was so similar to the night in Blackwater, to the animal-istic part of her that had risen to the surface. But where that had felt like something dark and dangerous, this felt like the lightness on the other side.

She touched the threads, grasping them between her hands and studying the woven web of power. Her smile widened impossibly as she raised her arms suddenly, tossing the ball into the darkness above her.

I gasped as the ball exploded into hundreds of pieces, filling the Void with burning embers of light.

The stars shimmered in the pure darkness, illuminating me fi-nally as Estrella's golden eyes met mine. They were the perfect echo of the gold in the stars as she took her first step toward me, the blue of her dress trailing along the surface of the water behind her. I met her step for step, approaching the woman I was certain thrummed through me just as much as I did myself. Her consciousness tickled at the edges of my mind, her eyes glowing as she smiled at me.

She swept her hand along the water beneath her feet as she moved, a line of golden thread appearing as she walked. She tugged at it, pulling me off my balance as I made my way toward her. A bright laugh bubbled up from her throat, lighting up her face in the way that made everything in my chest clench. It seemed so much stronger in the absence of the snake, as if the beating flesh itself swelled under her attention. She used it to pull me toward her, making my feet slip along the surface of the water until I stood just in front of her.

The gold faded from her gaze, shifting to the dark of the night sky with the twinkle of a galaxy contained there as she raised her hand and cupped my cheek in her palm. Her skin was warm, as if she herself burned with the fires of the stars she'd crafted from nothing.

"I've been looking for you," she said, tilting her head back to allow me to slide my hand beneath the curtain of her hair and cup her neck in my hand. My thumb grazed over her jawline, reveling in the shiver she loosed and the way her eyes drifted closed.

"And I've been *waiting* for you, min asteren," I said, leaning down and rubbing my nose against hers. Our bond was tremulous, pulsating between us as it begged to be completed. The moment we came together would be the moment it snapped into place, the thread becoming indestructible.

Unbreakable.

"I'm sorry I made you wait so long," she said, her voice tinged with laughter.

I sighed, lingering with my lips just off hers as I held her gaze. "You were worth every Gods-damned second," I said, leaning forward and closing the distance. My mouth touched hers, the heat of her spreading through me. Light tickled at my eyelids, the warm golden glow of it threatening to pull me from the moment. I shoved it away, letting my other hand fall to Estrella's waist and pulling her in tightly. She molded to me perfectly, as if her body had been carved from mine. The perfect fit, all of her hills and valleys nestled into mine to create a single being.

Two bodies. One soul.

She slid her hands around my waist, her nails digging into my spine and feeling like a claim on my physical being in the same way she'd already taken my soul for herself. I'd give her anything she needed, anything she wanted to take, if it meant that I would never have to leave this moment or this feeling. I slid my hands down over her hips, parting her dress at the slit in the thigh so that I could touch her bare skin. Her shiver in response pulsed through me, drawing a ragged groan from my mouth. She swallowed it, devouring it as she angled her head and deepened the kiss. I lifted her into my arms, reveling in the instinctive way she spread her legs and wrapped them around my hips.

"Everyone out," Medusa said, her voice breaking through the haze. Estrella pulled back from my mouth suddenly, her nails digging into my shoulders as her eyes flew wide. I smirked up at her as her cheeks turned pink, her gaze bouncing from person to person as they grinned at her and backed toward the doorway they would take to leave the cove. Estrella squirmed in my grip, but I refused to release her as her mother made her way to the door last. "The water is waiting for you, daughter. Make sure you enter it as you were always meant to be."

Her cryptic words seemed to strike something in Estrella, her eyes pulsing with golden light in acknowledgment. Medusa nodded thoughtfully; her face full of pride in spite of her daughter's incriminating position. She closed the rough, wooden door behind her as she disappeared, her voice trailing off as she spoke to those who had accompanied her to our handfasting.

"Well, that was awkward," Estrella said, her cheeks pinking all over again. I raised a single hand, keeping my other beneath her ass and using it to hold her steady, to brush my knuckles over the deep rose flesh.

"I believe you're the only one who was bothered by it, wife," I said, watching her eyes flare. I guided her over to the rock face that waited beside the lagoon, setting her upon it and standing before her.

"Say it again," she said, her fingers skimming over the skin of my shoulder as if she couldn't stop touching me. I understood the need, the itch that existed within us. We'd been separated for far too long, suffered in one another's absence for far too long.

I leaned forward, touching my mouth to hers with gentle ease and kissing my way over her jaw. I peppered every inch of flesh I passed with affection, spreading my love through her body as I made my way to the side of her neck. She bent back for me, her hair draping down behind her to scrape the stone. Grasping the knot at the base of her braid, I slowly worked the ribbon that had been tied there until it fell to the stone beneath her. My fingers speared through her hair, spreading it and allowing it to drape freely as my mouth found the hollow in her collarbone.

She let out the slightest gasp, the sound of her pleasure all the more satisfying after all the time we'd been forced to spend apart. I wanted nothing more than to feel her skin wrapped around me, to drag her into the waters of the lagoon and make her mine permanently. The final piece of our bond was so close I could taste it, the press of her mind on my own just the tiniest bit distant.

I could hear her; I could feel her, but it reminded me of someone speaking to me through a wall, one last barrier between us that needed to be demolished.

My fingers found the laces at the back of her deep blue dress, untying them as she ran her hands down the front of my chest. She scraped her nails over my abdomen, tormenting the flesh and leaving tiny pink trails in her wake. Those deft, cruel little fingers found the laces at the front of my trousers, tugging them open with fervor. I finished with her dress, moving my hand around her body to still her hand as it parted the fabric to slide into my pants.

"I want to take my time with you," I said, pulling out of her embrace. She cocked her head to the side as she looked me up and down, leaning back onto her hands so that she looked like a siren waiting on the rocks to bring me to my demise. Raising a single hand at the same moment she curled her legs up to point her knees toward the ceiling and cross her ankles delicately, she raised her dress to her thighs, revealing the expanse of her legs as she swept the fabric to the side and let it drape over the rock.

The dress slid down her left breast, the flesh puckering in spite of the warm, balmy air as she stared at me from beneath her lashes. I swallowed, shaking off the desire. The mating bond pulsed between us, her arousal meeting mine in the clash of a storm that felt tumultuous and chaotic.

"Are you sure about that?" Estrella asked, the smirk that played at her lips the only indication that she was aware of how she affected me. There was no question in that expression, no uncertainty in her gaze.

This woman knew she owned me, body and soul, and that she would retain possession of me for all eternity.

"My star . . ." I said, my voice trailing off with a groan as I closed the distance between us. I wrapped my hands around the backs of her calves, fingers splaying over the flesh and kneading it as I tugged on them until she lowered to lay herself flat over the rock. She spread her legs as I crawled over her, leaning into her space as she smiled up at me triumphantly. "What do you have against letting me take my time with you?" I dragged my nose up over the column of her throat as she arched beneath me, giving me better access to the most vulnerable part of her throat. Her other breast slid free of her dress and it bunched at her waist, revealing more of her smooth skin than I thought I could handle.

"We have an eternity to take our time," she whispered, reaching between our bodies to touch her fingers to the hollow of muscle at my hip. She slid them in a line over the curve there, moving slowly to the center until she found the fabric of my pants all over again. "For now, I just want you to fuck me."

She slid her hand into my fly to accentuate her words, wrapping her hand around my length and squeezing me. I groaned as I crashed my mouth into hers, swallowing her answering whimper and claiming it for myself. My hand found her breast, kneading the flesh as she arched up into me and worked my cock with slow rocks of her hand that threatened to steal every bit of my control.

I shoved my trousers down over my hips, cursing them when they caught at my knees. Estrella giggled into my mouth as I pulled away from her, maneuvering on the stone so that I could push them down the rest of my legs and tear them off. She took the opportunity to lift her ass up, pulling her dress down her thighs and tossing it to the stone beside her until she lay before me in all her glory.

She was Gods-damned beautiful, every inch of her skin taut with a mix of muscle and softness. The hollows in her body that had once existed as a consequence of her life in poverty had begun to fill, leaving her healthier as she smirked up at me. I reached into the pocket of my trousers, wrapping my hand around the short dagger that one of the Gorgon men had handed to me, explaining the final step to our hand-fasting. Estrella quirked her brow as she studied it, her gaze rising to mine. Her voice was all seduction and rasp when she spoke, her mouth forming the words as she laid herself flat against the rock again.

Her hand found her breast, gripping it and toying with her own nipple as I watched. She spread her legs slightly, giving me just a glimpse of the pleasure that waited for me there.

"So eager to be rid of me already, husband?" she asked, making everything within me clench. I set the knife on the stone by her feet, growling as I lowered myself into the waters of the lagoon. The warm water wrapped around me, going to my chest as the spark of pleasure tickled over my skin, elevating the arousal I already felt. Estrella studied my expression as I felt my eyes bleed to black, my own magic rising to meet the spark of Tartarus that existed within the waters.

I reached up, grabbing her by the feet and pulling them toward me. She sat up as I turned her, that hand that had tormented her breast moving to support her weight as I dragged her over the stone. It scraped at her skin, leaving it pink and irritated in a way that made me want to drag my tongue over it to soothe her, but I could not be bothered with gentleness as I shoved her feet apart and stepped

228

between them. My hands went to the inside of her thighs, grasping her and tugging her to the edge and positioning her right where I wanted her. Those dark eyes flashed with sparks of gold as she stared down at me.

"Do you still want me to rush this?" I asked, touching my mouth to the inside of her thigh. I kissed the sensitive, soft skin that met me, staring up at her as she sank her teeth into the inside of her cheek. She shook her head, spreading her legs wider as I grinned. "I thought as much."

I leaned in, inhaling the scent that I'd come to know as her and her alone. She smelled of darkness and earth, of the faint hint of a fire burning away on a summer's eve. Dragging my tongue through her folds, I let her wet heat envelop me as I groaned into her. Estrella sighed, wrapping her legs around my shoulders and placing her hands on the stone behind her to support herself as she watched me, that ember gaze burning where it touched. She rocked into me, fucking my face with her cunt as much as I used my tongue to drive her mad, tormenting her as her chest heaved.

I cupped a handful of the lagoon water in my palm, lifting it and letting it drip onto her thigh. She shuddered against me the moment it touched her, that magical sensation spreading through her. It was so similar to the way the tree of life had made me feel, a heightening of all the arousal we already felt for one another. I held her stare as I reached into the lagoon once again, pulling my mouth from her pussy in spite of her protest.

I grinned at her, my mouth wet with her arousal as I raised the water to above her body and watched the liquid pour down from my grip. It splashed against her pussy, coating her in the distinct sensation as she made a sound caught between a whimper and a scream. Those stunning eyes filled with molten gold, her hand reaching for me and grasping the hair at the back of my head.

She pulled me back to her cunt, making her desire very, very fucking clear. I dipped both hands into the water, wetting them before grabbing a breast in each palm. Her desperation drove higher, her writhing against the stone a thing of beauty as I slid my tongue inside her and fucked her like a man starved.

If I were ever to get to choose a last meal, if I were to die with her taste on my tongue, then I would step willingly into the abyss.

FORTY-THREE

ESTRELLA

I'd thought there would be an element of jealousy in sharing Caldris, in knowing that it wasn't only *me* in my body as he worked his tongue through me.

But the hand that gripped his hair was all mine, the thighs he buried himself between all me.

In accepting Aella as part of me, the two halves of me no longer existed. In becoming one, I could feel Caldris more firmly. I understood the bond better for accepting *her*, for she was the part of me that had access to the magics that were beyond Estrella. Where I'd only had glimpses of our bond before, the faint wisps of what Caldris felt, now I had it all.

Now I understood.

I tasted myself on his tongue, felt the deep satisfaction he gained from my pleasure. It coursed through him as it did me, reflecting back to me like the mirror. The growl that lurked in my moan of pleasure was all animal, all monstrous, as my hand tightened in his ashen silver hair, pulling him tighter to my body as my pleasure drove higher. Feeling what I did to him was the greatest aphrodisiac, far stronger than whatever magic lingered in this water, and I wanted the sense of his satisfaction when he brought me to orgasm. I wanted to return the favor, wanted to take him into my mouth and watch pleasure overtake him.

He growled into my pussy, the sound vibrating like a hum against my flesh as if he heard the thoughts in my head. But I knew he couldn't, not just yet, because his voice was a whisper on the wind, muffled by the bond we had yet to complete. I knew now what would come once he'd been inside me, once we joined together in the way the mate bond required.

The thought of hearing him in my head made me toss my head back, made me sink deeper into the way his tongue tortured my clit and worked it like the master he was. He knew my body as if he owned it, and I knew without a doubt now it was that it had been created for him.

Just as he had been created for me, long before I'd even come to be.

My orgasm lingered just out of my grasp, forcing me to bend forward and stare down at Caldris. He met my eye, smirking as he pushed back into my hand at the back of his head. The movement separated him from my core, drawing that wicked mouth away as he grasped me around the waist with a firm grip and dragged me over the stone. It scraped at my flesh, the bite of pain fading with a golden light that shimmered off my skin and lit the cove as Caldris guided me down. I sank into the water, the shimmering surface warming my insides as it surrounded me. The moment it reached the apex of my thighs, overwhelming, searing heat and desire flooded me, sinking into my belly as he lowered me until my feet touched the sand at the bottom of the pool. The water came to my chest, tickling the bottom of my breasts as I reached a hand between us to trail my fingers over Caldris's abdomen. His muscles retracted at my touch, twitching with a deep inhalation of breath. My nails trailed over the surface of his skin, tormenting him as that hand sank lower and lower into the water.

His eyes darkened as he stared down at me, the shadows in his gaze swirling around the blue of his irises. He stilled my touch with a hand on my wrist, the grip tighter than he had ever dared before. Not treating me like I was made of glass any longer, I realized, smirking up at him as he guided me down to where his length was hard as rock and curved up toward his stomach. He trailed the backs of my knuckles over him, controlling my touch when I wanted to take charge of the moment. I pressed closer, until my belly slid against our hands, and I felt the heat of his arousal against me.

He growled a warning, leaning forward to trail his nose up the side of my neck. He breathed deep, inhaling my scent in a way that was all feral and territorial. It raised the hair on my arms as I shivered, turning to smile at him in a move that made his gaze narrow in on the more pointed teeth at the corners of my mouth. A flicker of surprise crossed his face as he studied them, as if he could sense all the changes in me that weren't physical as well.

"You can play with me another time, min asteren," he murmured, the words soft against my skin. Another shiver wracked through my body, as if his voice reached deep into my soul and stroked it through my flesh.

He spun me to face the stone where I'd sat on the edge, leaving me with little choice but to raise my hands to catch myself against the rough surface. I stumbled forward a step, finding grooves in the stone and a ledge at the bottom. Caldris guided me up onto it, clearly having discovered it when he'd buried his face between my thighs. It accommodated some of the difference in height between us as I stepped up, letting my mate shove my legs apart slightly. Pressing into my rear, I felt the hard length of him against my lower back, his balls heavy against the swell of my ass.

"What if I want to play with you now?" I asked, my voice breathy. In another time, I would have been horrified by the want that was so blatant in my tone. I would have been appalled to give anyone enough power over me to know how desperately I wanted them. The human sense of shame would have interfered with that desire, but as I thought back to that girl now, I could find no trace of her. The human mentality about sex and sin was gone from me, leaving me to embrace the primal connection I felt to the male behind me.

Nothing we did together could be wrong.

"The next time you take me in your mouth, you'll be mine," Caldris said, lining himself up with my core. He stroked his length through the tight space between my thighs, rubbing himself through me slowly with gentle, teasing rocks of his hips. He stretched over my shoulder, taking the knife he'd deposited on the edge into his hand. He teased the edge of the blade over my arm, dragging it up to the side of my neck in a move that should have brought me fear. It should have given me that bitter tinge of distrust, of wondering if

I was about to be betrayed, but Caldris could never do such a thing to me. He loved me more than he loved himself, and I felt that love pulse down our nearly complete bond. "Until chaos reigns," he said, but there was a question in that touch of his knife at the side of my neck.

I didn't speak as I reached up, covering his left hand with mine. I guided the blade across the side of my neck where it met my shoulder, cutting deep into the flesh there so that my blood flowed in a slow, steady flow and slid down my breast. Taking the knife from his hand, I let the knowledge of the ancients fill me. Aella knew things Estrella did not, and she knew what the next step to this consummation would be. I brought it around the front as Caldris held his right hand out before me. I sliced the blade through his wrist at the exact moment that he entwined the fingers of his left hand with mine, wrenching it behind my back. He pinned my left arm there, his *viniculum* joining with mine.

Golden light flashed as I tossed the blade to the stone, guiding Caldris's wrist to my mouth. The taste of his blood coated my tongue, sweet and warm, in spite of the distinct reminder of winter that lingered at the back of my palate. His mouth dropped to my shoulder as he drew my blood into his mouth in the same way, bending his knees and angling his hips. He drove inside me without preamble, connecting us in more than just the physical.

Our *viniculum* pulsed, the white tendrils filling with the golden light of fate as Caldris's very being crashed into me. We collided at the center of our bond, our thoughts melding into one. I'd thought I'd known what it would be to be bonded in truth, thought I understood the implication of having another soul exist within the confines of my mind, but I hadn't had a clue.

Before, Caldris had ended where I began. Our threads had run as if in two segments of a line, meeting in the middle. In this, they intertwined, twisting around one another so fully they formed a knotted mess that would never be able to untangle. I did not know what was him and what was me, only recognizing the smooth glide of him through my flesh.

His pleasure blended with mine, as if we could feel both sides of our pleasure. I felt him draw back and then plunge forward, testing the new feeling of sex as a mated pair, but I also felt his immense completion. I felt what it was to be him, the tight, wet press of me as I parted for him and the vicelike grip of my pussy against his cock. I felt what it was to be both man and woman, and in the intensity of our first moments as a pair, I no longer knew who I was as an individual.

The power of the bond was all-encompassing, our pairing taking all that we were as people and making us somehow more as a collective.

"*Min asteren,*" his voice in my head was the same as if he'd spoken, but I felt it like a whisper against my mind, instead of a whisper against my skin. His mouth still pulled blood from my wound, drawing in deep gulps that only brought us closer.

"*Min oscura,*" I thought back. Whereas before, he may have questioned the choice to use the Old Tongue, he understood in the same way I did now. He understood that the Old Tongue was as much a part of me as the new. "*I see you now, my shadows.*"

"*A shadow cannot exist without his light,*" he thought, unpinning my arm. He kept our hands joined as he pulled his mouth from my neck finally, the wound healing as I released his wrist. With our bond complete, he continued to move inside me as he raised our arms so that I could see the shimmering gold of our *viniculum*. His lit with mine, a matching gold that glimmered off the surface of the water and illuminated the cave. I took my hand from his, watching and waiting for the moment that the magic faded from his Fae Marks, but it remained even without mine to touch his.

My magic was a part of him now, existing fully within the confines of his body as much as mine. Placing that hand on the stone beside the other, I leaned into it and bent forward, giving Caldris better access to my body as his hands dropped to my hips. He grasped them firmly, his fingertips pressing in to the point of bruising. I reveled in the roughness of it, loved every moment of the lack of control when he snapped his hips back and drove in hard.

Gone was any and all trace of gentleness, his body driving into mine with an uninhibited aggression that he couldn't have fucked me with before. He struck deep with each thrust, setting a punishing rhythm that he accentuated with a slow roll of his hips when he was fully sheathed inside me. "*Fuck,*" he groaned. "*I wanted to make love to you, not fuck you.*"

I pressed back into him, meeting him thrust for thrust as the water surrounding us splashed against the stone. "*Our love isn't gentle or kind. It's rough and all-consuming; it's a raging inferno that destroys the world in its wake.*" The words felt truer than I dared to admit as I thought them, feeling Caldris shudder behind me as they filled his head. The thread of our bond glowed with golden light, unbreakable with the force of a violent storm.

"I waited centuries for you. Waited centuries for this, and you still some-how manage to exceed every hope and dream I had." The words warmed me from the inside as he dropped a hand to my clit, stroking me as he fucked me. I wouldn't last long with both our pleasures swirling about as one, with that wicked finger working magic on my body while his cock worked inside.

"Caldris," I thought, tossing my head back to drape against his shoulder. He covered my throat with his left hand, and the searing pain of my *viniculum* spreading overwhelmed me. It was blinding, all-consuming as I felt Caldris's rise to match. He groaned through it, his cock twitching inside me as we both shattered over the edge of our orgasms in unison. He filled me, driving deep into me and pausing at the end as the Fae Marks worked over the front of our chests. The tendrils of black and gold combined into a swirling mass, forming an eight-pointed star just above my heart. It glowed with golden light at the center, shadows working through the light so that they formed one being.

My skin felt sensitive in the aftermath of the mark shifting, and Caldris drew me away from the wall to sink into the pool with him. The cool water was soothing against the wound as Caldris turned me to face him, touching his mouth to mine. It was the first kiss we'd shared since completion, the first time we shared breath, and I sank into the comfort of it.

The comfort of him. He shuddered as I ran my fingers over the new star on his chest, finding immense satisfaction in the added mark.

I was his star, and now his flesh was marked with the reminder of my ownership for the rest of his life.

Caldris was mine and mine alone.

FORTY-FOUR

NILA

Shadows pressed at the corners of the throne room, Mab's anger rising with every moment that passed. Caldris had not yet answered the summons she placed on him, and the men she'd sent to retrieve him had returned alone with hesitant apologies that he was nowhere to be found. I couldn't help the distinct feeling that he'd found a way to get to Estrella, that he'd managed to sneak past the daemons guarding the cove and dive into Tartarus. I knew he would stop at nothing to help his mate, and I hoped he'd managed to defy all odds to do it.

It might have been a small victory, one that came at the expense of those he'd left behind to face Mab's wrath in his absence, but it was only through those small victories that we would gain any kind of advantage against the Queen of Air and Darkness. For centuries, she had been a plague on this world. For centuries, I had forced myself to remain silent in the face of her wrath and kept out of sight and out of mind. I'd avoided her notice, done everything my father would have wanted of me after she took me from his home.

My father was dead, had been for more years than I could count now. The only tenuous connection I had to him had been through Rheaghan, the King my father had so greatly admired and been honored to serve as his adviser.

But she'd taken him, too, slaughtered him with no appreciation for the good man he was or the family lines that should have bound them together in love. I would have given anything to have my family back, to be reunited with my parents who had been taken far too soon. And yet there she stood, uncaring that she'd murdered her only remaining family in cold blood.

That she'd taken him from those of us who still loved him, and I wanted nothing more than to join him in the afterlife, to hope that I could be brave enough in my final moments for the father to grant me eternity in Valhalla after a lifetime of cowardice.

"Where is he?!" Mab screamed, her shrill voice lost to the depths of her madness. It echoed through the throne room as she paced at the top of her dais. The stone atop her crown pulsed with green light as if goading her on, contributing to the unhinged rage that would only worsen with time. No one knew who her mate had been or what had happened to him after Mab had managed to birth her heir, but the Queen had not fallen pregnant again after Fallon had vanished from her crib. In centuries of desperate preparations for the moment she could venture into the human realm beyond the Veil, she'd never attempted to replace Fallon with another child. Given her disdain for her own blood ties, it couldn't be due to any emotional attachment she felt for her daughter. She'd proven that theory in the time since Fallon returned from Nothrek.

Mab's mate was dead by her own hand, and the type of evil that took was incomprehensible. To lose a mate was to descend into madness slowly, to be the one who killed them . . .

If she felt no remorse for the life of her mate, for the other half of her soul, then the rest of us truly stood no chance of surviving her reign. Caldris and Estrella were our only hope, and now that she'd bound them both to her will, even that was a distant, impossible dream.

I pushed off the stone wall at my back, the red of my Fae Marks writhing like flames. They were as angry as I was, as deeply affected by the hole within me that would not fill again. Where I'd once felt the distant mark of another half within me, now there was just *nothing*. The secret we'd kept had been designed to protect me, to keep me safe from Mab's wrath.

Rheaghan believed in waiting out the evil that possessed his sister. He believed that his life could only truly begin once the stone was ripped from the top of her head.

Now he would never have the chance. He wouldn't be able to know what it was to hold his mate in his arms. He wouldn't know what it was to take me to our marriage bed. He wouldn't ever know the joy of children and watching them grow.

He'd never *live*.

I was determined to make it so that she didn't either.

A hand landed atop my arm, stopping me from taking the first steps to the dais where Mab had taken to marring the latest messenger to return with news of Caldris's absence.

"Where do you think you're going?" Eryx asked, holding me firmly. The messenger scurried off, retreating to the crowd at the back of the throne room as one of Mab's daemons stepped up to the foot of the dais. She glared down at him, descending the steps with haphazard steps. She moved as if she stumbled with each one, and it was as she lifted her dress out of her way that I realized she was barefoot upon the stone floor. Her hair was disheveled as she stepped beneath one of the torches hanging from the ceiling, pulled back into a braid that appeared as if she'd raked her hair through it. Stray strands of black stuck out from her head, deep circles etched into the lines of her too-beautiful face. I'd never seen her look so desperate, so lost.

"You let him escape!" she screamed, stretching her arm up as high as she could. She struck the daemon across the face, its figure unmoving in spite of the power I knew must have been in that slap.

"Nila, he wouldn't want this," Eryx said, making me turn my attention to him. His words were so similar to Dravenor's that for a brief moment, I felt the slick viscous coating of his blood on my hands all over again.

I didn't know how they *knew*, how they'd both seen through the deception that no one else seemed to spot. We'd been so careful, keeping our distance from one another. Never in the same room unless forced to be, never making eye contact or daring to look at one another when Mab forced us to be. He continued with his escapades and affairs, tearing my heart in two with every story that reached the Court of Shadows. It hurt even worse to know that he gave his body to others, that he shared it all while he hated himself for doing it, all because my father's final request had been that Rheaghan protect me in his absence.

He was not alone in the affairs, in the physical part of our deception that was agonizing. It was how I knew the pain he felt deep in his center with every person he took to his bed, because I felt the same every time I did the same. No mated pairs would bed another. No mated pairs would tolerate the scent of another on their loved one's skin.

Rheaghan bore it all to keep me safe, and somehow Eryx saw right through that to the pain tearing me in two.

"He did not suffer your absence all these years just to have you throw your life away now," Eryx whispered, not even looking at me as he said the words. It was too low for anyone else to hear, and his attention was so rapt on the scene playing out with Mab and the daemon that had knelt at her feet that none would suspect he spoke of anything but the scene before us.

"He did not pass, my Queen," the daemon said, his voice unnaturally deep and twisted into something dark and menacing.

"And what kind of life do I have? She won't just let me go now that he's dead. I'm her prisoner," I snapped, my throat tight with the burn of tears. Nothing in this life was worth having, not so long as Mab lived and breathed.

"As are we all," Eryx reminded me. He may have been free to return to the Autumn Court when Mab gave the go-ahead, but they just existed in a more distant cage. All who lived were condemned to this fate.

Even the humans in Nothrek were no longer safe from Mab's rule.

"Where is Twyla?!" Mab shouted, shoving the daemon back as she turned her attention to the group that had formed in the back. We all tried to hide from Mab's attention, but the Queen of Winter could not hide her bright, silver hair within the darkness of Tar Mesa. It was so like her son's, the silver more gleaming and bright than the dark-tinged silver that the God of the Dead possessed, but the similarities were undeniable in it. That was where the similarities stopped however, her skin brown where his was more golden. She stepped forward, a pale blue dress trailing behind her. She was all ice and sharp edges, poised and proper in the face of Mab's madness.

I couldn't shake the horror of the coming altercation. Of the centuries this moment had been in the making. Twyla's mate had been Mab's husband, but whereas any other Fae would release their spouse from the marriage bond, Mab had refused to allow Sephtis to be with his mate. They'd come together for one night, and that alone had been enough to conceive Caelum. It was a miracle where the witches' curse usually meant fertility struggles, and I'd believed that had been for a reason.

So many of us believed it was the Fates' hands twisting the threads to make it so, particularly when Caldris came into his power and revealed himself to be the only second-generation God in existence. That could not be for nothing, even if Mab had stolen him and bound him to her will.

"I am here, my Queen," Twyla said, curtsying to the other Queen in a show of respect she did not deserve. I remained back against the wall, letting Eryx's words offer me solace. I may not have been powerful, and I may not have had much to offer, but I could be there when Estrella emerged from Tartarus. I could offer her my assistance.

I could make my death mean something more than another frivolous casualty lost to Mab's rage.

"Where is your son?" Mab asked the Queen of Winter, refusing to pay her any sort of dignity in return. Her dark eyes were bottomless pits, glaring at the Queen who was all lightness and femininity.

"I do not know, Highness. I fear you greatly overestimate my closeness to my son. I am not his confidante, for I barely know him thanks to you," Twyla said, keeping her head bowed in respect. She couldn't give Mab the answers she wanted, and I knew that none who were here were people Caldris would have trusted. Even if he had, he would not have given them information that could be extracted from them. Not when so many were bound to Mab's will and the ones who were not were still able to suffer through her torments.

I was probably the last person she expected to have any information about his whereabouts, and yet I was the only one who could provide any sort of answers.

"Does it pain you to know that I raised your son as my own? That he has served as my weapon and I know him far better than you ever will?" Mab asked, a cruel smile lighting her face.

"And yet you still cannot find him now," Twyla said back, her voice deceptively calm in the face of the insult Mab paid her. They both knew that what Mab had done to Caldris could hardly be called raising him, that Twyla would have loved him with everything she had if he hadn't been taken from her. "If you know him so well, then where has he gone?"

Mab strode forward with quick steps, wrapping her hand around the front of the Winter Queen's throat. Her black nails dug into Twyla's skin as we watched in horror. Her eyes swirled with madness, Twyla's words bringing all of the monster to the surface. The challenge in them could not go unanswered, especially not when they'd come from the woman Mab already believed had stolen everything from her. Twyla had been her husband's mate. The woman who made their marriage into something Sephtis wanted desperately to escape. "He's gone after his little bitch of a fucking mate!" Mab yelled in the Winter Queen's face.

Twyla should have felt fear. She should have seen her death in Mab's eyes, but she didn't seem afraid of it. She raised her chin, arching her neck to give Mab a good angle as she smiled back at her.

"Then they are beyond your reach, and your own desperation for more power has brought your demise. If they are together in Tartarus, then you've already lost," the Queen of Winter said loudly enough for all in the throne room to hear her words. They were filled with knowledge that I did not share, as if her Lunar Witches had whispered the destinies of fate to her in all her years locked away in Catancia. It made me long to speak to Imelda once again, but the witch had vanished as soon as we'd failed to kill Mab—keeping hidden and out of sight to work in the shadows.

I had known, in the depths of my soul, that Estrella coming to Tar Mesa mattered. That her presence marked change, and that she was something more. Twyla's words confirmed it as Eryx shifted to meet my gaze, nodding as if he too read the words that Twyla did not speak.

"I will not lose to that sniveling child and your Godsforsaken son that should have never been born," Mab argued, her jaw clenching with her rage.

Mab's shadows twisted into a sword as she stepped back from Twyla, her movements slow and steady. Twyla had time to react and attempt to flee, but she stood with her head raised high as Mab paused, seeming to hesitate.

"I'll give my mate your greetings in Folkvangr," Twyla said. Her words were tangible, as if they could reach across the distance and stroke Mab's ire, stoking the flames of her madness. Mab screamed, the reminder of her husband and the woman he truly loved enough to send her spiraling over the edge.

Twyla wanted it—encouraged it even—despite the consequences she knew would come. She waited for her death . . . and the magic that would leave her as the Queen of Winter. The realization was a shock that nearly made me cry out, Twyla's intention to sacrifice herself for the greater good making my knees buckle. The magic of her court would spiral out into the world, seeking out the next body destined to contain it.

Seeking out her heir.

Mab's sword sliced through Twyla's neck.

Severing her head from her shoulders.

It fell to the steps of the dais at Mab's feet, rolling down in a mess of silver hair. It had twisted about to cover her face from view as her body toppled to the side, blood flowing freely to cover the steps. Her hand fell to the stone, the white snowflake covering her right palm fading from view. They dried like paint upon her skin, blowing off her in a harsh winter breeze as the Winter Court reclaimed what it had given. One of Mab's guards stepped up with his iron sword, angling it and shoving it down through the skull. It pierced the brain, leaving no doubt to Twyla's death.

No Fae, God or not, could survive an iron blade through the skull.

Mab was victorious as she cackled, tossing her head back with absolute joy that should have been reserved for children, but Eryx didn't allow her to have the peace of happiness for more than a moment.

"The Queen of Winter is dead," he said, his voice loud and ringing through the throne room as Mab's stare turned to him.

Her dark eyes widened as she realized what she'd done, what her rage had driven her to. She'd kept Twyla alive all these years for a reason, containing the magic of the Winter Court within her body and keeping it from Caldris. She shook her head, stepping back from Twyla's body as the shadows in her hand dissipated. She gazed out at the onlookers watching in the throne room, seeing the threat of her undoing in each and every one of us.

Eryx smirked at her when her stare turned back to him, as if she could feel the words he would speak. The condemnation that would come in them and the confirmation of everything she would lose.

"Long live the King."

Forty-Five

ESTRELLA

My mother and the other Gorgons had left the armor we'd both stripped off before our ceremony, and I eyed it with disdain as I finally forced myself to leave the blanket at the edge of the pool hours later. It was heavy in my hands when I lifted it from the rock, staring at it with all the hatred I felt for the situation. When we left this place, reality would press in again. The knowledge that I had to keep going through the trials and giving up pieces of myself to prove I was worthy of reaching the Cradle of Civilization.

I could turn back, return to the land of the living with Caldris at my side. We might stand a chance of fighting back now that we were both free from the influence of those snakes wrapped around our hearts—now that I wasn't limited by her ability to kill my mate with the clench of a fist.

I met Caldris's gaze as he stepped up before me, his brutal, handsome face soft as he gazed down at me.

"You have to keep going," he thought, sending his reassurance to

me in the moment I needed it. I knew he felt my guilt, the anger and pain I felt at leaving those we loved on the surface at Mab's mercy for even a moment longer, but there were answers in Tartarus that I was owed.

There were secrets that needed to be brought to light, and I knew there was only one person who could give me the answers to the questions that threatened to tear me in two.

Khaos had sworn those around me to secrecy, made it so only he could tell me why I was so different from my siblings. Why could I see the threads that Mab and Rheaghan could not, when they both shared the same father?

"What about the others?" I asked, warring with myself. *"Maybe I can return to Tartarus after Mab is dealt with."* Maybe we could free the Fae and then come and get the answers I needed.

"And risk needing to go through the trials all over again? You've already come so far, min asteren."

I chewed the inside of my lips, knowing he could hear the path my thoughts wandered. *"Medusa spoke of a weapon in the Cradle. She said it could help us,"* I admitted, even knowing that it would only encourage his belief that we should continue on. I didn't want to abandon the people trapped in Mab's clutches, but what if we weren't enough without it? What if returning without it would mean her death?

It would haunt me.

"Help us how?" he asked, his voice sounding cautious even in my head.

"She said it could cure Mab of the curse. It could return her to her natural state of being," I said, and even though I didn't dare to look at Caldris when I made the admission, I felt the weight of his gaze.

"You want to save her," he said, and while I'd expected judgment, there was only understanding. I felt nothing but warmth from him, in spite of all the harm Mab had caused him during his lifetime.

"She's a victim, too. Can you imagine what it's like to be trapped in your own body and not be in control of what you do with it? To murder and torture indiscriminately—even if it's not what you want? I'm not saying she's innocent. I know what she's done, but if there's a way to find out if there's any good left in her, then I think we need to take it. It's what Rheaghan would have wanted," I said, and that felt right. He'd given everything to be there for his sister and try to bring her back from the brink, and I felt like I needed to honor the brother I hadn't gotten to know.

"Even if all it does is make her easier to kill, I don't see how it could hurt

us," Caldris answered, nodding his head in agreement. *"But when the time comes, if she's beyond saving, I need you to promise me you won't hesitate. Our survival comes before hers."*

"*Our survival comes before hers,*" I agreed, and there was no hesitation in that. If it came down to us or her, I would always choose us.

I thought of the male I'd seen in the trials, the one who stared down at me from his throne while he forced me to perform, to prove my worth. It had to be sacrilege to think that the being who was responsible for the creation of the world was incapable of feeling, but I couldn't help but wonder if asking him to help was a more difficult task than asking Mab to stop killing.

We could only do what we were capable of, and a creature who was not capable of empathy would have no mercy to offer. Expecting him to help was a dream that would never come to fruition.

In this, we were alone.

But I nodded anyway, hating the way his brow furrowed with my thoughts. While I loved that I didn't need to try to explain my feelings to him any longer, that I didn't need to find the words to make them make sense to another being, I wished I could shelter him from the hard truth I already knew.

I stepped into my leggings, pulling the moldable fabric up my legs. It clung to my skin in the humid air of the cove, but I forced my way into the matching undershirt that donned me in black. Caldris dressed in his own trousers and tunic far more quickly than I did, given his weren't nearly as tight. He was the one to raise my armor from the stone, stepping forward to hold it out. I slid both arms in, turning to give him my back so that he could fasten the latches that ascended my spine. I ran a finger over the golden snake embroidered into the faint green scales of armor, the meaning of it having a far deeper effect on me than it had when the Morrigan first gifted it to me.

It was a symbol of my mother, of the parent that seemed to love me even though she'd been deprived of centuries with me. She wanted nothing more than for me to find my truth and reach my full potential, but I felt a kinship with her that I didn't think I would ever have with Khaos. Caldris's fingers skimmed over the bare skin at the top of my spine, the touch a gentle tease that made me wish for nothing more than to stay hidden away in the caves and live out our lives in peace here. He touched his lips to the tips of my ears, his breath soft and warm as if he understood the urge.

For once, I wished we could put ourselves first.

But neither my mate or I had that in us. Neither of us was capable of leaving those to suffer at Mab's hands and hiding away in this place.

Belladonna slithered up my leg, winding her way around my torso until she came to rest around my shoulder and bicep. She blinked at me, her pretty eyes holding mine for a moment before she closed them. Her entire body turned to a deep amethyst crystal as she hardened, her body shimmering in the dim lighting. She looked like a piece of jewelry rather than a familiar, hidden from prying eyes that might not expect her to be a living thing. I ran a finger over her, the crystalline surface unnaturally warm for stone.

"We have to go," I said aloud as I petted her, my voice far too weak sounding for the strength I felt physically. I'd thought I understood what it was to be strong, but the simple joining of my soul with Caldris's was enough to make me feel invincible.

"I know," Caldris answered, latching the final hook on my armor. He stepped around me, shoving his own on as I forced my feet into my boots.

He stilled suddenly, stretching his fingers out with a pained gasp. I felt the pain in my own palm rise in response as I stepped toward him, following his gaze to where he stared down at his hand in surprised horror. A white circle spread from the center of his palm, extending out into the shape of the points of a snowflake. It wasn't the same white that had been on his *viniculum* before it shifted to gold, but the kind that I expected to feel like ice when I touched a trembling finger to it.

"What is that?" I asked, cradling his hand in my own.

He stared down at it, not raising his eye to meet mine as I sifted through his thoughts. The knowledge of it settled in my gut, striking me like a punch.

Twyla was dead. Caldris gritted his teeth through the pain that followed, stumbling back as a winter breeze tore through the cavern. It bypassed me entirely, striking him straight in the chest. His blue eyes glowed white for a moment, magic settling in his body as I stared around at the swaying threads. The silver crown atop his head flowed with ice, turning from that metallic gleam to the sheer form of frozen icicles.

With his mother's death, Caldris had become the King of the Winter Court. The air around us was the shimmering light of the cavern, but the swirling vortex that surrounded him was all cold and ice. It came in a torrent of a storm, separating us and pressing in closer to his body as it tried to encase him in the eye. I could still see him through it, see the cool determination and blank expression on his face in the gaps between icicles as they formed, touching to his skin and hanging from his body like the melting waters rushing off a roof. They clung to him, hanging from his brow and his ears, from his forearms where they hung at his sides. The golden tone of his skin cooled slightly under the weight of that ice, paling as it spread across him in a thin layer. His lips turned blue as crystalline patterns of ice closed over his mouth, sealing off a final puff of warm breath in the too-cold air. The pool behind him froze over, white flakes of ice spreading from the shore to cross over the surface. The creatures living within froze in place, movement ceasing as the magic of the Winter Court found a new body to settle into.

I reached for him, snapping my hand back as the bitter cold burned my skin. The winds stopped as suddenly as they'd come, vanishing from Caldris as he inhaled another breath. The ice retreated from his skin far more slowly than it had taken him over, a single inhalation of breath warming his skin back to the golden hue I recognized. Warmth returned to his features as the snow left him, but his eyes were pure ice as he stared at me.

He crossed the gap between us, cupping my cheek in a hand that I half expected to give me frostbite. Instead, his warmth sank into me, leaving me to lean into the touch as I looked up at him. His thumb skimmed over the top of my cheekbone where it met my temple, and then he raised that touch along the curve of my hairline. He leaned down, touching his mouth to the top of my head as cold bloomed atop my hair. A snowflake spread from the point of contact, the feeling of the tiny pieces where they protruded from the center strange against my skin. More followed as Caldris twisted me to stare down at my reflection in the pool in front of us as it thawed, watching as they formed a headband across the top of my head.

My mate pulled the length of my hair into his hands, sweeping it back over my shoulders. Deft fingers worked to fix it into a braid, the gentle ease of the touch feeling just as much about his comfort as mine.

"It's beautiful," I said, my voice a soft murmur. I didn't know what to say to offer my condolences for the woman who had given him life, his own feelings more muted than I would have expected. He couldn't tuck them away and hide them from me completely, not with the fresh bond pulsing between us, but he did what he could to shield me from his pain.

"I had a feeling you would hit me if I fashioned you a crown fit for my Queen," he said, his mouth dropping down to my shoulder. I shuddered from the intimate contact even as everything else in me tightened. I hadn't stopped to think about the implications for Caldris becoming the King, hadn't even allowed myself to think past what waited for me in the rest of Tartarus.

If we managed to deal with Mab, if we managed to free the Fae trapped under her rule, that meant Caldris had a duty to the people of the Winter Court.

And as his mate, my duty was to be at his side.

So much for my quiet life.

"We don't need to think about that right now. We can't do anything to help the Winter Court in this moment, so you should take the time you need to gather your thoughts. Take the time to let yourself feel her loss," I said, forcing my anxiety over the future to the side so that I could focus on what Caldris needed if he would just stop being too stubborn to acknowledge it. I turned to face him as he finished with my braid, reaching up to cup his face in my hand that was far warmer than his skin. "You need to grieve."

"I barely knew her," he said, dismissing the sympathy with a shrug of his shoulders. He stepped past me, giving me his back as he retracted the magic of winter from the pool. The water unfroze, the ice melting until the fairies and serpents located within it moved freely once more, steam rising off the water in the wake of his winter.

"That doesn't mean you don't get to grieve her. She was your mother, and the ability to have a relationship with her was taken from you when you were so young. You're allowed to grieve the knowledge that you will never have the chance to repair that bond now. Even if you aren't grieving for what you lost, you still have the right to grieve for what will never be," I said, wrapping him in my arms. I held him firm, waiting for his tense body to soften and hug me back.

When he finally did, it was with a deep sigh of regret that I felt in every muscle of my body. His chin rested atop my head, his body going pliant as we stood there, and Caldris finally let himself feel the weight of the world on his shoulders.

We needed to go, but we took a few minutes alone to grieve together, for what might have been before and could have been in the future.

FORTY-SIX

ESTRELLA

The journey out of the caverns took far longer than the descent. There was no drop into the pools to rush the process, only the climbing of hundreds of crudely carved steps. As we approached the surface, the oppressive dry heat of Tartarus drifted down the tunnels to reach us, chasing away the humidity of the caverns. The coolness of the stone surrounding us slid away, replaced by scorching heat and fires that I knew waited just outside the sanctuary the Gorgons had called home.

Caldris led the way, stepping out into the blinding light beyond as I turned to look back at the majority of my mother's people. Of the family I hadn't been allowed to have, that would potentially always feel like strangers to me now. Another thing that had been robbed of me in my lifetimes cursed to a human existence, rather than the eternal one I'd been meant for.

Medusa followed at my back as I finally followed my mate into the light, blinking back against the red heat and light that felt unbearable to my eyes that had adjusted to the darkness. A figure crashed into my side, knocking me to the ground as a wet, canine tongue lapped at my cheek. Fenrir stunk of whatever meal he'd devoured while we'd been tucked safely away, but I couldn't bring myself to be angry with the familiar when I too craved his presence.

"You are almost who you were born to be," he thought, that deep voice echoing in my head. I watched Caldris snuggle into the two other wolves of the Cwn Annwn, smiling at the sight of my mate and his affection for the creatures.

"Almost?" I asked with a nervous swallow, but I knew better than to hope for an answer. As forthcoming as Fenrir was in some moments, there were others where he was as cryptic as the rest. The very notion that after everything I'd endured, I still had further to walk on my path of changes was horrifying.

"We kept him safe for you all these years, Child of Chaos, so that you may find yourselves united as one in this very moment." Fenrir's voice came as a deep growl in my head, his attention fixed on my face as he lingered over me. Instead of feeling suffocated by the cage his size might have created, I felt nothing but a sense of absolute safety.

He was both my weapon and my armor, the shield that would stand between myself and the dangers lurking in the depths. I reached up a hand, smoothing it through the silky fur of his coat at his neck. My hand came away wet with blood, a reminder of the meal he and the others had probably indulged in when they no longer had to worry about protecting me from all the things that went bump in the night.

"Didn't you bond to Caldris because of your bond with his father?" I asked him, wiping the blood from my hand against the leather of my armor. No matter how safe I felt with him, no matter how much I wanted to believe this massive creature was a docile house pet, there was the constant reminder of his capabilities. Of the violence that could consume him at a moment's notice.

His eyes burned a little darker as he felt that realization make me swallow, his nose nudging mine playfully as Caldris stepped up beside us. I was certain he heard my conversation with Fenrir through my own thoughts, heard it play out in his own mind that was simply an extension of mine now with the bond pulsating so brightly.

Fenrir shifted, nudging the thread of my and my mate's bond with his snout in a move that told me he too could see the threads that had so quickly come to define my life and my very existence.

"Why else would I abandon my bond with Khaos to protect a God?" Fenrir thought, his eyes shifting to look at Caldris midway. He knew

my mate could hear him through me, knew he could communicate with the male that he'd looked after since childhood. For the first time, what had once been Caldris's companion could speak into his mind.

Caldris reached out a hand to stroke Fenrir's face, the wolf leaning into the touch.

"Whatever the reason, I have been honored to have you at my side," Caldris said to the wolf, the moment of affection making everything inside of me tighten and then swell. My heart felt too big for my chest, the realization that my family was growing by the day something so unfamiliar to me that I didn't know how to cope.

Fenrir moved finally, allowing me to push to my feet. The sands beneath my boots felt unsteady compared to the firmness of the rocks within the caves, the muscles in my legs tightening ever so slightly. My body felt not its own, like it was battered and bruised, like it would never recover from the way it had changed so many fucking times in such a short period.

I was human, but not. I was Fae, but not. I was an odd jumble of contradictions that couldn't seem to settle. My skin tingled as I stepped away from the caves, drawn to the bright light shining in the distance as I peered over the top of the entryway.

Making my way up the bank, I clawed my hands into the sand to support my body as I fought against the loose grains that wanted to send me spiraling back into the ravine below. Caldris and Fenrir watched me climb, waiting in stillness as Medusa followed after me. I felt her at my side, ascending along with me even though I suspected she already knew what I might find.

Water poured out the other side of the caves, a steady streaming waterfall that rushed into an enormous lake in the middle of Tartarus. Something moved beneath the surface of the water in the distance, the shadow of it in the turquoise waters dark and larger than anything I'd ever seen. There were massive rocks carved into the cliffs at the side of the lake, altars where the glint of iron chains strapped moving bodies down and held them still.

Blood poured off the rocks in steady rivulets, bleeding down into the lake and staining that turquoise water with red.

"What is this place?" I asked, my voice a hushed whisper. I was used to the violence of Tartarus, to the endless suffering that existed in all the plains I had encountered. This punishment felt more real and raw than most of what Khaos exacted; it felt more personal.

"When your father asked me to move to Tartarus with him, to

bring my people to a place that was so defined by suffering and pain, I only had one requirement," Medusa said, reaching over to take my hand in hers. She guided me forward, leaving the ravine behind us as Caldris and the wolves began the ascent to follow in our wake. "I wanted a place that was all mine. A little corner of endless suffering where I could do whatever I wanted to the people who had hurt those I loved. To the very people who were responsible for my suffering." She guided me toward one of the rocks, looming just out of reach as we watched the figure of a male writhing on the stone. His innards had been torn from his body, draped over the stone. Even still, he breathed, staring off into the distance with eyes that had long since gone foggy with suffering. She closed the distance finally, bringing me closer until I stared down at the male.

He didn't respond to our presence, and Medusa reached into his torn-open stomach and wrapped her hands around flesh that made squelching sounds. She watched his face for a reaction, only removing her bloodstained hand when she did not get one.

"I was young when Pathos found me in the temple where I served my Goddess. Far too young when he took what was not his on her sacred ground. Definitely far too young for her to turn me into a Gorgon in punishment for tempting a God the way I had. All that I asked of your father was a place where men like him could suffer for eternity, but even Khaos could not grant me that. His mind has been broken for far longer than I care to admit, and yet I cannot bring myself to free him from his fate. I will not grant him the peace of the afterlife," she said, reaching down into the waters of the lake. She let it wash the blood from her skin and then stood, making her way to the stone that waited nearby. It was only close enough to see the body writhing on it, to hear the shrill, high screams of agony. "That is my choice, and it is one that I made long, long ago. And now it is time for you to make yours."

I followed after her, swallowing back my apprehension as we approached. "Is this part of my trials?" I asked, hating the familiar sight that greeted me. To have him thrown in my face once again for the purposes of testing me was a cruel punishment. Mussed salt-and-pepper hair was a tattered mess on the male's head, his form far thinner than I could ever remember it being. I'd been too aware of every curve of his body, of every flimsy, privileged muscle when it flexed as he forced me to watch him with the ladies of the night.

Byron lay strapped to the stone, the iron of his chains an unnecessary detail. He'd been human, a pitiful one at that in his life before Caldris ran him through and rid us of his presence.

I'd thought he would move on to reincarnate into his next life, but instead he'd come here. Come to suffer.

"No, this is not a part of your trials. This is your father's way of apologizing for all this man forced you to endure. This is a gift for you to do with as you please," Medusa said. She stopped me with a hand at my chest, keeping me from approaching him as the enormous shadow within the water approached his stone. It burst through the surface with a splash that would rival a tidal wave, sending buckets of water splashing over Byron's form. He screamed anew as the water sank into his open and gaping wounds, washing the stone clean as the creature stared down at him.

It was beautiful, covered in soft, iridescent pearly scales. It had two webbed wings that reminded me of a bat, and it fanned them out to the side before using them to push more water onto Byron's form. Its eyes glowed with turquoise light that reflected off the water. A thing of great and absolute beauty, the last thing I expected as it rose up from the water was for it to show pure brutality.

So when it struck forward and trapped Byron's leg within its gaping mouth, digging jagged, razor-like teeth into his flesh, all I could do was watch as it tore chunks of flesh from the bone. The sea serpent retreated back into the lake once more, disappearing from view as fresh blood pumped from Byron's wounds.

There'd been a time when all I wanted was my freedom. When I didn't care what happened to Byron so long as he no longer had the ability to torment me, but in the changes that had come over the last weeks since I'd escaped, I found I no longer had the maturity to be above watching him suffer.

His pain brought me peace. His suffering filled a karmic void that I hadn't known existed within me. Maybe it was Aella that I had embraced, maybe it was her bloodthirstiness that I hadn't wanted to acknowledge before, constantly trying to convince myself that I was above the brutality I'd seen in others.

But I wasn't. I was willing to sink to the depths of Hel if it meant I would get to bear witness to the suffering of those who had harmed me. My self-righteousness had been a lie, a deception to make me feel better about the monster hiding within me.

"What will you choose, daughter?" Medusa asked, staying behind when I took my first steps to close the gap between Byron and me. I paused at his side, waiting for his eyes to open. He'd squeezed them closed in pain, his fingers clenched into a fist at his side as if he wanted nothing more than to put pressure on his own wound.

I gave him what he sought, lifting myself onto the stone beside him and being careful not to touch him. His mouth stumbled as he gaped for air, mumbling beneath his breath.

"Please," he said, his throat dry in spite of the water that surrounded him. This close to the lake, the brine of salt assaulted my senses. Water that could not be drunk. Water that would make the sting of pain worse with every torrent the sea serpent poured onto Medusa's victims.

His eyes flung open when my hands went to the cloth covering his waist, the scraps of what had once been pants all that kept his manhood from the open air. I knew the moment he recognized me staring down at him, that flare of recognition in his gaze.

"Estrella," he wheezed, his mouth curving into the faintest of smiles. Believing the kindness and love he'd seen in me as a child would translate to all who were in need of help, when I wanted nothing more than to make sure he suffered for all he'd done. For all he'd hurt.

I reached into the fabric and grasped his length in my hand, ignoring Caldris's growl at my side. He may not have liked the situation, but his thoughts in my mind were a reassurance that he was willing to allow me this moment. To allow me to bring this pain, even though touching him made nausea swirl in my gut.

Byron's eyes widened as I dug my nails into him, making sure to cup him fully. "Is this how you imagined it? All those nights you pictured your future with me in your bed?" I asked, leaning forward to press my free hand into the wound in his abdomen. His guts were soft and pliant as I forced my hand to navigate through the gaps between them, digging deeper and deeper still and reveling in his gasps of pain. I angled my arm up, searching for the hollow where I felt certain his heart should have been. There was no possible way that the man capable of such evil even possessed one, no way that he could have a beating heart and not care for the suffering he caused.

But it beat within his chest, thrumming against my fingers in a fast rhythm as I angled up behind his ribs.

"I'll be honest, this is far better than anything I have ever dared to dream of for you," I said, sliding my hand back through his torso. I removed it just before I let my vision fill with thoughts of stone, with thoughts of rock so hard it would break into a million pieces and never recover. My hand pulsed with the cool, damp feeling of rock, reminding me of caves and darkness. Byron's scream was one of pure agony as the limp flesh in my hand hardened, turning to stone. He watched it, peering down over the tattered mess of his body to find the stone that had once been his cock. "The pain you feel now is nothing compared to what you did to me. To the agony I felt every time you touched me and promised to do more. I was a child," I hissed, wishing more than anything that I could reach inside of him and bring him the internal turmoil, the internal agony that came with such a violation.

That I could make his physical pain transcend into the pain of the soul that never went away. There was no healing.

"I intended to make you my wife!" he argued, grunting through the pain.

"And that would have been a fate worse than death. Just like this," I snapped, standing from his altar. I stood beside his stone, drawing one of my swords from the scabbard strapped across my back. It felt heavy in my hand as he writhed on the table, desperately attempting to escape the iron that I grasped in my palm. I adjusted my grip slowly, pulling the curved sword back before I sliced it through the air and tore through the skin at the base of his shaft. The stone fell heavy to the rock where he would linger forever, and I grasped it with my free hand. Guiding it to his face, I sheathed my sword once more and gripped his aging face between my thumb and forefinger, pressing into his cheeks and wedging my fingers between his teeth until he opened his mouth.

I shoved the stone into his open mouth, pushing it deeper and deeper until he gagged. Only then did I close his lips around it, pressing my palm to his mouth and holding it closed as I thought of stone once more.

The rock spread out from under my hand, closing his mouth permanently as it turned to stone. Never again would he hurl violent words. Never again would he give commands that resulted in the end of someone's life.

Never again would he be graced with the outlet of screaming to numb his pain, forced to suffer in silence the way all his victims had.

I turned away from him suddenly as the sea serpent broke through the surface of the water once more. Climbing onto the foot of the rock, I brought myself to stare back at him. "Estrella, get back!" Caldris snapped, the order making me wonder if I should feel fear as I stared at the brutally beautiful creature.

But I didn't as I met its turquoise stare. The sea serpent came closer, bringing its face only a breath from mine. That tongue snaked out, dragging over my cheek and the tears I hadn't realized I'd shed in my moments of violence before the serpent snuggled into my neck. I moved to pull my short sword free once again, moving cautiously so I wouldn't make the serpent fear me. It held perfectly still as I dug the tip into my forefinger, resulting in a single bead of blood that welled.

Touching that to the serpent's forehead, I held that touch as the serpent's eyes drifted closed. They flashed with gold when they opened, the color fading slowly as I held its stare.

"Make sure he suffers," I whispered, watching as the creature nodded its head once. It retreated into the depths as I climbed down off the rock.

The sound of splashing water reached my ears as I strode away, leaving my past behind.

I no longer had any use for it.

FORTY-SEVEN

CALDRIS

Estrella was quiet as we made our way toward the river Lethe, but her thoughts moved so quickly in a torrent of violence that I couldn't even hope to follow. It came as a comfort, seeing so deeply into the chaos of her mind in those moments when she was quiet. When she retreated into herself, I no longer had to struggle with the distance that it created between the two of us. I no longer had to wonder if she was angry with me or what might be going through her mind. Because even if I couldn't understand the deluge of thoughts that flitted from one subject to another more quickly than I thought humanly possible, I could feel the intentions in them and the emotions that motivated them.

My star was not angry or upset with me, and she squeezed my hand back as I slid my palm against hers and intertwined our fingers together. The emotion that surged through her was one of warmth to contradict the confusion of her thoughts. The jumbled mess that she'd become as she tried to reconcile the person she thought herself to be with the person she had shown at that lake hours before.

Her violence should have shocked her. It should have reminded her that she too was capable of terrible things, but instead all it did was remind her that eventually, those who deserved it finally received their justice.

Even if it meant that one day, such a fate may await all of us. Power was fleeting, drifting through the air like snow on the wind. Who was to say there would not one day come a time when she was not in control of Byron's suffering in Tartarus? Perhaps there would come a day when Mab ruled this place, too, and found a way to torture us even after our deaths.

I refused to believe it, refused to believe that the Primordials who hid here would allow her to infiltrate the home they'd chosen after they'd retreated and abandoned their own children.

But there was no telling what the Primordials, who were willing to abandon their own children, were capable of. It depended entirely on what suited them in the moment, and Mab would undoubtedly attempt to convince them that she was the strongest ally.

"*Caldris*," Holt's low, cautious voice hissed, the sound penetrating my thoughts so suddenly that I stumbled over my own feet.

Estrella spun to look at me, hearing it through the bond that pulsed with golden light between us. Her thoughts stilled immediately, the silence in their absence jarring as she studied my face. I stared down at her, my hand tightening around hers in an attempt to reassure her.

"*You have to come back. You've been in Tartarus too long to be safe, and Mab is on a warpath now that she knows you're gone.*"

His voice faded off with the muffled sound of footsteps in the silence. Estrella's eyes turned glassy as she spun away from me, hiding the emotion that came with the thought of being away from me. To be separated so soon after we completed our bond would be the greatest of tortures, and I could not bear the thought of leaving her behind at all, let alone so soon.

"It doesn't matter," I argued, even as my jaw clenched with the knowledge that I would be forced to leave people at Mab's mercy.

"Of course it matters! There are people we love there. What of Holt and Imelda? What of Fallon?" she asked, shaking her head.

I sighed, cupping her cheek in my hand and turning her attention back to me. In the distance, a raven flew above our heads, swooping toward the ground and finally bursting into the three women of the

Morrigan. Badb tapped her fingers against her thigh impatiently, eager to reach the next river in our journey.

"We do not have the time to dally," Macha echoed.

"Of course they matter. You know that is not what I meant," I said, sighing and forcing myself to ignore the intrusion of the Morrigan chiming their thoughts about the pause they could not understand. The conversation that had happened entirely within my head did not extend to those around us. "But what am I to accomplish by returning now? If I return without you, I will only put myself at risk. We're stronger when we are together, and we will need everything we have to fight Mab in any meaningful way. If I die, you die, and all hope is lost, min asteren. Having me there may be a temporary bandage for a gaping wound that will not heal on its own. Having us there together may at least give us the ability to cauterize it."

"But now you have the power of the Winter Court, and you're no longer under Mab's thrall. Maybe you could buy them some time until I can return," she argued, hating the thought that people were dying because of our actions. That my coming to Tartarus to help her had been disastrous for so many.

"What do you think she'll do when she realizes that she can no longer kill me at a moment's notice, min asteren? She will do whatever it takes to eliminate any threat I might pose. I hate it, too, trust that, but the lives lost now will be a fraction of those that are lost if she kills me before we have a real chance together," I said, hating the way she deflated. It was the reality, and we both knew our best chances of winning this war were by playing the long game and not allowing Mab's tantrum to influence our decisions.

"Okay, min oscura." She sighed, nodding and leaning her head forward until it touched my chest. She knew as well as I did that sometimes there would be sacrifices to be made in war. We wouldn't be able to save everyone from the wrath of the Queen of Air and Darkness, but Estrella had never been forced to live through the reality of war before. She'd never had to be the one making choices, all the while knowing that it was other people who would likely pay the consequences for them.

There was a reason those who had power, and respected that power for what it was, didn't want to keep it forever. There was a reason Kings and Queens who lived forever would one day pass on their rule to their heirs—a reason the Primordials had retreated from our world and given it to their children.

Nobody should bear the weight of that responsibility forever.

Estrella collected herself slowly, turning to continue on the path to the river. She walked at my side with her mother just behind us, the three wolves of the Cwn Annwn surrounding us and keeping us safe from any creature who might think us an easy snack in this treacherous place.

Together, we were formidable. Together, we would be enough.

Forty-Eight

ESTRELLA

The Morrigan quickened their pace as the sight of enormous, winding, and sprawling trees grew in the distance. We'd been walking for hours, making our way toward the next trial that would pull me beneath the surface to face a challenge that seemed to have no purpose.

"What will be expected of her here?" Caldris asked, and I turned my head to look up at him. His jaw was set tightly, squared and tense as he studied the three women who exchanged a look.

"That we cannot say," Macha said, pursing her lips that matched the red of her eyes. They glinted in the firelight, almost as if they were coated with the sheen of fresh blood. "The trials themselves change with each attempt. The Primordials and the Fates alter them as they see fit depending on the challenger."

"That sounds like the perfect way for corruption to be the ultimate deciding factor on who survives these trials," I muttered, hating the bitterness I felt for it. I didn't want to feel like I survived because of favoritism, but I also couldn't fight the feeling that perhaps my trials were on the opposite end of the spectrum.

Maybe I was the one who was being set up for death, the one who wasn't meant to survive this place. But I'd come too far, been through too much to accept the notion that the Fates had decided to just kill me off so stupidly, so without fucking purpose.

To die in this place was to be forgotten, to simply cease to exist and I refused to accept that.

If my time came, I would die in a blaze of glory and do everything in my power to take my enemies down with me. That meant I needed to escape the pit of Tartarus.

That meant I needed to survive whatever they put forth for me.

"What power does the Lethe contain?" I asked, knowing that was at least a question they could answer. I may not be able to know what awaited me in the river as we approached, the red sand beneath my feet quickly giving way to a sprawling and luscious grass. Moss coated the trunks of the trees as we strolled through them, curving our path to accommodate the plants that reached for the sky where it disappeared into nothingness. Light shone through the canopy their leaves provided, reflecting off the surface of the too-still water.

"It is known as the river of oblivion," Badb answered, bending down at the water's edge. She touched a single finger to the surface, and I watched in abject fascination as clouds of white drifted off from her fingers. They swirled through the water, the movements serpentine as it drifted away from her. She pulled her finger back, holding it above the surface and allowing us to watch as those tendrils rose and slithered along her skin until they faded back into her body like she absorbed them. "It will make you forget everything you know. Everything you are."

"How am I supposed to prove my worth if I don't even know who I am?" I asked, studying the way Caldris wandered closer to the river. He didn't touch it, simply staring at it in a daze. I watched as the surface rippled in small areas, like footprints appearing on the surface of the water as they came downstream. I blinked, squeezing Caldris's hand in my own and trying to pull him back.

He stumbled into me, blinking back confusion as he sighed. Following his gaze back to the river, we watched figures form on the surface. They were bathed in white, sheer cloths covering them from head to toe but there was no mistaking the humanoid form to them.

"What are they?" I asked as Medusa stepped forward, positioning herself between Caldris and the river—interfering should he choose to succumb to the eerie temptation the river presented.

"The memories of those who lost themselves to this river. They were never reunited with the physical form they belonged to, so they take on a half-life of their own. Tied to this place, and unable to move on," Macha answered. "Not all of them underwent the trials, some unfortunate souls have simply wandered too close and lost themselves. You are less susceptible since you have a physical form in this plane. Your mate, however . . ."

That explained the fuzzy look in Caldris's eyes, the distinct lack of his usually commanding presence. It was as if someone had watered him down, stripped out the power and personality that made him so *him*.

How could I wander into the river and leave him here, knowing he was susceptible to a fate so cruel?

"I'll look after him, Estrella," Medusa said, her green, serpentine eyes clear and uninfluenced by the power of the river. This place had been her home for so long, I wondered if the magic had any effect on her anymore. "I won't let anything happen to him in your absence. You can trust me to keep him safe, and I hope that gives you the strength to focus on your task."

"Can I focus on it at all though? I won't even remember that it's a trial, will I?" I asked, looking to the Morrigan for clarification.

"No, you will not remember why you have entered the river. According to those who have survived, you won't remember you're in a river at all. You will have to sort through what you are told to be truth for yourself, and I believe the aim will be for you to demonstrate who you are without your formative memories. Who you are at the very core of your being. Some may say that nothing is born good or evil, that life determines those things through circumstances and experiences, the Fates believe differently. They believe that one experience can alter two unique people in such profoundly different ways, changing one for the better and altering the other for the worst," Medusa explained, speaking far more freely than the Morrigan could. She reached out and brushed a stray hair behind my ear with the affection of a mother, and the intimacy of the moment reminded me of everything we'd been deprived of. All those moments we hadn't been allowed to have.

Formative moments.

"You will have to show them whether you are good or bad beneath your human desires. Without the emotions and relationships that have formed you as a human, who will you be if you become immortal?" she asked, the knowing look on her face making everything in me still. I was already not quite human but always partially human, but the way she said those words filled me with apprehension.

I had no desire to lose all traces of what made me human, to become as cold and calculating as I'd seen in so many Fae who were desensitized to the emotion that defined me as a person.

Still, I gave Caldris's hand one last squeeze and pulled free from his hold. Stepping up to the river, I stared down into the still abyss, attempting to see through the foggy waters to the bottom. My steps were slow and calculated, a complete shudder wracking my body as I watched the white swirls of memory spiral away from my body. They spread through the river as I forced myself to sink deeper, my mind a whirl of emotions as I searched for what I had already lost. I looked for gaps in my memory, holes that were not filled where they once had been. I couldn't even detect them, couldn't find what they surrounded to piece it all together. I strode into the river until all but my head was submerged, watching memories slowly fade away.

A woman stood at the edge of the riverbank, serpents writhing where hair should have been. I recoiled, stumbling back farther into the river until my chin sank into the warmth of it. It was preferable to the sadness in her green gaze as she watched me, far more comforting than the blank stare on the handsome, formidable male where he lingered behind the woman.

It was definitely preferable to the three other women lurking off to the side with eerie eyes, or the massive wolves lingering behind all of them.

I sank deeper, letting the water consume me. Letting it surround me. White wisps floated around me, like a veil swaying in the wind. I sank lower, leaving the surface high above me as I followed those tendrils as they sank to the bottom of the river.

Until I knew nothing at all.

The forest surrounding me was lush and vibrant, with trees so large they felt like they touched the sky. A rabbit hopped through the underbrush, the rustling of the dried leaves snapping my attention to the tiny ball of fur and the fluffy tail. It vanished into the tree line, bypassing feet that wore a pair of clean boots, the laces neatly tied. I followed the laces up over ankles, taking in the sight of the man before me. He was dressed all in black, his lithe form carefully still.

His eyes shone with gold as he stared down at me, an aura of the deepest midnight blue lingering around him like dark fragments. They shifted in the air, moving with the wind and revealing tiny, glimmering stars that matched his stare.

"What are you doing, silly girl?" he asked, the deep tone of his voice like a shock to my system.

Silly? I thought, reaching for the words to argue. I wasn't silly. I was . . .

My thoughts trailed off as I searched for what I was, for the empty pit of nothing that stared back at me. I looked down my body, jumping back from the bow I found my hand wrapped around. It shone with that same golden color, the thread somehow barely there as I trailed a single finger over the length of it and shuddered.

"I . . . I don't know," I said, shaking off my own confusion as I turned my attention back to the man studying me intently. He held my gaze for only a moment before he gave me a disinterested smile, nodding his head to the woods behind me. I turned to follow his stare, vaguely aware of figures I hadn't seen working in the distance. The people around me worked to make camp, fed and watered horses, and readied a fire, but they never quite came into view. They didn't fully form, as if only vestiges of something better forgotten.

I spun fully, staring at the hind that waited in the distance. She bent her head to eat the grass at her feet as her body twitched to flick off the flies bothering her. Her tail flicked to dispel them, a long feather-like thing that shimmered with the same gold as my bow. She was bright and vibrant in the green that surrounded her, standing out completely and not even bothering to hide.

The man with the golden eyes reached around me to grasp my bow, raising it. My own hands moved to follow, raising it to position as he placed a single arrow in my other hand. I notched it, guiding the string to my cheek and letting myself feel the brush of it against my skin as I breathed, trying to understand what was expected of me.

Trying to understand why.

"Our people are hungry. It is your responsibility to see them fed, huntress," he said, taking a step back. His hands fell away from me, the weight of his stare heavy on my spine. I sighed, glancing to my periphery of the people depending on me to provide them with meat for the night.

My stomach felt full and satisfied, no trace of hunger in it. I felt like I would know if I was hungry. I would know if I needed food, even though I couldn't ever remember a time when I'd been hungry.

I lowered the bow, turning to look at the man over my shoulder. "Feed them!" the man shouted, the command in that voice forcing me to turn back around and stare at the hind I was expected to kill.

I let out a deep exhale, preparing myself for what I had to do. It was the way of the world, the way of nature, and yet I couldn't bring myself to believe that this death was necessary.

The hind raised its head slowly, deep golden eyes connecting with mine. Something in me warmed at the way it froze solid, at the way it waited for me to make my decision. It didn't move to run away or flee the certain death staring it down, simply gave itself over to the instinct that made it wait.

I lost track of time in that moment, of the minutes that passed as the hind and I stared at one another. The people around me faded into the background, their translucent forms growing even more distant until it was only the hind and I.

I was not hungry.

The people I was supposed to feed looked happy enough for the night, and I . . .

I couldn't justify killing more than was absolutely necessary. I couldn't betray the trust the hind had placed in me by remaining.

I lowered the bow, shaking my head firmly as I turned away from the hind's trusting eyes once more.

"No," I said, tossing the bow to the ground at the golden-eyed man's feet. "I will not kill for the sake of it when there appears to be enough food to go around." All around me, the people working in the distance came into more focus than before, cooking over the fire. They were happy as they focused on their tasks, completely unaware of me disobeying the command I'd been given.

"You would leave them to starve?" he asked, crossing his arms over his chest.

"They look well fed enough to me," I said with a shrug, taking another step closer to the man. I stepped on the bow at my feet, snapping it in two as I glared up at him. "If you want the hind dead, then do it your fucking self. I will not be a man's weapon to be used at will."

FORTY-NINE

ESTRELLA

The man smiled, a curve of his lips that peeled them back from his teeth. I got the impression he didn't smile very often, that the twisted and malformed thing was meant to be one of approval, even though it came across as more menacing in his inexperience.

He laid a hand on top of my shoulder, squeezing the armor there softly. I barely felt it through the structure of my clothing, but the burn of emotion in those eerie golden eyes was what stole the breath from my lungs.

I didn't know this man, couldn't recall having ever seen him before. It was both unsurprising and a shock, considering I couldn't have told you my own name, and the wrongness of that was like a hollow within me.

But he knew me. That much was very clear.

"There's my girl," he said, the strangely familiar words pulling an unknown emotion from me. It swirled around in my gut, making my stomach sink into a pit I didn't understand.

When he finally pulled back and removed his hand from me, he waved his arms at his sides in a brief, smooth glide. Tendrils of white rose from the ground to follow the path his hands carved through the air, the warm glow of them drawing my attention as I studied the way they danced. They felt familiar even as they writhed through the air, like the missing piece of me that I needed returned.

They came toward me, moving with a slow and steady pace. I couldn't bring myself to fear them, to attempt to protect myself from those odd swirling lights as they reached me and brushed along my armor. Looking for skin, they coated my body in a vortex of light before they sank into the flesh of my hands, my neck, my face.

They slithered along the surface of my skin before sinking inside of me, disappearing from my view as my entire body pulsed with warmth.

Memories crashed into me so suddenly that my head exploded into blinding, sharp pain. I reached up with both hands, grasping my temples as a strangled scream tore up my throat and burst through the air. The man before me vanished, leaving me to suffer the pain of everything I'd ever lived surging through me once again.

The pain of loss and violation felt sticky on my skin, tears welling in my eyes as I sank to the forest floor. Sinking my hands into the dry underbrush, I let the abrasiveness of the crumpling leaves ground me in the reality of the here and now.

There were no flames of a funeral pyre burning my father's body in these woods.

There was no cane cracking against my back in these woods.

There were no thorns from the Twilight Berry bush tearing my hands into ribbons of flesh.

There was no death waiting for me at the Veil.

I cried as they flashed through my head like portraits of my memories, rocking as my sense of self returned to me.

Adelphia's voice was low and even in my memory, her words the driving force that made me push myself up off the forest floor. *There is beauty in knowing who you are.*

She'd been brave enough to know herself. She'd been brave enough to look at the adversity of her past and face life with her head held high. To do anything less would have been a disservice to her memory now that the life had been stripped from her too soon.

I knew myself. I knew my purpose, and I would not allow the Lethe to break me.

My legs wobbled beneath me as I stood, my knees bent to absorb the shock of shoulders that felt like they carried the metaphorical weight of the world. The hind came closer, her feathered tail swaying in the breeze with each step. It was only when she stood before me that she stopped, her golden stare meeting my own. She bowed her head ever so slightly, and I reached out a hand to touch the top of her face.

It felt like I'd failed, like I had spared her life but hadn't yet accomplished the side task of needing to bring something to the Cradle of Creation to present to the Primordials there in an offering they didn't deserve. Given that all the rivers required a trophy of some kind, the lack of one made nausea swirl in my gut. If I survived these trials and made it to the Cradle only to be turned away because of my desire to save a creature that didn't need to die, I couldn't begin to imagine the rage that would consume me. It terrified me to think of what I might do.

Who I might become.

My fingers moved over the hind's soft coat, her antlers glowing with golden light as she tilted her head farther. My hand slid along her head, allowing her to guide my touch to where she wanted it. I stroked the base of one of her antlers, shocked to find it smooth and almost polished as she moved away, tugging her head back until my hand grasped the end of her antler. I gripped it, studying the stare she kept on my face.

She jerked her head to the side, nearly tearing my hand open on the sharpened point of her antler. Instead of bleeding me, she tore it the other way until the antler cracked in my grip, the sound echoing through the woods as I held her stare, trying to understand what she'd done.

She was not afraid or angry, instead holding me pinned in that moment as she twisted her head one last time and the piece of her antler broke free, leaving me to stumble back from her broad form in shock.

I stared down at the antler held in my hand, the gold gleaming like the hilt of a dagger. It would make a crude but beautiful weapon, all sharpened edges and pointed tips.

"Why?" I asked, even though I did not expect an answer of any kind. I wanted to understand, to decide why the hind would injure itself so greatly and diminish its ability to protect itself from harm.

The hind tilted its head to the side as if listening to me, and we stood there for a moment until a woman's voice broke through the silence.

"For your kindness, Child of Fate," she said, stepping out from the trees. Her hair shone like silver silk, her dress a thing of beige that draped over her fair skin. One side of her face was beautiful, youthful and full of life, but the other was a gnarled mess of flesh and bone, an empty eye socket and skull protruding where the skin had seemingly melted away. Her hands twisted as she toyed with a spool of thread that she unwound and rewound, fidgeting as if she could not play with those golden threads.

My breath caught as I studied her, watching another creature toy with the threads that only I had been able to see until this moment. She did so with an absent mind, her familiarity with the texture of them and the way they moved so innate that I stuttered, unable to find any words.

Two more women with half-rotted faces stepped out of the tree line behind her, the same threads from her spool arching through the air where they too played with them between their fingers. The woman to her left was perhaps the youngest of the three, with dark black hair and a gray dress, her hair pulled back from her face with a crescent-shaped headband. The one to the right was the oldest, with deep red hair and a pair of golden shears held in her hand. I watched as she cut the thread she fiddled with, the gold of it leaching away to leave the fragment dull and lifeless. It fell to the ground, discarded and forgotten the moment it vanished into the leaves.

A life ended, a life forgotten.

I knew without a doubt that these three women with the rotting faces were the figures that had been toying with my life since before I'd been born. That they were the ones responsible for me and my creation.

The Moirai. The Fates themselves.

I swallowed, gripping the antler tighter in my hand as if I would be able to defend myself from any harm these women wished to bring me. There was no denying the Fates' influence, no movement that would be faster than their ability to cut my very thread and end my life.

"Those who seek to take from this place will always leave empty-handed," the oldest said, her voice clear and calming in spite of the grotesque way her teeth moved where her skin was missing. "But those who respect our creatures will always leave with a gift from the forest itself."

I raised my chin, needing the answers that I was afraid to ask the questions to get. "Why are you here?" I asked. The Fates had existed since the dawn of creation. They'd spun the wheel of time and the lives of Primordials, Gods, Fae, and humans alike for more years than I could count.

For them to appear before me now meant that they'd made the careful decision to do so.

They didn't bother to pretend that I was unaware of who they must have been, but the golden-haired one in the middle stepped closer, still twirling that spindle of thread around and toying with it. She approached me as the hind faded into the woods behind me, stopping only when we stood eye to eye. She was my height, an unusual fact I had come not to expect of the immortals that surrounded me. Even most humans were taller than me, leaving me feeling strangely uncomfortable with the proximity of her face as she stared at me with eyes that looked like molten gold.

She reached between us, raising a single hand to touch a sharp nail to my cheekbone.

Warmth spread through me at the touch, life and hope and magic blooming on my skin. I raised my hand to touch it, feeling my fingertips tingle as the magic spread. The darkened fingers lit with gold, my own magic rising in response as the color spread through the *viniculum* that covered my arm. "You asked a question of one of our children. We came to give you an answer," she said, but there was something more hiding in those words.

One of the others stepped forward, grabbing a golden leaf from the tree at her side. She crushed it into powder in her hands, pouring it into a vial that she pulled from her pocket. "Blow this into the face of your mate and it will reverse the effects the Lethe has had on his soul. His memories will return to him without consequence."

She held out the vial for me, and I took it from her without hesitation, staring down at the golden powder held within. "You came here to give me this?" I asked, unable to stop the odd emotion from bleeding into my voice. It was a bittersweet sort of appreciation that came with mixed feelings about their help.

Where had they been all the other times I needed help? Where had they been when I was suffering and had no one who could save me?

They'd been the ones to put me in those situations, to force me to live through defining moments so that I could become the version of myself that served their purposes.

"You have endured so much on your path to us, Estrella Barlowe," the dark-haired woman said finally, tipping her head up to look at the river where it appeared above my head. Ready to swallow me whole and return me to the surface so that I could continue on my journey. "You deserve to have him at your side for now."

The river lowered above my head, the water pressing in as time ran short. There were so many questions that needed answers, but I wouldn't have the time. The golden-haired woman spoke, her voice ominous. "But be warned, there will soon come a time where you must continue your journey alone. Your mate will not be permitted to pass through our temple to enter the Cradle of Creation. For that part of your journey, you will continue alone."

I nodded, even though I hated the thought of being separated from Caldris for a moment. "I understand," I said, and I realized I meant it.

I didn't know what the Cradle would hold for me or my Fate, but I knew it was mine alone to bear.

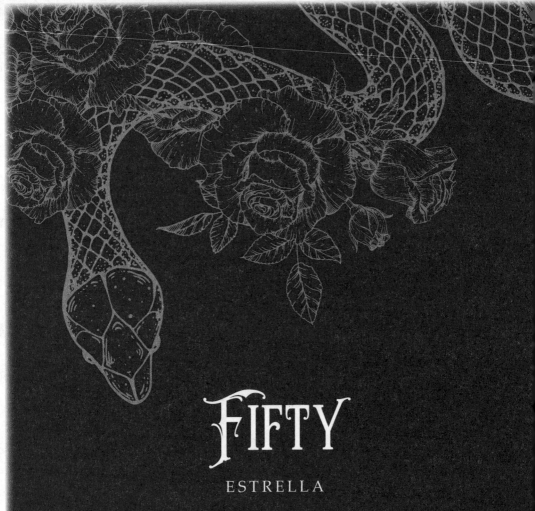

FIFTY

ESTRELLA

I crawled my way out of the sands at the river's edge, feeling the moment Caldris's stare locked onto me. There was no recognition in his face as he moved around Medusa and made to lend me a hand, not a hint of the man who recognized the bond pulsing between us.

I pushed to my feet, accepting his helping hand as his mouth parted on a startled gasp. It did something to me to know that even with my hair plastered to my face where it fell free from the braid, even without the emotional connection of our bond driving him or his memories of me, his attraction to me was sudden and immediate.

I'd felt the same with him, even with his human glamour in place when he'd deceived me. Caldris in all his glory was another story. He pulled me to my feet, keeping my hand in his as I dug into the pocket of my armor. I tossed the Morrigan the piece of the antler that I'd brought back as part of my gift for the Fates, grasping the vial they'd given me from the leaf in the Lethe. Yanking the cork free, I poured the powder into my hand as my mate watched me with curious eyes.

I held it out before him, letting him study the golden shimmer of it in the dim light. When he moved even closer to study it, I blew out a hard and fast breath, watching as the powder flew into his face and covered his lightly bronzed skin. He gasped, breathing it in and coughing as a single hand went to his throat. He released me immediately, taking a step back as some of the fog in his blue stare faded away.

My sigh of relief was immediate, knowing the moment that his memory returned in full. He moved to me, wrapping me in his arms and pressing a single hand to the back of my head to hold me to his chest with steady pressure.

"What the fuck happened?" he asked, pulling back just enough to look down at me.

"You're vulnerable to the Lethe even without touching the river. You're just a soul here in the end, so—"

"I'm more vulnerable to the punishments of the afterlife," he said, shaking his head as we walked away from the river.

"Where did you get that powder?" Macha asked, reaching out to take the vial from me. She smelled it, scenting the powder around the rim before handing it to Nemain who did the same.

"It was a gift from the Fates," I said, holding her stare as her brow rose.

"They came to you? In the Lethe?" Medusa asked, taking the vial from Nemain and studying it intently. Shoving it into her pocket, she started walking away from the river, leaving us to follow. I did so without hesitation, sliding my hand into Caldris's and needing the feel of him even as we moved.

Night would fall soon enough, and we would need to find a place to take shelter for the night. While we certainly had enough of us that we would be likely to survive the night, it didn't seem wise to tempt it when we could be resting more easily.

The memory of what had happened the night I hadn't been safely tucked away when night fell was too potent in my head for me to ignore the warning it gave.

Medusa and the Morrigan exchanged a look as they walked, leaving me to hate the feeling of being out of the loop.

"Is it a bad thing that the Fates came to me? I should think their gift would be a blessing," I said, following after them. Medusa sighed, stopping and turning to me slowly.

"It is not bad, as you said their gift was welcome," she said, exchanging another look with Nemain. The wolves prowled up ahead, searching the landscape for any signs of threat. They moved through the dim light like white flashes against a dark landscape, frolicking and having fun as they hunted. "It merely means that they were curious about something, and for the very beings who know all, curiosity is a challenge."

"What makes you think they were curious at all?" I asked, shrugging as I walked past Medusa. I spun to face her, walking backward with Caldris to guide me so I didn't trip. "Maybe they were just bored."

"They wanted to see you, Estrella. That means something has shifted, and they are trying to anticipate your new path. Seeing you in the flesh allowed them to play with your threads more intimately," Badb answered, her words sinking inside of me.

I considered her words, trying to find that place within me that cared. I couldn't find it, and for a moment I had to wonder if that was a consequence of embracing Aella. If the things that had once felt like they mattered so much to me would no longer make a difference in my life or cause me stress, instead embracing a careless attitude that was so different from the woman I'd come to know through my life.

I shrugged, a bitter laugh escaping me at the concern on Medusa's face. "They've been pulling the strings of my fate for longer than I'll ever remember," I said, continuing along the path Medusa had already set for us. "What difference does one more shift make in the grand scheme of things?"

Macha laughed, her head tipping back as she pressed a hand to her stomach. "Oh, Little Tempest. You will find that the moments when the Fates intervene and reknit things to suit their purpose have often led to great pain and destruction. All should fear their interest and curiosity—even those of us who are not the subject of it."

"What good will worrying do her?" Caldris asked, his deep voice calming the frayed edges that their words of warning left me with. Maybe my calm had nothing to do with Aella at all, but with completing the bond with the other half of my soul. Maybe he somehow grounded me, making those other concerns feel secondary and so much less terrifying.

Because we would face them together as one when they came. For the first time in my life, I had someone that I knew would always be by my side. Someone who would stand beside me no matter what I did. Even when the Fates forced us to separate as they'd warned the time would come, he would still support me from a distance and be the part of me I could not deny.

"If my fate has already been determined, then whether I worry or not will make little difference to the outcome of any of this," I said, continuing forward. Caldris allowed my hand to slip free from his as I approached the wolves, running my hand through Fenrir's fur as he approached me. He was tall enough that I could lean forward, touching my forehead to the top of his head affectionately. "I would rather not know what's coming for me. I don't want to feel the dread of knowing whatever loss or grief will hit me next. I want to just enjoy what I have while I have it, and for now, that's having all of you with me while I try to navigate my way through these trials."

Determination settled in my gut, fueling my words like a fire burning deep in my core. It spread through me like wildfire, consuming everything in its path until I didn't just want to *survive* the trials, I wanted to thrive and save my people.

Most of all, I wanted to prove it to myself. As harsh as the words of those in Mistfell had been, they would never compare to the ones I'd leveled at myself over the years. They were a tiny echo of the ones that bounced around in my own mind, the abuse I'd suffered at my own words.

I swallowed, raising my chin as I felt the weight of Caldris in my mind, sorting through the thoughts that I didn't bother to hide from him. His stare softened as he approached slowly, taking my hands in his. The thread of our bond shifted at the contact, wrapping itself around our joined hands and leaving us to both stare at the shimmering gold that bound us together for an eternity.

"You outshine even the brightest of stars, Little One," my mate said, leaning forward to touch his forehead to mine. His eyes blazed with an icy blue, the magic of winter even more present in him since the loss of Twyla and the transfer of her power. "There is not a trial in this world that you could not defeat if you so much as dared to try. It has been my honor to stand at your side while you discover yourself and your heart after all of this time. I have waited centuries for you, and I would have waited centuries more, because there is no one in this world or the one that we will create who could ever inspire me the way you do. You make me want to be better. You make me want more than I have ever dared to dream of, and you make me believe in light, when all I've known is night."

"Caldris," I said, the weight of those words lighting something within me. They soothed the flames of my own anger at myself, shifting it into something more comforting like the warmth of a hearth in winter rather than an inferno that felt untamable. "I love you," I said, swallowing back the burn of tears. The simple statement felt so insignificant compared to his lengthy declaration, but I couldn't find a way to communicate what they meant. I had to rely on the bond pulsing between us, what had once felt so invasive and like an intrusion of my privacy, becoming my only comfort when words failed me.

He didn't give me the statement back, his eyes crinkling ever so slightly. I could imagine the way his mouth curved into an arrogant smirk that conveyed every thought I already heard rattling inside his head. It pleased him to know just how much he disoriented me, gave him a twisted sense of male satisfaction to know that he'd rendered me damn near speechless.

It didn't happen often, and he viewed it as a triumph in and of itself.

He pulled away from me slowly, tearing his forehead from mine as his face came into better view. He still took my breath away, his brutal beauty the kind of face those poets wrote sonnets for, that women sang about around the fire, dreaming for themselves.

He was a song of beauty in the wind, a harmony moving enough to make listeners cry.

But it was me that he watched as he lowered himself to a single knee, raising my hand in his to press his mouth to my knuckles. He held out his hand to Medusa, nodding to her in some wordless communication that she seemed to understand. She smiled as she pulled a dagger from its sheath, pressing the tip into the pad of my mate's thumb. He turned my hand over as he traced the blood that welled in response into the palm of my hand. "I vow to be the sword at your back, to protect you from those who would stand in your way or make moves behind your back. I vow to support you in all you do, and to believe in the world you see for our future and our children's future. My sword and my life are yours, min asteren. In this life and the afterlife, in this world and what comes next, you are my guiding light—the answer to the questions I didn't know to ask."

I chuckled, the sound coming out hoarse and throaty as emotion swelled within me. The love he spoke of, the love he felt, would have been impossible to comprehend if it was not for the fact that I felt it, too. If it hadn't been for the incommunicable way that I knew nothing in this world would be worth having if I didn't have him at my side.

Freedom would not matter. Friends would no longer appeal to me.

Life for me would simply cease to be.

"You are the King of Winter," I said, attempting to pull him up from his feet. "Should it not be me swearing my loyalty to you as my lord and husband?"

"What kind of King would I be if my first priority was not to serve my Queen in all things?" he asked, allowing me to pull him to his feet as he touched his mouth to mine. The question rebounded in my mind, dancing around with the stark difference between the way he viewed me and the human men who'd thought to own me had seen me.

"You have a Kingdom to run. What is one woman compared to that?" I murmured against his mouth, smiling into him as he reciprocated the gesture, pulling away just far enough for me to see the softness in that icy blue gaze, the glacier melting only for me.

"You are everything, my star. None of this matters if I do not have you."

He waited for my response, and I felt a flicker of uncertainty from him. A moment where he worried I might reject him as I had done so many times in the past. My stomach cramped with the pain of knowing I had put that there, that I had no one to blame but myself for the way this gentle, loving man doubted himself. I reached up, cupping his cheek in my palm. His blood smeared against his skin with the touch, but he didn't care as he leaned into the contact. "You have me, Caldris. In this life and the next, I am yours."

His mouth touched mine, his thoughts swirling and mixing with mine until I couldn't tell what were mine and what were his. When we parted, we would continue on our journey.

But for now, I needed to feel.

FIFTY-ONE

ESTRELLA

We crested the curved hilltop, the grass beneath my feet offering the only cushion I would receive. I should have been used to the strenuous effort of travel at this point, of the way my feet ached in different spots depending on the terrain I navigated. But after hours of walking endlessly to reach the shelter Medusa drove us toward, I wanted nothing more than to find a random cave where I could rest for even just a few hours. The light was dimming in the horizon on the other side of the hills that formed before us, but it was the village that sprawled through the valley that caught my eye.

It was the open field at the center where figures of men and women fought. It was not screams of pain that lifted up toward the hilltops, but the ring of laughter and joy that reached me.

"What is this place?" Caldris asked as we all hurried down the hill. There was a fence surrounding the village, and while we could see over the top of it from our vantage point, I wondered how it might provide protection from the creatures prowling through the night in Tartarus.

"This is the Tithe settlement," Medusa explained, hurrying down the hill at our side. The wolves ran and frolicked through the trees that littered the hillside, and I made eye contact with Fenrir just briefly enough to nod him on. They would not be joining us in the settlement, instead enjoying the night to be free to hunt and be as wild as they were born to be.

"*Be safe,*" I told him, hoping he would convey the message to his sisters. It bothered me that my relationship with them was not as deep, that I couldn't share the same bond with them as I did with their brother. But as the girls circled back, brushing against Caldris as they went, I thought maybe that had its advantages. In some ways, it felt as if I had stolen Fenrir from him, at least I could not influence his bond with the other two.

"*Stole my fucking dog,*" Caldris said, but his voice was laced with humor. I could hear the taunting smile in it, and feel the way he did not fault me for the theft.

"*You cannot steal what was never truly his,*" Fenrir said, though his voice was sympathetic. A wolf belonged to no one, but our bond had the potential to eclipse the affection he and Caldris shared for one another. "*Do not worry for us tonight. It is I who must worry for you always, Tempest.*"

With those ominous thoughts, he and his sisters fled into the trees permanently, leaving me to make my way toward the valley. The gates of the wall spread open, allowing us to slide inside quickly and efficiently.

A slow river flowed down through the gap in the hills toward the settlement, seeming to come from nowhere. There was no magic attached to this river, no innate feelings and emotions that came to the surface from my proximity as I knelt at the riverside and scooped my hand into the waters there. Caldris did the same at my side, drinking deeply from his cupped hands. His spirit form did not require sustenance in spite of the magic that made him tangible and real in this place, so long as his body remained cared for, and with the way that time worked differently here, I imagined not enough had passed in Tar Mesa for it to be a concern.

But that didn't mean he could not revel in the feeling of cool water on his tongue, of the relief it provided after traveling through a land surrounded by flames.

"Greetings, Tempest," a man said as he stepped up beside us on the riverbank. I hurried to my feet, suspicion in my gaze as I stared him down. He'd pulled his gray hair back into a low ponytail at the nape of his neck, his eyes such a pale blue that they were almost white. His face was aged and weathered in a way I had not seen in some time given the proximity to immortal beings and Fae since coming to Alfheimr.

Human, I realized with a start. The man before me was mortal just the same as my own mother was where she hid away in Catancia.

"Hello," I said calmly, arching a brow to wait for him to tell me what he wanted from us.

"I have come to show you the settlement and all that we have done to prepare for your arrival," he said, sweeping out his arm in an arching invitation for me to continue toward the village that waited across the stone bridge. Caldris placed a hand at the small of my back in quiet encouragement, his comfort in this place sinking into me through our bond.

I couldn't explain why he felt so confident that this place and these people wouldn't bring us any harm, but I allowed myself to trust his instincts and follow after the man who turned on his heel and guided the way.

"Will the creatures that come out at night not harm us here?" I asked, looking back at the flimsy fences that seemed as if they would do nothing to barricade the hungry creatures.

"We are protected by wards created by Khaos himself. No harm will come to you during your time with us," he said, and I couldn't help the sigh of relief I felt with those words. If they were true, it was a reassurance of another night in a place of safety. Aside from the hours we'd spent in the home of the Gorgons, I'd felt riddled and haunted by dangers at every turn since arriving in Tartarus.

I just wanted to crawl into a bed beside the fire and sleep for a year until I felt recovered from this ordeal. In some ways, a night in a settlement felt like a blessing. In others, I knew it would be cruel punishment to wake in the morning and have to return to the reality of what my life was for the moment.

To have to wake and face another river.

"We have created an entirely sustainable community for ourselves within these protected walls," the man said, acting as a tour guide. He motioned to buildings as we passed, sweeping his arm out to a store where wild game hung outside for purchase. "The only ones who ever need to leave are those who hunt for meat. Our gardens are to your left, tucked behind the produce stand you see there.

If you keep going toward the edge of the woods, you'll find an ample amount of food that grows year-round to sustain us. Tartarus soil is some of the most fertile soil in the world thanks to the presence of the Primordials in the Cradle nearby."

"What did you say your name was?" I asked, wishing I knew how to address him with the questions I couldn't stop from forming in my mind.

"My name is insignificant, Tempest. I am merely here to guide you," the man said, his cheeks flushing with color as he lowered his chin.

"I'd like to know what to call you," I said, my brow furrowing at the odd response. Was it the Fae belief that there was power in a name that kept him from providing it to me? Or was there something stranger at work.

"My name is Leax," he said quietly. "I am a descendant of the humans who were brought here when the Primordials chose Tartarus as their place of eternal rest. My ancestors were tasked with ensuring that this settlement was prepared to house a population of their choosing. We are the keepers of the Tithe, and have kept them safe until your arrival."

"Until *my* arrival?" I asked, my brow furrowing. Caldris's confusion was an echo of mine, pulsating down the bond as he slid his arm free from the small of my back to entwine his fingers with mine and squeeze supportively.

"So that you might collect them," Leax said, continuing on his journey forward through the settlement. People milled about, a mix of humans and Fae working in ways that were so reminiscent of Mistfell that I was nearly catapulted back in time to when this simplicity had been my life.

I'd hated it at the time, and now I longed for the peace that came with it more than anything.

I reached out with my free hand, touching Leax's forearm to force him to pause and look at me. He stared down at where I touched him as if it was a crime, horror written into the lines of his face. "Please, I don't understand. Why would I come to collect them? What am I to do with them?" I asked, releasing him finally.

His attention swung to me, his eyes wide with fear. "I am sorry if I've upset you, Tempest. It was not my intention."

"I'm not upset with you; I swear it. I merely wish to understand what this place has to do with me," I said, trying to keep my voice soft and reassuring. I did not want to think of what whispers might have reached him to make him react so fearfully to me. Did they truly think me to be such a monster?

"They are yours," he said, guiding me forward. We walked through the streets of the settlement, the dirt beneath my boots well-packed from all those who had traversed it before me. The buildings that lined the street had been crafted from wood, the single-floor structures far more familiar to me than anything I'd witnessed since coming to Alfheimr and, in turn, Tartarus.

"Who is mine?" I asked as we turned a corner, navigating through the streets. The houses crested out into a circle around a field that was filled with people.

"They are," Leax answered, nodding his head toward the gathered crowd.

The field where so many sparred and trained and laughed was at the center of the village, and it was the gleam of dark hair that somehow shone with gold in the fading light that made my steps continue forward in spite of his odd words.

I didn't stop when someone stepped up to greet us, needing to see that hair for myself up close. I had to see the man that I knew would be attached to it, somehow so similar to that of his sister and so different all in the same breath. Mab had no hint of lightness to her, no remnants of the sun in her hair—only the cool depth of night and darkness.

Rheaghan turned to look at me as I hurried into the center of the field, approaching where he fought with one of the other sacrifices. His light green eyes were confused as I made my way toward him, not bothering to heed the swords swinging between them. His sparring partner hadn't yet noticed me, swinging her long sword with all her might. It was too late to stop the blow by the time I moved into its path, holding up my arm to block it from reaching anything vital. The blade was not iron, clanging off my skin as if my forearm was made from stone itself. Belladonna's eyes flashed with purple light at the exact moment of impact, glowing from the spot where she remained wrapped around my bicep. She did not shift from her stone form, but I knew who was responsible for the hardening of my flesh.

The sound of the sword cracking in two as it bounced back echoed through the clearing, and Rheaghan's eyes widened as he raised his own blade and pointed it at my throat in warning. I froze, staring down at the blade in confusion as I waited for recognition to come to his green eyes.

"Estrella!" Caldris's voice called, and he approached the clearing cautiously, grabbing my forearm only when he was certain it was safe to do so. He pulled me back, putting distance between Rheaghan's sword and my neck, studying the male he knew even better than I did. As much as it pained me to admit, my joy in seeing Rheaghan alive had clouded my judgment.

Even given what I knew now, he still didn't know that I was his flesh and blood, that we shared a father and Mab wasn't the only sister he possessed. That the sister who murdered him wasn't the only family he had.

"He does not remember you, daughter," Medusa said from the sidelines, her voice melancholy and a mirror of the sadness that I felt. I'd already deduced as much for myself given the knife to my throat, and the loss of everything that had made him *him* was one I felt in the marrow of my bones.

"Does he remember anything? Anyone?" I asked, thinking of the Sidhe woman who told such pretty lies to hide her love for him. Nila had done everything she could in an attempt to convince me that there was nothing between them, but I'd seen the careful avoidance they exercised when they were in court together. I'd seen the way they made sure never to look at one another too long, never to tempt the bond that they'd kept so carefully hidden.

She was his mate, and he had sacrificed so much to keep her from attracting more of Mab's attention. He had given everything he could to keep her safe from his sister's jealousy, only now to forget her altogether?

"None of them do," Medusa answered, sweeping her hand out to indicate the entirety of the village. There were far more who had been sacrificed to the Tithe than I cared to recognize, an entire community gathered here and for what? How were they being useful to the Primordials? How was any of this needed? "Only when they achieve their purpose will they regain the memory of who they once were." She guided us away, leaving them to train as another woman guided us to a handful of homes at the edge of the settlement. Rheaghan immediately resumed his training, fighting with the woman who gathered up another sword and continued in her efforts.

They were single-minded in their pursuit, training as if their lives depended on it when they were already dead.

Even in that effort, Rheaghan never touched his magic. Instead, he focused in on his technique and his breathing, remaining calm in a way that many of the others seemed unable to do. "Why doesn't he use his magic?" I asked, looking toward the mockery of a sky and the cave ceiling above my head. He couldn't reach the actual sun, so did that mean that his magic didn't exist here?

"He does not remember himself to be the God of the Sun, so why would he even think to attempt such a thing?" Medusa asked, and I realized just how stripped down the loss of one's memories left us. It wasn't just the loss of those he loved, but it was the complete and total loss of himself and everything that he was.

It was a fate worse than death, I thought.

One that I hoped one day I could free him from.

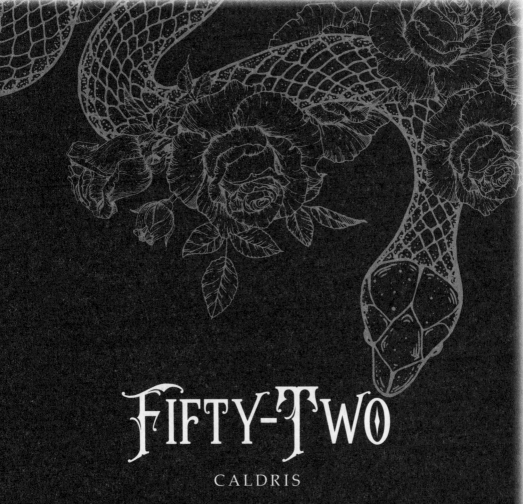

Fifty-Two

CALDRIS

Xela worked to pull Estrella's hair back into a loose ponytail as it dried from her bath, leaving my mate to wince as she forced her waves into submission. Leax had introduced the woman from the settlement who had barely spoken a word as she guided the others to the homes that they would occupy for the night, remaining behind in ours to help Estrella prepare herself for dinner.

Her presence was the only thing that kept me from making us very, very fucking late the moment Estrella had stripped out of her armor, sinking into the warm waters that filled the bathtub with a groan that sank straight into my balls. I grunted as I stood from the bath myself, ignoring Estrella's possessive glare in the moment before I managed to wrap a towel around myself.

Seeing the woman help her dress had made me jealous enough, the sight of her hands pulling and pinching at the white flowing fabric that she wrapped over one of Estrella's shoulders and guided down to enrobe her breasts and waist, before folding and tying it in a complicated pattern that left the rest to fall to her ankles in a cascade of fabric. It parted up the side of one of her thighs to her hip, revealing far more of my mate than I cared for.

The woman never so much as glanced my way, focusing all her attention on doting on Estrella. She was not one of the sacrifices from the Tithe, instead a human woman who had been raised within the confines of Tartarus and helped her family look after the land that eventually became home to the sacrifices.

"My family is all looking forward to finally meeting you, my Queen," Xela said, her chattering increasing the moment we were shut away in the privacy of our cabin. "We have passed down stories of your coming for generations."

"Why would your family know that I'd pass through the settlement?" Estrella asked, confusion lacing her brow with tension. Xela opened the drawer to the vanity where Estrella sat, pulling the headband I had given her from it and carefully weaving it into Estrella's hair. It was bright against the darkness, like a warm star in the night sky.

Xela did not pause before she continued on, adding golden adornments like large dangling earrings and a necklace as I dressed in the clothing she had provided for me. My own clothes were made of the same soft, billowing fabric as Estrella's, trousers cut from the cloth. A golden belt held them up at my waist, a single stretch of cloth hanging over one side of my chest. The clothing was so reminiscent of what I'd worn before the Fae and humans had gone to war against one another, so easy and comfortable compared to the restraining armor I'd begun to don during our war and never stopped wearing. This clothing felt vulnerable, whereas armor served as protection— even if it could not ever protect me from the worst of my enemies.

The swath of fabric kept my left side visible, the swirling marks of my *viniculum* purposefully revealed to display my place at Estrella's side.

All my life, I'd believed my mate would wear the symbol of my ownership on her skin. That it would be her who needed my protection, her who others needed to know belonged to me. I'd thought myself to be the greater power in our relationship, but in this world, in this place, I was merely the mate of the one who mattered.

It was oddly refreshing—satisfying in a way—to have the only expectation of me be to smile and look pretty. I grinned with the thought, earning a glare from my mate as she waited and listened to

Xela's half-coherent mumbling as she worked to decorate Estrella's face with kohl and paint her lips the color of blood.

She looked every bit the role of the Goddess adorned in these simple clothes, her face decorated with just enough embellishment to bring out the stunning green of her mossy eyes and make her lips look as if she'd fed from me.

The thought struck me with a pang of desire for that very thing, to feel her lips pressed against me as she licked blood from my skin and drank me down. Her glare heated as she recognized the thoughts, her pink tongue darting out to wet her lips as Xela tutted. Estrella ceased to hear her, instead focusing in on the portrait I painted for her in my mind—the way my tongue would feel on her skin as I unwrapped her from her gown like the greatest gift I'd ever received.

She turned away from me to look in the mirror as if that would stop her from seeing my thoughts, as if it would stop me from tormenting the woman who consumed my every waking moment. Even in my dreams, her figure haunted me, tormenting me with the memory of how she felt on the inside. The way she took me so fully, letting me sheath myself to the root in her pretty pussy that the Fates had molded just for me.

She gritted her teeth and tried to shut me out as I leaned against the edge of the bed, crossing my arms over my chest and watching my mate struggle to focus on what Xela was telling her. "My uncle Leax and I are both descended from the same line and have known of your coming for centuries, my Queen," she said, the words penetrating the haze of lust that I'd pulled Estrella and I into so easily.

Estrella blinked, trying to insert herself back into this moment, into the here and now so that she could comprehend the implication of Xela's words. She swallowed, wisely choosing not to bother asking. We both knew how Xela and her family had come to know that Estrella would pass through the Tithe settlement centuries before she actually did; we both already knew that the Fates were responsible for this understanding just as they had been for every other twist and turn her life had taken.

"Did the Fates happen to tell you why it was so important that I pass through this place?" she asked, twirling her hands in her lap. She made eye contact with Xela in the mirror, holding her gaze as the woman's hands paused with a soft bristled brush that she used to apply a quick sweep of golden rose to Estrella's cheek.

"To gather your army, of course," Xela said, her brow knitted with tension and confusion. She shook her head softly, smiling as she continued with her work and repeated the rouge on Estrella's other cheek. "Do you truly not know what this place has been intended for all this time?"

"My army?" Estrella asked, glancing toward the single window that pointed to the steps out from our cabin. It was, admittedly, the largest of the homes within the settlement, well-furnished even though it did not appear to have been used recently. It was clean and maintained, as if waiting for the time that someone would come to occupy it even if only for a night. Those who had been sacrificed were no longer sparring, the field at the village center empty and still, but I felt the way Estrella's gaze pored over it. She was imagining all those who had trained here, their dedication to being the best as we'd witnessed it, not understanding the purpose of why.

Most of them had been human in life, and while that hardly mattered in Tartarus, what good would it do to have an army of humans at her disposal?

Especially if they were already dead.

"We have no use for sacrifices here, contrary to what the Sidhe believe. We have more souls than we know what to do with," Xela answered, stepping back from Estrella and studying her handiwork. Estrella followed after her, staring at her reflection before turning to Xela and waiting for her to explain. "But the Fates knew that you would one day need allies to help you take back what was always meant to be yours. Few would be so brave as to risk Mab's wrath to support a single woman, no matter how powerful she may appear to the undiscerning eye."

"But they're human," Estrella said, echoing what I'd already worked through in my head.

"What has died will never truly be human, my Queen. Bringing them back, releasing them from Tartarus, always has untold effects on a being. There is no telling what they may be when they are finally free from this place," Xela said, moving toward the door.

Estrella stopped her, grasping her wrist with a gentle grip that the woman looked down at in shock. She covered Estrella's hand with her own, letting her eyes drift closed as if she truly believed herself to be touching a deity, to have the hold of a supreme being on her. I supposed in a way she was right, and while my grandparents might have been Primordials, I could certainly understand the way she would worship them.

After all, the humans of Nothrek had once worshipped me in the same way, believing me to be holy and worthy of adoration.

"What if the sacrifices no longer wish to fight for me once they remember who they are? Do they go free if this is not what they want for themselves?" she asked, bringing a smile to my face. For Estrella, free will was the most important gift she could give to anyone. She never wanted someone to serve her because it was required of them or because the consequences of doing anything else were too great for there to truly be a choice. Even if her entire army wished to leave her alone on the battlefield, she would let them leave her.

Because what they wanted mattered to her, in a way it had never mattered to me. That single trace of humanity within her was exactly why she would make the perfect Queen. Why my people would adore her so fully that I wondered if they'd even see me as their King.

"That is entirely up to you, my Queen, but I believe you underestimate the power of what you can offer them through their allegiance," Xela said, finally opening her eyes to guide Estrella out the front door of the cabin.

"What is that?" Estrella asked, and I didn't need to hear Xela's answer.

I felt it in my bones, felt the truth of it bang like a gong that would mark the turning of the tides.

Revenge.

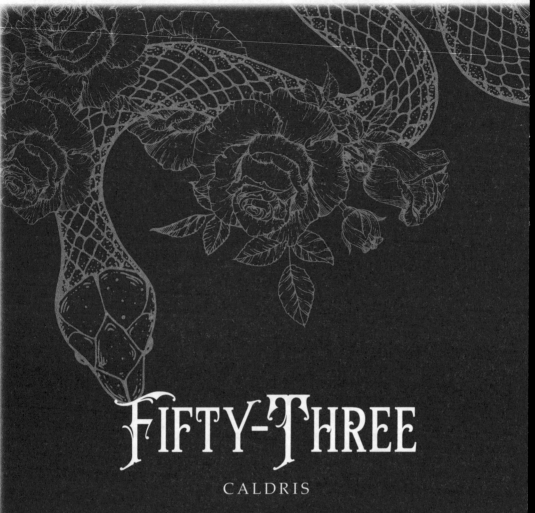

Fifty-Three

CALDRIS

The massive, long tables they'd pulled into the edge of the woods were decorated with vines that sprawled down the center. Flowers were dispersed through the vines, candles lit to offer dim lighting as darkness descended. Pieces of tree trunks were cut in perfectly uniform pieces, forming stools where people would sit. The plates were simple and white, crafted with painstaking precision to keep them as close to a perfect circle as possible. The same white fabric that Estrella and I wore was draped through the trees at the edge of the forest, cascading and framing the tables flawlessly. The trees were wound up in faerielights, strings of glowing embers that never burned looking like starlight.

"It's everything I've read about," Estrella thought, referencing the books she had buried herself in during our brief time with the Resistance in Nothrek. It seemed so long ago now, that she'd been unaware of who I was and fighting her own curiosity about the Fae and Alfheimr. She'd read about the festivals we celebrated, the meals

and the dancing that we'd all partaken in back before our world had descended into darkness. This kind of carefree celebration was before my time even, for Mab did not believe in joy. She chose only to celebrate the darker of our holidays, the ones that she'd twisted into sacrifices and a brutal version of sex. Some of our ceremonies were sexual in nature, but she'd taken the beauty of those moments and twisted them into darkness. She'd taken them from life to death.

Joy became punishment. Pleasure became pain.

The area beside the tables remained empty, a large space that was dedicated to nothingness. To Estrella, it probably looked like a place where the Fae and humans could dance together, could revel in the sounds of the human who played his lute with a soft and soothing sound, but the undercurrent of notes was sensual. It struck a chord deep within me, the magic of his music stoking the embers of a flame that I knew he would build over the course of the dinner.

If I was correct, that clearing wouldn't be where we danced the night away in celebration. It would be where Estrella was expected to accept pleasure. Where she was expected to enjoy herself and the knowledge that all who joined her here would wish to watch her with her chosen partner for the night. This was a celebration where an unmated woman would have chosen a partner from the crowd, where the rest would have wished it was her.

While they were unlucky enough that she would never be theirs to touch, it was fortunate for them that my little star loved to be watched. That she loved to come undone with an audience to bear witness to her pleasure.

All eyes were on us as we approached the head table, letting Xela guide us to the seat at the head. Estrella waited for me to sit, her eyes widening as I pulled out the tree stump and motioned for her to take it. The implication of placing her at the head was not lost on her, but she was the only one who was surprised by the act. Everyone around us knew that Estrella was the guest of honor, the one who would be at the center of attention for this night. She swallowed as she took the seat, carefully arranging the fabric of her skirt so she did not need to worry about the curious eyes watching her.

As the others took their seats, leaving the place to my mate's left for me, she scanned the group. Xela took the seat beside her to my surprise, but it made sense that the only other person Estrella knew would be the one to guide her through the evening. Rheaghan and Medusa were conspicuously absent from the feast, confirming my every assumption about the purpose of the strips of cloth in the little clearing. Someone must have told Rheaghan not to attend, more for Estrella's comfort than his as he did not know they were related.

Xela poured wine for both of us, and Estrella's nerves were obvious as she lifted the cup to her mouth and took a deep sip of the liquid. Estrella didn't ask any questions, hearing the facts in my mind as she raised the wine to her lips once again. The others at the table did the same, mirroring her movements. She groaned as she drank the liquid down, the magic imbued into it undoubtedly stroking the flames the music had already begun to build within her. A Fae woman snapped her fingers at the foot of the table, and Estrella jumped back on her stool slightly as her plate filled with food.

"Please, eat," Xela said, smiling as Estrella picked up a piece of fruit. She studied it cautiously, taking a gentle nibble at first before she dug in with more relish. While time moved differently here, while certain realities of the living were made less important in this strange place, it had been far too long since my mate enjoyed a meal.

Conversation started around us, casual and easy about the training or relationships that had begun among the people who called the village home. Estrella listened as she ate, grateful for the distraction from the trials that had been so stressful. Her thoughts wandered, the normalcy of the events occurring around her lulling her into a sense of calm, making her comfortable in a situation where she might have been on edge otherwise. She sank into the ease of it, the tempo of the music remaining calm and carefully sensual as she listened, offering a smile and partaking in the conversation where it called for her attention.

I slid my hand to her thigh beneath the table, sinking beneath the fabric where it parted. Her bare skin was as smooth as silk, gooseflesh rising in response to my touch. She smiled, though it was tense, as my touch wandered closer to the haven between her thighs. I didn't touch her there, but let my fingers play over the sensitive flesh of her inner thigh as she clamped her legs shut to attempt to dispel my touch. I grinned at her as her attention turned to me, leaning in to press my mouth to hers so sweetly that anyone watching might have thought it a moment of affection had it not been for the scent of her arousal on the air. I couldn't say for sure that anyone else would notice it, but I was far too attuned to my mate's desires to miss it.

"How did you two first meet?" a woman halfway down the table asked. Her face was lit with a bright smile, her eyes crinkling in the corners as she raised her wineglass to her mouth. "Was it love at first sight given your mating bond?"

The Fae who were in the settlement were limited, and I hadn't seen any mated pairs since we'd arrived. The understanding of our bond was probably limited given the erasure of all the memories that had come before, a bit of a fascination to the humans who either had never experienced such a thing or couldn't remember a time when they had.

"It was for me," I said, locking eyes with my mate. She rolled hers in response as my thumb stroked against the seam of her pussy under the table. She jolted at the contact, her body primed and ready for me so that even the faintest tease felt like a jolt of lightning in her veins. "I obviously had the privilege of knowing about our bond before I ever found her, so the moment I laid eyes on her, I was done for."

"Cheating, if you ask me," Estrella said, the mumble earning a laugh from the rest of the table.

I couldn't help but smile at her, sinking my teeth into my lip. "But even if I hadn't known, she was still the most beautiful woman I'd ever seen."

Estrella rolled her eyes again as her lips pursed, ignoring the sound of women swooning at the sweet moment. She knew it to be true now, could feel the genuine emotion behind the words, but that didn't mean that Estrella allowed herself to feel that. It didn't mean that her own self-conscious nature could accept them fully.

"What did you think of him, my Queen?" Xela asked, her eyes finally straying to me. Her stare wandered for the first time, but it wasn't entirely with the weighted gaze of attraction or the burn of lust. Instead, it was strangely calculating, though she did seem to conclude that she approved of what she saw.

Determining if she thought me worthy of Estrella, measuring me to decide what my mate might have seen the first time she looked at me.

It didn't stop Estrella from growling possessively, the sound rumbling in her chest. She placed her hand on my bicep, squirming when I finally brushed my thumb against her clit beneath the table. A quiet admonishment and reward all in one, I couldn't help the feral grin that took over my face at the sound of her jealousy.

"I thought he was absolutely fucking terrifying," she admitted finally, earning a laugh from those down the table. Xela glanced down, scolded for her wandering gaze, and I almost felt bad for the woman. "He snuck up on me in a barn when I was resting—"

"I tried to comfort her, but she's too fucking stubborn. She tried to run from me, even though I had taken great lengths to make myself appear less intimidating," I admitted, watching as she chewed another bite from her plate.

"Great lengths," Estrella scoffed. "You made yourself appear human, I will give you that. But less intimidating would have meant reducing your attractiveness, and you are far too vain to allow something like that, my love," she said with a chuckle, the affection in the words warming something in me.

"Are you insinuating I am arrogant?" I asked, pressing my free hand to my chest to feign offense.

"I'm not insinuating anything. I'm stating plain facts," Estrella argued, picking a berry from her plate and throwing it at my face. It bounced off my nose, landing on the ground beside me as I leaned in and placed my elbow on the table.

Invading Estrella's space came so naturally, the power play we constantly engaged in humming beneath the surface. In this place, she might have been the Goddess they all sought to worship and believe in. But at the end of the day, when we all retired to our beds, it would be me she obeyed. There was something powerful in that, in knowing that this strong woman followed my orders and obeyed my commands not because she had to, not because she was weak or needed direction.

But because she chose to. Because she wanted to be submissive to me and me alone because I was the only one who could make her kneel at my feet and do what she was fucking told.

"Have I somehow not proven to be worthy of all that I've claimed?" I asked slowly, letting her feel the torment in each word. I leaned forward, catching her bottom lip between my teeth and biting just hard enough to bleed her. That single well of blood was enough to charge the celebration with sex, her scent reaching even the humans as I licked it from her mouth and let it sink inside of me. Her taste on my tongue was the greatest aphrodisiac as the music increased in tempo, even the musician not immune to the magic of her. "Have I not made good on every single promise I've made you?" I asked, watching her pupils dilate with desire. She glanced away from me to the table of people watching our interaction with rapt fixation, my thumb stroking her beneath the table to drive her to the point of madness. I craved nothing more than for her to find that place where she was so lost to her own wants that she would embrace the discomfort that came with being watched, that she would revel in the attention that she deserved.

I wanted her wanton. I wanted her lost to anything but the feel of me moving inside her.

I wanted her to crave me to the point of desperation.

"Caldris," she said, her tone hesitant. It amused me that even after I'd fucked her in front of countless people before, she could still have that moment of insecurity. She could still wonder if this was what was right, if the desire to know that she was the point of fixation and desire for so many was what I wanted.

I lived for the knowledge that what they wanted would always be mine. I lived for the moments where they realized how blessed by the Fates I truly was to have her soul entwined with mine, to know that there was nothing I would not do for the woman that possessed me as much as I owned her.

I brushed the fabric off her shoulder, watching the white slide down her light brown skin. She was stunning as it slipped over her bicep, and she caught it and held it there as she studied me and tried to make her choice. If she wanted it, I would take her back to the cabin and fuck her there, but she and I both knew that she wanted to prove a point just as badly as I did. I wanted every man at this table to know she was mine, and she craved that same possession over me.

She wanted Xela to watch me fuck her, so that the woman whose gaze had lingered too long would understand that I would never even see her outside of when she existed in my mate's periphery. Estrella burned so bright she eclipsed every other woman from the world, casting them into the shadows of her light.

"They want me to prove that I am worthy of touching you, min asteren. They want me to prove that I am worthy of being your mate," I said, slowly sliding out of my chair. Everyone at the table stood as one, getting to their feet out of respect as I held out a hand for Estrella and waited to see if she would take it. If she would accept this ceremony willingly or if she would want to retreat to our private quarters. I would support her choice either way, revel in the feel of her body moving against mine.

She slid her palm into mine, letting me guide her to her feet finally. The fabric that had been draped over her flesh slid to the ground as she stood, leaving her nude as eyes fell to her. I led her through the gathered crowd, letting the onlookers have their view of the Goddess who walked among them. She moved with feline grace, her steps fluid and in time with the rhythm of the music that continued to play. She eyed the clearing as we entered, the strips of cloth hanging from the trees in two lines at the center. Waiting between the two largest trees that formed an archway, a ceremonial table had been crafted from stone. It was long and wide, intricate carvings of a faceless woman and a man etched into the stone on the side.

The woman took her pleasure from the man she'd tied down to the altar, her head thrown back in the throes of ecstasy.

I stripped out of my clothes while Estrella watched, her gaze bouncing between me, the audience who now watched us carefully, and the altar beside us. I knew the path her thoughts had wandered, that her uncertainty came from a place of insecurity.

While she knew I loved her and desired her more than anything, I had always been the one in control. I'd always guided her where I wanted her, particularly when we played with people to watch us.

She connected the pieces of the puzzle easily, understanding making her mouth drop open as I stood naked before her and turned my back to the altar. Lifting myself up onto it, I laid myself out along the surface.

Estrella hesitated beside it for only a moment before she climbed up onto it along with me, settling herself over my hips so that she straddled me. I raised a single hand to cup her behind the neck, bringing her down close so that her mouth touched mine as I spoke into our bond. *"It's just you and me, min asteren. Take what you need from your mate."*

Estrella twisted her hands at her sides, the thread of our bond pulsing in gold as she guided my hands up over my head. The thread dug into my flesh, warm and comforting in spite of the steady pressure as Estrella wound it around my wrists and fed it through the loop at the top of the altar.

For the first time in my life, I felt like the lamb that had been led to slaughter. Like the sacrifice I had seen so many times throughout my long history. This was an offering I would gladly give, my love and my body to the mate that I wouldn't have changed for anything.

"You're so beautiful," I murmured as she placed her hands on my stomach and stared down at me, studying her handiwork and deciding what she should do with me.

"I don't know what to do," she said, the nerves in her voice making my heart clench. Estrella had stepped into her own power in so many ways, but in this she still struggled to understand exactly how much power she wielded over me.

"Yes you do," I insisted, smiling up at her in encouragement. *"Get your cunt wet for me."*

"Your hands are busy," she snarked, but her mouth twitched in the barest hint of a smile.

"My mouth is not," I argued, bucking my hips ever so slightly to motion for her to shift her body. She did so, carefully inching her way up my body and settling herself when her legs were above my shoulders on the tableau. She stared down at me for a moment before she reached down, burying her hand in my hair and angling my neck as she lowered her pussy to my mouth.

I worked her over with my tongue, letting her guide me where she wanted me as she whimpered, her voice hoarse and throaty. Her arousal coated my tongue, and I could feel it simmering in her blood, the way her entire body needed this moment.

I was hers to touch. Hers to taste if she wanted. Hers to fuck.

She shivered above me as my tongue slid inside her briefly, gliding through her until I reached her clit. She shivered above me as I flicked it against her, adding pressure where she needed it most. *"They want to watch you come undone, my star. They want to watch you rearrange the heavens with your chaos,"* I spoke directly into her mind as I worked her over with my tongue, reveling in the feeling of her hand in my hair and the way she manipulated me for her use.

She was so fucking wet as I devoured her, sliding my tongue into her once more. Her body responded immediately, pulling me in as deep as she could and contracting around me, constantly seeking out more like the greedy thing she was.

"Please," she begged, her tongue darting out to lick her own lips. I gave into her, licking her until she was a writhing mess above me, her hips undulating so that she rode my face and took her own pleasure. Drawing her clit into my mouth, I sucked gently until she came, her entire body shaking with the force of it.

She all but collapsed after, maneuvering herself down to straddle my hips. She rested there for a moment, her chest heaving with the force of her breaths as she laid her body atop mine.

Touching her mouth to mine, she murmured a single gentle word of ownership for all to hear. "Mine."

She smirked at me as she pulled away, the look one of pure seduction, a quirk of her mouth as she rose to sit on top of my hips. The wet heat of her pussy touched my cock, making it twitch in response and the need to drive inside her. But no matter how I shifted my hips, I couldn't get the right angle with the way she'd positioned herself.

She grinned as if she understood exactly how much that tormented me. Her orgasm feeding down the bond had driven me to the edge.

"Fuck me," I said, the word an order that earned a startled gasp from the crowd watching.

They didn't understand that *this* was exactly the way my star liked me.

And it was exactly the way she would fucking have me, even as the little Goddess shook her head at me playfully and dragged a single finger down the center of my chest.

FIFTY-FOUR

ESTRELLA

I knew what they would say behind me, heard enough of the whispers to know that they thought him daring and bold for commanding me this way, that they thought him foolish and naive to think he could ever maintain control.

They didn't understand that I didn't want control in this, that when my clothes came off, I wanted nothing more than for my mate to tell me exactly what he wanted, but I would play their games for the moment. I would use him and take what I wanted from him, but I would do so knowing that when we returned to the privacy of our little cabin, I'd pay the consequences for toying with him.

It was in both his nature and mine, the very bones of our relationship. By day, he followed my whims, but by night, he led the way.

I grinned as I stared down at him, shifting farther down his thighs. The motion brought him farther from my core, the place that he'd wanted to be, until I straddled his shins and leaned forward, taking him in my hand and working his hard flesh.

I slid my grip up his shaft twice, rubbing my thumb over the head and gathering the precum that had accumulated there. I slid that thumb inside my mouth, tasting him as it spread over my tongue. Leaning farther forward, I replaced my thumb with the length of his cock, slipping him between my lips as I spread to accommodate his girth. He was warm as I guided him over my tongue, tilting my head instinctively to take him to the back of my throat with ease. He curved up toward his belly button naturally, making this angle difficult for me to take him as deep as the heat in his eyes said he wanted. He watched me anyway, enjoying what I could manage as I swallowed around him. His hips jerked upward, his body constantly seeking more.

I placed a hand on each side of his hip, pinning him down as I slid my mouth up and down and took him in shallow thrusts. Each one made my eyes water as I used my mouth to torment him. I made no effort to keep quiet as I pleasured him, the sounds obscene and erotic as I struggled to breathe through my nose. I held his stare through it all, the heat of his light blue eyes fading to black as I gazed up at him through my lashes. This was not an example of a woman being a hole to fuck, of being willingly used.

This was where a woman offered her mate pleasure, serving him because it brought her joy to watch him come undone and be able to do *nothing* to stop it.

He grinned at me as he heard my thought, groaning as I drew him deep. He struggled against the threads keeping him tied to the altar, and I drew my own pleasure from the growl that rumbled in his chest when he couldn't break free from them.

I swallowed as I finally drew back off of him, shifting to linger above his cock as I straddled him. I reached forward, dragging his hands down so that they rested upon the stone beside his shoulders, the threads shifting to do my bidding and retightening once I finished positioning him. I threaded my fingers through his, using his hands to support myself as I lowered down onto his cock, angling my hips to slide him in.

I worked him in bit by bit, my body needing time to adjust to the feeling of him inside of me. He spread me open as I worked over him, releasing one of his hands to rest mine upon his chest and get better support. "Fucking Gods," I gasped, rolling my hips over him as the head of his cock brushed against the end of me. I wanted it to stop and never end all at once, the distinct pinch of pain that came with taking him so deep had become something of an addiction. I knew that no one would ever make me feel this way, no one else could make me feel this way.

I pinned him still, keeping him where I wanted him as I held his stare. His blue eyes burned with lust as he breathed with me, my hips setting a hard, fast pace as I rode him and took my pleasure from his body. Another orgasm built in my core, my body moving to shift until the angle was just right and he stroked over that spot within me.

I came on his cock, trembling and gasping as I shook above him. He filled me with his own release when I lowered to lay upon his chest, loosening his bindings with a twist of my hand so that he could grip me by the ass and drive up into me in quick thrusts that brought him his own release quickly.

His grip was tight on my skin as he growled, the familiar warmth of his release flooding me. He kissed me, the embrace turning tender as I finished unknotting the bindings that kept him still.

My mate scooped me up into his arms and stood, carrying me from the clearing and heading for the privacy of our cabin for the night.

I smiled against his chest even as my exhaustion tickled at the edges of my awareness, because I knew before the night was over, he'd wake me so we could do it all over again.

Insatiable, insufferable male.

I woke with a start, my lungs heaving as I struggled for breath. The pain was indescribable as it tore through me, making me feel like I may burst into flames if I did not get up from the bed and *move*.

Caldris slept peacefully beside me as I tossed off the covers, getting to my feet and padding silently from the bed chamber. The sitting area was separated by a narrow-arched doorway, my armor freshly washed and waiting for me. Xela had draped it over the back of a chair by the door, the scaled armor resplendent in the moonlight shining in through the open window.

Crossing my arms over my chest, I covered my breasts from view as I leaned forward to look outside. The land around the house was still, the air quiet as a contradiction to the way it felt like I was boiling from the inside. Nobody else seemed to feel it, seemed to notice the need to move.

I winced as I stepped back, my thoughts a chaotic array in my mind. *"The Phlegathon calls you,"* came Fenrir's voice, his calm ease soothing my nerves that something had gone terribly, horribly wrong within the confines of my body.

"If this is how it calls to me, I don't think I have any desire to answer." The sarcastic tone was rich, even in my mind, coating the thought with my intent as Fenrir huffed in response. It was as close to a laugh as the wolf could come, a few rapid breaths to convey his amusement with me.

"The River of Fire," he said, the words sinking deep into me with all the ominous nature of a prophecy I did not want to come to bear. *"The call will be nothing compared to the pain of the river itself, Tempest."*

"Wonderful," I snarked, closing the window in my mind to shut the wolf out. As much as I adored the reality of having companionship with me at all times, of having a wolf and a mate who could help me through my darkest moments, there was something to be said for silence as I dealt with the pain in my body.

I grimaced as I lifted my armor from the chair, stepping into the pants and then the top, doing my best to lace everything as tightly as possible without any assistance. I didn't wish to wake Caldris so that he could watch me suffer, instead hoping that at least one of us could find the peace that came with a good night's rest. As another surge of lava flooded my veins, I closed the window on our bond as well. The sill wouldn't shut completely, leaving the window slightly ajar where the thread was determined to keep us linked. I had to hope it would be enough to dilute the emotions and the pain, keeping him blissfully unaware until morning came. While I needed to move because of the restless energy consuming me, I had no desire to leave him behind and make my way to the river in the danger of night.

I sat as I tugged my boots on, lacing them up my shins and then opened the door with a wave of my hand. It parted for me, brushed aside by the ease of magic that flowed from my fingers. The winter breeze that accompanied it reminded me of simpler times, of those too-brief days when I'd believed Caldris's magic to be the only magic I possessed. It was a wistful memory in spite of the complicated emotions I'd felt back then, the difficulty I'd had in accepting his role in my life and the future that had been carved out for me.

The loss of my humanity had always been something I'd struggled with, from the very first day. I didn't know how I would face the reality that the part of me I'd known for the majority of my life was gone in truth. I didn't know if it was possible to lose her any more than I already had.

I turned toward the field where we'd seen the warriors training when we arrived, ignoring the still ongoing party at the wood's edge. The sound of revelry and dancing was more than enough to keep me away from the celebration on its own, but the knowledge of what those people had seen was inescapable.

I would face them the following morning, in the light of day when my desires didn't feel so close to the surface. When the starlight didn't reflect off my armor in the same way it had shone on my skin while Caldris fucked me for all to see.

A lone figure stood in the center of the field, moving through a series of well-practiced movements. He was careful and controlled, precise in a way I had never seen. He wore no shirt, the lines of muscle crawling up the sides of his spine flexing with each motion.

I paused at the side of the field, watching him go through the dance-like movements with rapt fixation. This was so far from the male I'd thought I'd come to know in life, the humorous jester who thought he was amusing even when he stood in my way.

Rheaghan's head snapped to the side as he saw me watching him, his sword lowering to point toward the ground as the rest of his body turned to follow. "Shouldn't you be at the celebrations?" he asked, quirking a single brow.

His mouth didn't curve into the bright smile I knew, and that made me even sadder to admit. I'd been waiting for any trace of Rheaghan, searching for a mannerism that would make me believe he was still in there.

But he wasn't. He was just a shell of the man who'd once lived, a body without the memories that made him *him*.

"I'm not much for parties, I guess," I said, taking a few steps toward him. He must have trusted my intentions after our moment earlier, nodding as if he understood that.

He glanced down at his sword, hefting it in his hands. That green-eyed stare that was so like mine didn't rise back to meet me, and I felt deprived of it in the moments I waited. "Why is that?" he asked finally, running his thumb over the flat side of his blade.

I turned to stand beside him, staring out at the settlement he called home. He followed my stare, tensing when I didn't give him my attention again. "It seems so foolish to celebrate like this," I admitted, scoffing as I realized the truth in the words. I understood why the others needed it, why they craved the light in the darkness, but the weight of the night surrounding me was too heavy to ignore for a few hours. "There's so much pain out there. So much suffering, and I know it's only a matter of time before it steals someone else from me. The more time I waste, the more I think I'll lose in the end."

The tension in Rheaghan's body bled out, his muscles relaxing finally. He turned to face me, his entire body pivoting with the movement. Even though he kept his distance, I felt the intimacy of the moment, his eyes roving over my face as if he saw me for the first time.

"Then maybe you should grab a sword," he said, gesturing to the table with weapons strewn on top of it.

I furrowed my brow as I turned to look at him, studying the tense lines of his face. "Why would I need a sword?"

"Because our time is much better spent training to survive what may come tomorrow, so that we stand a chance of protecting the people we love when the battle comes," he said, watching as I nodded and took the first step toward the swords. I'd left my own in the cabin with Caldris, not intending for anything like this to occur. I hadn't known what drove me to this place, what brought my legs here when I'd wanted to leave the settlement entirely and begin my journey to the Phlegathon. It would have been a foolish choice to leave on my own in the middle of the night though, and even I knew that.

I hefted one of the short swords into my hands, the others looking too long and heavy for me to wield properly. I tested it in my grip for a moment, weighing it before I sank my teeth into my bottom lip and placed it back with the others.

I spun to face Rheaghan, leaving the table at my back as he tilted his head to the side. "Are you afraid to fight me, Estrella Barlowe?" he asked, my name sounding too familiar and too strange on his lips. His mouth curved with the challenge he issued to me, the woman I assumed he knew he was meant to follow into battle.

"No," I said, answering his smile with one of my own. "I am not afraid to fight you, Rheaghan. In fact, I don't need a sword to beat you in this arena. Here and now, you with your sword and just me." He couldn't know that my intent in using my magic against him was to attempt to draw him into that place where instinct and muscle memory took over. If I could only remind him of what it looked like to fight with things that were unseen and misunderstood, then maybe I could remind him just a bit of the man he'd once been.

The man he would be again.

"Are you sure you want to do that?" he asked, the confusion on his brow earning a grin from me. He had no recollection of the things he himself was capable of, no memory of what I could do.

I raised my chin, imagining that we were siblings who'd been gifted with the ability to know one another all our lives. Imagining everything we'd been deprived of as I smirked. "Unless *you're* the one who's afraid."

He smiled, shaking his head before lunging so quickly he thought to catch me off guard. I sidestepped his swing, letting it crash to the ground where I'd stood only a moment before. The speed of my movements surprised me, his shock mirroring what I felt as he spun in a slow circle to look at me.

He repeated his strike, darting forward at a run as I swept my hand along the grass at our feet. Wrapping my fingers around the threads I found there, I raised them up until the ground responded. The lump that formed between us tripped him, leaving him to spiral toward the ground.

"What the fuck," he mumbled, catching his balance just in time to avoid the crash.

I lashed out with a thread, using it like a whip that cracked against his face. The tiny bead of blood that welled on his cheek was a testament to the control I'd learned, and his hand reached up to touch it for a moment before he laughed.

We moved in tandem, his body moving with sharp thrusts and lunges meant to maim. I dodged them all, using the threads around us to defend myself. He jabbed his sword at my face, leaving me to wrap it up in threads that I snatched from the sky. They were golden when I grabbed them, gleaming with light as I twisted them around Rheaghan's sword and focused in on the hardness of earth. The threads turned to stone, the weight dragging Rheaghan's sword down to the ground as something fell from the sky.

The crow landed beside us, shattering into bits of rock upon impact. I swallowed back my remorse, hating that I'd been so wrapped up in our sparring session that I'd forgotten the implications of my magic. The threads controlled life itself, controlled fate and the universe.

It was not something to be toyed with, even if doing so would result in me having a better understanding of my magic. Rheaghan laughed as he got to his feet, the joy on his otherwise empty face almost worth the consequences of my stupidity.

He didn't seem oblivious to the way I stared at him, searching for signs of the man I knew. He released his hold on his sword finally, shoving his hands into the pockets of his pants.

"Did we know each other before I died?" he asked. The words were confirmation that he at least knew he was dead, that as much as they'd been stripped of all they knew, these people were at least given that much.

"Not well," I said with a sad smile. It was the truth, as much as it pained me. We'd been robbed of having more time together.

"I think I would have liked to know you better, Estrella Barlowe," he said, earning a smile from me as I stepped forward and held out my hand.

He met me halfway, grasping me by the wrist and leaving me to do the same. "Well, you can know me now instead," I said, offering him the only consolation I had.

That part had been a lie for the moment, but maybe not forever. If I survived long enough, if I was able to claim the army that had been intended for me, maybe both versions of Rheaghan would have the opportunity to know me.

Maybe, just maybe, I'd get to know my brother in the end after all.

FIFTY-FIVE

ESTRELLA

The journey to the Phlegathon took the entire morning after we bid the residents of the Tithe settlement goodbye with the rising sun. It had only taken a couple of hours for Caldris to awaken without me, seeking me out the moment he realized I was gone from the bed we'd shared. I'd spent those hours trying to draw Rheaghan into using his magic, exposing him to my powers constantly to no avail.

He'd still never thought to attempt them, and the reflexes I knew he must have remembered didn't kick in to accomplish the task either. It had made for a very bittersweet farewell, even if we both suspected it would be a temporary thing. I wanted nothing more than to convince him to come with us, to take the brother I'd never known away from this place and attempt to remind him of all he had once been. Instead, I'd left him behind, offering him the peace that came with not remembering the circumstances of his death.

Not remembering that it had been his own sister, the very

woman he'd desperately tried to protect from herself for centuries, who ended his life.

I reached up, holding out a hand for Belladonna as she shifted back to her living form and wound herself around my hand. As I passed her off to Medusa so the tiny creature could avoid the river and subsequent trial, my arm felt empty without her.

Caldris was quiet but supportive as we approached the river, words not needed between us in the moments where I stared down into the next river I would need to face. The river itself ran red, the water a mix of molten lava and hardened rock where it cooled as it flowed through the icy waters. The riverbanks were littered with skulls and bones, horrifying statues carved into the cliff face itself. A great winged beast with three heads perched atop the cliff where it had been carved into a collection of five skulls, his great, leathery wings spread wide as if preparing to take flight.

It was scaled like a serpent, so similar to the sea monster we'd seen only a day prior. But whereas that one had been beautiful and ethereal, this creature was molded from darkness and menacing even though it did not move. The craftsmanship that had been needed to craft such a statue was incredible, the dedication making me stare at the creature far longer than I should have.

I stared down at the lava, my blood boiling within my body already making me feel as if I was burning from the inside. The call of the river in my veins was what drew me forward, standing at the edge of the pointed cliff. The drop down to the river was too large for a human to survive, a blow that would shatter the bones of any mortal on impact. Caldris guided me toward the narrow, winding steps down to the riverbank that was made of human remains, the bones scattered about like sand.

I didn't leave that cliff face as I stared down at the river below, unable to tear my eyes off the burning water. Flames burned atop the water, steam hissing through the air to form little clouds. If the fall wouldn't have killed a mortal, the burning river would have certainly done it. With a swallow, I slipped my hand out of Caldris's grip, following the instinct that had me pressing closer to the edge. He knew my thoughts, watching me with apprehension as I prepared to do the very thing that he would warn me not to attempt.

But there was no arguing with the need inside me, no more patience now that we'd come this close.

I sprinted the rest of the distance to the edge, diving off it face-first. My arms stretched above my head, angling my body so that I could slip through the surface of the water as smoothly as possible. I had to hope that the water beneath the lava wasn't boiling, that it would only hurt for a moment before offering me a blissful reprieve from the pain I knew I would feel on impact.

I fell, time seeming to suspend in those moments when I closed my eyes and waited to feel the pressure of the water against me. I waited to break through the surface, feeling like I just kept falling.

And then I broke through, immense pain tearing through my body. First it was the horrible ache of the impact, the shattering of my bones that immediately worked to reknit themselves back together. My skull felt like it shattered into a million pieces, jagged edges putting pressure everywhere at once. That faded as I healed, the distinct scent of sizzling flesh reaching me through the water. My body burned, the lava and boiling water temperature consuming me in the flames. It felt as if my skin blistered, as if I would never reach the bottom and be freed from the eternal torment of brutal, endless heat.

I sank deeper into the water, my body unable to move through the pain, even though the panic that had started to consume me demanded I turn around. It warned of an impending death even I could not survive, a body melted into the Phlegathon never to be seen again. I'd reached the point of no return, the knowledge that I would never make it out of the water before it was too late.

So I swam deeper, heading for the volcanic rock at the bottom of the river. There was nothing to greet me there, no trial or Primordials waiting to cast judgment over me. With trembling fingers, I reached out to touch the rock at the bottom. My hand was red, the skin melted from my flesh to reveal the bleeding muscle beneath.

My finger stroked the rock finally, feeling as if this was my last breath. I didn't allow myself to feel the panic or the fear, sinking deeper into the pain and just wishing it would end. I knew Caldris would feel it, that he would know exactly what my last moments were filled with, so I worked to pull the window closed on our bond, sheltering him from the moments that *had* to be the end.

My palm sank into the rock, fingers splaying across the surface as a current snatched me up, sweeping me away from it all.

I tumbled into icy waters, the temperature difference cooling my burns. My entire being throbbed as it healed, the cold putting my system into something of a shock. I trembled, my entire body shaking as I spun in a circle in that current, tossing head over feet and lost to it completely.

When I fell to the ground finally, the river spitting me out onto red sands beneath me, I felt like I could barely move. I wanted to cease to exist, the agony in my form making me lie limply for a minute as I fought to look around the place I had landed.

I knew I was not safe. I knew that this trial would not wait for me to recover, but I couldn't bring myself to move.

A rush of wind hit the side of my face, capturing my attention as a great bird eclipsed the sun. I rolled to the side just in time to evade the mouth that opened wide enough to tear my head from my body, forcing myself to my feet. My hand perched on the ground supportively as I squatted, my gaze traveling up the winged creature from the cliffs beside the river. A giant winged serpent with four legs, I recognized it from the books I'd explored as a child. It was one of the myths Nothrek had no qualms sharing about Alfheimr, a monster straight from anyone's nightmares.

Each of the hydra's three heads watched me as it opened its mouth and roared its fury, making me move slowly as I stood to full height. I fought to keep my movements cautious, not to alarm the beast with any sudden threats as I reached behind my head to grab my swords. The creature lunged anyway, forcing me to pull them free with more speed. I swung them in an arc, narrowly missing the beast as I dove sideways. The gaping hole of its mouth stunk of rotting meat as it grazed by my head, the second mouth heading for me the moment I dodged. I struck with brutal efficiency, curving both blades inward in a calculated strike.

Each highly sharpened blade cut through the creature's neck, slicing a narrow piece from the center of its throat as they ran parallel to one another and emerged out opposite ends as my arms crossed. Ducking out of the way the moment the head rolled to the ground, I recentered myself and turned back to face the beast once more as I readied my stance and brought my swords back to their natural position at my sides.

The hydra floundered for a moment, a deep, rumbling roar coming from one of the mouths that still waited for me. Blood bubbled from the gaping wound where the third head had been, dripping like acid down its scales as something moved within the neck. My horror knew no end as the scales regrew, extending the neck from the place where I had cut it. But instead of simply regrowing the head I'd already disposed of, the neck grew longer, diverging into two paths where there should have been one. It was a slow, meticulous growth that I could do nothing but watch as each scale appeared, the top of the neck curving as the bones and flesh sprouted to form two new heads.

"Fuck," I muttered, dodging when one of the new heads lunged for me. The ferocity in the movement was all revenge, all hatred and anger. Before the creature had simply wanted to eat me, but now as it chased me around the arena, I knew the matter had become deeply fucking personal. A tail whipped into the side of my ribs, knocking me sideways as the bones shattered. One of my swords flung from my hand, skittering across the mix of sand and rocks to land at the hydra's feet. The monster stepped on it with a massive taloned paw, scowling down at me with too-intelligent eyes.

I adjusted my grip on the only sword that I still held in my hands, considering my options as I worked to evade the next strike. I was too slow, leaving me with only one choice.

I ducked beneath the creature's mouth, grasping the hilt of my remaining sword in both hands as I slid beneath the hydra's belly. I stabbed at the scales there, desperately trying to penetrate what I had hoped would be soft underbelly. The sword bounced off, the vibrations of the impact rattling my wrists and arms and making them ache. The hydra moved its massive body, huge feet coming for me as I scrambled to get out from beneath it.

It knocked into me with the side of one of its necks, curving and colliding with itself as I tried to race out of its grasp. There was no freedom, no vulnerability to be found as I turned to face the thing. I released my sword that would prove useless to me, letting it fall to the ground as I focused in on the power at my disposal. Without my magic in this trial, I'd have been dead on sight. I wouldn't have stood a chance, and the injustice of that knowledge fueled the fire of rage in my belly.

For all the Fates claimed they had plans for me, those plans seemed to involve my death more often than not.

I screamed at the beast, matching the roar it emitted as it moved. It was too fast for its size, seemingly an impossible feat as it raced to cross the distance between us. The threads slipping off of it felt too hot to touch, burning my palms and as hard as rock as I grasped them in my hands, the sizzle of my flesh distracting me from my purpose.

When the first head came too close, I wrapped the threads of its own life around it, holding it still and squeezing with all my might to hold it against all the odds. The threads tore at my palms, drawing an anguished scream from me as it sank into my burning flesh, cutting through muscle and bone alike. I did the same with the next head that came for me, wrapping it up in the threads and holding it still. Pinned between the two heads, I waited for the others to maneuver toward me, holding my position until the last possible moment. Only when I held the red-eyed stare and watched flames gather in the depths of the third's throat did I finally release them, moving with all the speed in my legs to duck beneath them and *run*.

Fire followed in my wake, a trail of flames that caught each of the two heads I'd held prisoner, engulfing them as they screamed in pain. The hydra writhed in pain as its own fire sank into its open mouths, traveling down its throats, distracted by the death I hoped would be permanent. I watched from the corner of my eye, waiting for the two heads that burned to regrow.

The hydra was weakened by the loss, stumbling sideways as it fought to regain its balance. As it looked for how to continue forward with the stumps that did not seem to heal. The flames eventually died out, instead burning like embers that spread down to the hydra's chest. I suspected I could wait for it to continue spreading, but there was no telling how much damage the hydra could do while I waited for that. Using the distraction to my advantage, I searched for my blades. The sword I found gleamed in the red sand, the metal red and overheated from the fire it had been caught in. I swallowed as I glanced down at my already burning palms, at the mess that had once been my hands.

Pushing through that pain, I raced toward the hydra, grabbing the sword up off the ground as I went. The pain was immediate, an agony I could not tolerate spreading up my arm. The flames engulfed me, giving me mere moments to react. With a single sweep of my sword in a wide arch, I severed the two remaining heads from the creature. Touching the blade to the top of the wound, I forced it down into the sizzling flesh with both hands, cauterizing the wound and hoping that it would be enough.

I did the same with the second, dropping the sword and stumbling to fall onto my back on the sand. The flames left me, my *viniculum* glowing with gold as it fought to fix the damage to my body. Skin slowly reknitted, covering the flesh that made us all. My body felt weak and drained, but I used the last of my energy to raise my head and stare at the hydra, watching for any signs of life. It remained still on the ground, the embers spreading through its body until it turned to dust and bone, a breeze catching it and spreading ashes on the wind.

I sighed, dropping back down to the ground beneath me. Relief was immediate.

As was the exhaustion that tore me into the depths of sleep, the vague foggy vision of a man stepping up beside me. His golden eyes gleamed as he smiled down at me, telling me to rest now as he gathered some of the ashes from the hydra into a vial.

Using the last of my energy, I let my eyes drift closed as I raised a hand, the sight a gruesome mix of flesh and bone, of skin and muscle.

I gave Khaos the finger as I fell into darkness.

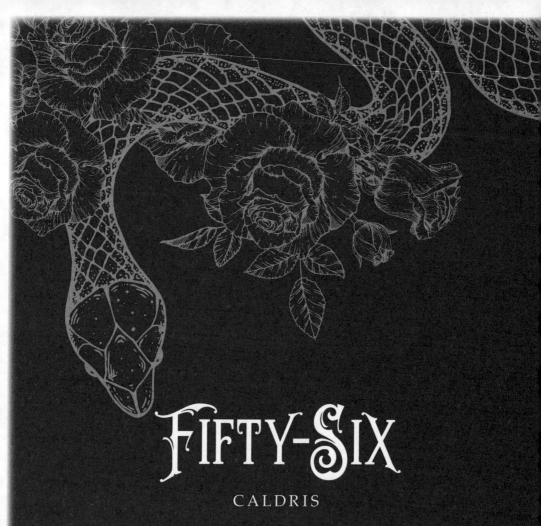

Fifty-Six

CALDRIS

Estrella did not emerge from that river. There had been so much pain in the moments before our bond went dark, absolute agony and burning. The very idea that the Fates and Primordials had decided to subject her to something that would bring her this much suffering made me murderous.

What purpose could there be in this? What could she possibly prove by surviving pain the likes of which no creature should ever feel?

How could her own fucking father decide that this was what was right for his daughter?

She was his own flesh and blood, the one child he had supposedly borne with the woman he loved.

I paced at the riverbank, having descended the narrow path the moment Estrella dove into the river. The skulls and bones crushed beneath my feet as I moved, the crunch and snap of them drawing a wince from Nemain with every step. In her inability to speak, she seemed far more greatly affected by the noises around her, as if her own forced silence amplified all else. "She should be back by now," I hissed, turning to Medusa with a glare.

The Gorgon woman met my stare, her mouth twisting in her own concern as she nodded. "You feel nothing in the bond?" she asked, taking a step toward the river as if she might jump in after Estrella.

As if I wouldn't have done it myself if I'd been able, but only those who were called to the trials could enter the rivers without risking being lost to them. If I entered, I would never find the path to the trial.

I would simply perish for daring to interfere.

"It's silent. Like she's asleep," I said, shaking my head. Medusa paced along with me, her own anxiety rising in response to the silence. Minutes turned to hours, leaving me with nothing to do but wait and hope.

When change finally came, it was in the parting of the river. The red waters and lava split down the middle, revealing a narrow path of rock at the bottom. A man emerged from the river, walking upon the sands with casual ease.

It was the woman cradled in his arms that made me take a step forward, stopping only when Medusa thrust her arm out in front of me, ceasing my progress. Estrella was limp as he carried her, and if it had not been for the deep, intuitive knowledge that she still breathed, that our bond still remained, I would have thought her dead. Her head hung back where it was draped over the man's arm, her arm dangling at her side. As he made his way out of the river, the waters crashed back together behind him, a wave rocking through it that somehow never reached us. Instead, it lapped against the cliff on the other side, leaving behind a stain of red that looked like blood smeared along a wall.

Khaos shifted Estrella in his hold, glaring at me as he handed her over. She moaned, a deep, pained sound as I took her from his arms, cradling her close. She smelled of fire, that burning acrid scent clinging to her skin in a way that made me clench my jaw.

"Was she successful?" Medusa asked, approaching the man she shared a child with. Khaos nodded, reaching into his pocket and pulling out a single vial filled with ash. He placed it in Medusa's open palm, allowing the woman to cradle it for a brief moment before she handed it to Badb, letting the Morrigan put it with the other items Estrella had collected in her trials.

"She was," he said, his voice deep and emotionless. He didn't seem to regret the obvious pain Estrella had suffered, didn't seem to care one way or another that she would continue to put herself in danger for the sake of proving her worth to him. He should have valued her for who she was, not only needing to see what she could do. "Only the Cocytus stands between her and the Cradle of Creation now, God of the Dead. You would do well to remember that she is not a damsel in need of saving. She is a catalyst who will change everything about the world as you know it. These trials—"

"Are the product of a male who does not care for his own child," I snapped, ignoring the cautionary hand Medusa placed on my forearm.

Khaos studied me for a moment, his face impassive. There was nothing there for a moment, and then his burnished golden eyes burned deeper, his nostrils flaring.

"I care," he spat, the response coming with more emotion than I'd have thought him capable of. "There is not much in this world I care for in the slightest, but for my wife and my daughter." He reached out with his hand, cupping Medusa's cheek in his palm. The genuine affection as she leaned into that touch was everything we'd been told Primordials could not feel, everything my parents had claimed they'd never had from their own sires.

Love didn't exist for the very beings who were not human in any way, but simply wore a human form as they wished. They were the personification of the world, pure power contained into one creation.

"You have a funny way of showing that love," I said, adjusting Estrella in my grip. She groaned as she snuggled into my chest, sinking deeper and recognizing the familiarity of my arms. I wanted nothing more than to lay her down and snuggle up with her, to offer her a comfortable place to heal, but there was nothing but rock and bone nearby.

"One day, you may understand that we have greater responsibilities to the world than we do to our loved ones. Estrella may be my daughter, but she is also capable of bringing great harm to the world if I do not weigh her carefully. I must know what she is capable of to know if she is ready for the responsibility I will soon lay at her feet," he said, releasing Medusa finally to give me the full force of his glare. "Your world depends on it."

He shook his head, taking a step back from us. I thought he might disappear into the river once more, but instead he let his eyes fall closed. His body burst into darkness, exploding out into the night of a thousand stars before my eyes.

It was the perfect reminder that the body that housed him wasn't truly *him*, that he existed beyond physical confines. He was so much more than he appeared, a destiny in the wind.

And then he was gone, fading into the dim light and leaving us behind. I hiked Estrella higher into my arms, turning to her mother fully as my mate slept.

"Whatever you're hiding, whatever you have planned for Estrella, know this," I warned, my voice a stern command that I knew Estrella would scold me for if she'd been awake. "She will not tolerate your secrets or your lies. She will not allow herself to be a pawn in whatever game it is the two of you are playing. You may think you have her right where you want her, but I promise you, if you back her into a corner, she will make you regret it."

Medusa's answering smile was sad and the way she reached up to pat my cheek was motherly rather than condescending.

"Unfortunately, Estrella's time in Tartarus will be the extent of my time with her. I will not leave my home to journey back to your world with her. Whatever consequences there may be for doing what is necessary to guide her to her destiny, they won't matter for me in the end. Estrella will leave Tartarus as she came," Medusa said, her look pointed. I understood the message in it, the warning she wanted to convey, even if she didn't elaborate.

I understood the word she didn't speak, the one that hung between us that neither of us wanted to lend voice to.

Alone.

I opened my mouth, fully prepared to risk it all to have that conversation. But a figure raced down the steps carved into the cliff, hurrying and looking over his shoulder as if he expected to be followed. I'd have recognized him anywhere, even if I'd only seen him briefly in that first night after I found Estrella.

He'd died so quickly, a fact that I both regretted for my mate's sake but could also appreciate, given his hesitation in allowing her to be near me. Had he lived, I had no doubt he would have proved to be a large inconvenience to my interest in her.

Had he lived, I might have needed to kill him myself, and when that truth came out, Estrella would have never forgiven me.

He hurried across the bones, wincing and jumping as each one cracked beneath his feet. Medusa rolled her eyes toward the sky, as if she too couldn't find any joy to be had in his presence. But I knew that Estrella would likely be pleased to find him safe.

"Why is he not suffering?" Medusa asked, and I wondered what she meant.

Badb laughed, crossing her arms over her chest as he approached. "Your daughter freed him from the eternal torment Khaos gave him," she said, making me smile.

Of fucking course she had.

"Brann," I said, leaning down to run my nose alongside Estrella's. The feral urge to lay claim to the woman was illogical, particularly knowing that she viewed Brann as nothing more than a brother even if they were not blood related. He paused, studying me intently and measuring me up. His eyes widened as realization dawned, and it occurred to me that Estrella had not informed him of who I was. I'd assumed he'd known, that he'd been able to see through my glamour and that was why he'd been so adamant that they needed to leave me behind that night. But the shock written into the lines of his face said the opposite, that he was horrified to see the bond between us glowing bright and completed. I couldn't help the arrogant smirk that I knew transformed my face, watching him so disturbed by the sight of my mate in my arms.

"Caldris," he breathed, my name coming out as a horrified sigh. "What have you done?"

"Bold of you to assume I would do anything to harm my mate, Lunar Witch," I snapped, watching as Medusa rolled her eyes. She shucked off the cloak she'd draped over her shoulders in spite of the heat, laying it down on the smoothest patch of bones and dust she could find. I followed without a word, laying Estrella down on it so that she could rest in peace. Positioning myself between her and Brann, I crossed my arms over my chest. "Whereas the last I saw of you, you attempted to drive a knife through my mate's heart."

Brann swallowed, pursing his lips as if ashamed of his actions. "Can you really blame me? You of all people know what Mab is capable of. I was trying to save her from that fate," he said.

"You were trying to save yourself from being dragged into that situation along with her. You never cared if Mab found her. It was only a matter of time before she did and you knew it. She was never meant to remain in Nothrek forever. She was meant to be with me," I hissed, hating the futility of the argument. None of it mattered now in truth, except that maybe, just maybe, we could have defeated Mab centuries ago. We could have saved countless lives and spent decades together.

We could have had children already, the thought hitting me with a pang of longing. Instead, I had a mate who thought herself only to be in her twenties with an eternity spread out before her. We had all the time in the world, and I would not allow her to rush into mother-hood for the sake of my desire for children.

All because of what he'd robbed me of. All because he'd been selfish and stolen her from the other Lunar Witches so that he could remain hidden away and never have to face Mab.

"That isn't true," he said, shaking his head. He looked around the side of me, studying Estrella's face with a somber expression. "I never wanted this for her. I wanted her to have a normal life. To just get to be without words like *fate* and *destiny* hanging over her. You don't understand what it's like to watch someone grow. To help raise them from a baby to a woman over and over and fucking over again and then watch her die. She may have seen me as a brother, but she was always more like a daughter to me. And there was never any-thing I could do to stop the ticking of the clock, but at least I knew she would come back. I knew she'd reincarnate, and I'd get to see her again. But if the Veil came down and she died . . ." He trailed off.

"She'd be gone," Medusa said, finishing the thought as under-standing filled her face.

"And what excuse did you use to justify not returning her to Alfheimr when she came into her last life? There would be no rein-carnation for her after that final death, and you tried to kill her," I said, half hoping I could drive the man to violence.

It would have been stupid, and it wouldn't have taken even a flick of my finger to knock him on his ass, but sometimes, you just wanted to punch another man in the fucking throat and watch him choke.

"I wanted one last life with her, and I wasn't willing to let that go until I had no choice. When the time came, I knew death would be a kindness compared to what Mab had in store for her," he admitted, shrugging his shoulders as Estrella stirred behind us. "She may be your mate, and I understand that her place is at your side now. But for thirteen lives, she has been my responsibility. I couldn't bear to admit that I'd done wrong by her when I took her from the rebellion. I couldn't return her to Imelda and just say I was sorry for taking her away."

"Yeah, I'd have been afraid of what Imelda would do to me, too, if I'd pulled the same shit you did," I said, letting the conversation fall into silence. I moved to Estrella's side, sitting next to her and pulling her head into my lap so that she could be more comfortable. Her skin was pink where it was visible, like it was fresh and new and warm to the touch.

I didn't dare to think of what she'd survived in that trial. What she'd had to accomplish to survive yet again.

FIFTY-SEVEN

ESTRELLA

My skin felt too tight as we approached the Cocytus the next day. Brann and Caldris had been mostly silent after I finally awoke, but I didn't have the energy to ask what their conversation had been while I was asleep. For them to practically ignore one another's existence while we traveled together by foot did not bode well for me at all. I reached up, removing Belladonna from where she'd wound herself around my bicep. The purple snake slithered down to the ground, making her way to Medusa who would look after her while I was gone. She was almost as comfortable with her as she was with me, and it brought me strange comfort to know with absolute certainty that she would be looked after if something happened to me.

That out of all the creatures in the world, at least the little snake would have a place to belong. She'd return to the home she'd had before me, and I wasn't too proud to admit it was probably a safer one than I could offer her. The river gleamed with a blue that reminded me of sadness, the surface rippling as I stepped into the water. My muscles twitched with the shock of cold, but I forced myself to move deeper into the waters.

This was my final test, the final trial standing between me and the Cradle of Creation. I moved quickly, hoping to get through it sooner rather than later.

It was only the knowledge that the end to these struggles was so close that kept me moving, my irritability and exhaustion threatening to make me give up. I wanted nothing more than to rest for a week, to allow the bone-weary tiredness I felt take control and hide beneath the covers. These trials were not meant to be survived, because anyone who had less to live for than I did would no longer want to win.

I fought back tears as I moved into the water, grateful for the moment without Caldris's watchful eyes. I knew he felt everything I did, knew the sympathetic, soft stare he leveled me with constantly came from a place of understanding. There was no hiding how deeply that last trial had wounded me, both physically and emotionally. It had weakened all my resolve, sinking deep into me and making me doubt myself in ways I hadn't thought ever to do again. I'd been so close to death, so close to burning alive in that river and then the battle with the hydra.

If my life was always going to end in flames, if I was always going to be destined to die, then why was I fighting so hard to stay in the world of the living?

The only answer I had was love. It was what motivated me to push through and submerge myself in the Cocytus.

My ears rang as the water poured in, surrounding me and suffocating me. The sound of wailing filled me, an ear-piercing shriek that surrounded me and forced my hands to cover my ears in an attempt to shut it out. My mouth opened on a silent scream that matched the one I heard, my voice joining the cacophony of sound. My lungs burned as the water filled them, setting me aflame from the inside out as darkness pressed in.

I landed on the grass beneath me, sputtering and spitting out the water I'd swallowed. My stomach purged itself, emptying in a wave that felt like it would never end. The water itself tasted of salt, acrid and burning as my eyes watered.

Pushing myself to my feet as soon as I stopped vomiting, I looked around the garden surrounding me. Lush plants and trees were artfully arranged into neat patterns, a circular clearing at the center. It was covered in cobblestone, a natural pool in the middle with water the same blue as the river above my head. The waters rushed over me, carrying spirits and spectral forms down the current. Their mouths were opened into silent screams that I could no longer hear from my place beneath the waters, but the memory of that sound was one that I knew I would carry with me always.

It was the pain of grief, of loss and agony so thorough it knew no end.

The waters in the pool rippled, the branches of a tree hanging over it swaying as it bubbled. I stepped up beside it, staring down into the pool that seemed to have no bottom. A lone figure swam toward the surface, forcing me to back away as the male came closer and closer and then finally emerged from the depths. Water dripped down over his features as he flung his head back, flinging droplets of water at me as he tossed his hair out of his face, running strong fingers through it.

He was nude entirely, his body more on display than I'd ever seen it in my past. In our nights tucked away in the privacy of the woods, we'd never bothered to fully disrobe. It wasn't safe, not when the risk of discovery came with too many consequences. We'd needed to be ready to flee at a moment's notice. I averted my gaze quickly, focusing in on his face even though he didn't seem at all perturbed by his stark nakedness.

"Loris?" I asked, hating the anguished expression on his face. It was one that matched the wails I'd heard in the river, and now that he'd presented himself to me, I could make out his voice in the memory. The deep, mournful cry that I'd never heard in life struck straight into my chest.

"Why?" he asked, his face pinching with the word. It was barely a whisper between us, so sad and heartbroken that I floundered for an answer. The last time I'd seen the man who had once been my lover, I'd killed him.

I'd been the reason he died, the one to send him to the afterlife. I'd never imagined he might come to Tartarus instead of reincarnating, never dared to think of what might have become of him. The guilt was too great to bear when faced with his new reality, plunging into my heart like icy talons gripping my heart.

"Why what?" I asked, shaking off the thoughts that wouldn't help either of us. The question seemed obvious, but I couldn't stand to make assumptions about what he may need answers to. Not when I'd already taken so much from him as it was.

"Why did you kill me?" he asked, his face twisting into a sob.

"I didn't mean to," I said, the truth strangling my throat. "You were trying to kill me, and the *viniculum* couldn't allow that. I wouldn't have hurt you intentionally. You know that."

"Do I?" Loris asked, running a hand through his hair that was darkened by the water clinging to it. There was something violent in the motion, an energy that was barely restrained. "Why is that exactly? Was it because you loved me so much you couldn't bear to live without me?"

The sarcastic tone of the words made me flinch, the harshness seeming completely out of nowhere. Loris and I had been clear from the very beginning of our physical relationship that what we shared was never going to be about love. It was never in the cards for us, and we'd only wanted to taste what was forbidden. "You were my friend," I said, letting him feel the genuineness of those words. He may not have been the love of my life, but I'd cared for him in my own way.

"Right. Your friend," he said, sinking his teeth into his bottom lip. "Because you have a filthy fucking Fae mate, and I was just the placeholder."

"How was I supposed to know that I had a mate or that the Veil would fall? What I felt for you was an entirely different situation that had nothing to do with him," I argued, wincing as he took a step toward me. I backed away instinctively, not wanting his hands to touch me. I didn't know what Caldris could feel when I was in the river, if he could hear the thoughts. Our bond was silent for me when I was gone, only the barest of impressions coming down the bond as if the river muffled it.

"That's not entirely true," he hissed, his steps continuing as I backed over the flowers behind me. I raised my feet, trying not to trample them as I watched tears track down Loris's face. "You may not have been aware of his existence before the Veil fell, but that doesn't mean your heart was ever yours to give. You were never going to be capable of loving me."

"We agreed when we decided to get physical. We both knew it was only a matter of time before you chose a wife, and I had to marry whoever they decided for me. Love was never going to be mine to give whether it was with my mate or a human husband," I said, my back striking the trunk of one of the trees at the edge of the grove. The bark dug into the back of my head, my hair tangling on the rough surface as I tried to keep my distance.

"The difference, Estrella," he argued, his head tilting to the side. I didn't know if I should expect anger or sorrow, his features flashing between the two emotions so quickly that I couldn't keep track. They were so entwined together, a horrible mix of emotions that was so strange on Loris's face. In life, he'd been so carefree. He'd been the gentlest of the Mist Guard, completely different from the rest of the harsh men who had made up that force. "Is that you would have hated your husband for the rest of your life. I would have been the only man you ever *chose* for yourself. I accepted the fact that they wouldn't allow me to marry you. I accepted the fact that one day, I would have to watch you bind yourself to another, because I knew we would always have those nights in the woods. I knew I would find a way to continue to meet you and continue our relationship in secret. I knew nothing needed to change, and that I would spend every day for the rest of my life looking at your children and wondering if they were his or mine."

I fumbled for words, trying to grapple with understanding. None of what he said made any sense with the man I knew, none of it lined up with any of the conversations I remembered us having. We'd planned to go our separate ways once there was a spouse involved, because neither of us wanted to hurt innocents who might have had real love involved. Not when we were just in it for pleasure that could be found in any body. "That was never what I wanted."

Loris reached out, running his thumb over my cheek. "And what of what I want? Does that not matter to you at all?" he asked, glancing above his head.

Three golden apples hung from a tree branch higher up, too far for him to reach but more enticing than I could ever recall a simple apple looking. His stare came down to mine once again, his eyes burning as he leaned into my space more. With his mouth only a breath from mine, I turned my head away and gave him my cheek. "Stop it," I hissed.

"We can still have those forbidden nights in the woods, Estrella. That's my price," he said, the bitterness and pride in the words making my heart sink into my stomach. That was the one thing I could not do, the one task that I would never complete. I wouldn't step out on my mate, wouldn't engage in any activity that would hurt him or bring him shame.

He came before everything else.

"Your price?" I asked, swallowing as the world spun at my feet.

"You cannot reach the apples without *my* help. You were the greatest betrayal of my life, and now it brings me great joy to know that you will never leave this place without me. You may want to return to your mate, but I will do everything in my power to make sure you never see him again. If I must suffer here, then I'll at least do it with you at my side," he said, pressing his hand to the front of my throat. The touch was far more aggressive than anything Loris had ever done before, harsh where he was usually sweet.

"Loris, please. This isn't you," I said, shaking my head and trying to squirm away from his grip without causing him any more harm than I had already done.

"You want my help? I want you to go back to your fucking mate and be forced to tell him what you've done. I want to fuck you one last time, Estrella. I want to know what a Goddess feels like on the inside, and I want to go into my afterlife with the joy of knowing I have ruined you for him," he said, angry tears accompanying the words.

"No," I said, my voice catching with emotion. My throat closed, the pressure around me feeling like a hand on my neck and squeezing. My mouth opened on a scream but didn't allow any sound to pass, my lungs filling with water I could not see.

"Then I reject you, Estrella Barlowe. You have failed the Trial of the Cocytus," he said, his voice strengthening as he stepped away. I sank to my knees, clawing at my throat as the water burned through my lungs. It was so cold, so brutal as I sank into the depths of the river once again.

I'd failed, and that was how I died.

Fifty-Eight

CALDRIS

Estrella sputtered as the river spat her out, washing her ashore. She struggled to breathe as the sand scratched at the surface of her armor, leaving me to haul her away from the riverbank. Her body was limp as she fought for breath, the lack of response from her making worry settle in my gut. There was nothing held in her hands, no sign of her victory, but a loss shouldn't have meant she survived.

In all the trials I'd seen her survive, in all those I'd seen play out in her head as she thought back, she would have died if she had not won. This felt different, her body weakened greatly even though I couldn't find an injury on her. I ran my hands over her, waiting for her to react or cry out in pain.

But there was nothing except her blank stare as she blinked up at me. Medusa stepped up beside us, turning back to the fishing village we had passed on our journey. "We need to get her to safety for the night," she said, the seriousness of her voice making me nod. I lifted Estrella into my arms, hating the way she hung there limply. Her eyes were open, staring at the river as we left it behind, but I wasn't certain she truly saw any of it. She dug the side of her head into my shoulder, raising an arm to cover her other ear as if she needed to drown out a sound that I couldn't hear.

Focusing in on our bond, I followed it down the thread to her mind, flinching the moment the screams of agony reached me. They were lessened in my mind, and even that was bad enough to make me crave the silence.

"Make it stop," Estrella mumbled, her voice broken. She whimpered as she squeezed her head tighter, and it was all I could do to turn to her mother helplessly.

Medusa paused, turning back to us. "Some distance will help her," she said, but the sad expression on her face told me it wouldn't be enough. That it wouldn't drown out the sound of that wailing in her head. It was enough to drive anyone to the point of madness, to make them wish for the end. I picked up my pace, desperate to do what I could to diminish the strength of it at least.

"What happened?" I asked, glaring at the Morrigan where they moved in silence at our side. The three of them exchanged a look between them, debating what they should tell me.

"She failed," Badb said finally, her gaze locked on Estrella's pained face. "It is a token to her strength that the river allowed her to leave at all, but every failure will take something from her. She will grow weaker, until she isn't strong enough to fight the pull of the river. If she does not find a way to win this trial, the Cocytus will be her final resting place."

I looked down at my mate as we entered the village, Medusa conversing with one of the fishermen. He pointed us toward an empty cabin, leaving us all to share a single roof for the night. I moved into the doorway quickly, laying Estrella on the bed and checking on her through our bond. The wailing was less potent, to the point that she could hear us around her and try to focus on the words we spoke. But that wailing was ever present in the back of her mind, a reminder of what waited for her. "And what if she doesn't go back? What if she abandons the trials altogether?" I asked, unable to fathom the thought that she might have come all this way just to lose at the very end. That the last trial might be the one to defeat her.

"Then she will never enter the Cradle of Creation, and she will slowly lose herself to the screams of the grieving. Once a trial has been lost, I'm afraid there is no turning back to the land of the living. She can no longer simply leave. She will either try again, or she will remain here forever," Macha explained, her voice solemn.

"Leave us," Medusa snapped, ordering the Morrigan out of the cabin. They disappeared into the dim light outside, but she didn't dare to try to command me away from my mate's side. "Tell me what happened. Tell me so that I can help you win when you go back."

Estrella cleared her throat, forcing herself to sit. When she spoke, her voice was hoarse as if she'd spent an eternity screaming. Her stare on me was hesitant, and I considered offering to leave so that she and Medusa could talk it through more comfortably, but the first word she spoke guaranteed that I could not leave.

"Loris," she said, the name sinking inside of me. Even if we hadn't discussed her once lover, just the name of a male would have been enough to raise my hackles. "He was the only other man I ever . . ." She trailed off, looking at me from the side of her face.

My fists clenched, gripping the bedding fiercely as I fought to keep my anger off my face. "You hurt him," Medusa said, earning a wince from Estrella.

"Not exactly," Estrella said, explaining the circumstances of his death to her mother. It hadn't been her fault, and she knew that logically. There would have been nothing she could have done to prevent the *viniculum* from protecting her life, from keeping her safe for me. It was *my* magic that had killed Loris, that had eliminated the threat to my mate. I felt no remorse for it given what he'd been willing to do for the Mist Guard he served, and knowing that while it had never been love, Estrella had once held him in a form of affection guaranteed he would never have my sympathy.

He should have been honored to die to protect her, not been willing to make the killing blow.

"The Cocytus takes a person's every sorrow and magnifies it," Medusa explained, sitting on the edge of the bed. "He is no longer the man you remember. He no longer remembers things accurately. In his mind, you killed him to free yourself of your entanglement because you had a mate waiting for you. In his mind, he sees his every insecurity. He will never measure up to a God; he will never be good enough to deserve you. It no longer matters that he never even wanted your heart in life, because the river has made you into his obsession in death. Give him what he wants. That is what he needs to move on with his afterlife. That is what he needs in order for him to give you his assistance."

Estrella imagined the three apples in her head, the way that they were just out of reach. She needed his help, and he hadn't offered it.

"I can't," she said, her voice cracking. She wouldn't meet my eye, her window slamming shut in her mind to try to shove me out of her head. There was something in her memory of that trial that she didn't want me to see, something she thought to protect me from. "I cannot give him what he needs."

Suspicion made my hackles rise, my magic tickling along my skin in warning. My *viniculum* pulsed, the tendrils writhing on my skin as if our very bond felt the affront that had been committed. Carefulness forgotten, I shoved at the other side of Estrella's window and thrust it open, shoving my way into her head once again. She gasped as I slid inside, the memory of the trial slithering between us like something insidious. I hadn't dared to peer into this part of her past, hadn't wanted to see the man who'd touched what was mine, just as I suspected she hadn't tried to look into the women that had come before her.

There were some memories better left forgotten, some people not meant to be shared. He stood before her in the trial, entirely nude and trembling. His pain was tangible even as someone who did not know him, the emotion surrounding him enough to smother the air with darkness. His jealousy drove his words, motivated them as he made his demand of Estrella.

He wanted to touch her. He wanted her to touch him.

Out of spite for me, out of sheer, absolute hatred for what I represented, he wanted to use Estrella to strike at me. He blamed me for everything that had gone wrong in his life and led to his death, and wanted to take the one thing that mattered to me more than anything.

My mate.

Our bond would never recover from an affair, no mate bond could tolerate such an injustice. There were those who agreed to practice nonmonogamy within their relationship, but it was a mutual decision that they came to based on their own sexuality and needs as a unit. Those pairs tended to be well-matched. They tended to share those needs so that they could find absolute completion within one another. It would have been tragic for a monogamous Fae to be paired with someone who wanted nonmonogamy, ending in nothing but heartbreak all around.

Estrella and I would never be nonmonogamous. We would never tolerate the touch of another. She was all I wanted and my desires did not require other relationships to keep me content, and I knew she felt the same. The disgust that slithered through her at Loris's proposition only confirmed that.

What he suggested would be nothing short of rape, a manipulation to get her to give him her body under threat of death. That the Fates had allowed *this* to be her Trial only worsened my already shit opinion of them, making me want to tear her father's head from his shoulders.

"He wants her to fuck him," I snapped, turning to Medusa. "Is this what your husband wants for your own child?"

"Just because that is what he claims to want does not mean it is the actuality. When you return to the river and see him again, he will have no recollection of your previous encounter. He won't remember giving you an ultimatum. It is up to you to maneuver him to the place where you need him, Estrella. You have to guide him to wanting to make peace with you," Medusa said, her voice soft as she watched Estrella curl into me. The fight had gone out of my mate at some point in that river, her guilt becoming a storm inside her.

"He blames me for his death. How could he ever want to make peace with me when by your account, he is never going to remember it accurately," Estrella said, shaking her head. I hated the defeat in her tone, hated the way that it felt like she'd given up entirely and accepted that this was her end.

"So he is never going to see the events that led to his death the way you do. Does that matter? Is his opinion of you more important than giving him what *he* needs so that you can walk away with what you need more than anything?" Medusa asked. "I did not come with you so that I could watch you tuck your tail between your legs at the first sign of failure. Why aren't you fighting?!" The anger in Medusa's bellow shook the cabin walls, forcing me to stand from the bed so that I could attempt to intervene in the coming fight. If Estrella wasn't up to standing up for herself, then I would be the one to do it for her.

I was the one she could lean on. I was the one who carried her when she was too weak to stand.

"Because I've never won! I have never been able to fight back in any way that fucking mattered!" Estrella snapped, her face pinching with the anguish that I felt echoed in her head, that incessant wailing bringing her own sorrow to the surface. "What am I supposed to do? Keep fighting when we all know I'm going to fail? When we know that this is just going to keep getting harder and fucking harder until I can't take it anymore?"

"And what makes you so certain that you'll fail, Estrella?" Medusa asked, her voice too calm in the face of Estrella's anger.

"Because what if he's right? I killed him. What if there had been another way, and I was just too selfish to see it?" she asked, and a little piece of my heart broke for the weight she'd been carrying. The concern and guilt that all of this had brought back to the surface. No matter how much she'd been forced to shove aside to survive in the life she'd been thrust into, Estrella had lost everything she'd ever known and had people she'd thought cared about her want her dead. There was no erasing the damage that could cause.

Tears streamed down her cheeks as she broke, her chest heaving with the words I didn't think she'd even intended to speak out loud. I sent comforting thoughts down the bond, trying to reach her as she stood from the bed. Her legs buckled beneath her, tearing a whimper of frustration from her lungs as she caught herself on the edge of the bed and forced them to stand straight and support her. She paced, the movement awkward and jilted, stunted by the weakness in her body that she refused to allow to force her to bed.

"There she is," Medusa whispered with a smile, staring at the version of Estrella that was one breath from a breakdown, her lungs heaving with the force of trying to suppress the emotion that clogged her throat.

"I don't know what I'm supposed to do in this trial. How am I supposed to win if I can't even blame him for hating me?" Estrella whispered, fear coating every word. She didn't think she could win, didn't think she could come back to me after she went back in and the very notion that she'd survived so much only to die like this was tearing her in two.

"He may not be the man you knew anymore, but he is still a man, Estrella," Medusa whispered, stepping up to my mate. She placed a hand on each side of her face, staring down at her as Estrella nodded. "Men can be manipulated, especially if they believe you to be out of reach. You do not need to fuck him to give him what he wants. All you need to do is make him believe he matters for one more moment, and then you can forget he ever existed."

"I don't want to forget," Estrella whispered, those words causing a clench of pain within me. Even *knowing* what she felt for him wasn't romantic, even feeling that for myself, I wanted to erase him from her past and make it so he was never a thought in her mind again. "He deserves better than this. He deserves better than to be manipulated and forgotten. I hate them for making me do this. I hate every last one of them. How do I continue on, trying to prove my worth to beings that I despise with every fiber of my being? I don't want to be worthy to them if this is what it takes."

Medusa smiled, and Estrella was too far gone to her rage to see the pride in it. The joy it brought her to know her daughter weighed her own worth by her own standards, that Estrella's morals and self-worth would be worth more to her than any approval the Fates could ever give.

"Then you make them bleed for what they've done to you," she said, the resolve on her face hinting at what she hadn't dared to hope for, the very thing none had dared to consider.

"And when they call me a monster, too?" Estrella asked, forcing her mother to raise her chin. Her snakes slithered around her head, seeming to respond to the word that the Gorgon woman had learned to hate.

"Prove them right," Medusa said with a shrug. "Sometimes a monster is exactly what the world needs to right the wrongs that have been committed for centuries. You have let your fear of what you could be hold you back for far too long. You didn't even think to try to remove the snake from your mate's heart because you feared you would fail."

"I could have killed him. The risks were too high—"

"And what would have happened if you succeeded? Who might you have saved in the process? Your fear of yourself is your greatest weakness. Be the fucking monster, Estrella. For they will judge you as one either way."

Medusa left the cabin, leaving us blinking after her. Estrella didn't try to follow the bond to see what I thought of the altercation and for that I was grateful.

I wasn't sure she was ready to know that her mother was right.

Fifty-Nine

ESTRELLA

The grove remained unchanged as I approached the natural pool at the center. My legs were wobbly beneath me, as if the loss I'd suffered here had stolen the energy from my body. I wondered if I'd get it back if I was successful in my task, or if I would need to continue on through the rest of my life feeling this weak. It was impossible to think of being victorious in any meaningful way with the loss of power, the way it seemed to linger just out of reach. I didn't know if it would respond if I even tried to touch it, for it didn't matter in this moment.

In this trial, my humanity was what was needed. My care for someone I had once known, who had mattered a great deal to me in his own way, would have to be what guided me through this. I didn't know if I had it in me to lie and manipulate, to insinuate that I would offer something that wasn't mine to give. My body belonged to my mate, just as his belonged to me. I would have gone to the ends of the earth to ruin any who dared to touch him, to demand such things of him.

The water bubbled as Loris moved toward the surface, his body emerging in a sudden burst. He dragged in a deep lungful of air, the sorrow in his eyes shining as soon as he met my stare. He opened his mouth to speak, but I didn't wait to hear what he would say. I met him as he stepped out of the edge of the water, the grass of the grove bending beneath his feet. Wrapping my arms around him, I ignored the nudity that made me uncomfortable and squeezed him into a tight hug that I felt like I needed just as much as he did. He froze, going still in my embrace before he finally raised his arms and wrapped them around me. They were gentle as they encircled me, his cheek coming to rest on the top of my head.

"I'm so sorry," I mumbled into his bare chest, pulling back so that I could stare up at him. My face was wet with tears as he studied me, raising his hand to capture the moisture for himself as he considered those words.

"You're sorry?" he asked, a bit of his anger bleeding into his features. The words weren't enough, and I dreaded the rage that would follow. "I'm dead thanks to you."

"I know," I said, admitting my guilt in the role I'd played. Whether or not I'd wanted it, it was my fault. He was dead because I lived, because my life had been deemed more important than his in the game of the Fates. "I never wanted this. I would give almost anything to change it."

"Almost anything," he scoffed, his brow twisting with indignation. "Anything but him, right?"

"Do you want me to lie to you? Is that what you're looking for? Do you want me to lie and say that I would sacrifice my mate to bring you back? It wouldn't matter. No matter what I say, you'll still be dead, Loris," I said, spinning on my heel. The flash of gold in the trees bolstered me, forcing me forward in this game of carefully crafted words. I didn't want to lie, but I could be more vocal about the truth. I could offer comfort in the form of encouragement, bolster him in what he'd lost. "And I have to find a way to live with that."

"I'm sure it pains you," he said, crossing his arms over his chest.

"It does," I said, admitting the truth that I didn't want to speak out loud. "Everything that has happened is all because of me. All those people who died when the Veil fell, I carry the weight of their lives with me. They're a reminder that the choices I make are never my own. They always have this greater purpose, influencing the things around me in ways I can't predict. It's a weight I wouldn't wish on my greatest enemy, so yes, I carry that with me every day. Because forgetting that comes at too high a cost."

"Is that supposed to make me feel better?" he asked, but the way he fidgeted told me that he wasn't unaffected by it. Not as much as he wanted me to believe.

"I don't think there's anything I can say that will make you feel better. There's nothing I can do to make any of this okay. It's the truth regardless." We stood in a moment of silence, allowing the weight of the conversation to settle between us. Loris shuffled his feet as he thought over my words, measuring them carefully and judging each and every one. The scales were imbalanced, working against me from the very onset.

"I didn't expect you to apologize," he said, shrugging his shoulders as he held himself more tightly. All confidence was gone from him, as if the shock had brought him back to reality in some way.

"Then maybe you never knew me as well as you thought you did. We were so naive, Loris. I feel like a different person when I look back at that girl now. I didn't understand what was coming," I admitted.

"There's no way you could have known," he said, stepping alongside me. He looked up to the apples, pointing at them as I watched with a hollow in my heart. "The apples are what you need to continue on, but I have a price."

My heart dropped into my throat, thinking that after all of this, the way I'd tried so hard, it would be for nothing. I swallowed. "What's your price?"

He turned to me more fully, leveling me with the full weight of his stare. "Promise me you won't forget. Promise me you'll make our deaths matter," he said, the words drawing a strangled sob from me.

That was a price I could pay. A cost I would have accepted even without his request. He may not have agreed with the way I would make them matter in the end, given his hatred for the Fae of Alfheimr, but ridding the world of Mab would save humans as well. "I promise," I said, letting him hoist me into his arms.

"Then I forgive you," he said, our faces too close as he murmured the words. The affection there felt genuine, and I wondered if I'd missed it in life. If I'd misinterpreted our agreement as being mutually beneficial or if he truly had been twisted in the river. I hoped that whatever the case may have been, this brought him peace. I hoped forgiveness was the path to moving on, to freedom from Tartarus. He didn't deserve to suffer here for eternity.

He held me higher, letting me pluck the apples from the tree. The moment the final apple was freed from the branch, cradled in my hands, I felt like I was suspended in midair. Looking down to where Loris had held me, I watched him disappear. His arms no longer supported me, billowing away like a whisper on the wind.

"I promise," I repeated, watching his face twist with fear. Whatever came next for him, he was going into the unknown just like I was. There was no certainty in life or in death, only the unexpected.

He faded away as if he'd never really been here at all, leaving me floating in darkness as the wails of mourning filled my ears once more. They stayed with me, even as I crawled my way onto the riverbank, a distant howling in my ears.

A voice that I would never forget.

SIXTY

ESTRELLA

We continued on in a hurry, moving in silence as I tried to escape the wailing in my ears. We walked until we reached our next destination, the next place where we would find safety to rest for the night.

Even if the trials were behind me, Tartarus still wasn't safe for me.

The village before us was enormous, a city the likes of which I'd never seen in its prime. But whereas I imagined the cities in Nothrek had once been filled with towering structures and vertical buildings meant to optimize the limitations of the space to house its people, this village was filled with single-story dwellings.

The Temple of the Fates was carved into the cliffside, a gleaming thing of white marble. The structure was too large for the village surrounding it, the doorway alone feeling tall enough that I could stand on top of Caldris's shoulders five times over and still never even touch the top of the doorway. Interspersed with the more permanent homes that had been crafted out of any manner of natural objects that could be found in the surrounding landscape: wood, straw, mud, clay, there were tents made from rough fabric, linens swaying in the wind that tore through the encampment.

In some cases, the tents appeared larger than the homes themselves, entire households crammed into them to sleep together. A child ran through the settlement, her hair blowing behind her as she raced through the space. The giggle she emitted was one of pure joy in spite of the temporary housing that surrounded us, and she met a friend on the other side of the path before they raced off together.

"Who are these people?" I asked, turning to Medusa. The woman I logically knew was my mother, but had not yet quite managed to reconcile that way in my head, smiled at me wistfully.

"They're waiting for the Fates to call them into the temple," she said, nodding her head forward. I followed her gaze to the way they worked together in the center of the settlement, a miniature temple emerging from behind the tents and homes as we approached. "Some of them have been waiting for longer than you have existed, Estrella. Some of them will never leave this place or feel the grace of the Fates upon them. They would tell you to be thankful for their favor, that they've deigned to shine their golden light upon you and guide you through your destiny."

We approached the smaller temple, the words scrawled above the door making my steps falter. I tripped over my own feet, as I stared up at the language written in the Old Tongue. They were a reminder of the wolves at my back, of everything my bond with Fenrir symbolized and reminded me of what I had always been destined to be. The choice that had been torn from me before I'd even been born, staring me straight in the face as I studied the temple that these people had clearly built their village around.

But they'd been here longer than I'd existed . . .

Teampal a'le Tempestrua Moirai.

Temple of the Child of Fate.

"How long has this been here? Who came before me that would lay claim to those words?" I asked, taking the first step up to the temple doors. There were only a dozen of them compared to the never-ending cascade of steps on the temple of the Fates themselves, but Medusa did not move to follow. Instead, Caldris and I stood alone on the white marble, all those who had traveled with us remaining behind. The message was clear, this place, this temple, was for me and me alone. But my bond with my mate pulsed brighter than ever, the magic seeming to recognize that he belonged with me in this.

I was grateful for it, knowing that the other temple would not welcome him. I wanted to cling to him for every moment I could, wanted to remember what it was to have him beside me when the time so quickly approached where I would have to say goodbye once again. Even if for just a while, being separated from him at all was almost too much for me to bear.

"The temple has stood in the shadow of the Fates since the dawn of time," Medusa said, looking to the temple at her back where it was carved into the mountain. "They have known of your existence since they drew their first breath. They have seen your destiny since the first thread was spun. They created your father from the darkness, not so that *he* might be born, but so that one day, you would be."

"I don't understand," I said, shaking my head as I tried to wrap my mind around the reality of that. The implications of what it meant would never be something I could understand, not with the idea that spanned centuries and time. Not with the understanding that this had all been written in a time that I could not even begin to fathom.

There was a distinct, burning question in my gut. One that I needed the answer to but didn't think anyone but the Fates could give me, and whether or not they would offer the answer was another question.

"Ask it, Estrella. Whatever question you have, ask it of me, and I will do my best to answer," Medusa said, holding my weighted stare.

Caldris stepped up behind me, pressing his chest into my spine and offering me his strength. I knew my breathing was ragged, the words feeling torn from the depths of my soul. Like some part of me knew the answer already, knew that it would forever change me and my outlook on what I would do with my life.

"Why?" I asked, the single word sitting between our group so heavily. It was such a simple question, open and closed all at once, and yet . . .

The answer would change everything.

Medusa raised her chin, her green eyes shining bright. It wasn't tears that made them seem to sparkle, but the hidden sheen of gold within the green. Serpentine, they slithered through the grass of that stare as she watched me.

"All cycles have an end," she said, her bottom lip trembling slightly as she moved to approach the steps. She stopped just before them, reaching out with a hand to touch her palm to the center of my chest. Even in the armor I wore that covered my skin, I felt something move within me in response, a golden thread writhing over her skin in response. I yanked at the collar of my armor, tugging it away from my chest as Caldris fought to untie it to give me the space I needed to maneuver. Something played beneath my skin, a thin line of gold that was so like the threads I'd touched on so many occasions. But where those had all been straight and smooth, this was a knotted bundle at the center of my chest just above my heart. It was not connected to the thread of my life that I could see swaying in the wind if I focused, but something else entirely. "All things must die, Estrella. All lives must end."

"I don't understand," I said, my voice a deep rasp. Caldris pressed tighter, and I knew that he'd understood the words I couldn't seem to grasp. I wasn't sure if it was because I didn't *want* to understand yet, or if I was missing information that would somehow prove to be vital.

"You will in time. It is your destiny to end the cycle that has existed since the dawn of creation. It is your destiny to remake the world as you see fit and begin anew. It is your destiny to destroy us all, so that we can be reborn from the ashes of your wrath," she said, making me furrow my brow. She made me sound like a monster, like a villain meant to do the very thing I wanted to condemn. Her earlier words repeated in the back of my mind, the comfort she'd given me in my moments where I'd feared how the world would see me.

Every hero is a villain of someone else's story.

"You, my love, are the Tempest of the Fates. You were born to shift the balance of power, for you carry a piece of the Fates inside you that can never be carved out," she said, pulling her hand away from that knot all over again. I felt the tangle inside me now, felt the well of power brighten now that it had been recognized. Now that I saw it, I could not imagine how I'd ever missed it before.

"How?" I asked, touching my hand to my chest to soothe the ache it left behind.

"They told me it was the only way I would ever have the child I so desperately wanted. It was the only way to fortify you and I so that you could survive pregnancy. They placed the knot within my womb and sent your father and I into that very temple," she said, nodding her head to the place where I knew Caldris and I had to go. "The place that was your beginning and when the time comes, this will be your end as well."

She turned her back on us finally, running her hand through Ylfa's fur as the wolves sat on guard at the bottom of the steps, watching over the entrance to the place that I knew I needed to go. I didn't want to, didn't want to face whatever waited for me within, yet Caldris tied my armor and took my hand, guiding me toward the temple at last.

No more hiding.

No more secrets.

These were the days where I uncovered the truth of my creation, where my destiny laid itself bare at last, and I couldn't have been more fucking terrified.

His hand was heavy in mine as he guided me up the steps, pausing at the top to look down at me from his place beside me. "You can do this alone, if that is what you wish," he said. Even though I knew it pained him to make such an offer when all he wanted was to remain at my side, his love pouring down the bond in such deep waves I thought I might choke.

I wasn't ready for this. Wasn't ready to know the truth. The thought of facing that alone was too great a burden, so I tightened my grip on his hand and took the first step.

My palm touched the heavy doors crafted from molten rock, a circle at the center glowing with gold at the moment of contact. They spread open before me, creaking with their weight as I stared into the darkened temple. There was no light to be found within, no sun to be had as night descended on the village at my back. It came with a swift, heavy darkness that seemed impossible, and I took in a deep breath of air that I held in my lungs until they burned. With a sigh, I took the first step and crested the threshold of the temple, dragging Caldris behind me.

It was a darkness without stars within, a night so true I couldn't see anything.

Then my *viniculum* pulsed with golden light, traveling from my hand and to my arm and shoulder in a wave that then flowed into Caldris. There was a thud somewhere in front of us, a noise that made me believe we were not alone in this strange place. A creak of something that seemed to be everywhere at once, the noise permeating the darkness as I spun in place.

Another thud from somewhere behind me, the click of a locking mechanism snapping into position as the doors sealed shut.

Trapping us inside.

SIXTY-ONE

ESTRELLA

The world plunged into absolute darkness, the likes of which I'd never known. I gripped Caldris tighter, clinging to the one lifeline I had when it felt like I was suspended within nothing. Words rippled across my skin, a voice I couldn't account for whispering through the breeze that stole through the entryway.

"From chaos, she was born."

The voice was soft and feminine, gentle and haunting. Gooseflesh rose on my skin, raising the hair on the back of my neck. I wished more than anything that I could see. Wished that I could find the person responsible for the voice, but I somehow knew it wasn't a tangible person.

"And in chaos, she will reign."

It was my mate's turn to shudder, the words so similar to the refrain that we had adopted as *ours*, as a statement of our love. Never had either of us considered that it might be part of a bigger riddle, a piece to fit into the puzzle of my existence. *"Until chaos reigns,"* he muttered in my head, and I felt the weight of his gaze on my profile. I couldn't stand to turn to look at him, couldn't handle the fact that I wouldn't be able to see him in this darkness, that the black ink of night stole everything from the world and plunged it into a void of nothingness.

Even with his hand in mine, in this place, in this time, I was alone with only his voice inside my head to ground me and keep me floating into the darkness.

"Welcome home, Tempest of Fate. We have waited eons for you."

A torch lit on the wall beside me, one matching on the opposite wall beside Caldris. The fire pulsed, casting his face with golden light that made him look starkly beautiful. He shimmered like a statue in the sun, his *viniculum* responding to mine. In a synchronized wave, torches lit on the wall one by one creating a path down the narrow entry. In the distance, the hall opened into an enormous, cavernous room that was filled with light. There was no denying the impulse to make my way there, to follow the guide that had been set out for us. Caldris squeezed my hand reassuringly as we took our first step as one, moving together as a unit. My steps were slow, cautious, and uneasy as we made our way toward the truth waiting for me in that room.

The golden light bathed a statue in the center of the room ahead, the figure of a woman appearing as if she'd been encased in molten gold. It poured over like liquid, burning like the fires of starlight in the night sky. Her gown was a drapery of fabric, falling off her shoulders and cascading down her torso before pooling all the way to her feet. Dark hair had been pulled back into a braid on top of her head, waves tangled into a clip at the back so that they could hang down over her shoulders.

It was the same gown they'd dressed me in for dinner at the Tithe settlement.

The face staring down at me was impassive, carefully neutral as if the weight of so many stares upon her would be judging and looking for weakness. She was a Queen in a sea of faces, the kind you would never forget. Calculating and cold, but a tiny smile played at her lips, hinting at lightness that had no place on her face.

"It's you, min asteren," Caldris said, speaking the words out loud as if the temple itself needed the recognition from him. I studied that face intently, hating to admit that the features as a whole were familiar. They looked like me, but didn't.

Couldn't, not when I wore my heart on my sleeve so clearly for all to see. Maybe she was a version of me that had lived in the past or one that had yet to come, but this woman, this statue, was not me in the present.

I moved to deny it, shaking my head once as my mouth opened. My voice caught in my throat as the statue moved, shifting to turn her neck to face me with a creak of metal scratching against itself. I froze solid, staring at the statue in horror as she raised a hand. Her palm faced me, her fingers splayed as the shimmer of those golden eyes held my stare.

"Ready yourself tonight, Estrella Barlowe. For tomorrow, you die."

The voice in my head was the same, the attachment to this woman undeniable. I raised my hand, letting it linger just before hers. They were the same size, down to the very last knuckle. Every detail of our hands lined up and matched so perfectly it was like she'd been carved with me as a model. The words, the meaning of them, echoed the warning the Morrigan had given me when I first arrived in Tartarus. I glanced to Caldris from the corner of my eye, studying his face to see if he'd heard them. I had to know what he knew, had to know if that was something that had played in his head, too, or if he would hear it in mine.

As the panic coursed through me, there was no way he could *not* know of what was coming.

"Some secrets are better left in the dark, Little Bird," the woman's voice said, and it felt like time stood still. My father's words, echoed in the ferryman and then repeated to me in this temple that had existed since the dawn of time. I didn't know what came first or last, floating in this timeless space where nothing made sense.

I swallowed my fear, drinking down my own apprehension and moved my hand closer to hers, our fingers finally brushing against one another. Her gold melted from her hand, spreading my skin like liquid—viscous and thick. It poured over me, sliding down my fingers and coating my hand, enrobing my wrists and sinking into the marks of my *viniculum*. I could not tear my hand away, instead trapped within her grasp as those metallic fingers entwined with mine. She trapped me as the liquid covered me, crawling up my arm to encase my shoulder and my neck, eating away at the armor that covered my body. It was warm to the touch, the heat almost melting my flesh as I shoved Caldris to the side with all my strength, forcing him to release me before the gold could touch him.

My heart hammered in my chest as the gold touched the spot where that knot existed within me, my mouth parting on a silent scream as the gold rose up my throat to cover my face. It sank into my mouth, making its way up my nose and into my eyes. When it covered me entirely, I could not move. Caldris's voice was a quiet murmur in my head, and I wondered what he saw.

Had this all been in my head? An imagination or imagery meant only for me? But it couldn't explain the way my lungs seized, turning solid as the gold hardened. I couldn't breathe, but Caldris was calm, reassuring as if it was nothing. I felt the edge of his own fear lingering at the side, a tangible thing he shoved away to try to help me through this prison. I drew in a deep breath, feeling my lungs expand with it. The gold filling them cracked and shattered into dust, and I pulled away with a jerky step back as everything returned to me.

Gold fluttered off me as my eyes opened to see, flakes of it billowing in the wind like leaves in autumn. Beyond them, the statue of the woman was gone, as if she'd poured her very essence onto me. Something inside of me felt hardened, as if I could still feel the presence of that molten gold within me as it cooled, changing me for the future in a way I could not anticipate.

The armor I'd worn was gone, leaving me nude as I stood at the center of the temple with Caldris at my side. At the forefront of the temple, one of the walls shifted. The stone cracked and crumbled in on itself, drawing me forward without care for my own nakedness. Caldris stepped before me, moving into the space that it created as if to defend me. But when he stepped to the side, the twin moons shone in the night sky above a courtyard. A galaxy of stars sparkled next to the moons, shooting through the darkness and surrounding us and lingering so low that they seemed to be in the very air around us. Grass tickled my feet as I stepped out onto it, turning to draw my mate into the starlight with me.

The statues words at the back of my mind, there was only one way I wanted to spend my night if it were to truly be my last.

"My star," Caldris murmured against my mouth, the words soft and reassuring as I grasped him by the waist of his pants and dragged him into the center of the courtyard. There was a bed and blanket already made up there, a place to sleep beneath the stars as they tore through the night. "We have all the time in the world."

I didn't know if the statement was meant for me or for himself, but nothing could have stopped me from pulling him closer, grabbing him around the back of the neck and tugging him down to my height.

"Come fuck me beneath the stars, King of Winter," I murmured against his mouth, pressing my own to his teasingly. He groaned into me, trying to control himself for me. He knew what this was, even if he didn't know the true reasons behind my insistence. He may not know why I believed this would be our last night together or that I'd be going into the Temple of the Fates alone the next day, but he knew me well enough to know what drove me.

I needed him, needed to feel him, before I faced the greatest of my fears.

My fate.

"I wouldn't want to make them jealous," he said, finally giving in enough to wrap me in his embrace, sliding his hand down my spine and over the curve of my ass. His other hand followed, a slow tease as he lifted me into his arms. I wrapped my legs around his waist, letting him carry me as he knelt on the edge of the bed and used one of his hands to support me while the other crawled forward, laying me down at the center carefully. He held himself over me, shielding me from the light of the moon and stars above. His hair fell around me, his nose touching mine as that blue-eyed stare became my entire world.

"Why should a star be jealous of me?" I asked, the words a whisper.

"Because as beautiful as they may be when they dance like that, they'll never be my favorite," he argued, touching his mouth to mine. It was gentle at first, a teasing caress coaxing me to open for him. When I did, he deepened our kiss quickly, leaving me to untie his tunic laces and tug it over his head, letting him work his pants down his legs in haste.

He wasted little time guiding himself to my center, finding me already wet and wanting. A look from him was all it took, and I'd be ready. He took me more slowly than usual, letting me feel every inch as he worked his way inside me. His tongue tangled with mine, his breath sharing the same air, with every shallow thrust. He glided through me, sinking in to the hilt and moving with the casual ease of a man who wanted to take his time. I clung to him, letting him take and give and everything in between. Our connection was all that mattered to me, feeling him inside my head and inside my body at the same time the most intimate of acts I could share with any person.

He was mine, and I was his, and when he finally buried his face in my neck and drove us both over the edge, I watched the stars dance in the sky above—their movements restless and chaotic.

Knowing the destruction that would follow in their wake.

Sixty-Two

ESTRELLA

I moved through the village the next morning, feeling naked in the golden dress that the temple had set out for me at some point in the night. It was the same one the statue of myself had worn, the same shimmering fabric that moved with me like liquid gold. I'd taken it as a sign, styling my hair in the same way in spite of my misgivings. Honoring what the Fates saw in my future couldn't hurt whatever was about to occur, at least. Especially not for something as simple as my hair. I had no choice but to wear the dress since my armor had vanished, wiped from existence.

I would miss it in the battles ahead, the comfort of it having all but convinced me of my immortality. I felt like I could do anything with that armor, but even my swords had been stripped from me for this.

There were no weapons allowed in the Temple of the Fates, the Morrigan claimed, offering me a quiet reassurance that I would receive both my armor and my weapons when the time was right. That they would always be there for me when I needed them most, but the battles were won and this was my reward.

So why did it feel like my death sentence instead?

We scaled the hilltop, making our way through the garden of boulders that seemed to litter the path. The slope was steep, the path uneven beneath my bare feet. There was nothing to protect me from the sharp edges and dirt at my feet, making my skin ache and throb with each step, but the walk was blissfully short before we reached the bottom of the temple. The entrance was guarded by two figures to either side of the door, statues that I couldn't help but see differently after the night before. I was all too aware of the magic that existed here, of the potential for them to move and harm and hurt. The Morrigan lingered at the back of our group, and I turned to face them. They'd already told me that they would not be joining me in the temple, and as Nemain raised the bag with the items I'd collected in my trials, I took it. Slinging it over my shoulder, I pulled the silent woman into a fierce hug, hating all that she'd lost because of me. Badb and Macha were next, all three of the sisters clearly uncomfortable with the physical affection that I forced on them. I didn't know if I'd see them again, or if this was my final moment with the guides that had been all I'd had for a time. Since Medusa had joined our group of travelers, they'd become more quiet and distant than they'd been prior to her appearance. Part of me wondered what may have come if Medusa hadn't joined, or if there was perhaps bad blood between my mother and the three Goddesses of the Morrigan.

When I pulled back from Badb, she surprised me by touching a gentle hand to the side of my neck, cupping me there in a move that felt like it was meant to bolster my resolve. I knew that they knew enough about what was going to happen to know I needed it, to know that the contact would be welcome as I fought to suppress all thoughts Caldris might overhear. Whatever the Fates had done to protect this, I couldn't know.

I only knew that if he'd heard the words the statue had spoken in my ear the night before, if he'd heard even the echo of them in my memory, he'd be doing everything he could to drag me from this place kicking and screaming. He'd never allow me to make it to the temple doors, and yet here I stood, with him a quiet sentry at my side, fully prepared to step into the temple alongside me.

"It has been a pleasure to know you in this life, Estrella Barlowe," Badb said, her voice choked with emotion that felt strange in her ethereal tone. She was always tinged with a bit of darkness, a deep and smoky voice that conveyed absolute strength.

"It has truly been our honor to know this version of you before the Cradle changes you," Macha reiterated, stepping back and taking Badb along with her. The three of them moved to stand beside Nemain, pausing briefly before they looked toward the sky and blended into their singular raven. They took off in flight, their form quickly disappearing into the light in the distance as they curved through the air above the temple.

Medusa stood at the doorway when I turned to face the temple finally, the gleaming white marble taking my breath away. It was the same as the temple that had been dedicated to me somehow, but the sheer size of it was so enormous I thought I might lose my ability to breathe standing before it. Never had anything else made me feel so insignificant and small in the face of it.

She was the first to make her way through the entry, waiting for me on the other side. I saw it for the deception it was, for the manipulation to convince my mate and Brann where they followed at my back. The simple act would make them think that they too could pass through the entry, when I knew it would be the opposite. I didn't know how, but I knew that this was the moment when we separated. I felt it in my bones and in my blood. I couldn't afford to turn to look at Caldris, knowing that he would see the devastation on my face even if he couldn't hear it in my thoughts. I pressed forward, the fabric of my golden dress skimming the dirt beneath me as I crossed between the two statues on either side. Their swords were crossed peacefully, guarding the place that didn't belong to the people who wanted entry. The cruelty of having sanctuary exist right in front of you and being unable to reach it was not lost on me, and I hated that for the people in the encampment.

I stepped forward, crossing through the entryway. My skin tingled as the barrier felt me, the air heavy at the point where the temple met Tartarus. I forced myself through, not giving it any hesitation so that Caldris's ever-watchful stare could fixate on my reaction. When I made it through, I turned to stare at him on the other side. He was faded from view, clouded by mist as he stepped up. While I could still make out his features, the separation between the interior and the exterior of the temple was plain to see from this side.

He took a step, attempting to enter the temple only to spring back from the soft surface he met. He bounced back with a look of shock on his handsome face. "Estrella," he whispered, a question in the name. His brow furrowed with agony as he searched my face, and I felt the wall the Fates had placed within me fall away.

It crumbled like stone, allowing him to finally see the truth of what I'd known. It let him feel the fate pressing down on me, the truth of what would become of me here.

That I'd known he wouldn't be able to come and gone anyway.

"Estrella!" he shouted, raising a fist and pounding at the boundary. His hand bounced back, the gelatinous surface repelling him with as much force as he gave. "*No,*" he pleaded in my head, flinching away as Brann attempted to pull him back from the temple.

A woman from the encampment stepped up, her face shrouded in a white cloak. She waited behind my mate, silent and peaceful as he stared at me with those begging eyes.

I held a hand up to the boundary, pressing against the surface that was hardening with every moment that passed. Stone spread from the bottom, climbing up to seal the doorway off.

"I love you," I whispered, hoping he could hear the words on the other side. I could say it in our bond, but I wanted him to hear it in my voice. I wanted him to know in case I never saw him again.

His hand touched the boundary, pressing against mine through the barrier between us. "Don't you dare," he said, shaking his head as he looked down at the stone. The panic that filled his face would haunt me for the rest of my days, haunt me in whatever afterlife I found.

"I need you to say the words. I need to hear them one last time."

His face twisted with pain, with rage so full that I couldn't imagine ever being leveled with that hatred. Even in this, his anger was not with me. "I love you, my star," he said, holding my stare as the stone came up and cut the connection of our hands, one step closer to taking him from me.

"I'll see that he gets back to the land of the living, Tempest," the Priestess said, her words a reassurance in the background.

"Do not let Mab see you," Medusa said, her words an order as she spoke them behind me. Caldris never took his eyes from me but I knew he heard the order, watched his cheek twitch. "Gather forces quietly and be ready for Estrella to return. She will have need of them when she's completed her final trial."

The words were a shock to me, having thought that the final river was my last trial. It was a secret I knew had been kept from me intentionally, the one I wasn't likely to walk away from.

I couldn't stop to process, couldn't look at anything but him as the stone came up between Caldris and I, stealing his face from my view completely.

The bond went silent as the stone filled the doorway, trapping me in the Temple of the Fates.

There would be no escape now that I had entered.

The only way out was through.

Sixty-Three

ESTRELLA

The inside of the Temple of the Fates was similar to the outside, the lowest level a sprawling entryway filled with marble columns and detailed carvings. I stepped into the marble, feeling out of place in my shocking golden dress that was so vibrant compared to the white that surrounded me. But as we walked farther toward the opposite end of the room, a splash of color appeared on the backdrop.

The tapestries that hung from ceiling to the floor were larger than any I'd ever seen, larger than anything that was practical to create or even use. The colors were a myriad, splashes of every color of the rainbow mingling with the delicate golden thread that I recognized intimately.

I stepped away from Medusa where she lingered in the center of the room, drawn to the colors and the way the gold was woven into them. A part of the fabric of life but not the entirety of it, the thread was a statement of absolutes in a world of color. It was life or death in a sea of possibilities.

The bottom right of the most recent tapestry was of a woman who looked too similar to the statue in the temple, the back of my head all I could see as she studied the tapestries before her. I spun to look at Medusa, shock written into the lines of my face. All around me more tapestries descended, falling from the ceiling to line the columns and the walls.

My face peered back at me in each and every one, something I recognized even in my differences. "Is this me?" I asked, stepping away from the tapestry that had first called to me. To the right of it was the woman I'd recognized so immediately, the me of my first life.

Aella stood with Brann at her side, his figure never changing in his time that we'd spent with the rebellion. He hadn't needed to hide who he was or what I was, instead focusing on teaching me the ways of touching magic even when it did not exist in Nothrek, purely for the sake of readying me for the day the Veil fell.

"They all are. These are your story, Estrella. All the threads and the lives that led you to this moment," Medusa answered, but I studied the gathering of tapestries that seemed to expand with each passing moment. They hung in layers that I felt like I could spend an eternity walking through, learning the ways of my lives and the past that I could not grasp in my mind on my own.

These versions of me were strangers, and yet I recognized them all the same. I felt the pull of them on my soul, though I could not touch them. They stirred within me, the phantom of a memory that was no longer mine at all.

There were tapestries that didn't even have me in them, aspects of fate that had been woven before my time. The lines of destiny that had guided me here twisted and knitted the world to suit my creation, and I hated every fucking second of it.

This was wrong. This level of interference and manipulation should not have been.

"I don't understand," I said, shaking my head. I both did and I didn't, because none of this effort made sense with anything I could reconcile in my head. What purpose could be so great to go to this? To spend *centuries* manipulating the lives of thousands . . .

"The answers are just ahead, through the temple pass," Medusa said, guiding me to a narrow passage that ascended the stairs. From the way the temple had been carved into the mountainside, I knew that there were three main vestibules to the temple.

"You're not coming with me?" I asked, almost ashamed of the way my voice cracked. I'd known as much, or should have anyway. They'd told me this was a journey I had to make alone.

"I will see you very soon, daughter. I will be waiting for you within the Cradle, but the words of the Fates are for you and you alone to hear," Medusa said, stepping up to the wall of the temple beside us. It opened for her, letting her step into the sunshine in a beautiful valley, filled with a waterfall and still pond, an Eden within Tartarus.

I took to the stairs the way I'd entered this Hel.

Alone.

SIXTY-FOUR

CALDRIS

There was no trace of the thing that had once been Estrella's father remaining in the ferryman while he rowed us up the tangle of rivers to the secret entrance to Tartarus. It was the impossibility of the situation that kept me quiet, kept me from prying and trying to find the man who would have been horrified to know that his daughter was prepared to die in the Cradle of Creation.

That whatever her purpose was and whatever destiny had drawn her to this place and this time, she accepted that her life was the price the Fates demanded. I knew now the words that had made her believe that was true, and my fingers danced along my thigh as I stood on the boat. Even Brann, who seemed incapable of shutting his mouth, didn't dare to speak to me for fear of the consequences, his own face twisted into a sorrowful expression that reminded me of the hole where my heart had once been.

My heart beat outside my chest, because it thudded within hers. Without the ability to feel her, with the bond silenced by this strange barrier between us, I felt as if I were alone all over again. As if the Veil still existed and I could only feel the faintest of whispers of her existence. My heart was still, my life feeling pointless.

I had to have faith in her ability to return, in the fact that her mother would not have brought her into that temple knowing that her death would come. Estrella had been warned of her coming death since that night in the woods of Mistfell when Adelphia had warned her that death was coming for her after her candle fell from the stone. There was no other choice but to accept that two types of death existed, that Estrella still clung to the woman she'd been as a human. There was a figurative death in that loss that she failed to anticipate the power of. Letting go of that version of herself would feel like a sacrifice, it would feel like she was being torn from her body if she were to ever give that girl up in truth. I loved that human girl, the innocence of her gaze when it had found me staring at her in that barn. While life may not have been kind to her, there was a certain quality to her that could only exist because of her young life.

Age hardened you. It tore the kindness from your soul and ripped the care from your bones. It had long since made me cynical and forced me to see the worst in people, but Estrella always hoped for the best. She hoped people would prove her right and be as gentle as she would be to any who loved her, but she hadn't yet felt centuries of disappointment when people acted for their own selfish gain.

Age tore the innocence away. Age took your ability to be hurt and morphed it into a fever dream, a breathing, tangible thing that you could never seem to shake. Age made it so that you anticipated the pain of that betrayal with every step you took.

I didn't know that I had it in me to believe that the people who had my mate were *good*. I just had to hope that their own self-interest aligned with mine, that they needed my mate alive far more than they needed her dead. In that, I had to trust.

Otherwise I'd have flung myself into the closest river, gladly joining her in this Hel forever.

Instead, I stood in silence as the ferryman guided us out through the cave we'd entered, returning Brann and I to the land of the living as the Priestess had requested. It was a bittersweet thing to be returning to my home, knowing that my mother was dead and I was the King of Winter. That I'd had to leave my mate behind after all my desire to help her. I didn't think I'd managed to do anything for her in this place except to be a shoulder for her to lean on, a comfort to her emotionally. These trials weren't for me, and the helplessness of that fact and my helplessness in what would come didn't sit right with me.

"Do you think she'll be okay?" Brann asked as we emerged into the light of day. The sun was far too bright on my face, after the time spent in the dimness of Tartarus, and I turned my head to stare at the floor of the boat as the ferryman continued to row.

"She will be," I said, letting my resolve power the words. If there was one thing I knew about my mate, it was that her ability to survive anything life threw at her was her true magic. She would adapt and change as she needed, serving whatever purpose was necessary so that she could come back to me. She'd *live* through sheer determination alone, bending the will of the Fates to hers.

That was who she was. That was her strength.

Holt and the rest of the Wild Hunt waited on the shores when we finally reached the sands of the coast where Brann had once fallen to certain death. I'd been prepared for a great many things when we finally returned to the land of the living, all that was left to reunite my spirit with my body.

What I hadn't been ready for was the reality that Holt and Brann clearly knew one another, their glares a matching set as they sized one another up. "Brander," Holt said, his voice stern and unforgiving. It was so unlike the male who was usually full of lightness and humor even in the darkest of times.

"Huntsman," Brann returned, the bite in his voice matching his lack of desire to use the man's real name. He reduced him to his title, a disrespect that would have been equivalent to calling Brann a witch.

Reducing him to his magic, or in Holt's case, his curse.

"I've a name," Holt snapped, turning to his horse. There weren't enough horses to carry us, so I sighed as I guided Brann up to ride at my back. He shook his head, denying the ride.

"She never referred to you by anything other than Huntsman," Brann said.

"What I allow Imelda to call me is none of your business, and you are not gifted the same courtesy," Holt said, staring down at where Brann seemed determined to go his separate way. To escape the coming war, I had no doubt.

The fucking coward.

"Why not?"

"Because I like *her*," Holt said, guiding his horse into a trot up the narrow path. I followed after him, leaving Brann behind. There wasn't time to reason with him, to convince him that Estrella would want to find him with the rest of her loved ones when she emerged from Tartarus. If he didn't already know that, if he didn't want to be there when she walked the earth again, then he didn't fucking deserve her in the first place. I had better things to do than babysit an immortal, stubborn witch. I had an army to gather for my mate.

He could rot, for all I cared.

SIXTY-FIVE

ESTRELLA

The bag clutched in my hand felt impossibly heavy as I ascended the stairs, making my way into the second vestibule of the Temple of the Fates. Filled with the offerings I'd gathered from each of the rivers: the horn from the bull, the hair from the lion, the antler from the hind, the ashes from the hydra, and the apples. This level was far smaller than the one below, cradled atop the cliffside with gaping, open windows that revealed the Cradle of Creation on the other side. The waterfall ran down the opposite cliff on the other side of the valley, the shine of water running through the loose forests of trees that surrounded the gardens at the center. They were teeming with life, all things natural flourishing within the valley in a way that made me think of all the seasons coming together. Of all the places and times in the world condensed into one garden that somehow pleased everyone.

In a single corner, winter reigned. The plants were encased in snow and ice, the cold descending to freeze the water of the stream and the lake where it sprawled out between the four corners. Human figures moved within the valley, their bodies tiny pinpricks on the scope of what I watched. But there was no denying the man who stood before the lake, shadows surrounding him like the midnight of a galaxy. His eyes gleamed with gold as he met my stare through the open window, raising a single hand to hold it palm out.

It felt like a mockery of everything I'd left behind, of the mate I'd tried so desperately to touch through that barrier as it slammed closed between us and locked him out. Medusa stepped up beside him, wrapping her arms around his waist and tilting her chin to stare up at him. I couldn't make out her face from this distance, her features too lowly contrasted to travel through the space between us aside from the writhing serpents in her hair, but something in that posture was familiar.

It was a look of love on her face, I was certain, because that was how I looked up at my mate to tell him I loved him without words.

She too raised her hand into a still wave, her head turning to face me. The noise of footsteps behind me made my heart catch in my throat, the reality of what I'd come here to do pressing down on me. Would they watch, when the Fates killed me? Would my parents bear witness to the end of my life in this temple that promised nothing but pain for me.

Death was my price. It was my salvation and my end, and I could only bring myself to regret what it would do to my mate if and when it came to pass.

I spun slowly, my hands curving in a sweeping motion as the gold of my dress moved with me. It cascaded over the floor, a liquid energy that I could not quite contain. The Fates stood before me, neatly arranged into their group of three in the same positions as I'd seen them in that meadow in the river.

"Aella, we have long awaited this moment," the woman at the center said. Her half-rotted face moved grotesquely, her fingers constantly fiddling with the spool of thread she held in her hand. Even now, even in these moments, the three of them worked to knit a new tapestry, sewing the threads of life together bit by bit as if they were simply unable to help themselves.

"I am Clotho, and I stitched your name into the tapestry long before the night of your birth," the woman at the center spoke, that spindle twirling to give her sister more thread. To allow her to take more of the magic of the Fates and spin it into creation and destiny itself.

"I am Lachesis, and I have guided you through all your names and all your lives," the one to the left said, her fingers working over the new tapestry with a speed the likes of which I'd never seen. She did not need needles to tie the thread into knots, her deft, calloused fingers doing the work alone.

"I am Atropos, and I am the cutter of threads and ender of lives. I am the one that meets the living when their destiny has met its end," the one to the right spoke. She cut her scissors through the air, as if she could not stop the motion that was endless. There were no threads to be cut in this moment, no lives to bring to the end of their days, but still she cut.

"You're the one who will kill me when I've served my purpose here," I said, keeping my voice calm. Even as I looked for confirmation of what was to come, I would not show them fear. Fear for the afterlife, fear for any pain that I might feel in my final moments. Fear that I might live and have to go on forever changed.

Silence was my only answer, a refusal to give me the gift of knowledge. I swallowed, nodding in acknowledgment. I should have expected nothing less. I raised the bag I had brought, the gifts I'd worked so hard to gather for these women so that they might grant me passage into the Cradle. So that I might find the answers I sought in the family that waited for me there. Atropos reached out and accepted it, never bothering to open the pack and look at the items I'd gathered. I supposed they didn't need to, for these women knew every step of my trials. They knew what gifts I'd brought long before I ever brought them.

"Do you think yourself worthy? Of what you will become after you enter the Cradle?" she asked, the words catching me off guard. What did it matter if I thought myself worthy of my fate? Fate did not care for my wishes or wants, my insecurities or faults. It only saw how to use them to its advantage, only saw a being that could be manipulated to suit.

"How am I to say if I am worthy when I do not know what it is I will become? I don't think there is anyone who is worthy of the kind of power the Primordials and Gods possess. All I can do is endeavor to be fair and just, to give those around me the best life possible and not allow my magic to corrupt me in the same way it has so many others. Does that make me worthy, or does that make me blinded by my own idealism that I might be different than those who came before me?" I asked, sighing as I spoke the words. It felt like blasphemy to insult the Primordials and the Gods, especially in this place, so near to where the Primordials had chosen to hide away from the world they'd created like cowards.

Clotho moved, breaking free from their triad to take a step closer to me. She touched a hand to my chest, that bundle of threads rising within me as it recognized her touch. Her head tilted to the side, studying the thread intently before her eerie eyes rose to my face once more.

"When we knit the threads, we see only facts. We see actions, but the thoughts behind them are lost to us. We have long since stopped understanding the facets of human emotion, if we ever had the ability to begin with. Do you not wish to have everlasting life and power? It seems so many of your kind would give anything or anyone to have such things, and yet you seem angry that we have presented you with them."

"No," I said, scoffing as I considered how I could make them understand. If it was true that they did not understand human feelings and things such as love, then how could a choice that was purely rooted in emotion ever make sense to a being like that? And what business did a being with no concept of love have determining the fates of men? "I do not want either of those things. I want to live my life in peace and not be consumed by the knowledge that my decisions carry the weight of the world. I don't want to live for an eternity knowing that I could make a difference, and wondering if it will be for the betterment of man or the downfall of everything I love. I want to be no one and nothing in the grand scheme of this world, and when I die, I want my memory to fade into obscurity. So if that isn't the answer you wanted, if it does not serve your purpose or make me worthy, then just kill me now. I tire of these fucking games that are never-ending. I am worthy or I'm not. Make your choice already, because I have made mine."

Atropos grinned, handing back the bag I had given to her. "The trials were never meant for us, Estrella Barlowe. Our choice was made so many centuries ago that they have always been irrelevant to us and the knowledge we have. These were the events that were necessary for you to be in the position to make the choices that aligned with the path we chose. These trials were so that you could come to understand your own worth and the weight of that worth on the world," she said.

"You mean they were your manipulations to get me here, because I did not want to come here on my own. Without those trials, I would not be the woman you need me to be for whatever reason.

You did what was necessary to serve your purpose and get me here, but it was never about what I needed to discover. Do not frame it as such when you could not even begin to understand the damage you have done. You have spent so long manipulating these fucking threads like we are all puppets on a string, and you've forgotten that we are real people. That we want things you will never understand. We love and we hurt and we feel the pain you cause us for your sick amusement." I paused, waiting for an answer I knew I would not get. They would not feel sorry for the things they'd done, for the lives they'd ruined.

"You do not even begin to understand how deep our manipulations go, Estrella Barlowe," Clotho said, her face shifting and morphing as I watched. Her skin knitted back together on the rotten side, her cheeks filling in as her features shifted around into a magical glamour that became far too familiar. My anger dissipated, my lungs sagging as I expelled the air from them in surprise.

Macha stood before me, her face twisted into a sad sort of smile as her sisters shifted at her sides. Where Lachesis had stood was Badb, her raven hair gleaming. Where there had once been Atropos, there was Nemain, her throat healed from the damage they'd let me believe Khaos had caused.

It was Badb who finally spoke as my jaw clenched, fighting back the sting of betrayal in my throat. "I warned you that even we had our own reasons for aiding you, Child of Fate," she said, acting as if it were my fault that I'd come to care for the three women who had served as my guide. Their distance after Medusa came made more sense now, if she did not know the truth of the Morrigan's identity, they probably wanted to keep it that way.

"And what were yours?" I asked, forcing myself to push through the hurt to get the answers I needed.

"Curiosity," Nemain said, and her voice sounded so strange after so much time spent in silence. I'd barely gotten to hear her speak before her voice had gone, and now here she stood, speaking as if it had never happened at all. "We were impatient to meet you."

"You told me the Fates appeared to me because something shifted, but you'd been there all along. You didn't need to make yourself known. Why bother?" I asked, hating the need to understand.

"It would have been expected of us. You stole your power back from Tartarus and chose to stay anyway. You chose forgiveness over hatred, and that is not a trait we would expect from any of the Primordials. To not appear to you would only have raised suspicions to Medusa, and we were not ready to reveal ourselves yet," Macha said, her face twisting as if she felt the tiniest sliver of guilt for their deception.

It wasn't enough.

"You are my reason. You are why I will never want the power you have. Because I will *never* allow myself to become like you."

"You are far more like us than you could possibly understand, Tempest. That is why you are here, about to enter the Cradle when we grant no access to others of your lineage. We are not your reckoning, Estrella," Lachesis said, her voice tinted with something dark and almost angry. It never struck the point of feeling like emotion, but the window behind me opened to the Cradle, the Fates pressing closer to force me to take a step back toward it if I wanted to keep my distance from the monsters approaching.

Clotho finally opened her mouth again, her lips tipped up into an arrogant smirk as she watched my face fall. As one they reached up, touching a hand to my chest and that knot of thread there. They pushed, shoving me back through the open window so that I staggered over the edge and my feet touched the grass of the Cradle. I stared at the Fates in shock, realizing that they'd granted me passage. But it was Clotho's last words that hung in the air as the glass rebuilt, shards snapping together to seal the temple off once more. "You are ours."

Sixty-Six

ESTRELLA

I walked down the hillside, making my way into the valley that spread before me. Primordials stepped from the trees, emerging into the path that I walked so that they too could stare at me. The weight of those gazes upon my skin felt like the heat of a thousand suns, a judgment when I'd hoped the trials were done.

But the sinking feeling Clotho's words left in my gut, made me wonder if maybe my trials had only just begun. Golden eyes studied me, from each and every corner of the Cradle, forming a line along the path to welcome me. By the time I finally reached Khaos and Medusa, I felt that sinking pit inside of me open into an eternal well—the depths of which I could not feel. *What was this?*

Khaos stepped forward, the harshness I'd come to know gone from his face. "Welcome home, daughter," he said, closing the last distance between us. I backed away from him as his hands came to touch my face, to cradle it in a moment of intimacy he had not earned. His lips pressed together, a swallow working through his throat at my rejection. "You're angry with me."

"You stood there, and you watched me suffer. You never once tried to help me; you never once intervened," I snapped, turning to look at where Medusa was cuddled into his side. She was quiet in the face of this argument, not bothering to offer any help to the father I'd never asked for. She didn't need to help him understand, and for once, I appreciated that there was no one to help me communicate my pain.

I wanted him to hear it from me. I wanted him to hurt the way I had.

"Not all of us are as impervious to the influence of the Fates as you are, Estrella. I did what I could, when I could, without compromising your success. It was imperative that you make it here—to this place. In this moment, as you are. Had I stepped in and helped you, you never would have known what it is to stand alone. You would have never learned to trust in your own strength, and the strength of your resolve. You, and you alone, can defy them, Estrella. You and you alone can fix what we have wrought, but in order to do that, first you must kill Mab and rid the world of her stain. That is what is foretold, that is what will bring the turning of the tides," Khaos said, his hands finally dropping to his sides as he realized I would not allow the embrace he sought.

"She is your daughter, just as I am. How can you speak of her death and not care what that means?" I asked, his impassiveness regarding Mab only confirming what I'd already suspected.

Whatever Khaos was capable of, it wasn't the kind of love I related to. I could never condemn my daughter in that way.

"Any part of Mab that was my daughter has long since been erased. The crown she wears, the crown we fashioned for *you* at the insistence of the Fates, has cursed her beyond recognition. We made it so that only the child we had together could wear it without consequence. I never imagined it would be stolen or used in this way. I never thought someone would tolerate the weight of it at all, but Mab is half me, and she connected to it just enough to gain power from it, but it did not save her from the madness it causes, only delayed it. It is only a matter of time before she slaughters everyone in her path," Khaos answered.

"You are the Primordial of chaos. Why not stop her yourself?" I asked, the words a condemnation. All the suffering he could have ended if he'd only just taken responsibility for what he caused.

"The Fates condemned us all to live out our days in the Cradle," he said, stepping forward again. He ignored my attempt to jerk back, finally laying his palms on my cheeks. His eyes closed at the contact, a buzz of familiar energy humming through me where he touched. "We did not willingly choose to leave our children. We did not willingly abandon the only one we were capable of caring for. You believe this to be a prison where Mab sends her enemies, where the Gods and the Primordials drag those who've wronged them, but it was our prison first. Our dungeon that we cannot escape. We will never walk the earth so long as the Fates control us all."

"All things must die, Estrella," Medusa echoed, her words from the night before tickling at the back of my mind.

I was their reckoning, and they were the jailors.

Khaos turned me to face the Primordials who watched us, laying his hands atop my shoulders. "They do not watch because you're a curiosity. They watch you because you are the only one that can free them from this pit. They watch you because you are our savior," he said, forcing me to watch as the Primordials bowed their heads to the ground beside the path where I'd walked.

"Why would the Fates guide me here if I'm meant to kill them? How is that even possible?"

"It is possible because of the tangle they placed in my womb the night they sent me into that temple so that you could be conceived. The knot that was my price for having the daughter I so desperately craved, is the very thing that they set into motion all those years ago. You can kill them, because you are one of them, Estrella. You may be our daughter by blood, but you carry a piece of each of them inside of you as well," Medusa explained.

"They know. They know that I'm going to be the one to kill them," I said, the realization dawning. Their reckoning, *their end.*

"All things must die," Medusa said again as Khaos turned to me, his hands leaving my shoulders.

Only one of his hands cupped my cheek this time, and I couldn't help the way I leaned into the touch, seeking out a moment of comfort from the father I'd never known.

"I wish we'd had more time. I wish they hadn't kept you from me for so long," he said, his lips pursing and nostrils flaring. Alarm bells rang in my head as Medusa whimpered, the sound of a sob forcing me to turn from Khaos's burning stare to look at her. I never saw the knife coming as she covered her mouth, only felt the blinding, searing pain as it tore through my chest. Khaos stabbed me, shoving it to the hilt as he held me still with his hand on my shoulder, his face twisting as if he'd been the one to be stabbed.

The iron lit me on fire from inside, shredding through tissue and muscle, puncturing my heart where it slowed. He pulled the knife back, a rush of blood pumping out of the hole he'd created. Staring up into those golden eyes, I watched his face twist.

"I'm sorry," he said, his eyes shining with unshed tears. His arm moved, as he shoved the knife into my chest again, creating another wound next to the first. I gasped for breath, struggling as Medusa came up behind me and held me up. She supported my weight, keeping me standing when my legs buckled beneath me.

"Why?" I asked, my mouth wet. The coppery taste of blood filled it as I gurgled, my hand moving at my side. Trying desperately to cling to that thread, to hold onto the bond I shared with my mate.

Caldris.

One last time, Khaos pulled his knife free and stabbed me a third time. I stared down at the hilt, at the blade protruding from my chest as Medusa lowered me to the ground finally. She lay my head upon her lap, running gentle fingers through my hair as I clung to the thread, using that bond to keep me here. To keep me from leaving him.

He would never forgive me.

Khaos knelt beside me, staring down at me as he wrapped his fingers around the knife and tore it back again. Tossing it to the side, his bloody hands came to rest on my face, smoothing hair back from my cheeks as my face wet with tears. There was so much pain, so much burning inside of me as my lungs fought for breath. As my heart pumped blood out the wounds. The golden dress was stained with red, a deep spreading pool gathering on my torso.

"Why?" I repeated, waiting for the answer to the question that they hadn't given me. How could I save them if I was dead? And if I was meant to save them, then what was the purpose of this? What could I do in death that I could not in life?

"All things must die," Medusa repeated, and I wondered if the words were her mind's attempt to understand the loss. Her way of coping.

Khaos touched his hand to my wound, his human figure fading into a darkness that spread over the Cradle. Only his face remained as I choked on my own blood, a dancing whisper in the night as the thread held in my hand turned gray and lifeless. The bond snapped, my heart beating for the final time.

There was no more pain, only eternal darkness, a night sky without stars, and Khaos's voice to follow me into death.

Sixty-Seven

CALDRIS

The return to my body came with immense pain. The kind of pain that I never wanted to experience again. Everything hurt, as if I was punished for leaving unattended, but it welcomed me back anyway.

On the ground at my side, there was the stone figure of a snake. It held perfectly still, a mirror of the snake Medusa had pulled from my heart in Tartarus. Holt's eyes dropped to it, a question in them as he raised his gaze to mine again. I merely nodded, rubbing at my chest with my palm.

Gone was the incessant wiggling of that serpent inside me. Gone was the tug of Mab's call to accomplish her every whim.

I was free.

I stood, making eye contact with Holt as we moved toward the doorway to the dungeons. The Wild Hunt waited amid the cells, watching as we emerged.

"What's the plan?" Holt asked me finally, and I knew that they would stand with me. That they would help me gather forces for Estrella so that I could be ready when she returned to me.

"I'm not supposed to be seen. I cannot risk death before Estrella has done what she needs to finish in Tartarus." I rubbed at my chest where my *viniculum* brushed against my collarbone, a faint pain lingering there that just would not quit. The bond was still silent between us, making me unable to feel her in any way. I cleared my throat and continued on, though it felt like I was attempting to swallow endless water, like I was drowning in it. "But we need to quietly gather people who may be willing to fight. It's almost time," I explained.

"We should find Imelda," Holt said, and while I couldn't argue with the fact that the witch would be useful in this fight, it was not lost on me that he had his own selfish reasons for wanting to find her.

"Still no sign of her?" I asked, not truly daring to make eye contact.

"No," Holt grunted, his dissatisfaction at the fact very clear. He was determined to make up for lost time with the witch, but she was having none of it.

"Then we need Nila. If anyone is capable of helping us gather people who are willing to fight, it will be her. Estrella will bring an army with her, but it won't be enough on its own," I said, making my way to the stairs.

Holt stopped me with a hand on my shoulder, looking up to the stairs. "Let us go find her. If you can't be seen, then you should stay here for the time being." He didn't hesitate to abandon me, fleeing up the stairs to the throne room and leaving me to pace back and forth in the dungeon. The bodies had piled up in my absence, and it took everything in me to focus and not return to my purpose.

They'd waited this long, and they would have to continue to wait. If a battle was truly coming, there would be more where they came from.

Death was inevitable in war.

I only hoped we could keep it as minimal as possible.

I dragged my hand over the stone, the feeling of the porous rock the only thing that grounded me in those few moments where Holt was gone. I wished I could follow after him, the urge to move and do something like an itch in my skin that I couldn't scratch. It left me restless, my worry over Estrella making me need to do something productive with myself in her absence.

I needed to move.

The door to the dungeon opened as Holt guided Nila into the room, the smaller woman making her way down the stairs hurriedly. "Estrella?" she asked, taking in the sight of only me standing and waiting in the dungeon.

"She'll be here soon, and she's coming to fight. We need those who are willing to fight alongside her—"

My entire body jerked back, the pain in my chest like a physical blow as it morphed into more pain.

"Caldris . . ." Holt said, his stare locked onto the side of my neck. His eyes were wide, his mouth open as he floundered for words.

Cold spread through me, a cold the likes of which I'd never known. I tore at my shirt, shoving it down over my shoulder to watch as my *viniculum* faded away, sinking into my skin and then disappearing from view entirely. Holt reached for the bottom of my sleeve, shoving up my forearm so that we could watch as it spread from my elbow and slowly made its way to my wrist. My arm had never been free from those marks, my skin looking too bare in their absence. Even before she'd been born, I'd had that part of my mate with me.

Instead now, there was only nothingness, a tingle on my skin where the sign of my love had once been, as if she'd never existed at all.

"No," I muttered, touching my hand and trying to hold those marks on me. Trying to cling to the one last piece of her as the thread tied around my finger turned gray. It lost its vibrance, my world lost its color as I felt that thread snap.

It took my soul with it, my heart.

I screamed, feeling that loss so deep in me that I felt like half a person. Half a being. I touched my fingers to the frayed edge of our bond where it writhed in the wind, dead and useless.

"Caldris," Holt said, patting my cheek to try to get my attention as I stared down at the remains of what had once been my everything.

Now there was just nothing. A dark world with no hope. Nothing to live for, and my only comfort was that my death was certain. I would follow after her, and we'd be reunited in the afterlife.

A place without pain. A place without loss. A place without this horrible, numb emptiness.

For now, all I knew was that my mate was gone.

Estrella was dead, and I'd have done anything to die faster, because every moment I spent without her was a moment too long. I'd waited centuries to find her.

Even death couldn't keep me from her now.

ACKNOWLEDGMENTS

To my readers, who stuck with me through the delay that I'm certain felt agonizing after the cliffhanger in *What Lurks Between the Fates*. I cannot thank you enough for staying supportive and continuing to share your love for this series. It has meant the world to me as I fought battles within my personal life. It's funny how sometimes when you're in the moment and desperately trying to find the words, it can be so impossible to see what's causing the writer's block. But then when the book is finished and you read it through, everything becomes crystal clear. I wasn't in the right place to write the second half of this book a year ago. It's all about Estrella's journey of self-discovery and learning to love herself as she is—after a lifetime of negative thoughts and influences. Her journey is a fantastical one that mirrors my own experience over the past year, and if I'd forced myself to write those moments before I was ready, I don't think I'd have been able to do her journey justice.

Art mirrors life. This one is mine.

To Caitlen, for sharing the other half of my brain cells and taking good care of it when it's lost to me. For keeping me on schedule when no one else can and for giving me a safe place to land when everything feels heavy. For being the best friend every woman should have.

To my little family for supporting my dreams and thinking I'm something to brag about. I hope you never stop being delusional in your belief in me and the things I can accomplish. You are my reason, and I love you to the moon and back.

To my agent, Josi, for always believing in me even when I came out of nowhere with this fantasy romance idea that was so off-brand people told me I should stick to what I knew.

To Monique Patterson, Susan Barnes, and the rest of the team at Bramble, I will forever be thankful for the chance you took on me. For the love and appreciation you've shown my characters and my stories and the willingness to work together to make them shine.

To every woman out there who has had to overcome what fate threw at them . . .

This one's for us.

ABOUT THE AUTHOR

Harper L. Woods is the *New York Times* and *USA Today* bestselling fantasy romance alter ego for Adelaide Forrest. Raised in small-town Vermont, her passion for reading was born during long winters spent with her face buried between the pages of a book. She began to pass the time by writing short stories that quickly turned into full-length fiction. Since that time, she has published over twenty-five books and has plans for many more. When she isn't writing, Woods can be found spending time with her two young kids, curling up with her dog, dreaming about travel to distant lands, or designing book covers she'll never have enough time to use.